BEST MUSIC COMPANY
548 - 12th STREET
OAKLAND 7, CALIFORNIA

Rhythm and Tempo

Books by Curt Sachs

THE RISE OF MUSIC IN THE ANCIENT WORLD

WORLD HISTORY OF THE DANCE

THE HISTORY OF MUSICAL INSTRUMENTS

THE COMMONWEALTH OF ART

RHYTHM AND TEMPO

OUR MUSICAL HERITAGE (Prentice-Hall)

Rhythm and Tempo

A STUDY IN MUSIC HISTORY

By CURT SACHS

W · W · NORTON & COMPANY · INC · New York

09-0103

Contents

Rhythm and Tempo

CHAPTER 1

Elementary Principles

Books on any subject reflect of necessity a limited range of vision, in which some parts and qualities stand out while others retreat or vanish altogether. The readers expect to find their familiar, personal ranges of vision—ranges that might be very different from that of the author.

The danger of facing such discrepancies is especially great in the field of rhythm, whatever this doubtful term conveys. Rooted deep in physiological grounds as a function of our bodies, rhythm permeates melody, form, and harmony; it becomes the driving and shaping force, indeed, the very breath of music, and reaches up into the loftiest realm of aesthetic experience where description is doomed to fail because no language provides the vocabulary for adequate wording. Disenchanted, the author is, alas, compelled—as more or less is every writer on art—to describe the technical traits, the dactyls and double dots, *proportiones* and metrical patterns, rather than the elusive, indescribable essence of rhythm.

This being as it is, the present author has no hope of giving satisfaction to every reader; and when he thinks of the discontent with which he himself has laid away the writings of other men on the subject, he fancies with horror the reaction of his own prospective readers.

A foretaste of what might be in store for the author appears when it comes to defining the scope of the vocable 'rhythm,' which, so far, has been used in at least "fifty different meanings." [1]

[1] A. W. de Groot, *Der Rhythmus*, in *Neophilologus*, Vol. XVII, 1932, p. 82.

WHAT IS RHYTHM? The answer, I am afraid, is, so far, just—a word: a word without a generally accepted meaning. Everybody believes himself entitled to usurp it for an arbitrary definition of his own.

The confusion is terrifying indeed.

Teachers take their pupils to task for not playing 'rhythmically.' Rhythm, they imply, is inexorable strictness of time values, and they enforce it by counting, clapping, stamping irritably: *one, two, three, and four.* But other musicians tell us just the contrary: their "rhythm" is the willful deviation from deadly strictness. While they call 'meter' a metronomic, mechanical norm, their 'rhythm' is the human touch of freedom that makes 'meter' non-mechanical, non-metronomical . . .[2]

But even the Greeks, who coined the word 'rhythm' in early antiquity, and the Romans who followed them, gave it not only inconsistent, but outright contradictory, meanings. *Rhythmós*, like so many terms, changed scope and connotations from age to age, from man to man, in Hellas as well as in Rome.

In view of this confusion, it would be in the best scholarly tradition to repeat here all the different meanings that authors have given to the word 'rhythm' in two and a half thousand years. But such a tedious rehashing would have no positive result except, at best, the doubtful merit of completeness as against the very definite disadvantage of uselessness, boredom, and waste of precious space.

Also, most of these definitions would be useless for the purpose of the present book. Juxtaposing and contrasting the notion of rhythm with meter, *Takt,* or similar concepts is inadmissible where all these concepts, in very different civilizations and ages, must be described under one general, all-comprehensive concept of which they are mere parts or facets.

That this concept must be called rhythm cannot be doubted. In every language, and in spite of technicalities, the equivalent of rhythm has a character more general than any other term. We can, and do, discuss the rhythm of a building, a statue, or a painting; but we cannot discuss their meter or *Takt.* The very etymology of the word 'rhythm' is general enough to give it a commanding position.

[2] Cf. Jaap Kunst, *Metre, rhythm, multi-part music,* Leiden, 1950.

The derivation of the Greek term *rhythmós* leads back to a verb for 'flowing'—*rheō, rhein,* an early relative of the German *Rhein* or Rhine and even of the English word 'river.' Thus Fowler could tersely state: "Rhythm is flow." [3] But evidently this flowing is not, and never was, a smooth, inert, continuous movement without articulation. It is, rather, a fluency due to some active, organizing principle, to ever renewed impulses whose very orderliness at once gives life and ease to the flow.

This organized fluency is reflected in the various Greek connotations of the word. They start from movement, gait, and dancing, and—via the intermediate connotation of a treatment of such motion in art—reach beyond to the almost opposite meaning of restraint and moderation.[4]

The two extremes—movement and moderation—are connected in a charming formulation by the Roman grammarian, Charisius (*ca.* 400 A.D.): *Rhythmus est metrum fluens, metrum rhythmus clausus,*[5] or "rhythm is flowing meter, and meter is bonded rhythm." Here, flux and dam are united in one definition.

This latter meaning is obviously at the bottom of the most recent discussion on rhythm in its proper sense. Werner Jaeger, the famous classics professor, has made it convincingly clear that, far from denoting motion as such, the oldest use of the word indicated on the contrary a pause, a steady limitation of movement.[6] Among his examples are a poetic monologue by Archilochos from the seventh century B.C., who urges himself to "understand the rhythm that holds mankind in its bonds" (fragment 67 a 18); and Aeschylos (525–456 B.C.), whose Prometheus complains: "I am bound here in this rhythm."

As a consequence, Dr. Jaeger does not believe in the allegedly figurative sense in which the word 'rhythm' has been used in the visual arts of space. With the notion 'bond,' it would naturally apply to all the arts, and its preferential use in music and poetry would only be a later shrinkage in scope.

[3] H. W. Fowler, *A dictionary of modern English usage,* Oxford University Press, London, 1926.

[4] Ernst Graf, *Rythmus und Metrum,* Marburg, 1891, pp. 1 ff.

[5] Charisius Flavius Sosipater, *Institutiones grammaticae,* § 289, printed in Lindemann, *Corpus grammaticorum latinorum veterum,* Leipzig, 1840.

[6] Werner Jaeger, *Paideia,* transl. by Gilbert Highet, New York, 1939, pp. 122–124.

In itself, to be sure, the word 'movement' would seem to restrict the concept of rhythm to the so-called arts of time, to music, poetry, drama, and dancing. But this time-honored classification is not unchallenged today.[7] We no longer believe in a rigid separation of time and space in the arts. Movement, at least in a psychological sense, is never quite absent from the visual arts. Giving shape to things and thoughts with pencil, burin, or brush, the hand is in restless motion; up it goes and down and left and right. And since in a way most art perception retraces the creative process, the observer perceives the lines of the artist as live and moving forces: to him, they rise and fall, converge, diverge, intersect, and draw the viewer's eyes to the fore and the back. No work of art can simply *be;* it always stirs and acts and forces the spectator to follow with his senses the many directions that it suggests.

Factual coexistence in space does not necessarily mean coexistence in our vision or, for that matter, in our aesthetic experience. It often dissolves into a sequence of perceptions, both physiologically and aesthetically.

"The normal eye," in the first place, "does not try to see a large area at a time, never a whole line, for instance. . . ."[8]

In the second place, quite a number of visual works demand aesthetically a moving eye to read them section by section over a period of time. We will not even speak of the landscaping art, whose very reason of being is the moving visitor to behold its ever changing scenery. But we might speak of the allegedly static art of architecture. "Are there instantaneous monuments? Are there monuments in which we perceive in a flash, and not by slowly followed routes, the various elevations, the outer and the inner views, the perspectives, the successive vistas?"[9] When the Gothic cathedral emerges unexpectedly from the tangle of lowly, narrow-set buildings, it takes a couple of seconds before the eyes, obeying the surge of the tower, have reached the tip of the steeple. Many

---

[7] Cf. also Marcelle Wahl, *Le mouvement dans la peinture,* Paris, 1936, Etienne Souriau, *La correspondance des arts,* Paris, 1947, p. 77; Gisèle Brelet, *Le temps musical,* Paris, 1949, pp. 3 ff.

[8] Harold M. Peppard, *Sight without glasses,* New York, Garden City Publishing Company.

[9] Étienne Souriau, *La correspondance des arts,* Paris, 1947, p. 77.

sculptures must be 'developed' by walking around and examining them from every angle—so much so that recently Michelangelo's statues were made a subject for 'movies' in the proper sense of the word. And in medieval paintings, on glass, or wood, or stone, the phases of the Passion are often set in a single common scenery and require a moving eye to read the episodes from the Last Supper via the Crucifixion to Christ's Entombment and Resurrection. Indeed, the earliest rhythmologist proper, Aristotle's pupil Aristoxenos of Tarentum, who wrote around 330 B.C., attributed rhythm to an art as visual and spatial as sculpture.[10]

This book deals little with rhythm to be seen or to be felt. It is concerned rather with the steady, orderly recurrence of audible impressions only, that is, with rhythmical sounds. And it is concerned with rhythmical sounds exclusively as an element of art, as an aesthetic experience.

In keeping with the 'bonding' element in the Grecian concept of rhythm, Aristoxenos called rhythm the *taxis chronon,* the 'order of times.'

But there had already been a better, broader definition: one generation before Aristoxenos, Plato had explained that rhythm was a *kinéseos taxis,* an 'order of movement.' [11] It would be safer, however, to add what Andreas Heusler added to the Aristoxenian definition: *Gliederung der Zeit in sinnlich fassbare Teile,* or "organization of time in parts accessible to the senses." [12] For art cannot live but in the realm of perception.

Plato's kinetic definition excludes implicitly two forms of movement as non-rhythmical:

kinetic chaos, such as an avalanche produces while thundering
     from landing to landing; and
kinetic continuum, like that of a smoothly gliding sailboat, car,
     or plane.

[10] An experimental research into visual rhythm is: Jean Weidensall, *Studies in rhythm,* Chicago, n.d. Cf. also: Willy Drost, *Die Lehre vom Rhythmus in der heutigen Aesthetik der bildenden Künste,* Dissertation Leipzig, Leipzig, 1919.
[11] Plato, *The Laws,* II, 665.
[12] Andreas Heusler, *Deutsche Versgeschichte,* Vol. I, Berlin, 1925 (in *Grundriss der germanischen Philologie,* Vol. 8, i), p. 17.

It includes, on the contrary, kinetic intermittence at regular intervals, which, perceived through ears or eyes or feeling, makes our minds aware of a well-organized expanse in time or space. Such intermittence amounts to a steady, orderly recurrence of visible, audible, palpable stimuli; as, in the tactile field, of strong and weak; and in the visual field, of light and dark, or up and down, or left and right.

Recurrence appears in its lowest form as an undifferentiated pulsation like the throbs of the heart, the even tick of a clock, the regular flash of a blinker, or the nerve-racking drip from a leaking faucet.

Some authors have been unwilling to accept such simple pulsation as rhythm.[13] Still, recurrence of this kind complies with the basic requirement: to be kinetic, intermittent, and perceived through one of the senses. Indeed, their intermittence is of the strongest kind. They do not alternate between a more and a less, but between yes and no; not between stronger and weaker, or lighter and darker, but between a push and a pause, or presence and absence.

RHYTHM AND FORM. It has become a truism that the notion of rhythm has been expanded to encompass the whole 'form' or structure of a piece. The basic idea of such expansion is this: In dealing with rhythm, we find a generating, time-organizing pattern in two phases, say long and short, or strong and weak, or heavy and light, or dark and clear, or whatever the contrast may be. If, as usually, this pattern is repeated, the two phases recur on a higher level: the first pattern may play the role of the strong phase, while the repetition may be the weak phase, or vice versa. The easiest example is our 2/4 bar with the generating pattern *one*–two. Repeated, it forms a greater pattern of 4/4, in which the one–two group is stronger than the three–four group. And so on in double bars, phrases of four, and periods of eight or sixteen measures—a process that can theoretically be continued ad infini-

---

[13] François-Auguste Gevaert, *Histoire et théorie de la musique de l'antiquité*, 1875–1881, Vol. II, p. 14; Eduard Sievers, *Metrische Studien*, I, in *Abh. d. k. sächs. Ges. d. Wissensch.*, Vol. 48, 1901(03), p. 28. For the opposition: Rudolf Westphal, *Elemente der musikalischen Rhythmik*, Jena, 1872, p. 3.

tum. Hence the old idea that rhythm and 'form' are more or less two names for the same thing.

Alas, not many composers have been acquiescent enough to comply with what the textbook writers demand. The square formation—2^x—is frequent, to be sure. But it is neither general nor, as a rule, consistent. And when we leave its rather restricted realm, the equation of rhythm and form becomes unwieldy and dangerous. Indeed, it would be purest nonsense in the analysis of any symphonic poem by Strauss or Debussy or, for that matter, an organum of the earlier Middle Ages. Even in so well-wrought a form as that of a Bach fugue we would be at a loss to find the prevailing rhythm or form prefigured in the rhythmic cell of the theme. Does the second, C minor, fugue of the *Well-tempered Clavier* reproduce as a whole the tiny anapaest of the theme?

Ex. 1. Bach, *Well-tempered Clavier*, Fugue I, 2

Let us not quarrel over the trifles of words. Everybody is entitled to call the ABA of a da capo aria a rhythmic structure or, if he so chooses, even the four movements of a symphony. They represent indeed what Plato called a rhythm: *kinéseos taxis*, an 'order of movement.' At a pinch, they might represent even Heusler's "organization of time in parts accessible to the senses," if the structure is unusually clear-cut. But the accessibility to the senses is open to doubt. For any longer piece is very definitely at variance with the findings of modern psychology that "the maximum filled duration of which we can be both distinctly and immediately aware" is twelve seconds, which is the reason why the ancient Greeks limited the length of a verse to twenty-five time units.

While we concede—and gladly—that any structure has rhythmical qualities, we must not expand a rhythmical microcosm into a rhythmical macrocosm. Rhythm weakens the more we widen its concept and scope—not only because the perception of rhythm must needs deteriorate with its expansion, but also because the basic requirement of rhythm—regularly recurrent accents, lengths, or numbers—is no longer fulfilled in the larger forms. The four movements of a symphony have accents only in a figurative sense, and their arbitrary, not recurrent, lengths can no longer be said to conform to a rhythmical pattern.

The concept of form, on the other hand, includes a number of non-rhythmical qualities that may be just as strong as rhythm, if not stronger. In the first place, there is pure melody. The form of a rondo depends upon the recurrence, after separating episodes, of a certain leading melody, in which the exact correspondence in the sequence of notes seems more important than their rhythm. In the second place, there is pure harmony. The title "Symphony in C major" implies the outstanding, structural role of C major— as a starting point, an ever-recurring feature, and an end and goal. Of late, our analysts have found tonality to be the structural principle even of operas, particularly Mozart's and Wagner's, with the C major of the *Meistersinger* as the best-known example. And the basic formal principle of a fugue by Bach is its plan of modulation from key to key.

Thus—at least in the eighteenth and nineteenth centuries— harmony as much as rhythm could be said to be 'form.'

Rhythm, like melody or harmony, must not be said to be form. But it can contribute to form as one of several elements, which all concur in creating musical structure. It might even be one of its facets. But we will not dilute the topic of this book by allowing rhythm, the 'bond' of flow, to peter out and lose itself in the infinite.

THE AESTHETIC EXPERIENCE derived from regular intermittence can be twofold, active and passive.

Active experience is directly connected with the work and will of man: all repetition of a motor act at regular, easily perceivable intervals simplifies the work of the limbs. It automatizes the impetus necessary to drive them on and consequently saves considerable energy of motion and volition. The resulting relief implies that pleasurable sensation that we find at the bottom of all aesthetic experience.

The passive aesthetic value of regular intermittence derives from empathy; this word, according to the *Oxford Pocket Dictionary*, denotes "the power of projecting one's personality into (and so fully comprehending) the object of contemplation." The pleasurable sensation passes from the doer to the beholder. It conveys not only the satisfaction of ease and control, but also the gratification that mankind draws from order.

The details belong in the domains of aesthetics and psychology, which lie outside the scope of this book. The interested reader can find a masterly "inventory of the sources of pleasure in rhythm" on half a dozen pages of Carl E. Seashore's *Psychology of Music*.[14]

History, however, shows that aesthetic satisfaction has no absolute, unconditioned character. It is subject to factors that change from man to man, from age to age, from country to country. Rhythm is a 'bond'—a discipline imposed on music and poetry in order to convert unshaped raw material into a well-wrought art. And therefore the satisfaction that it gives depends upon the degree to which the interference of form with formless nature is desired or at least tolerated.

Thus the aesthetic appreciation and the fate of rhythm must needs agree with the appreciation and the fate of form in all the history of art and with its foremost rule: the more a style leans to the classicistic side, the more does it stress form at the cost of naturalness and of the striking power of nature's haps and passing moments. The less a style is classicistic, the more does it stress the here and now of reality at the cost of form. Classicistic styles, both in poetry and in music, will readily sacrifice a good deal of natural speech inflection to the beauty, flow, and cadence of meters. And in instrumental music, they will sacrifice many impulses that might conflict on the spur of the creative moment to the smoothly running evenness of recurring lengths and accents. Non-classicistic styles, on the contrary, would readily sacrifice the even flow and cadence of regular meters to natural speech inflection and conflicting impulses on the spur of the creative moment.

Examples are not hard to find: the steadily growing victory of speech inflections over the formality of even, recurrent meters in Greco-Roman antiquity; the decay of Gregorian meters in the naturalistic times of the Romanesque; the 'oratorical' style with emphatic offbeats or *senza misura* in the naturalistic Early Baroque; the prose texts of operas—*Louise, Pelléas, Salome*—in the naturalistic age around 1900; and the ever-changing, not recurrent

14 Carl E. Seashore, *Psychology of music,* New York, 1938, pp. 140–145.

time signatures in the primitive world as well as in the primitivistic world of Stravinsky and Bartók.

Counter-examples on the classical side are: the strict regulations in the so-called classical times of ancient Greece; the imposition of rhythmic modes on the polyphony of the earlier and middle Gothic Age; the rigid accents in the High Renaissance of Italy; the even beats of Luther's chorales in the time of Bach; or the strictness and consistency of Mozart's rhythms.

FREEDOM AND STRICTNESS. Order is the vast expanse between the deadly extremes of chaos and mechanization. There are numberless shades within this expanse, some of which draw closer to one of the poles, and some to the other: freedom is often not far from chaos; punctilious, frigid strictness stands next to mechanization. The present author does not share in the view of the Swiss philosopher, Ludwig Klages, that the two sides (he calls them, not quite successfully, *Rhythmus* and *Takt*) are different in essence.[15] Shades of the same phenomenon, they stretch between the extremes of chaos and metronomic lifelessness; and whatever we call music is nearer to one or to the other extreme, in a gradation similar to that in human locomotion between a leisurely stroll and stiff-legged goose-stepping, with a light-footed, effortless walking pace somewhere in the middle.

Rhythmical freedom must therefore not be looked upon as lawbreaking with a judge's contemptuous eye. It is neither inferior nor rudimentary, but just dissimilar. Far from being chaotic or defective, the rhapsodic strains of a shepherd lonely on the hills can have the wild, exciting beauty of horses, unbridled and panting, that gallop across the savanna. And again they have the soothing, tender, often melancholy charm of a streamlet rippling forth in dreamy monotone. Indeed, they might not even suggest that much motion; wide-spun and often with long fermatas and rests, they seem to defy the lapse of time and to hover motionless in the air. Nor could you or would you lift your baton to the song of a lark, although you sense its perfect, lawful orderliness, irrational as it may be. Indeed, you feel that any 'normalcy' of song and motion would kill their charm in an unnatural mechanization.

[15] Ludwig Klages, *Vom Wesen des Rhythmus*, Kampen, 1934.

A good number of sophisticated composers in the nineteenth and twentieth centuries, tired of deadly, inhuman normalization, have tried again and again to retrieve this pristine charm of nature.

The passage from freedom to strictness is smooth; no sharp-drawn border keeps them apart. Mechanical rhythm cannot last for any important length of time, either in music or in poetry. The strictest orchestral performance in western concert halls under the pitiless beat of the baton accepts those often imperceptible shades of driving or checking for which Hugo Riemann invented the pseudo-Greek word *Agogik;* and whoever tries to adjust his mind and fingers to an evenly ticking metronome feels strongly handicapped, even in the soulless execution of etudes, to say nothing of romantic, emotional music. To repeat a striking expression of Ralph Kirkpatrick's, one falls "below the human level." [16]

Free rhythm, a precious heirloom from our animal ancestry, is doubtless the earlier quality. Strictness comes with man.

CLASSIFICATION. Rhythm appears under many very different forms. The word, in the sense of our definition, evokes the even beats in most of our present western music and the almost chaotic arbitrariness in jazz and modern art music; it applies to the regular squareness of East Asiatic melodies; to the weird, irregular patterns of the Near East, of India, and of Negroes all over Africa; to the tidy feet and meters of ancient Greece; to the rigid Gothic *modi* and *ordines* of the Middle Ages; to the complicated polyrhythms of the Flamboyant; to the almost stressless flow of Renaissance polyphony; and to a great many other forms of organization.

In the field of rhythm, approaches and solutions change from country to country, from culture to culture. But they also change from age to age within the same civilization; and we have no lesser difficulties in understanding and performing the almost unaccented polyphony of Palestrina's age within the traditions of our own historical area than in perceiving and comprehending the 7/16 time of a Bulgarian folk song or the breath-taking drumbeat combinations of African Negroes.

It is mainly for this reason that the historian finds but little help

[16] In J. S. Bach, The *"Goldberg" Variations,* ed. Ralph Kirkpatrick, New York, 1938, p. xxiv.

in the diligent studies of experimental psychologists who have been interested in rhythm ever since Ernst Meumann's pioneering approach of 1894.[17] The human guinea pigs of our psychological laboratories, even if carefully shuffled, belong in our time and in our own civilization and yield useful material only for this very limited section of the whole expanse in time and space in which the historian is interested. The history of rhythm teaches, on the contrary, that different generations and different cultures react very differently. When the German psychologist Dietze, for instance, finds that even numbers of beats or stimuli are more easily grasped than odd ones, his statement is valid for hardly fifty per cent of mankind: the whole east of Europe, the north of Africa, the southwestern quarter of Asia, India, and other regions give preference to odd-numbered rhythms and seem to grasp them quite readily.

It is not easy to stake out the diverse forms of rhythm. In all their divergence, they overlap enough to make the classifier's life uncomfortable. Yet we cannot shun the task. A mere description of rhythmical concepts and devices as we find them here and there in the world would be useless and impossible. For only a sound classification can show us what to describe.

The following paragraphs outline the main approaches of mankind to the problem of musical rhythm, albeit tentatively. But the discussion will be brief and will leave details to the chapters in which they find their natural places.

Ex. 2. Beethoven, Seventh Symphony, slow movement

Ex. 3. Schubert, D minor Quartet, slow movement

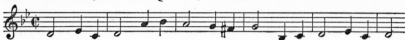

[17] Ernst Meumann, *Untersuchungen zur Psychologie und Aesthetik des Rhythmus*, in *Philosophische Studien*, Vol. X, 1894. Cf., for example, Kate Havner, *The affective value of pitch and tempo in music*, in *American Journal of Psychology*, Vol. 49, 1937, pp. 621–630.

In either one of the slow movements of Beethoven's Seventh Symphony and of Schubert's quartet *Death and the Maiden* we face actually two very different, indeed opposed, kinds of rhythm: in the first place, we can describe the two pieces as moving in 2/4 time, with a stronger accent on every odd-numbered quarter; in the second place, we can describe them as moving in a dactylic or adonic pattern (dactylic being long–short–short, and adonic, long–short–short–long–long).

The first statement means that within a (practically unlimited) pulsation of motor units or quarter notes, an ever so light accent stresses the odd-numbered units. This recurrent accent couples every two quarter notes to form a structural group—*one*–two *one*–two, and so forth. The second statement means that the piece appears as a sum of recurrent configurations, each of which comprises one long and two shorts (♩ ♫).

In a similar way, the scherzo in Beethoven's Ninth proceeds in 3/4 time in dotted, so-called cyclic dactyls (♩. ♪ ♩); Bach's Brandenburg Concerto No. 3 moves in ¢ and anapaests (♫♩); and the second section in Brahms' German Requiem—*Denn alles Fleisch ist wie das Gras*—in 3/4 and iambs.

Ex. 4. Beethoven, Ninth Symphony, first movement

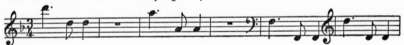

Ex. 5. Bach, *Brandenburg Concerto*, No. 3

Ex. 6. Brahms, *Deutsches Requiem*, second movement

The two statements are obviously not just two different ways of describing the same quality; the dactyls may appear under two different time signatures, 2/4 and 3/4; and the signature 3/4 goes with both dactyls and iambs. Rather, the two descriptions mark two different regulating principles.

The first of these principles, closest to westerners, is easily understood as a progress in even steps: again and again western musicians have measured their time and tempo by normal, leisurely strides. And they have used the stride, not as a simile, but to cover an actual unit of motion. A series of beats at equal distances is organized in patterns of two beats through evenly recurring accents: *one*–two *one*–two (2/4).

This 'striding' form of rhythm may be called 'divisive.' A stride, in the words of Webster's *International,* is "an act of locomotion . . . completed when the . . . feet regain the initial relative positions." The stride is hence a concept that exists before we divide it into two components or phases of equal length, the step of the left foot and the step of the right. In a similar way, its musical counterpart, the 2/4, exists as a basic pattern before we divide it into one accented and one less accented step or beat, as we usually call it for the conductor's motion. The 2/4 exists as a basic, ruling pattern before the details of melody take shape in the head of the composer. In the simplest cases, in marches, hymns, nursery songs, etc., the actual melody coincides with the beats. In more complex pieces, the melody proceeds without too much regard for the stepping frame. Theoretically, the first beat of a group or bar is meant to carry the strongest accent or weight. Indeed, the conductor's baton moves energetically down. What the ear perceives is often very different and contradictory: all accents, indeed all notes, may fall between the beats; and, ignoring the conductor's gesture, the composer might place a rest or else let die the fading remainder of a previous note tied over the bar line where properly the strongest beat should be. Actually, the rest is in this case not a repose, not a cessation of activity, but rather what the late-Latin, French, and Italian terms for quarter rests suggest: a *suspirium, soupir,* or *sospiro,* that is, a 'sigh' or a 'breath,' indeed, an active function of our body.

Whether or not the regulating beat in divisive rhythm is perceptible or else contradicted by a freer span of the melodic line, it exists as an all-present function of the organizing forces in our bodies and minds. It reflects and expresses the regular alternation in which we arrange our movements, be it the actual tension and relaxation of muscles or a steady reciprocity of the right and the left foot in striding. Consciously or subconsciously, we relate the music to this physiological rhythm and overlook its vagaries, or else we enjoy them as such for giving us the aesthetic delight in order with freedom.

Along with divisive rhythm, the examples given above—iambs, dactyls, and anapaests—show a different concept of rhythm. The regular recurrence on which such patterns rest is not a certain duration to be divided into equal parts, but rather a grouping (in poetry: foot) composed of longer and shorter elements (in poetry: syllables), such as $2 + 1$, or $3 + 3 + 2$ units, or any other arrangement of shorts and longs. These rhythms are 'additive.' As a consequence, disturbing offbeats, ties, and rests in accented places are inadmissible in principle. They would destroy the identity of an additive pattern.

Divisive rhythm shows how the parts are meant to be disposed. It is regulative. Additive rhythm shows how the parts are actually disposed. It is configurative.

Another consequence is that these aggregates of dissimilar elements cannot be called 'striding.' Their physiological equivalent is rather the tension and relaxation that we experience in breathing in and out—a motion to and fro which is under normal conditions regular but hardly equal.

The simile of respiration forced itself upon writers on rhythm as early as the nineteenth century. Alas, pent up in the music of their time or, worse, in the music of "our classical masters" Bach and Handel, Mozart and Beethoven, and smilingly nescient of anything else, they misused, like Mathis Lussy in Paris, respiration for a divisive, binary rhythm which did not need or even stand this simile. A more important statement has to hide in a footnote of Lussy's: that "when we hear a person breathe in a quiet sleep, the time between expiration and inhalation is twice as long as that between inhalation and expiration. Consequently [says Lussy] a person in a state of quiet breathes in ternary time." [18] The audacious dictum that respiration is by nature just ternary seems

[18] Mathis Lussy, *Die Correlation zwischen Takt und Rhythmus*, in *Vierteljahrsschrift für Musikwissenschaft*, Vol. I, 1885, p. 144.

to be doubtful even if we do not secure the testimony of a physiologist. I am afraid that Lussy yielded to the lure of tampering somewhat with the irrational durations of nature, since the only uneven
time he knew was ternary. But the essential facts in his argument
are these: (1) binary rhythm is *not* breathing, as Lussy had stated
before; and (2) respiration belongs to ternary rhythm.

The latter point demands clarification. The words "in principle"
and "purest form" in the preceding paragraphs were necessary to
avoid confusion. The very examples from European music at the
head of this section, from Bach and Beethoven, Schubert and
Brahms, show that the two elementary concepts of rhythm can
unite and have united, in the East and the West, in the past and
the present. The spondee, the dactyl, and the anapaest of the
Greeks may be meant to be 'additive,' but since they can be divided by two, they are also divisive. And our, and Lussy's, 3/4,
although divisible by three, is even in modern western music
as a rule iambic or trochaic, that is, 'additive' in the sense of $1 + 2$
or of $2 + 1$.

Rhythmology—especially in the field of poetic versification—
has coined a pair of terms to cover the two forms of rhythms just
discussed: it calls 'qualitative' the rhythms based on equidistant
accents, and 'quantitative' the rhythms based on impulses at different distances. 'Qualitative' refers to intensity—to strong or weak,
accented or stressless; 'quantitative' refers to duration—to long or
short.

The present author hesitates to use these terms. For even educated musicians and experienced philologists pause a moment to
make sure which is which. The two words are too similar in sound
to express the contrast graphically and too vague to denote duration and accent as unmistakably as they should. Thus, the present
author finds in his faithful *Petit Larousse* that in French the verses
following *la quantité* of syllables are called *métriques,* but the
verses following *le nombre* of syllables are called *rythmiques.* Alas,
when you care to look up *quantité* in the same dictionary, you will
find it to be a *nombre.* Incidentally, is not, in logical language,
'quantity' very definitely one of the 'qualities' of a rhythm? Since

Le petit Larousse is on the desk, let us see . . . and indeed: *quantité* is a *qualité* of that which can be numbered. . . .

Instead of the later term 'quantitative,' the Greeks invented, and most scholars have kept, the word *metron* (in Latin *metrum*), derived from the verb *metreo* (in Latin *metiri*) 'to measure.' In full agreement with this term, the later Middle Ages called 'mensural' a notation especially devised to show the relative lengths of its notes, its longs and its breves; and to this day, the terminology of the French, leaders in versification, has retained the names of *vers mesurés* and *vers métriques* for poetry in long–short patterns. Hence meter has the backing of a tradition strong and good enough to justify its use for rhythm by length, and nothing but rhythm by length.

What, however, should rhythmic organization by stress be called? Here, too, the coexistence of conflicting definitions runs one into serious difficulties. Even the ancient Greeks and Romans, who laid the foundations for every discussion on rhythm, have left a rather confusing picture. Most of them do what we can and will not do: they juxtapose 'meter' and 'rhythm,' as does for instance Aristides Quintilianus around 100 A.D.: "Meter is only in words, but rhythm is in the motion of bodies" (*metrum in verbis modo, rhythmus in corporis motu est*). Saint Augustine, the Carthaginian Church father (A.D. 354–430), has been quoted as opposing this terminology when he rightly says that "every meter is rhythm, but not every rhythm is meter" (*omne metrum rhythmus, non omnis rhythmus etiam metrum est*). What he, as a representative of late antiquity, actually means is something very different: 'meter' has at least two verse feet and not more than four; 'rhythm' is an aggregate of several meters. However, he adds, musicians call all feet and meters 'rhythms.' [19] This amounts more or less to what Servius (late fourth century A.D.) tersely states in *De accentis:* Metricists accommodate duration to their syllables; rhythmicists accommodate their syllables to time.[20]

The Greek distinction between 'rhythm' and 'meter' does not

[19] Aurelius Augustinus, *Musik*, transl. C. J. Perl, Strassburg, 1937, p. 89.
[20] Quoted from Rudolph Westphal, *Fragmente und Lehrsätze der griechischen Rhythmiker*, Leipzig, 1888/89, p. 43.

help us, since it opposes a musical to a poetical concept. On the contrary, what we need is a couple of terms for different aspects of the one musical concept of rhythm.

The present author thinks that the best antonym of 'metrical' would be 'accentual.' This word is by no means his invention; it has been used here and there, and notably in the timeless controversy on the rhythm of Gregorian chant; but it is buried under heaps of inadequate terms. Unfortunately, this word is not quite adequate either. Actually, we accent very little unless there is a *sforzato* mark on a note; and a considerable part of our allegedly accentual literature is played on the organ, and another part was in earlier centuries performed on the harpsichord, where accents are outright impossible. Metrical music, on the other hand, including the most metrical melodies from India and Greece, can seldom do without accents, even where stresses are not compulsory. The term 'accentual' is, however, acceptable as long as we keep in mind the basic fact that, as pointed out before, accent, albeit regulative, is not necessarily perceptible, provided that we ourselves project into music our awareness of an accentual pattern.

It should be made clear from the very beginning that a strict separation and opposition of meter and accent contradicts the facts. With a few exceptions—such as the so-called Scotch snap and the prosody of the French language—there has always been a natural trend toward the lengthening of accents and, on the other hand, toward bestowing an accent on lengths.

To sum up: pure accent and pure meter are mere extremes, not opposite classes. They meet and merge in ever new combinations.

From an orthodox viewpoint, accentual rhythm ought to be binary: two beats, not three, are connected and comparable with our even strides to the left and the right. Ternary patterns like 3/8, 3/4, and 3/2 stand halfway in the metrical camp. Not being divisible by two, they necessarily consist of two unequal parts in the ratio of 2:1; they are two *plus* one (trochaic) or one *plus* two (iambic) just as much as they are three times one.

Meters, on the other hand, are not estranged from bodily motion either. In the Orient, they are inseparable from accentual hand-clapping and drumbeats; and in ancient Greece, they were members of the complex art of 'orchestics,' in which words, music, dancing, marching, and gesture combined the expressions of the mind and the body.

In their common relation to the stride of man, the two approaches to rhythm overlap. 'Meters' of two equal members such as in Greece the pyrrhic ♫, the proceleusmatic ♫ ♫, the spondee ♩ ♩, and the dispondee ♩ ♩ ♩ ♩, are divisive and multiplicative rhythms in need of an accent to keep their identity.

While the contrast of metric and accentual patterns is striking enough for ready distinction, there exists an important and somewhat embarrassing third group of verses and melodies in which no metric organization and hardly any recurrence of accents are considered.

Philologists have tried to comprehend this group as a third, independent class along with the metric and the accentual group. They have taken the number of syllables in a verse as the distinguishing trait—eleven for the Italian *endecasillabo,* twelve for the French *alexandrin*—and called the verses 'counted' or 'isosyllabic.' The latter term can hardly be commended. In the first place, 'syllabic' cannot be extended to textless musical rhythms; in the second place, it might suggest an invariable number of units in each of the lines as well as a uniform length for each of the syllables.

Andreas Heusler [21] has denied this group an existence in its own right. Its main characteristics, as he sees them, are: a sequence of syllables in principle equally long; a (suggested) alternation of up and down, with one down between two ups (as iamb and trochee), or with two downs between two ups (as anapaest and dactyl): actual accents infrequent. He says: "Usually, like the Romance verse, the last up before a caesura and the end of a line must bear a syllable accented in speech. Otherwise the verse does not need any coincidence of up and natural accent."

Seen from this angle, the alleged third group would be nothing but a shade of accentual verses, in which the voice is allowed to ignore a number of suggested accents in the interest of one or two essential stresses in a line. This, however, is hardly an exclusive feature. It has been done in a goodly number of verses that we would unhesitatingly call accentual. Every well-built verse runs

[21] Andreas Heusler, *Deutsche Versgeschichte,* Vol. I, Berlin, 1925, p. 85.

to a single peak; and we do not know how often the performers might have bestowed this one-peak on quite respectable verses in order to avoid mechanization and enhance a speechlike flow.

On the other hand, it must be conceded—against Andreas Heusler's authority—that a feel of rhythm can doubtless be conveyed by an even or alternate recurrence of numbers, if they do not exceed the limit of easy perception.

The *Rigveda,* most sacred book of India, and the *Avesta,* the holy book of ancient Iran, are uniformly composed of sixteen syllables in two equal half-verses, without any meter or accent. A similar organization is common in Chinese, Korean, and Japanese verses; it recurs in Byzantine chant, in Middle English, French, Spanish, Portuguese, and Italian poetry. The original Alexandrine verse of France was established in the twelfth century as a non-metrical and non-accentual set of twelve syllables in two sections of six syllables each, after the manner of the Avestan verse.

But the best example of numerical rhythm is the national verse of Italy, the *endecasillabo* or line of eleven syllables. During the seven hundred years of its existence—from Guittone d'Arezzo and Dante to G. Carducci and d'Annunzio—it never leaned towards meter; all syllables have in principle identical length, although the Italian likes to dwell on accented syllables even in ordinary speech. The organization is purely accentual, but in various arrangements. Theory distinguishes between an *a maiore* and an *a minore* form: *a maiore* denotes the form 6 + 5 syllables, *a minore,* on the other hand, 4 + 7 syllables. There is always an accent before the caesura, and another on the next to the last syllable. The classical *a maiore* verse is the first line of Dante's *Divina Commedia:*

> *Nel mezzo del cammin di nostra vita*
> .   .   .   .   .   !   .   .   .   ! .

The *a minore* verse has an additional accent in between:

> *Per me si va nella città dolente*
> .   .   .   !   .   .   .   !   . !   .

or:

> *Per me si va nell' eterno dolore*
> .   .   .   !   .   .   !   .   . ! .

(The *endecasillabo* recurs in Spain as the *endecasílabo;* its *a maiore* form is *común,* and its *a minore* form, *sáfico.*)

Within the *endecasillabo,* the accents have changed in number, place, and intensity; but the eleven syllables have not changed. This number, then, is the essential quality of the verse.[22]

It is, however, outside the scope of a musical book to establish verse classifications. Whether or not this kind of rhythm is a sub-division of accentual poetry should be left to the decision of philologists. The phenomenon as such cannot be ignored, be it co-ordinated or subordinated. And since a phenomenon must have a name in order to be discussed, we choose 'numerical.' Too bad that the only adequate name, 'quantitative,' has been misused for other purposes.

Numerical rhythm, with its three qualities,

> (1) a counted number of syllables,
> (2) absence of meter,
> (3) absence, scarcity, or vagueness of accents,

accounts for an impressive number of musical structures at variance with those which we take for granted. This applies essentially to the most characteristic music of eastern Europe, especially Russia.

Ex. 7. Mussorgsky, *Pictures at an Exhibition, Promenade*

When we try to analyze the *Promenade* from Mussorgsky's *Pictures at an Exhibition* (1874), we realize the failure of our wonted criteria. The composer gives to the first measure 5/4, and to the second one, 6/4. But these signatures are arbitrary and illogical. There is definitely no special accent (as there should be) on the first beat of the second bar. Rather, there are *sforzato* marks on each one of the notes. On parsing the phrase, we might find a suggestion of alternately up and down, five complete and one catalectic iamb, while the opposite sequence is musically impos-

---

[22] Cf. also Emilia Fiorentino, *I ritmi della poesia italiana sono quelli della musica,* in *Rivista musicale Italiana,* Vol. 23, 1916, pp. 73–114.

sible. But an actual alternation of strong and weak would be against the consistent *sforzato* marks as well as against all musical logic. The only admissible description is: a phrase of eleven quarter beats with a suggested but not realized stress pattern.

There are hundreds of similar examples; Mussorgsky's and Stravinsky's scores are full of them, and a few will be quoted in the last two chapters of this book.

Here, it will suffice to say that, while numerical rhythm is poetically a nuance of accentual organization, it is musically a shade of additive patterns.

TEMPO. The natural stride of man, important in matters of rhythm, is inevitable in matters of tempo.

Men of today are generally unaware of the fact that there was, is, and must be, an average normal time—*tempo giusto,* as the time of Handel called it. Without the concept of normalcy we would not be able to rate a tempo as fast or as slow. Again and again, each chapter of this book will have to record a standard tempo recognized as 'normal'; and again and again, each chapter of this book will have to mention that the regular stride of a man walking leisurely has provided the physiological basis. This implies a rather consistent time unit or 'beat' of 76–80 M.M., which means 76–80 pendulum ticks a minute on Johann Nepomuk Mälzl's commonly used metronome.

It is obvious that we call fast all tempi expressed in higher metronome numbers, and slow, all tempi expressed in lower metronome numbers. Still, things are not that simple.

The complication and confusion in modern times derive from our elaborate gamut of tempo shades *prestissimo, presto, un poco presto,* and so on all the way down to *molto adagio.* Such a variety of tempi implies a ratio of about 1:8 between its extremes: the fastest tempo is meant to be eight times quicker than the slowest tempo.

Such a range does not, and actually cannot, exist. For it conflicts with physiological conditions of tempo, with the range accessible to marchers' steps, to dancers' *pas,* to conductors' beats. No human being is able to stretch or to shorten steps and beats within so enormous a span. Dancers, marchers, conductors would automatically take a number of all too rapid units on one of their steps or beats or else divide an all too sluggish unit into a number of steps or beats in order to re-establish a physiologically acceptable meaning and basis. In other words, the conductor would in a medium tempo beat quarters, in a faster tempo halves or wholes, and in a slower tempo eighths. Therewith he would reduce an alleged difference in tempo to an actual difference in symbols. We know this change of symbols without a change of tempo best from the practice current around 1500: quite a number of pieces of that time are written with a certain time unit in one manuscript, and with a different time unit in some other source without the slightest implication of different tempi.

An actual change of tempo, a true acceleration or retardation, is possible only in much narrower limits. The maximum of slowness, which still allows for a steady step or beat, is possibly M.M. 32, but probably a higher metronome figure; and the maximum of speed, beyond which the conductor would fidget rather than beat, is probably M.M. 132. These two extremes are not at a ratio of 1:8, but at best only of 1:4, and probably less.

Incidentally: the present author has tried to metronomize Bach's B minor Mass, each movement separately and on various days, and found that his beat was consistently near M.M. 80, covering now a quarter note, now an eighth, now even a half note, including the "fast" triple-time pieces like the *Gloria,* in which two of the three eighths follow one of these beats (which would amount to ♩. = M.M. 53).

And, once more, incidentally: The belief that from the oriental layers of history down to the eighteenth century in Europe the throbbing heart has provided a physiological basis of musical tempo is widely open to criticism. The present author, for example, has a pulse somewhere in the sixties, and sometimes even below sixty; but his usual, 'personal' standard tempo in performing or reading music is approximately 80 M.M. And a similar lack of agreement between the alleged physiological standard and cause and the actual personal tempo could be observed in the tempi of nearly all of the tested musicians. This irrefutable fact belies the musical influence of heart pulsation. Is it not rather the other way round: that in determining musical tempo, civilizations without a mechanical metronome have always availed themselves of the ticking clock that nature has given to the heart? The pulse can certainly measure music. But just as certainly it does not rule it.

It seems, therefore, that the word 'tempo' covers two very different concepts. One, the real, physiological tempo, varies within the rather limited range of feasible steps and beats. The other one is psychological. It is less a tempo proper than a mood: the Italian word *adagio*, misused for a tempo, implies moderation and leisure; and *allegro* means, basically, gay and content. When J. J. Quantz (1752), who will be quoted and discussed in a later chapter, apportions M.M. 80 to the half note in *presto*, to a quarter note in *allegretto*, to an eighth note in *larghetto*, and to a sixteenth in *lento*, he misleads the reader completely. For all his alleged tempi are simply the assignments of different note symbols to one and the same beat—in fact, *proportiones* in the sense of the Renaissance. They do not become actual tempi without those imponderables that every good performer knows: the same metronomic tempo can be given a driving or a hesitant character.

Not frigid metronome figures, but "the movement's inner measure is the sole determinant," said Robert Schumann.

CHAPTER 2

Beginnings and Primitive Stage

THE BODY'S MOTION. When Hans von Bülow, the great conductor and pianist, boldly decreed: "In the beginning was rhythm," he took advantage of the prerogative of so many pointed sayings: to be pithy, impressive, and unfounded.[1]

Organization of rhythm came long, long after men—like the birds—had given melodic shape to mirth and to mourning.

As long as singers stand alone, without other voices or instruments to join, the urge for strictness in rhythm and tempo is very weak. The melody of backward civilizations, in America, the South Sea Islands, Asia, and Africa, seldom has the mechanical discipline for which all higher cultures strive. Attention of primitive singers and listeners does not, as a rule, carry beyond the short, individual verse and reawakens only after a few irrational moments of respite.

Western concepts that a modern transcriber might be tempted to suggest for the sake of easy reading are dangerous; bar lines and time signatures at the head of a staff give a false account of this freedom and irrational character. Even where *we* think that a certain song "is" in 2/4, or one–two one–two, a subsequent verse line could easily have a few syllables more or less and force the melody to follow suit. And the listener is left in doubt whether the singer has switched to 3/4 or to 2½/4, where he actually has not switched at all.

Moreover, the same melodic line would often serve for poems

[1] Bülow's opinion was shared by Vincent d'Indy (*Cours de composition musicale,* Paris, 1912, Vol. I, p. 20).

entirely different in character. A good example is the music of the Gond, a tribe in Central India. "Each Gond melody is sung to several sets of verses—that is, a melody is sung to one set of verses at one time and to quite a different set of verses at another. The basic melody remains the same, but in a particular combination we may find four notes in a 'measure' while in another there may be three or five or any other number—as many as the syllables of the different verses require." [2]

In most solo singing of the primitives we are at a loss to detect a binding principle or pattern in any western sense except for an emotional stress here and there or for the to and fro, however irregular, of tension and relaxation.

Still, rhythm can be, and often is, the essential part of music, even in primitive society. As Frances Densmore states in her discussion of the music of the Algonquin Chippewa Indians, "The words of a song may be slightly different in rendition, or the less important melody progressions may vary, but a corresponding variation in rhythm has not been observed. A song when sung by different singers, shows an exact reproduction of rhythm." [3]

There is no contradiction; even in the world of primitive man the basic motor impulse must in many styles be more important than the interest in words.

Where this is not the case, the rhythmical weakness (as seen from a western viewpoint) yields in general to the shaping force of habit; melodies repeated over and over again—and most of them are—freeze into strictness with the lapse of time. An excellent example is the songs of the extremely primitive Veddas in inner Ceylon, who despite their undeveloped culture achieve a rather reliable rhythm with every two beats in the rudimentary patterns of spondaic or dactylic 2/4 feet.

They also achieve a rudimentary co-ordination with the body. Mrs. Selenka, who recorded Vedda melodies early in 1907, saw how, "while singing, they rocked the upper part of the body slightly, as if in empathy with the rhythm. One of them moved clearly the thumb in cadence, and the older man beat time with

    [2] Walter Kaufmann, Folk-songs of the Gond and Baiga, in The Musical Quarterly, Vol. XXVII, 1941, p. 280.
    [3] Frances Densmore, Chippewa music, Washington, 1910, p. 6.

the big toe, which he appeared to move quite independently." [4]

The body's motion, actual or suggested, is indeed a general concomitant of rhythm, sometimes seemingly a result, but oftener its cause.

Karl Bücher, in his well-known book *Arbeit und Rhythmus*, often reprinted after its first edition of 1896, appears to have been the first among recent authors to insist on the elementary fact that rhythm is by no means inherent in either poetry or music but solely, he says, in the movement of human bodies, whence it passes on to verses and singing or playing.

The ancients, it is true, had anticipated this statement. Plato had expressly assigned *harmonía*, or melodic organization, to *ōdē* or singing, but *rhythmós* to *órchesis*, or art in man's bodily movement.[5] And five hundred years later, Marcus Fabius Quintilianus had unmistakably said: *metrum in verbis modo, rhythmus in corporis motu est*—"meter is only in words, but rhythm in the body's motion." [6] Marius Victorinus said the same in similar words.[7] Almost two thousand years later, the contrast recurs in what the French today call *rythme de la parole* and *rythme du geste*.[8]

It is the Aristidian *rhythmus in corporis motu* and *le rythme du geste* that the Swiss philosopher, Ludwig Klages, expresses from his point of view when he says: "The world of sound is to a much higher degree dynamic than the world of color, light, and shadow; it cannot but side with the world of motion. Hence, there is, so to speak, a psychical [*seelische*] gravitation between sound and motion, which causes every rhythmical sound to create rhythmical movements, and every rhythmical movement to create a rhythmical sound." [9]

But much as rhythm and bodily motion act and react on one another, rhythm cannot depend directly on muscles and sinews. Plato, two and a half thousand years ago, was already aware of the absence of rhythm in a narrower sense from the lives of

[4] Max Wertheimer, *Musik der Wedda*, in *Sammelbände der Internationalen Musikgesellschaft*, Vol. IX, 1909, pp. 300 f.

[5] Plato, *Laws*, I, 653–654.

[6] *Marcus Fabius Quintilianus, Institutionum oratoriarum*, libri duodecim, 9:4.

[7] Marius Victorinus, *Ars grammatica*, in Heinrich Keil, *Grammatici latini*, Leipzig, 1874, Vol. VI.

[8] Vincent d'Indy, *Cours de composition musicale*, Paris, 1912, Vol. I, p. 28.

[9] Ludwig Klages, *Vom Wesen des Rhythmus*, Kampen (1934), p. 39.

animals,[10] although their bodies are functionally similar to ours. Man is the first animal to dominate rhythm. For "rhythm comes from the mind and not from the body." [11] Man does not follow a body-made rhythm in blind passivity. He himself, on the contrary, creates the law of rhythm and forces it upon the motion of his body in walk and dance, in work and play. Music and poetry accept this law to a greater or lesser degree, according to their greater or lesser nearness to bodily motion.

ADAPTATION. The dance, all-important in primitive life as a magic, musical, social, indeed a gymnastic, athletic phenomenon, presents itself to the mind as the most vital link between the flowing melodic impulse of singing and the regulating rhythmic impulse from bodies in motion.

Language, so often the truest mirror of thoughts and events, confirms this linkage. The better part of rhythmic terminology has come from dancing or from the indispensable limb that serves all motion and station: the 'foot,' or *pous* and *pes* in Greek and Latin, which in all the western languages serves to denote the smallest rhythmical unit. The aggregate of feet, the 'verse,' derives from Latin *vertere*, and the aggregate of verses, a 'strophe,' from the Greek word *stréphomai*, both being verbs denoting the act of turning. 'Stanza' stems from *stare*, 'to stay'; and 'period' or *períodos*, literally a 'roundabout way,' meant in Greek a circuit or rotation.

Organized in regular patterns, motor impulses pass from the moving limbs to the accompanying music, only to revert from voices, clappers, and drums as a stronger stimulus to the legs and torsos of those who dance. For, in Heusler's words, "the recurrence of equal sections [of time] stimulates our muscle sense." [12] Often, music seems to be in the lead: melody begins, and the dancers follow as if obeying the rhythm and tempo imposed on them by the singers and players. This is quite customary among the North American Indians. Actually, the musical introduction only antici-

[10] Plato, *Laws*, I, 654 B.

[11] Gisèle Brelet, *Le temps musical*, Paris, 1949, Vol. I, p. 260.

[12] Andreas Heusler, *Deutsche Versgeschichte*, Vol. I, Berlin, 1925 (in *Grundriss der germanischen Philologie*, Vol. 8, i), p. 17.

pates the usual rhythm and tempo of the well-known, often-performed movements of the dancers. The unprepared reader must, however, be warned that these tribal rhythms have very little in common with ours; primitive dancing does not know the regular 2/4, 3/4, or 6/8 times that the West takes for granted.[13]

Aside from dancing, certain forms of regulated work, such as cradle rocking, manioc grinding, rice peeling with pestles, have forced a regular beat on accompanying melodies—although the all-dominating influence that Bücher assigns to manual work in shaping music and rhythmic organization seems to be greatly exaggerated.

A similar impulse in man's evolution towards a stricter rhythm appears to have come from choral adaptation. One single sentinel in front of a palace is hopelessly ridiculous when he goose-steps back and forth between the gate and his sentry box; but a goose-stepping battalion can be convincing and perhaps impressive. The lonely singer, in the fields or the vineyard, does not need, or want, or stand a rational, countable rhythm; but an accompanied singer —or, for that matter, a chorus—requires a rhythmic principle to regulate the partnership. When the rather primitive Andaman Islanders, to the east of India, sing their unpretentious songs, the verse has the freedom of recitative, but the chorus is strictly rhythmical.

In later strata, another decisive impulse came from instrumental accompaniment. It is true that breath, as the medium of singers and pipers, is a continuum almost independent of actual respiration and directly under the impact of emotive, melodic inspiration. The word 'almost' can even be dropped in the case of reed pipes: oriental pipers need not and do not interrupt their play to refill the lungs once in a while; in and out, they breathe through the nose as glass blowers do and use the mouth as a wind chamber under pressure as if it were the bag of a Highlander's pipe.

But unlike singing and blowing, activities such as rattling, scraping, stamping, striking, plucking, and later even bowing will easily if not compulsorily follow the rhythmic impulse latent in man's psycho-physiologic constitution and settle in even beats or recur-

[13] Cf. Sachs, *World History of the Dance*, New York, 1937, pp. 175–203.

rent patterns. Erich M. von Hornbostel and Robert Lachmann were probably the first to see this.[14] Thrasybulos Georgiades, who had hardly known their statements, tells us in his book on Greek rhythm that within the basically metric folk music of modern Hellas players of plucked and percussion instruments tend to give accents.[15]

POLYRHYTHM. These musical accents allow us to understand the highest form of adaptation: polyrhythm. It has developed out of the rhythmic impulse derived from the shape, the size, and the playing position of instruments, and hence from the specific work of the muscles required to play them. But this physiological basis must not overshadow the psychological disposition of the people whom nature has driven to delight in the combination of con-tradictory rhythms and to convert disorder into a planned art.

This conversion might explain the seeming paradox of the initial sentence: that polyrhythm (which is of necessity counterrhythm) is the highest form of adaptation. Does not adaptation imply agree-ment, and counterrhythm, disagreement? Actually, all counter-rhythm is the agreement, on a higher artistic level, of disagreeing rhythms. It means sameness in variety.

Such counterrhythms are in the primitive world exclusively instrumental—a proof that, technically, they stem from muscular impulses.

In Indonesia and in Africa, counterrhythms attain an almost unique complication. There is the clicking, clattering pestle play of rice-pounding women in the Malay Archipelago—*tingtung tutung-gulan gondang* in the onomatopoetic description of a native poet [16]—where the third pestle stamps in uniform halves; the second, in uniform eighths; the first, in uniform offbeat eighths; the fourth, in those additive patterns of $3 + 3 + 2$ sixteenths which we will find in almost every chapter of this book; and the fifth and last, in a free series of alternately three and two sixteenths.

[14] Robert Lachmann, *Musik des Orients,* Breslau, 1929, pp. 67 ff.

[15] Thrasybulos Georgiades, *Der griechische Rhythmus,* Hamburg, 1949, p. 49.

[16] J. Kunst, *Music in Java,* The Hague, 1949, Vol. I, p. 195, after J. S. Brandts Buys. Also Curt Sachs, *Geist und Werden der Musikinstrumente,* Berlin, 1929, p. 206.

Ex. 8. Indonesian pestle-play

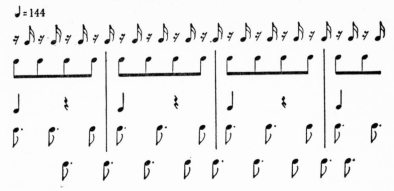

And we also think of the dual rhythm of South African xylophone players who—in a way reminiscent of Ockeghem's *Missa prolationum*—would beat four quarters with the left hand and nine quarters with the right hand to find a 'consonance' every thirty-six beats.[17]

But African drummers seem to reach the climax in their breath-taking drum toccatas. Often a number of large and smaller drums will act together, each one with its independent rhythm against the lead of the principal drum. The players combine accentual rhythm with a rudimentary kind of meter. They constantly alternate between 2/8 and 3/8 groups, with the 3/8 forming now a dotted quarter, now a triplet within 2/8; and they indulge in off-beats and the inversion of long and breve such as in iambs versus trochees.[18] There is even the South Indian *rūpaka* pattern 2 + 3; indeed, there is the 3 + 3 + 2 articulation of eight beats, which we find in practically all civilizations.

An even more incredible example comes from Northern Rhodesia.[19] The second drum proceeds in even 12/8, not without oc-

[17] Melville J. Herskovits, *Patterns of Negro music*, n.d., p. 2. Cf. also E. M. von Hornbostel, *African Negro music*, reprint from *Africa*, Vol. I, 1928, pp. 24 f.

[18] Rose Brandel, *Sounds from the equator*, New York University master's thesis, 1950, with transcriptions from *Belgian Congo music*, recorded by the Reeves Sound Studio, 1937.

[19] A. M. Jones, *The study of African musical rhythm*, in *Bantu Studies*, Vol. XI, 1937, pp. 295–329, App. II. Cf. also a paper on *African drumming* by the same author, *loc. cit.*, Vol. VIII, 1934.

casional accents on the third eighth of a group. The fourth drum agrees, but articulates the second part of each measure in hemiola: three groups of two notes each replace two groups of three. The third drum has measures of 12/8, too; but they are organized in six eighths, one half note, and two eighths and, furthermore, are shifted by two eighths to the right. The first drum has a 6/8 meter of $2 + 1 + 3$ coincident with the measures of the third drum. The voices, finally, have alternately one bar for the soloist and one for the chorus. They agree with the twelve eighths of the second drum, but are shifted by four eighths to the right and have duplets in the solo measure. The two dotted quarters of the chorus are marked by clapping hands.

Ex. 9. North Rhodesia, Bemba dance

Formally, African Negro drumming is somewhat related to the more sophisticated Indian drumming, which will be discussed in a later chapter of this book. And there is even—very vaguely— the possibility of a prehistoric connection via Sumer or otherwise.

If there is such a connection, a second question would be whether the polyrhythm of the Negroes represents a primitive, prehistoric stage of Indian rhythm or else the degeneration, in primitive surroundings, of a ripe, historic stage. Modern anthropology has become very cautious; it is often inclined to see in "primitive" phenomena distorted remainders of a higher civilization from abroad rather than indigenous stages in the bud. Much as this Indo-African drumming resembles certain aspects of American jazz, a reserved attitude in establishing direct links still seems necessary.

While we are doubtless allowed to speak of intricacy in African drum rhythms, we should avoid the confusion found in popular thinking between the much-abused and undefined notions of simplicity and primitiveness, which seem so closely related in the minds of people who still do their thinking in the evolutionary terms of the eighteenth century. Bach's and Mozart's rhythms are incredibly simple in comparison with many Negro and other primitive rhythms, to say nothing of India and her rhythmical sophistication.

He to whom everything outside his glorious western world is 'savage' will find it hard to accept this fact. Still, the causes of much of the emphasis on rhythm among primitives and in the oriental civilizations are obvious. The West has developed harmony, counterpoint, orchestration, and long-drawn-out forms so thoroughly that rhythm became stunted: the traits that a style enhances are won at the cost of other traits; every gain implies a loss. Moreover, it must not be forgotten how prominent the role of the body is in lower civilizations, how essential it is in man's expression and the forms of his life. Rhythm, as the body's artistic function, cannot but share in this prominence. Thus it would often occur that some rhythmic feature, almost artificial in the works of Beethoven or of Brahms, is perfectly easy-flowing and natural beyond the frontiers of our modern western culture.

NON-ADAPTATION. Much as the co-operation of voices and instruments enhances a common rigid rhythm, we have to accept the bewildering fact that the two media often remain independent of one another. The perceptions of simultaneous percussion and singing are often kept apart as two different, unrelated sensations, which do not call for fusion and, hence, for mutual adaptation. The bliss that the rhythmic organization of clappers or drums conveys can be felt without in the least encroaching upon the coincident song.

In Australia, rhythmically free and independent singing is often accompanied by the rigid, uniform clatter of boomerangs struck against one another. But the point is brought home less by the contrast of freedom versus strictness than by discrepancies in movement. One of the most unexpected experiences in the music of North American Indians is to hear the regular drumbeat of the accompanist follow a tempo entirely different from that of the voice. In one song of the Chippewa,[20] the singer would proceed, say, in quarter notes of M.M. 168, and the drummer, much more slowly, in M.M. 104. Or, the other way round, the voice would sing its quarter notes in M.M. 96, while the drum, much quicker, accompanies in M.M. 152.[21] In a discussion of Yuman and Yaqui music, Frances Densmore says that the voice proceeds "in the same tempo as the accompaniment in 51 per cent, faster in 16 per cent, and slower in 32 per cent of the songs recorded with drum or other instruments."[22] This means that in 49 per cent the drum follows a course of its own.

Such astonishing lack of adjustment must certainly not be looked upon as a self-conscious counterrhythm to compare to the well-wrought double patterns of drummers in India. It rather testifies to a more or less total independence of the two media and their perception. Perhaps this independence is similar to that found in our own church services, where we would not dream of co-ordinating the organ and the choir inside a church with the bells above.

The principle is most fully illustrated in one of the songs of the Chippewas. There the time units of voice and drum are so nearly alike that in Frances Densmore's book the same metronome number is used for both. "At the beginning of the record the drumbeat is slightly behind the voice, but it gains gradually until for one or two measures the drum and voice are together; the drum continues to gain, and during the remainder of the record it is struck slightly before the sounding of the corresponding tone by the voice."[23]

We witness similar incongruities in other parts of the world. "The Bafioti in Loango," in the present author's words, "keep their hopping quite independent of melody and time; and the same is reported of the modern Greek *tratta*. Among the Eskimo the rhythmic accompaniment is not the same as the song (it may be 9/8 as against 4/8, or otherwise), and the East African Was-

[20] Frances Densmore, *Chippewa music*, Washington, 1910, p. 28. For similar evidences from the Indians in Montana cf. Alan P. Merriam, *Flathead Indian instruments and their music*, in *The Musical Quarterly*, Vol. XXXVII, 1951, p. 374.
[21] *Ibid.*, p. 58.
[22] Frances Densmore, *Yuman and Yaqui music*, Washington, 1932, p. 36.
[23] Frances Densmore, *Chippewa music*, Washington, 1910, p. 6.

segeju dance more slowly as the tempo of the accompaniment in-
creases. . . . It appears almost as though an actual unity is not
a natural heritage." [24]

From the more primitive western Caroline Islands in Micronesia,
George Herzog relates (and shows in his transcriptions) that the
natives often sing without a steady rhythm while the clapping
hands beat out some strict though simple pattern.[25]

Obviously a certain cultural growth is necessary to fuse two
different perceptions into one complex experience. And a certain
musicological growth is necessary to understand that in more
primitive civilizations singing and percussion can be two independent activities and independent sensations.

ACCENT AND METER. The lower civilizations, living more
completely through the actions of the body and receiving their
rhythmical impulses from the bodily processes of tension and
relaxation, keep on the whole to pulsating accents. Sometimes
such accents crystallize in regular, ever recurrent patterns. In
Samoa, "the beating of the mats [used as percussion instruments]
sounds like the trotting of a horse, the first tone struck with both
sticks, the second with only one—a trochaic pattern." [26]

But not always are the accents equally spaced. In the music of
North American Indians, as elsewhere too, songs with changing
time are much more frequent than melodies with a strict, consistent time. Frances Densmore, in one of her useful analytic-
statistical surveys of Amerindian music, indicates no less than
811 pieces in the changing category as against 134 in the consistent category [27]—or about six irregular pieces to one regular
melody.

One of the reasons for varying time—and perhaps the principal
reason—is the varying length of text lines, which again depends
upon the ever varying number of syllables necessary to express
an idea. "At first these changes of time seem erratic, but when the

[24] Curt Sachs, *World history of the dance*, New York, W. W. Norton & Company,
Inc., 1937, p. 176.
[25] George Herzog, *Die Musik der Karolinen-Inseln*, Hamburg, 1936, p. 266, ex. 44.
[26] Augustin Krämer, *Die Samoa-Inseln*, Stuttgart, 1903, pp. 315 ff.
[27] Frances Densmore, *Pawnee music*, Washington, 1929, p. 13.

song is regarded as a whole, and especially when it becomes familiar, the changes of measure-lengths are merged in a rhythmic unity which is interesting and satisfactory." [28] As a matter of fact, this kind of change is typical of numerical rather than of accentual rhythms; and this is what probably the majority of primitive melodies are.

As far as it is at all permissible to speak of time signatures in a western sense and what they imply, duple time is, both in the straight and in the mingled species, much more frequent than triple, quintuple,[29] or septuple time.

Metric expression, less closely related to the body than accents, is rudimentary in the primitive world. When it occurs at all, it is most often essentially in the form of dwelling on notes with a stronger tonic accent and emphasis—just as in the older forms of oriental cantillation. But the elements of actual metric patterns are not totally absent. Examples from the Caroline Islands prove that at least percussion is familiar with metrical patterns in algebraic ratios. North American Indians often beat their drums in orthodox 2:1 trochees with a strong accent on the first beat.[30]

In vocal melodies, not subject to the regulating force of the arm and leg muscles, actual meters are rarer. Consistent iambic songs as they appear among the Sebop of Borneo [31] have not many parallels. Iambic patterns can be heard in the liturgy of Mongolia. Still rarer are the persistent trochees, dactyls, and anapaests that we find in melodies of the Maoris of New Zealand.[32] But then, the Maoris as well as the Buddhist Mongols belong to the upper crust of primitive civilization, closest to the oriental high cultures and probably their retrogressive descendants. And even in New Zealand metrics are on a low level, very far from the leading position and thoroughness that they have been granted in the Near and Middle East as well as in ancient Greece.

[28] Frances Densmore, *The American Indians and their music,* New York, 1926, Women's Press, p. 133.

[29] An illustration of quintuple time is found in example 10, from the Solomon Islands, in Curt Sachs, *The rise of music in the ancient world,* New York, W. W. Norton & Company, Inc., 1943, p. 38.

[30] Frances Densmore, *Northern Ute music,* Washington, 1922, p. 101; also *Mandan and Hidatsa music,* Washington, 1923; Merriam, *op. cit.*

[31] Transcribed by Charles S. Myers, A *study of Sarawak music,* in *Sammelbände der Internationalen Musikgesellschaft,* Vol. XV, 1914, p. 306, No. IX.

[32] J. C. Anderson, *Maori music,* New Plymouth, N.Z., 1934, pp. 435 f.

Still, anywhere in the world, some metric, rather than melodic, inspiration might appear as the actual structural nucleus on which to build a musical form. Either alone or together with a few other, contrasting patterns,[33] it would be pregnant enough to be repeated and to generate a musical form.[34] There is no more beautiful illustration of such generation than one of the legends of the Papuas in British New Guinea: "Once," it reads, "an old man sat gazing at the waters of a river when suddenly something lifelike appeared on the surface. A crocodile? No, it was a tree trunk which kept rising from the waves, then disappearing, at definite intervals. The old man reached for his drum and softly beat out the rhythm, and as he struck the drum, the picture of a new dance took shape in his mind." [35]

In the field of rhythmical predominance and pristine inspiration, there is a surprise in store for the reader. The Menominee Indians in North America construct true isorhythms very much

Ex. 10. Menominee Indians, isorhythmic song

like those constructed by the French in the thirteenth and fourteenth centuries. Some characteristic metrical pattern, say of four measures, is forced upon a melody, say, of twelve, sixteen, or more measures. Consequently, measures 5 and 9, though melodically different, have the exact metrical organization of measure 1; and

[33] Frances Densmore, *Papago music*, Washington, 1929.

[34] Cf. Curt Sachs, *The rise of music in the ancient world*, New York, 1943, p. 50, ex. 27, from Lifou, Loyalty Islands.

[35] Curt Sachs, *World history of the dance*, New York, W. W. Norton, 1937, p. 177, after F. E. Williams, *Orokaiva society*, Oxford, 1930, p. 234.

measures 6 and 10 follow just as strictly the metrical pattern of measure 2; and so forth, with measures 7 and 11 after 3, and 8 and 12 after 4.[36]

This surprising appearance of isorhythm in a primitive society is not at all confined to the Menominee. It occurs very often also in the music of the Arapaho Indians in the Great Plains, now as a thorough, now as a partial form of organization.[37]

All over the primitive world, accents and meters, their strength and their nature, are conditioned by factors sometimes beyond our insight and reasoning powers.

MOTOR TYPES. Musical rhythm depends to a great extent upon the motor type that a primitive people builds up in striding, working, dancing, gesticulating. In Erich M. von Hornbostel's words, "The style of Indian music . . . is only one expression of a trait . . . which distinguishes the race most sharply. This is so deeply rooted in the physiological that it persists for thousands of years and withstands the influences of natural and cultural environment and even of miscegenation. It determines equally the body movement of the dancer, the arm movement of the drummer, and the throat and mouth movements of the singer and speaker." [38]

The present author has distinguished in his *World History of the Dance* between closeness and expansion as the fundamental dualism in the field of motor type. Close movement relies on a carefully kept center of gravity, on centripetal gesture and a well-rounded, soft-flowing outline. Expanded movement has vehement, centrifugal gestures, a vigorous stride, and a bulging, jagging, projecting outline. Close movement is basically calm and serene; expanded movement is wild and passionate.[39]

"The intense excitement and passion of the expanded style are expressed not only in the compass and leap of the melody but also very strikingly in its rhythmic freedom. Wherever songs in this style have had to be transcribed into our notation, the musicologist

[36] Cf. Frances Densmore, *Menominee music,* Washington, 1932, p. 30.

[37] Cf. Bruno Nettl, *Musical culture of the Arapaho,* master's thesis, Indiana University, Bloomington, 1951.

[38] Erich M. von Hornbostel, in Theodor Koch-Grünberg, *Vom Roroima zum Orinoco,* Stuttgart, 1923, Vol. III, p. 416.

[39] Curt Sachs, *World history of the dance,* New York, 1937, pp. 24 ff., 34 ff.

has had great difficulty in putting in the bar lines to make a pattern intelligible to the modern student." [40] One song from eastern Flores, only ten measures long, appears in Jaap Kunst's skillful transcription [41] under no less than nine time signatures: 3/2, 7/4, 3/2, 4/4, 5/2, 5/4, 3/2, 7/4, 3/2. "Yet with all these efforts justice is not done the mysterious accentual character of these songs. They simply do not fit into any time scheme, they are rhythmically irrational." [42]

Nowhere is 'expansion' better exemplified than in Mongolia. In their 'expanded' dances, the Mongols sing in purely melodic, passionate, irrational rhythms. They follow neither poetical prosody nor the disciplining influence that dances exert. Not even the principal accents coincide with those of the text, although the singers sustain the final note of every line and put in a rest before the following line begins. Binary and ternary measures alternate, and within these patterns frequent syncopation excludes the simplest form of recurrence. Any stricter rhythm in Mongolian music, particularly 2/4 with essentially stronger accents on the good beats, betrays a recent Chinese influence. [43]

Ex. 11. Mongolian song

Very slow

"In the province of close movement, on the contrary, the rhythm is strict and regular. A measure of a certain count, once established, is generally retained. And strangely enough, this measure is nearly always even [binary]. Of twenty-one Semang melodies [from the jungles of Malaysia], seventeen have even [binary] measures. And the greatest single territory of the close dance, eastern and southeastern Asia, is at the same time the center of quadratic rhythm." [44]

[40] Sachs, *op. cit.*, p. 193.
[41] Jaap Kunst, *Music in Flores*, Leiden, 1942, p. 23, No. 38.
[42] Sachs, *op. cit.*
[43] Cf. P. Joseph van Oost, *La musique chez les Mongols des Urdus*, in *Anthropos*, Vol. X/XI, 1915/16, pp. 358–396; Madame Humbert-Sauvageot, *Dix-huit chants et poèmes mongols*, Paris, 1937; Ernst Emsheimer, *Preliminary remarks on Mongolian music*, in *Reports from the Scientific Expedition . . . of Sven Hedin*, Stockholm, 1943, pp. 75 f.
[44] Curt Sachs, *op. cit.*, pp. 193 f.

SEX. Motor types differ not only from country to country; even within a tribe they vary according to sex. "There is a fact known to all gymnasts and athletes which is fundamental: the man strives for release, for motion forwards and upwards and is better adapted to it than the woman. . . . The inference is not to be drawn that the expanded dance is the exclusive province of men, and the close dance that of women. Men may dance the close dance, too: in many cultural groups, in fact, they do so exclusively. With a very few exceptions, however, the expanded dance is left to the men. The women participate without concern for what the men do and do not permit themselves to be drawn from their own true natures." [45]

"In the same way, the sexes also form opposite singing styles. . . . Out of innumerable examples, the Northwest Siberian Voguls may be cited; the men do almost all the singing, and their melodies are free in rhythm and structure; the women, confined to the so-called Songs of Fate, arrange their melodies in simple and regular verses. Both examples confirm an innate tendency in women to neatly regulate the songs of domestic life also, in doing which they—and their daughters—have faithfully preserved archaic traits that the men have lost." [46]

Out of the almost embarrassing riches of examples, only three distinctive specimens within otherwise different realms of rhythm may be presented. One is a song of manioc-rasping women of the

Ex. 12. Macusí, Manioc-rasping song

Ex. 13. Pangwe, women's song

[45] Curt Sachs, *World history of the dance*, New York, W. W. Norton & Company, Inc., 1937, p. 31.
[46] Curt Sachs, *The rise of music in the ancient world*, New York, W. W. Norton & Company, Inc., 1943, pp. 40 f.
[47] Erich M. von Hornbostel, in Theodor Koch-Grünberg, *Vom Roroima zum Orinoco*, Berlin, 1916, Vol. III, p. 431.

Macusí tribe on the border of Venezuela and British Guiana.[47] Another example is a women's song of the Fang or Pangwe in the Cameroons, in which a soloist alternates with a chorus measure by measure.[48] And a third example is taken from Arabian peasant women on the northern tip of the Sahara.[49]

Ex. 14. Arabian women's song

Though it seems safe to attribute to woman a greater sense of neatness and order, it is necessary to realize, as Bücher has already done,[50] that in practically every primitive culture women, rather than men, have been connected with regular, rhythmical work within or near the house, with cradle rocking, kneading, grinding, pestling, seeding, and weaving. All these occupations settle in an even to-and-fro and force their rigid times and accents—in 2/4 mostly—upon the gentle songs they elicit.

In this connection, one fact has particular interest: The drummers of the Chippewa and other North American Indians leave war dances unaccented, but give accents to moccasin and women's dances.[51] There is hardly an explanation except that the war dances, exciting and tense, need the relentless strain that impatient beats of even distance and even intensity impart; that the women, on the contrary, take refuge in the unexciting orderliness that a uniform alternation of strong and weak conveys.

Plato saw this sexual antithesis two and a half thousand years ago: "Both sexes have melodies and rhythms which of necessity belong to them; and those of women are clearly enough indicated by their natural difference. The grand, and that which tends to courage, may be fairly called manly; but that which inclines to moderation and temperance may be declared both in law and in ordinary speech to be the more womanly quality."[52]

[48] Erich M. von Hornbostel, in Günther Tessmann, *Die Pangwe,* Berlin, 1913, Vol. II, p. 345.
[49] Béla Bartók, *Die Volksmusik der Araber von Biskra und Umgebung,* in *Zeitschrift für Musikwissenschaft,* Vol. II, 1920, p. 504.
[50] Karl Bücher, *Arbeit und Rhythmus,* Leipzig, 1st edition, 1896, Chapter VIII.
[51] Frances Densmore, *Chippewa music,* Washington, 1910, p. 6.
[52] Plato, *Laws,* VII, 702, transl. B. Jowett, New York, 1892.

CHILDHOOD. Closely related to women's songs are the melodies of children. Many, maybe most, of them are ruled by simple, strict, divisive, and usually binary rhythms. All continents and the islands in between provide examples. The four children's songs that Dr. Jaap Kunst has appended to his monumental book, *Music in Java*,[53]

Ex. 15. Javanese children's song

are particularly characteristic, although their binary rhythm is, in Indonesia at least, a common trait of musical form. Next of kin to the young Javanese are, across the straits, the children in Bali, on whose endeavors in music Colin McPhee has written a special study.[54] The four binary children's melodies from the Malabar Coast in southwest India published by Otto Abraham and Erich M. v. Hornbostel [55] are the more significant since they come from an almost anti-binary environment. The picture may be rounded

Ex. 16. Malabar children's song

off with children's songs from the rather primitive civilization of the Baining in New Britain, Melanesia.[56]

Ex. 17. Baining children's song

The examples are herewith presented for what they are worth. It is tempting but dangerous to conclude from the unsophisticated age of their singers that simple, strict, divisive, binary rhythms

[53] Jaap Kunst, *Music in Java*, The Hague, 1949, Vol. II, pp. 534 f.
[54] Colin McPhee, *Children and music in Bali*, in *Djawa*, Vol. XVIII, 1938, No. 6.
[55] O. Abraham und Erich M. v. Hornbostel, *Phonographierte indische Melodien*, in *Sammelbände der Internationalen Musikgesellschaft*, Vol. V, 1904, pp. 360 ff.
[56] George Herzog, *Die Musik der Karolinen-Inseln*, Hamburg, 1936, pp. 340 f.

are "natural" and represent the original rhythmic attitude of man-kind. It is dangerous because the child is under the irresistible in-fluence of the mother and must be supposed to shape its early melodies in the style of maternal, womanly tunes. No child forgets what its mother has sung.

OTHER CONDITIONS OF RHYTHM. There are other topics allied to that of sex differences in rhythm.

The nearest at hand would be the tempting theme of geograph-ical differences in rhythm, which, so far, has been an easy prey for well-meaning amateurs.[57] A scholarly research into this question is still remote. He who tries his hand at a problem so extremely com-plicated should be aware of the very grave dangers that the favorite contrasts of mountains and plains, heat and cold, fertile and in-fertile soil hold in store. He should take to heart the moral of that classic example of two South American Indian tribes, of the same race and living side by side on the same spot of the northeastern Gran Chaco. One of them excels in wildest dance leaps, vigorous rattle swinging, and loud, violent singing. The dances of the other tribe are "a hesitant, indolent weaving to and fro; their musical instruments sound weak and timid; their drum, as though muffled; and their flutes, never shrill; and even their war horn makes less noise than a toy trumpet. . . . No effervescent enthusiasm ap-pears in their melodies. Their singing is soft and listless." [58]

There are, then, two neighboring tribes of the same race in the same climate diametrically opposed in their motor and sounding behavior. Indeed, geography and race are easy catch words which are unreliable guides in the labyrinth of styles. The tools of meteor-ologists and craniometrists seldom open an insight into the secrets of musical life.

Another topic, character differences in rhythm, has met with a slightly better fate as far as scholarly treatment is concerned.[59] The same is true of a closely related theme: Rhythm and Health,[60]

[57] E.g., in the *University of Arizona Bulletin*, Vol. VI, No. 8, Tucson, 1935, pp. 1–44.

[58] Herbert Baldus, *Indianerstudien im nordöstlichen Chaco*, Leipzig, 1931, p. 106.

[59] Werner Aulich, *Untersuchungen über das charakterologische Rhythmusprob-lem*, Halle dissertation, Halle, 1932.

[60] Charles W. Hughes, *Rhythm and health*, in Dorothy M. Scullian and Max Schoen, *Music and medicine*, New York, 1948, pp. 158–189.

albeit only in an historical survey. Short remarks on Rhythm and Physics, Rhythm and Chemistry, Rhythm and Biology, Rhythm and Psychology, Rhythm and History can be found in a Berlin dissertation on the Morphology of Rhythm.[61]

[61] Gotthilf Flik, *Die Morphologie des Rhythmus,* Berlin dissertation, 1936, pp. 12–28.

CHAPTER 3

The Far East

THE HISTORICAL SITUATION. The Far East in a narrower sense comprises the countries and civilizations of China, Korea, and Japan. In a wider sense, it extends westward to the Mongols and Kalmucks,[1] and southward to Burma, Siam, Indo-China, and Malaya on the continent, and to the islands of Indonesia.

These civilizations are by no means of one cast; they differ strongly in origin, race, religion, and language. Buddhism, Hinduism, Taoism, Shintoism, Islam, and, of late, a number of Christian denominations, stand side by side in this enormous territory; and even in its center, China's monosyllabic language with three or four inflections of pitch is opposed to the polysyllabic, little-inflected languages of Korea and Japan.

Notwithstanding all these basic differences, China, the common mother civilization, has put its indelible stamp on all these cultures. Her momentous influence was strongest when, during the second half of the first one thousand years A.D., Japan adopted Indo-Chinese Buddhism as her official religion, the pencil script of China, the Chinese language (in the same way as Latin was adopted in Europe during the Middle Ages) as the idiom of scholars, and the elaborate music and dances of the continent for the ceremonies of the imperial court.

Things are very different today. Buddhism is no longer the leading religion of Japan; Chinese writing symbols have been trans-

[1] Cf. the rhythmical surveys in Ilmari Krohn, *Mongolische Melodien,* in *Zeitschrift für Musikwissenschaft,* Vol. III, 1921, p. 79 ff.

formed to serve the purposes of the native, polysyllabic language, which has totally replaced Chinese, even in scholarly works; and Chinese music exists essentially only in the carefully sheltered *Tōgaku* branch of the imperial court music, which has till recently not been accessible to any research.

In rhythm, though, all of East Asia shows amazingly homogeneous traits, whose beginnings are lost in the darkness of ages.

THE ABSENCE OF METER. The languages of the Far East know long vowels and short vowels, long and short consonants, and hence both long and short syllables, but do not allow them to play a formative role in poetry. In China as well as in Korea and Japan, the unit of verse is the individual syllable, be it long or short; and nothing matters except their number. The *haiku* form in Japan, for instance,[2] has three lines of five, seven, and five syllables, and the *tanka* form [3] has thirty-one syllables in five lines of five, seven, five, seven, and seven syllables. Poetic rhythm is purely numerical.

This implies that dynamic accents are absent, too. Officially, neither language knows such stresses. They have, rather, 'tonic accents'—that is, the stress that a higher intonation confers upon a syllable. Actually, differences in intensity exist; but weak and unimportant as they are, they have not had the force to create accentual patterns.[4]

The Chinese T'ang Dynasty (618–907 A.D.) seems to have admitted exceptions at least in the metrical field: some poetry—and probably music, too—followed definite meters in sophisticated, elegant forms. To give one example: [5] a certain poem of the eighth

---

[2] Schott, *Einiges zur Japanischen Dicht- und Verskunst*, in *Philosophisch-Historische Abhandlungen der Königlichen Akademie der Wissenschaften zu Berlin*, 1878, Berlin, 1879. Harold Gould Henderson, *The bamboo broom*, Boston, 1934, p. ix. Kenneth Yasuda, *A pepper-pod*, New York, 1947, p. xxix.

[3] Miyamori Asatarō, *Masterpieces of Japanese poetry*, Tokyo, 1936.

[4] Rudolf Lange, *Lehrbuch der japanischen Umgangssprache*, Stuttgart, 1890, p. xxiv. Masatoshi Gensen Mori, *The pronunciation of Japanese*, Tokyo, 1929. P. M. Suski, *The phonetics of Japanese language*, South Pasadena, 1942, p. 93. Joseph K. Yamagiwa, *Modern conversational Japanese*, New York, 1942, pp. 5–9. William Montgomery McGovern, *Colloquial Japanese*, New York, 1942, p. 11. Serge Eliséeff and Edwin O. Reischauer, *Elementary Japanese*, 2nd edition, Cambridge, Mass., 1943, p. 2. Joseph W. Ballantine, *Japanese as it is spoken*, Stanford (*ca.* 1945), p. 5. I am indebted to Mr. J. W. Paar of the Oriental Division in the New York Public Library for his advice on things Japanese.

[5] Heinz Trefzger, *Das Musikleben der T'ang-Zeit*, in *Sinica*, Vol. XIII, 1938, p. 58.

century A.D., "The Drinker in the Spring," is written in the following affected meter:

⌣ ⌣ ⌣ ⌣ ⌣

‒ ‒ ‒ ‒ ‒

⌣ ⌣ ‒ ⌣ ⌣

‒ ‒ ⌣ ‒ ‒

But then, the period of the T'ang was widely open to influences from India and the Middle East, and this poetic style, no doubt, may be due to foreign models too.

Today, the only kind of accent in Chinese poetry is the tonal accent resulting from the various pitches given to syllables in speech.[6]

RHYTHMICAL WEAKNESS. Wherever rhythm is more or less of the numerical type without accentual or metrical patterns, the urge to express oneself by means of rhythm must be comparatively weak. This is certainly true of the eastern region of Asia. The very dance, except some extant tribal dances and the Indo-Sino-Japanese court dance *bugaku,* has lost the irresistible drive that it once had in the primitive world. Many, if not most, of its forms proceed in narrow steps and measured gestures and lend themselves to a highly stylized suggestion of persons, objects, and scenes.

East Asiatic music has a similar lack of drive. The most archaic piece that we have, the venerable hymn to the Emperor of China, moves in its orchestral parts by uniform quarter notes without the slightest attempt at rhythmical grouping. And the hymn to Confucius—composed, possibly, as early as the Chou Dynasty, though it was given its exclusive position in the liturgy only in 1743,[7] two thousand years after the end of that dynasty—proceeds, as it is written now, in nearly two hundred whole notes in an almost timeless adagio, not unlike the European organum of the Christian service in the days of Charlemagne.

Even outside the realm of ceremonial music, the necessity for strictest rhythm that the mutual adaptation of singers and instruments entails has led to an unparalleled poverty: the whole gi-

[6] Information from Dr. Lee, then of Yale University, on July 30, 1948, at Ann Arbor, Michigan.
[7] J. S. van Aalst, *Chinese music,* Shanghai, 1884, p. 27.

gantic area of the East and Southeast of Asia knows hardly any form of rhythmic organization except an eternal, mildly accentual, duple time in all the fields—for voices and for instruments, in the dance and the opera, in orchestral, chamber, and solo music.

Indo-Chinese folk music knows 3/4, too, but apparently as an exception.[8]

SQUARE RHYTHM. In the numerical rhythm of Chinese poetry, the individual syllable is the unit of time; and since its verses are extremely short, with only four or five or six monosyllables, each verse in a poem is musically rendered by a single measure of as many beats as syllables, not, as elsewhere, by a whole phrase.

Such musico-poetical forms are either symmetrical (*shi*) or else asymmetrical and rhapsodic (*ch'i*). The purest realization of symmetrical form is the Hymn to Confucius in the Confucian liturgy.[9] Temple singers perform it in incredibly long-drawn notes of equal value, each of which carries one monosyllable of the text. Four such notes form a verse, and eight such verses, a strophe—a strict organization in powers of 2, which is to musicians known as 'square.'

The East seems to have been the only oriental country with 'square rhythm' as an absolute ideal. The Chinese prince, Tsai Yü, who wrote his famous treatise on music shortly before 1600 A.D. but drew from sources that might go back to times B.C., describes the rhythm of sacred music as an even division and subdivision of wholes into halves, quarters, eighths, sixteenths, and thirty-seconds. The stringed instruments are plucked in thirty-seconds, with the plektron moving in a regular to-and-fro alternation; the drum beats in sixteenths, with a stress on every eighth; various percussion instruments strike the two halves; and likewise, the players of mouth-organs inhale and exhale in two halves. Only the singing voices proceed in solemn whole notes.

China's so-called classical operas—that is, the operas written between 1530 and 1860 A.D.—were as a rule composed in regular

[8] G. Knosp, *Rapport sur une mission en Indochine*, in *Archives internationales d'ethnographie*, Vol. XX/XXI, 1911.

[9] See music examples in Curt Sachs, *The commonwealth of art*, New York, 1946, p. 41, and *The rise of music in the ancient world*, New York, 1943, p. 123; also van Aalst, *op. cit.*, pp. 27 ff.

4/4, more seldom in 2/4, and never in ternary or any other odd-beat time.[10] And the same is true of practically all branches of Far Eastern music.

This inherent predilection for squareness in beat is alive not only all over the Far East in the narrower sense of the word, but also in the glittering music of the gamelan orchestras in Java and Bali, even when some accompanying singer feels free to ignore such inexorable strictness and to meet it in careless rubatos. How triple time can seem deficient to those who are 'duple' by trend and tradition, appears from one of Mr. Colin McPhee's experiences in Bali: after a party for his friends from the West, the natives deemed the dance music heard on this occasion not to be music at all; the bars (if we are allowed to use this modern word) had been incomplete without the fourth beat.

CLASSICISTIC STATICISM. Duple and quadruple time are the natural result of a steady motion in even steps—left and right, left and right. Expressing an imperious need for static rest and symmetry, it is to an astonishing degree linked up with 'close' and restful movement in the dance: people whose dances keep to measured symmetry, to smooth and rounded lines, to calm and static motion, give a marked preference to binary rhythm, indeed, to a square organization where every group of beats can be divided by two for the next lower unit, and multiplied by two for the next higher unit.

Close and restful movement, measured symmetry, calm and static motion are the leading traits of styles on which the modern history of art has conferred the much-abused titles 'classic' or 'classicistic.' In this sense, the prominent attitude of China, Korea, Japan has been classicistic. It may suffice to think of the truly Platonic mind of Confucius, Buddhist contemplation versus action, the ideal of dignity, serenity, and timeless staticism, the emphasis on 'being' instead of 'growing.'

Musically, this classicistic attitude appears, beside the square, divisive rhythm, in the quietude of all the spokesmen of good music: in Confucius' tirades against loudness, crescendo, decrescendo,

[10] Kwang-chi Wang, *Ueber die chinesische klassische Oper*, Bonn dissertation, Geneva, 1934, p. 14.

and speed, because they upset the nerves of the listeners which music was intended to soothe; furthermore, the attacks of the poet Lü Pu-we against the ones who "overstep the limits"; and again the fiat of Confucius that music be mild, serene, and dignified.

To this day, the Chinese, or half-Chinese, music of the Japanese court proceeds, partly at least, in *nobe,* a tempo not more than M.M. 32 to the quarter note; [11] and despite a traditional stretto in the later part of a piece (which Confucius would probably have disliked and condemned), any tempo change within a movement would be considered vulgar.

Square rhythm at a moderate speed has been a characteristic trait of classicistic civilizations far beyond the limits of Asia. A later chapter will show how in Italy the fifteenth century reflected the decline of the Gothic age and the advancing classicism of the Renaissance in a steady decrease of ternary rhythms and an equally steady gain of binary time, until the matchless classicism of the High Renaissance early in the sixteenth century decided the victory of 4/4 time. It is important to realize that this 4/4, which seems so natural and self-evident to us, exists nowhere in the countries between the Far East and Renaissance Italy, except occasionally in a quite accessory form.

The simple, regular, and square character of East Asiatic rhythms is not only classicistic, but also, and maybe preponderantly, feminine in the sense outlined in the preceding chapter. The Far Easterner is indeed 'feminine,' although of course not in any derogatory sense that an inveterate misogynist might give to this word. Anatomically and physiologically, the difference between the two sexes is less than anywhere else. The body of 'yellow' man is hairless, short, and often graceful, light-footed, slim; and—with the exception of archaic dances like those of the court of Japan—the eastern dancer, in all his vigor, has ideals of motion which in closeness and restraint are very similar to those of the female sex.

UNCLASSICISTIC DYNAMISM. East Asia has been the realm of binary rhythm, classicistic, quiet, and peaceful. But are we allowed to project this fact backwards through the three thou-

[11] After practical demonstrations by Mrs. Eta Harich-Schneider, New York, 1951.

sand or more years of East Asiatic history? One point, to be sure, is in favor of such an inference: that the 2/4 time is a common possession within the Far Eastern world, from northern China to Bali, from Japan to Indo-China—an identity hardly possible without a common heritage from ancient times.

Still, the evolution of the visual arts rouses some doubts. Whoever approaches them with a preconception of Far Eastern—or let us just say Chinese—classicism, static, quiet, and peaceful, must be soon disillusioned. The whole first thousand years A.D. and several centuries before and after, belie this. A glance at the grotesquely decorated mirror backs from the end of the Chou Dynasty in the third century B.C., at the galloping horses on stone reliefs from the Han Dynasty (206 B.C.–220 A.D.), or at the "tremendous vitality" and "savage restlessness" [12] of animal representations during the Wei (386–557 A.D.) at the time when Buddhism entered the country—and the belief in the eternal stoic calm of the East will be hopelessly shattered.

If the visual arts reflect long ages of exuberant vitality and restlessness, the binary rhythm of quiet staticism can hardly have had an exclusive sway in three thousand years.

Unfortunately, the earlier stages of Far Eastern music are practically unknown. In other countries, they would, at least in traces, survive in folk and semi-folk expression. But in the East, such evidences are scarce; most of them have withdrawn to recesses beyond the reach of musicology.

We know at least one indicative story. Wên, a prince at the court of Wei (426–387 B.C.), sighed: "When in full ceremonial dress I must listen to the Ancient Music, I think I shall fall asleep, but when I listen to the songs of Chêng and Wei, I never get tired." [13] There is probably no prince today in Asia, Europe, or Africa who would not enthusiastically endorse a similar impatient reflection. And yet it shows that even the court of China needed a livelier style to counterbalance the frosty stateliness of the official music.

The southern border of the square-rhythm area, Indonesia, prob-

[12] Leigh Ashton and Basil Gray, *Chinese art*, London, 1935, p. 90.
[13] R. H. van Gulik, *The lore of the Chinese lute* [should read: *zither*], Tokyo, 1940, p. 37.

ably never knew the ideal of such stateliness. With a substratum of primitive civilization still closer to the surface and with decisive influences from the West, and particularly from the Indian subcontinent, it had a strain of dynamism foreign to the classicistic spirit of China. There is the frequent accelerando and ritardando in the playing of native gamelan orchestras under the driving or restraining leadership of the conductor's drums (which in shape and playing technique are of Indian origin [14]), in spite of an imperturbable East Asiatic rhythm in powers of two.

Indian, too, are probably the riches of officially recognized tempo shades. The less sophisticated Sundanese regions of western Java have names for no less than seven different tempi: extremely slow, very slow, slow, fairly slow, moderately quick, quick, and very fast.[15] Characteristically enough, the more 'classicistic' East of Java knows no more than five such grades. They have names, too, but are increasingly often called by the figures 1, 1½, 2, 3, 4,[16] which indicate their proportional speeds and thus remind the Westerner, in a curious parallel, of the tempo *proportiones* of the European Renaissance.

Moreover, Java bases its tempi on a smallest time-unit or *chronos protos*. This unit is called the *keteg*, which denotes a heartbeat.[17] The pulse as the regulating standard of tempo, which will be mentioned often in the chapters to come, presents itself for the very first time.

DRUM PATTERNS. No doubt it was India, too, that gave her metrical drum patterns or *tālas*, but this time to the whole of Eastern Asia, including Indonesia, China, and Japan. They have their principal stronghold in the archaic court music of the Mikado, and particularly in its oldest branch, the gorgeous *bugaku* dances,[18] which came to Japan from the Asian continent in the second half of the first millennium A.D. together with the Chinese script and language and with the Buddhistic religion of India. While wind and stringed instruments play the melody and an accompanying

[14] Cf. Curt Sachs, *The history of musical instruments*, New York, 1940, Pl. XI, opposite p. 192.
[15] J. Kunst, *Music in Java*, 2nd edition, The Hague, 1949, Vol. I, pp. 409 f.
[16] *Ibid.*, p. 335.
[17] *Ibid.*, pp. 162, 170, 205, 296, 350.
[18] Cf. Yutaka Ishizawa, *Introduction to the classic dances of Japan*, Tokyo, 1935. Makoto Sugiyama, *An outline history of the Japanese dance*, Tokyo, 1937.

ostinato motif, the rhythm is provided by a triple percussion: the large and shallow drum *taiko*, suspended inside a sumptuous stand; the "barbarian" barrel drum *kakko* "from Turkistan," lying horizontally on a low bench; and the small gong *shōko*, hung, like the *taiko*, in a circular frame on a stand.[19]

Both *taiko* and *kakko* are played with two sticks each, the right stick being 'male' and the left one 'female.' On the *taiko*, the right-stick beats are strong, and the left-stick beats are weak. On the *kakko*, the difference is negligible.

Thirty-six rhythmical patterns performed on these three instruments (with the *kakko* occasionally replaced by an hourglass-shaped *ikko*) are preserved. There were probably many more in earlier times. Some patterns extend over sixteen measures, some over eight, some over four, and a few even over six. The author owes the following four examples to Mrs. Eta Harich-Schneider, who during a stay of nine years not only copied and studied the old scores in the archives of the Mikado, but also used to play them with the court musicians.

As an eight-bar pattern, let us select *Nobeyohyōshi*:

Ex. 18

Taiko:

Kakko:

Shōko:

Our four-bar pattern might be *Hayayohyōshi*:

Ex. 19

Taiko:

Kakko:

Shōko:

[19] The three drums are depicted opposite p. 160 in Sir Francis Piggott, *The music of Japan*, London, 1909.

Indeed, there are, in actual performance, a few five-beat bars; or, better, a few among the oldest four-bar patterns alternate between three and two beats, as in *Yatarabyōshi:*

Ex. 20

In a curious variety, called *Ranjo*, from *ran*, 'revolution, anarchy,' the *ikko*, a one-headed drum replacing the *kakko*, plays in offbeats, with the strongest stroke on the fourth beat, as (one), *two*, (three), *and FOUR.*

Ex. 21

This is certainly unusual. But it has a near parallel in ancient India, where, as the Indian chapter will show, the accented strokes or slaps fell on the end, not on the beginning of the duration of a 'member' within a meter.

Like the Indian *tālas*, all these patterns are repeated from phrase to phrase throughout a piece without separating rests except those which are a part of the pattern. Meanwhile the melodic instruments proceed in even measures, in whole, half, quarter, and eighth notes, and sometimes with ties over the bar lines and subsequent offbeats.

It is in dance music that even China, which has lost so much of its older music, shows traces of rhythmical patterns. Examples are found in the ancient "rustic dances" that the Chinese musical scholar, Prince Tsai Yü, discovered and presented to his emperor in 1595. One of them gives to the two accompanying drums the short recurrent pattern

small drum: ♩ ♫

big drum: 𝅗𝅥

which in its 'divisive' organization of eight time units in halves, fourths, and eighths was characteristic of the eastern Orient.

In another of Tsai Yü's examples, the pattern runs against the regular 4/4 of the melody: in each section of eight bars, the drums mark two halves in the first bar, but in the following seven bars proceed almost regularly in the sequence

small drum: ♪

big drum: 𝅗𝅥 𝅗𝅥· 𝅗𝅥

which is the 'additive' organization of eight beats in 3 + 3 + 2, characteristic of the Near and Middle Orient, India, ancient Greece (as the 'dochmiac'), the European late Middle Ages, Renaissance, and twentieth-century jazz.

Despite the importance occasionally given to the drums, rhythm was in the Far East quite certainly less pregnant than in India and the western Orient. The surprisingly great number of percussion instruments in all the parts of the East should not mislead our judgment. Only a few of them provide some actual rhythm; most of the rattles, scrapers, clappers, cymbals, bells, and sounding stones were rather meant to separate the verses of temple hymns or to assume, in the liturgy, symbolical duties of a non-rhythmic or hardly rhythmic character. The very drums, beaten with sticks save a few exceptions, lend themselves less well to elaborate metrical patterns than the hand-struck drums in India or in the western Orient. One of these exceptions, in Java, has been mentioned in the preceding section.

FREE RHYTHM is not absent from the Far East, despite the prevalence of strictness in all its member countries. As a rule it seems to belong to archaic forms. There are, of course, the unaccompanied liturgies of all Asiatic religions, of which we know best the Buddhist cantillation, with a clacking beat of wooden clappers between two lines as the only ruling agent.[20] Outstanding in the

[20] Information from Mrs. Eta Harich-Schneider, New York, 1951.

secular field are the recitatives at the beginning and the end of every scene in China's classical opera.[21]

More interesting and characteristic types of rhythmical freedom have been preserved in Japan, where—as often—older forms have had a greater chance to survive. In her masked, half-operatic *nō* dramas, the music, vocal and instrumental, is in an archaic way as unfettered in rhythm as it is in the steadiness of pitch. To be sure, even in *nō* some solos and all the choruses are rhythmically simple and rational and assume quite regular bar forms under the control of evenly striking drums. But most of the solo parts, "gliding and tense," [22] elude any rational sequence of stresses or meters so much that the singers now push forward, now slow down, now break off without apparent reason and against the regular prosody of the text.

Specifically Japanese, too, is the curious rhythmical shift between the singer's melody and the accompaniment. Frequently, for long stretches the instrument will keep slightly ahead of the singer, by an eighth note more or less, whether it anticipates his

Ex. 22. Japanese song with koto accompaniment

actual note or plays a different one in 'heterophony.' This shift is quite definitely not a case of syncopation or rubato proper in any western sense; there are no good beats or bad ones. The melody flows as smoothly as the accompaniment does; they have the same rhythm, though not in coincidence.[23]

Although this practice is truly Japanese, western music has known quite similar shifts. One of the most striking examples is Elsa's submission to Lohengrin's will in the third scene of the

[21] Kwang-chi Wang, *op. cit.,* p. 15.
[22] Robert Lachmann, *Musik des Orients,* Breslau, 1929, p. 67.
[23] Cf. also Robert Lachmann, *op. cit.,* ex. 9.

first act in Wagner's opera, where the singer's voice repeats three times the notes of the clarinet with a delay of an eighth or a sixteenth note. Perhaps we had better say it should repeat. For the passage, a notorious stumbling block, is not often done as the composer has written it.

Ex. 23. Wagner, *Lohengrin*, Act I, Scene 3 (Elsa: *"Mein Schirm"*)

Once more, freedom is most outspoken in the border regions, where primitive substrata are closer to the surface. Burma is a good example. And Dr. Jaap Kunst has given us a truly fascinating example from Java: "Upon a perfectly solid instrumental foundation of quadratic structure, and with unfaltering adherence to the tonality, both the female voice and that of the [flute] *suling* move with the sureness of a somnambulist in unrestrained freedom. . . . All rhythmic contact between the two seems to have been broken off." [24]

Unrestrained freedom over a perfectly solid quadratic foundation—is this not the truest jazz? It seems to be the fate of this book that wherever we stop a boundless vista opens across the oceans and continents.

[24] J. Kunst, *Music in Java*, 2nd edition, The Hague, 1949, Vol. I, pp. 398 ff; Vol. II, pp. 537 ff.

CHAPTER 4

Ancient Israel and the Beginnings of the Eastern Church

RHYTHM IN WORDS AND IN MUSIC. Philologists have been asking why rhythmical poetry, as opposed to music, is allowed to violate the evidently fundamental quality of all rhythm: the exactly equal distance between stimuli or entire groups of stimuli. Indeed, unless the reciter rambles on and on, even a regular pattern—dactylic, iambic, or otherwise—is very far from the theoretical fiction of exactly equal units of time: the actual lengths of spoken syllables and their emotional stresses are rather different. Often not even the theoretical pattern is left intact, and the poet will speak in groupings so irregular that the very word 'foot' seems out of place.

The answer derives from the fact that rhythmic organization, a purely formalistic quality, is necessarily at loggerheads with any intellectual or even emotional 'content.' The words of a children's song can be so insignificant that a child hardly cares to understand them. A definitely unintellectual poem like "Ring around a rosy, A pocket full of posy" thrives on its regular iambic accents and its equally iambic melody. And the situation is not very different when it comes to church hymns and national anthems. Words can, on the other hand, be so pregnant in meaning that we would not even like to set them to music—hardly any musician has composed music for the poems of Schiller. And in such a case, rhythm, though existent, recedes in importance and is not allowed to attract attention.

68

A parallel release from strictness exists in painting: a Madonna and Child describing a geometrically exact triangle would be unbearable. Even where She approaches a triangular outline, as in the classicistic style of Raphael, She is basically meant to convey a being in feminine form, human, regal, or divine. She loses 'content' and interest when stress on outer form prevails and makes Her a lifeless ornament.

And yet there is rhythm, in intellectual poetry as well as in painting. Only, this rhythm is suggested rather than worked out: the law that any rhythm imparts is well brought home, not in a crude, mechanical way, but, more subtly, in the disguise of freedom.

The degree in which rhythm is merely suggested corresponds to the ratio between form and content (be this content action, feeling, thought, or images). Therewith the whole question becomes a matter of classicistic or non-classicistic attitude. Classicistic art entails worked-out rhythm; non-classicistic art represses formalistic rhythm.

As a consequence, formalism is not only a question of shaping, but also of showing, the immanent rhythm. The present author remembers vividly how around 1900 the French and the English stage seemed archaic to him in their style of reciting Racine and Shakespeare, while at the same time the naturalistic actors of Berlin, almost ashamed of the formal verses in the so-called classical drama, tried to ignore their rhythm completely and to "speak" them as nonchalantly as possible.

BIBLICAL POETRY. This chapter deals with the rhythm of Biblical poetry, both in its Hebrew texts and in the traditional cantillation of the oldest Jewish congregations in Yemen and Iraq; and it also discusses the secular songs of oriental Jewry.

Biblical poetry means in this chapter the lyrical parts and episodes within the framework of the Old Testament—in its epical, narrative sections from Genesis on to Esther and Daniel, in the prayers, plaints, and praises of the Psalms, and in the sermons and lamentations of the older Prophets.

This poetry, composed at different times between the beginning and the end of the first millennium B.C., is the classic example of a free accentual rhythm. It never squeezed emotion or meaning into formal, regular patterns of meter or stress. No frigid, monotonous sequence of uniform iambs or dactyls, no constant number of feet in a verse, no even distribution of accents was allowed to distract attention from the words themselves and to dilute the power of diction. Every word, indeed every sentence, kept its natural flow without interference of any kind from outside. Biblical poetry was naturalistic and in a way almost an uplifted, poetical prose. For "perfect prose," says Klages (although without referring to Hebrew literature), "has a rhythm just as perfect as perfect poetry . . . and needs high mastery to create the free harmony that despite the lack of helpful rules bears witness to the flow of language." [1]

Hebrew prosody, in Elcanon Isaacs' words, "differs fundamentally from classical prosody. No poem is written according to a repeated meter scheme. The rhythm of Hebrew poetry depends, not on the relative position of the prominent syllable with respect to the surrounding syllables, but on a certain relative position of the important syllable in the verse. Classical verse, comparatively, is mechanical; Hebrew verse is dynamical." [2] Rabbi Salomon Herxheimer's translation of the Psalms calls Hebrew rhythm "a rhythm of thought" (*Gedankenrhythmus*).[3] And a learned priest in France explains that "just as the thought of the Hebrew poet is in one piece [*d'un jet*] and forms an indivisible whole, thought itself becomes his rhythmical unit." [4]

Seven hundred years before, Yehuda ha-Levi (born *ca.* 1085 in Spain), the greatest Jewish poet of the Middle Ages, had already made clear the Hebrew point of view: that meter appealed to the senses only, but impaired comprehension and the intensity of expression.[5]

This viewpoint touches upon the basic contrast of Judaism and,

[1] Ludwig Klages, *Vom Wesen des Rhythmus*, Kampen, 1934, p. 53.

[2] Elcanon Isaacs, *The metrical basis of Hebrew poetry*, in *The American Journal of Semitic Languages*, Vol. XXXV, 1918, pp. 29 f. The word 'mechanic' is used also in Andreas Heusler, *Deutsche Versgeschichte*, Vol. I, Berlin, 1925, p. 80.

[3] Salomon Herxheimer, *Die vier und zwanzig Bücher der Bibel*, Berlin, 1848, Vol. IV, p. 11.

[4] Edmond Bouvy, *Poètes et mélodies; étude sur les origines du rythme tonique*, Nîmes, 1886, p. 9.

[5] Jehuda ha-Levi, *Sefer hakusari*, ed. David Cassel, Leipzig, 1853, book II, § 69 ff. (pp. 181 ff.).

say, Grecianism: thought against perception, the infinite against the finite, character against a merely formal beauty. And one might add: passionate dynamism against serene staticism. "Hebrew does not behold an object in rest; everything is in action, everything is in movement; and this action rushes on, and this movement is quick as a thought." [6]

Outside poetry proper, the Greeks themselves agreed with the Hebrew principle: Aristotle has said that orators should refrain from meter since its pedantic punctiliousness would impair the force of expression.[7]

The non-mechanical rhythm of Israel, on the contrary, allowed the poet to create adequate dynamic tension by placing now one, now two, three, or exceptionally four unaccented syllables before the packed energy whipped down in an accent. Whether these unstressed syllables were phonetically long or short did not matter. In the rare cases when a monosyllabic word stood at the beginning of a verse, the line started forcibly on a downbeat. But as a rule, the verses were 'rising,' since almost all the Hebrew words had a stress on the last syllable; they appeared either in iambic form with one unstressed syllable—Psalm One: *a-shrê*—or, oftener, in anapaestic form with two unstressed syllables before the first accent—Psalm 33: *rannenú zadikím*. St. Jerome (*ca.* 400 A.D.), theologian, creator of the authorized Latin translation of the Bible (Vulgate), and the only man in antiquity to discuss the Biblical rhythms, confirms indeed that Hebrew verses were essentially "dactylic"—a term that in Greco-Roman terminology applied equally well to anapaests and to dactyls proper.[8]

If we take the liberty of calling 'feet' the groups of syllables having one accent each, there are either two, three, four, or six feet in a line, of which those with four feet are organized in 2×2 feet, and those with six, in 3×2 feet.

As a rule, two lines form a period. A period is either symmetrical, with three or four feet to a line; or else asymmetrical, with three

[6] Bouvy, *op. cit.*, p. 8.
[7] Aristotle, *Rhetoric*, 1403 B.
[8] A fact unknown to Eduard Sievers. Cf. his *Metrische Studien*, I, 1901, in *Abhandlungen der königlich Sächsischen Gesellschaft der Wissenschaften* Vol. 48, Leipzig, 1903, pp. 151, 169. Cf. also Ernst Graf, *Rythmus und Metrum*, Marburg, 1891, p. 87.

and one or, oftener, with three and two feet (the latter being known as the *qīnā* or lamentation verses).

A few examples from the Psalms may show what this means.

Three feet:	. ! . . . ! . !	Ps. 1:3
Four feet:	. . ! . ! / . ! . . . ! .	Ps. 1:3
Six feet:	. ! . ! / . ! . . ! / . ! . . !	Ps. 1:1
Three and two feet:	. . ! . . ! . !	
	. ! . . !	Ps. 5:2
Four and three feet:	. . ! . ! . / . . ! . !	
	. ! . ! . !	Ps. 4:2

Periods of twice three were the most frequent.

SHAKESPEARIAN AND OTHER PARALLELS. It would be an exaggeration to call unique the freedom of Hebrew poetry and its contempt for metrical patterns in the interest of correct and emotional, indeed, of passionate accents. Do we not know very similar poems, say, from Shakespeare's tragedies? What variety in meter, what clashes of accents, when the Clown sings:

> Come awáy, come awáy, déath,
>   and in sád cýpress let me be láid;
> Fly awáy, fly awáy, bréath;
>   I am sláin by a fáir cruel máid.
>   Shakespeare, *Twelfth Night*, II, 4.

When Macbeth, in the last act (scene 5), on hearing that "the queen, my Lord, is dead," recites:

> Tomórrow, and tomórrow, and tomórrow
> Créeps in this petty páce from dáy to dáy
> To the lást sýllable of recórded time,

he totally abandons regular iambs. "To the last" is an anapaest; "syllable" is a dactyl; and "last syllable" allows two accents to follow without a short in between—as in Hebrew. Some lines have eleven syllables, some have ten.

The terms 'iamb' and 'anapaest' seem to need an apology. Some authors [9] maintain that the Greek words refer exclusively to short–

[9] E.g., Thrasybulos Georgiades, *Der griechische Rhythmus*, Hamburg, 1949.

long meters, and they therefore oppose the use of these words for dynamic, accentual patterns lest their readers should think that the two principles of rhythm were psychologically or even genetically related. Does not this scruple go too far? Homer's dactyls and the other meters of early and middle antiquity have been read in purely accentual scansion all over the Greek- and Latin-learning world ever since metrical reading was lost in late antiquity; and yet they are called dactyls or whatever they were in metrical times. Neither does anybody hesitate to call the accentual verses of Goethe's epos *Herrmann und Dorothea* plainly dactyls.

Even the 'classical' Alexandrine of the French in the seventeenth century was in its inner structure not very far from Hebrew principles. The outer organization, it is true, was uniform: the Alexandrine had twelve syllables in two equal sections; each section was subdivided into two feet. But the inner structure of the two sections reminds one of Biblical verses: the two feet within a section were of equal or of unequal length; each of the four feet had the accent on the last syllable; a foot could have from one to five syllables in any arrangement; examples:

$$! \ldots ! \cdot ! \ldots ! = 1 + 5,\ 2 + 4$$
$$\cdot ! \ldots ! \cdot ! \ldots ! = 2 + 4,\ 2 + 4$$
$$\cdot \cdot ! \cdot \cdot ! \ldots ! \cdot ! = 3 + 3,\ 4 + 2$$

The situation is hardly different in older German poetry before the equalization of accents under classicistic and other influences. In Germanic verses stress is given to the most significant syllables. Here are (1) one arrangement of accents from the Old Saxon epic *Heliand* (ninth century A.D.):

$$\cdot ! \cdot ! \cdot \cdot ! \cdot \cdot \cdot ! \cdot ! \cdot$$

and (2) two lines from an Early Middle High German poem:

lébentigez brót, wāriu wīnrebe
sō tuot der wégemüede gást ein ríuwige dánnekēre.[10]

which yields this plan of accents:

$$! \ldots ! ! \cdot ! \cdot \cdot$$
$$\ldots ! \ldots ! \cdot ! \cdot \cdot ! \ldots$$

[10] From Andreas Heusler, *Deutsche Versgeschichte*, Vol. I, Berlin, 1925 (in *Grundriss der germanischen Philologie*, Vol. 8, i), pp. 35, 39.

BIBLICAL CANTILLATION. The two lines of a Biblical period often carried a *parallelismus membrorum:* the half-verse is answered by another half-verse that expresses either an intensification or an antinomy, not in the same meters, but in similar words.[11] The Seventieth Psalm may serve as an example:

Make haste, O God, to deliver me;
Make haste to help me, O Lord.

Let them be ashamed and confounded that seek after my soul;
Let them be turned backward, and put to confusion, that desire
 my hurt.

The musical associate of this parallelism was the antiphony of two answering half-choruses, which, via the churches of the East, eventually reached the western Catholic Church and had its climax in the often overwhelming polychoral settings of the Baroque.

But the musical facets of the question are unknown to the rhythmologists. The historians of Biblical rhythm, including even the music-minded Eduard Sievers in his monumental work, have clung to the philological aspect. They have analyzed texts and nothing but texts. It is true that most of them wrote at a time when reliable sources of music were not yet available.

In the meantime, and particularly owing to Idelsohn's diligent research, we possess invaluable recordings and transcriptions [12] of the melodies with which those texts are actually sung in the Orient, in Yemen and Iraq, in Iran and Turkistan, by communities with traditions so old and intact that we may call them Biblical.

Oriental-Jewish cantillation of the Scriptures confirms but also supplements the results of philology. The musical lines are just as irregular in length as the poetical verses. Within, accented and unaccented syllables are carefully kept apart, both in stress and in duration. Unaccented syllables are rather evenly, though never mechanically, rendered by short notes, which we transcribe as eighths. Rarely are such notes replaced by ligatures or groups of

---

[11] See *Studies in Biblical parallelism,* in *University of California Publications, Semitic Philology,* Berkeley, 1918–1923; Arnold Merzbach, *Ueber die sprachliche Wiederholung im Biblisch-Hebräischen,* Frankfurt-am-Main, 1928; Charles Franklin Kraft, *The strophic structure of Hebrew poetry,* Chicago, 1938; David Gonzalo Maeso, *Contribución al estudio de la métrica bíblica,* in *Sefarad,* Vol. III, 1943.

[12] A. Z. Idelsohn, *Hebräisch-Orientalischer Melodienschatz,* 1914 ff.

two slurred sixteenths on one syllable or else reduced to only one sixteenth. There can be four shorts and even more before a long. The accented syllable, on the other hand, is rendered by a long or quarter note, or else by a ligature of two or three eighths, which might expand to lengthy coloraturas on holydays, just as do their counterparts in the chant of the Catholic Church. Sometimes a long and a subsequent short shrink to a triplet. An unaccented long before an accented long is treated as if it were short.

Thus Hebrew music fuses rhythm by stress and rhythm by length. It follows the natural trend to stress the long and to lengthen the accent.

A very simple instance of archaic cantillation is the creed, *Harken Israel,* in the version of the Babylonian Jews: [13]

The text, in English translation "Harken, Israel, the Lord, our God, the Lord is One," reads in Hebrew:

Shemá yisraél adonái elohénu adonái ehád.

Every unstressed syllable is rendered by a short, every accented syllable by a long, with an extra lengthening on the final, most important syllable, -*had.*

Ex. 24. Babylonian Jews, *Harken Israel*

Hardly more complicated is the Babylonian version of the Song of Songs. The King James version of the beginning reads: "The song of songs, which is Solomon's. Let him kiss me with the kisses of his mouth. . . ." In Hebrew:

Shír hashirím ashér lishlomóh:
yishshaqéni mineshiqót píhu.

All the accented syllables appear as quarter notes, undotted or dotted.[14]

Ex. 25. Babylonian Jews, *Song of Songs*

[13] Idelsohn, *op. cit.,* Vol. II, p. 82.
[14] *Ibid.,* p. 81.

If there is any need for corroboration that a lawful alternation of longs and shorts matters also in ancient Jewish music, it will be found in the 'tropes,' in Hebrew: *ta'amīm* or *nginót*. They are, so to speak, 'melodicles' or conventional groups of notes out of which all cantillation is composed in ever varying arrangements as a mosaic is composed of tesserae. The tropes are very different from one another, not only melodically in the sequence of their notes, but also metrically in the sequence and balance of their time values. In modern transcription, they contain whole notes with fermatas, gliding thirty-seconds, and all the values in between; they know the finer shades of dotting and the lively, flexible mingling of different lengths; they form concise and clean-cut patterns, now stricter now freer in accent and meter, but always characteristic and well defined.[15]

But with all the careful discrimination of long and short, not one of these patterns has ever followed the mechanical rule of Greek and Greek-inspired rhythm that there should be a rigid ratio between the two. Nor are they ever recurrent in the sense of Greek polypodies.

STRICTER RHYTHM. The Old Testament presents a few examples of stricter rhythmic organization, such as the Song of the Well in Numbers 21:17–18—"Then Israel sang this song, Spring up, O well; sing ye unto it"; or, more complicated and irregular, the Song of Lamech, Methusael's son, in Genesis 4:23–24—"Adah and Zillah, Hear my voice Ye wives of Lamech, Hearken unto my speech." Perhaps the most striking example is the parable of the Lord's vineyard from Isaiah, Ch. 5: "Now will I sing to my well-beloved a song of my beloved touching his vineyard. My well-beloved hath a vineyard in a very fruitful hill. . . ."[16] The Hebrew text, *Ashírah gá ledidí*, follows the pattern

$$. \mid . \mid . . \mid$$
$$. \mid . \mid . . \mid$$

---

[15] Cf. the table in A. Z. Idelsohn, *Hebräisch-Orientalischer Melodienschatz*, Vol. II, Jerusalem, 1922, p. 81. But it should be known that the melodicles are different in the various provinces of Judaism, although the symbols are the same.

[16] In a conversation on this matter, Miss Mildred Pearl of Philadelphia drew my attention to this passage.

! . . ! . . ! . (.) ! . . ! .

. . . ! . . . ! . . . ! . . (.) !

etc. But even here no more than two consecutive lines follow the same meter.

Elcanon Isaacs [17] considers such pieces to be early, while, according to him, the freer rhythm is a later "movement away from a strict regard to form to the freer movement of prose." Sporadic examples of actual songs in the earliest books of the Bible—such as the hymn on the early defeat of Moab in Numbers 21:27, 28, *Bonú heshbón tibanêh,* "Come into Heshbon, let the city of Sihon be built and prepared," are, in his words, "vigorous folk poetry—often lyrical, with metrical feet of three morae predominating, and great regularity of beat. The verses are short, very distinct, and of uniform length. The accent is for the greater part on the ultima, and the word-foot units are similar in their form."

Elcanon Isaacs' examples are certainly correct. But his chronological conclusion is rather doubtful. The songs in folk style within the older, epical books of the Bible have an unmistakable choral character and were, it seems, accompanied by drumming and dancing. This was the form in which Jephthah, the judge, was bidden his tragic welcome: "And Jephthah came to Mizpeh unto his house, and, behold, his daughter came out to meet him with timbrels and with dances." [18] And it was again the form in which the women "of all cities of Israel" hailed the victors after the battle against the Philistines. They came out, "singing and dancing, to meet King Saul, with tabrets, with joy [?], and with instruments of music. And the women answered one another as they played, and said, Saul hath slain his thousands, and David his ten thousands." [19] They "answered one another": to singing, playing, and dancing they added the "answering" antiphony of two half-choruses in the traditional *parallelismus membrorum* of words and music.

Such antiphonal group singing in strictest rhythm is still alive in the most archaic styles of (modern) oriental Jewry, as in the wedding songs of Yemenites to the accompaniment of dancing

[17] *Op. cit.*
[18] Judges 11:34.
[19] I Samuel 18:6, 7.

men and drumming women [20] in regular beats—sometimes five in
3 + 2.[21] Other living examples of archaic Hebrew music in strictest rhythm can be found—at least in description—in Robert Lachmann's excellent study, published posthumously, on the music of

Ex. 26. Yemenite Jews, wedding song in antiphony

the Jewish inhabitants of Djerba, an island off Tunisia in the central Mediterranean:

"The women's songs . . . are essentially dependent not on the
connection with the text but on processes of movement. . . . This
type of song . . . goes back to prehistoric times. . . .

"In the Jewish communities not only in Oriental-Sephardic districts but also, for example, in Yemen, the women accompany their
songs on frame-drums or cymbals. . . . The beats follow at regular
intervals; they fall on each period of the melody. They . . . only
give the length of the unit of line [as obviously the cymbals in the
Temple did], but they do not divide the melody into bars, nor do
they bring it within the limits of a systematic rhythmic figure. . . .
The songs group themselves partly in 4/4 time and partly in 3/4
time—i.e., in the two simplest forms." [22]

Notwithstanding the strictness of rhythm, tempo can be very
irregular in the Orient. "This irregularity," says Idelsohn,[23] "derives from the wild and erratic enthusiasm of the singers." Oriental
Jews sing slowly at first and thereafter in an ever increasing tempo
up to a frantic prestissimo.

Altogether, Jewish music has known a strict accentual rhythm
in dance and dancelike songs, and freer rhythm in cantillation.
Meter, though not absent, is unimportant; and recurrent patterns

[20] The *New York Times* of April 20, 1952, has on p. 81 an article, *Israel develops dances of Yemen*, by Dana Adams Schmidt.
[21] Cf. Abraham Z. Idelsohn, *Hebräisch-Orientalischer Melodienschatz*, Vol. I, Leipzig, 1914, e.g. Nos. 142, 145.
[22] Robert Lachmann, *Jewish Cantillation and Song in the Isle of Djerba*, Jerusalem, 1940, pp. 67–82 and *passim*. Unfortunately, the music appendix does not include any women's songs.
[23] Idelsohn, *op. cit.*, p. 49.

of short and longer elements in the sense of ancient Greece and the Muhammedan Orient have been unknown.

There were, to be sure, quite a number of musical species between the extremes of cantillation and popular airs to be danced to: the songs to the accompaniment of the lyre, instrumental music inducing trance in the prophets, the solos on the lyre like David's to soothe King Saul's depression, the dirges of pipers hired for funerals, the elaborate music in the Temple, and the (often foreign) music at the royal court. All this music is lost, and the sources merely relate *that*, not *how*, it was performed. They would say that the music in the Temple included cymbals, and the modern reader might conclude that the presence of percussion instruments indicates rigid beats. But there is little doubt that the cymbals, as elsewhere, marked the end of a line and not the beats inside a verse. Only one remark allows for a rhythmic interpretation, modest as it may be: at the inauguration of the Temple under King Solomon, "it came even to pass, as the trumpeters and singers were as one, to make one sound to be heard in praising and thanking the Lord." [24] But then this would be just a confirmation of our earlier statement that any ensemble tends necessarily to rhythmical strictness, while solo music is by nature free.

An Assyrian bas-relief in the British Museum represents the royal orchestra of Elam (north of the Persian gulf) in the act of welcoming the Assyrian conqueror in 650 B.C. All musicians march, and two of them dance in a strictly cadential hopping step; [25] there is no doubt that the music, too, was strict in rhythm. Non-Jewish evidence of rhythmical strictness in ensemble music is not directly conclusive for the music of Israel, to be sure. But it might have an indirect bearing on Hebrew practice, since the ancient Middle East had many common traits in music and the courtly life of the Jewish kings was closely related to that of other western oriental kingdoms.

A word for rhythm seems not to exist in the Hebrew language. Only one passage—and Greek at that—speaks of rhythm in ancient Israel: Philo describes a congregational supper of the Essenic or

[24] II Chron. 5:13.
[25] Curt Sachs, *op. cit.*, Plate 3, opposite p. 80. Cf. also Curt Sachs, *Zweiklänge im Altertum*, in *Festschrift für Johannes Wolf*, Berlin, 1929, pp. 168–170, with plate.

Therapeutic sect and says: "They all stand up together and . . . form two choruses . . . one of men and one of women, each chorus . . . under the best and most distinguished member as its leader. Then they sing hymns in honor of God in many *meters* and tunes. . . ." [26] But then, Philo was an Alexandrian Jew, born about 20 B.C. and reared in Greek surroundings. Whether we can depend on this Hellenistic philosopher, to account for a single word of musical terminology within a world of Grecian metric conceptions, is more than doubtful.[27]

THE EASTERN CHRISTIAN CHURCH may be touched upon in brief.[28] The state in which the music of ancient Israel has been found was more or less the state of music in probably all, and certainly in one, of her neighboring countries: Syria. The cantillation of the Syrian Church, to a great extent provided by Jews, became subsequently the nucleus of all the oriental-Christian and Byzantine-orthodox liturgies with their many ramifications. It was just as antiphonal, responsorial, accentual, and non-metric as the chant had been in Jewish Palestine.

Any re-application of the ancient meters of Greece would be erroneous. Most church languages in Asia and Africa, as Syriac, Coptic, Abyssinian, had no meter anyway. Byzantine chant, it is true, had Hellenic texts. But Greek had had to pay for becoming the official language of the Eastern Roman Empire. In its diffusion to Asia and Africa and its steady contact with oriental languages, it had lost the refined concepts of vowels long and short and therewith the essential condition for metrical organization.

The non-metrical rhythm of Byzantine chant has been characterized as a counting of syllables, that is, as numerical. The earliest great explorer of Byzantine church music, Cardinal Pitra, writes: "Without regard for hiatus, longs, or breves, a syllabic rhythm governs all the stanzas." Often, the stanzas have some refined pat-

---

[26] Philo, *De vita contemplativa*, 1. II, § 83.

[27] On Jewish-medieval thought about rhythm, Cf. Eric Werner and Isaiah Sonne, *The philosophy and theory of music in Judaeo-Arabic literature*, in *Hebrew Union College Annual*, Vol. XVI, pp. 286, 300–303.

[28] Egon Wellesz, *Byzantinische Musik*, Breslau, 1927; *A history of Byzantine music and hymnography*, Oxford, 1949; *Die Rhythmik der byzantinischen Neumen*, in *Zeitschrift für Musikwissenschaft*, Vol. II, 1920, pp. 617–638, Vol. III, 1921, pp. 322–336.

tern, such as this one: two verses of eleven syllables are separated by a set of six verses, in which three of seven syllables alternate with three others, growing from six to nine syllables:

<pre>
11   11
        7   7   7
            6   8   9
</pre>

"This, then, is the secret of the hymnographers: Neglecting the distinction of classical meters and doing away with the fleeting shades of longs and breves, which possibly had become obsolete in common pronunciation, they turned to an element invariable, visible, palpable: to the number of syllables as it has eventually come to prevail in the poetry of all modern languages."

The adopted rhythm, continues Pitra, "does not lack in flexibility, variety, or precision. The strophes, now weighty now light-footed, would march with the heavy steps of seven-syllabic verses, and again would rush on with tripping small and hasty steps. . . . In ever varying combinations, strophes might have from three to thirty verses and, within a verse, from two to fourteen or fifteen syllables. We doubt that classical poetry ever proceeded with greater ease in its boldest attempts.

"If it is true that classical poetry offered a kind of double melody to trained ears, one resulting from the sequence of longs and shorts, the other from the rhythm of tonic accent, it is permissible to believe that the former one, inaccessible to the common people, was exclusively reserved for delicate, educated minds, while the tonic accent appealed to the masses and incited the acclamations and the whistles of the amphitheaters. The Church has faithfully preserved this popular heritage." [29]

The tonic accent was indeed important in Byzantine music and poetry.[30] In general, the accents of the main words were rendered by lengthening out the accented notes or replacing them by melisms—just as in Hebrew cantillation. For the rest, an even sequence of eighth notes prevails, including accents of minor importance.[31]

[29] J. B. Pitra, Hymnographie de l'église grecque, Rome, 1867, pp. 13–25.
[30] Cf. Melpo Merlier, Etudes de musique byzantine, Paris, 1935, p. 9.
[31] Cf. Egon Wellesz, Die Hymnen des Sticherarium für September, in Monumenta Musicae Byzantinae transcripta, Part I, Copenhagen, 1936, pp. xxxiii ff.; H. J. W.

A loss of meter and a gain of accent similar to that of Byzantine chant occurred also in the western Roman world in the times of the emperors. The ancient world had no meter to leave to the Middle Ages, in the West as little as in the East.

Tillyard, *The hymns of the Oktoechos*, Part I, in the same *Monumenta*, Vol. III, Copenhagen, 1940.

CHAPTER 5

The Near and Middle East

He who makes a mistake is still our friend;
he who adds to, or shortens, a melody is still
our friend; but he who violates a rhythm unawares can no longer be our friend.

Ishaq ibn Ibrahim (767–850 A.D.)

The western part of the Orient taxes our vocabulary more than
other regions do. Shall we speak of Arabian music? But the Berbers
are not Arabs, and still less so, the Persians, Turks, or Pakistanis.
Shall we speak of Muhammedan music? But considerable numbers of the Arabs, in Egypt, Syria, and Lebanon, are Christians.
Not even the notions Near and Middle East are consistently defined. And yet there is very definitely—at least in the cities—one
musical style in the gigantic area that houses the Muslim and the
Christian Arabs west of India.

Hence the author should be pardoned for using terms that may
be too narrow in scope: his 'Arabs' will often include non-Arabs,
and his 'Muhammedans' often non-Muslim.

EARLY POETIC METERS. Arabian music, like that of other peoples, originally followed the rhythms of poetry. Still as late as the
ninth century A.D., Ziriab, a famous singer-composer, impressed
this general rule on his pupils: in studying a song, to memorize
first the rhythm of the text, then to beat it out on a drum, and

only in the third and final place to learn the melody proper.[1] Which reminds us of Plato's words, requoted in the early Baroque, that "music is in the first place speech and rhythm, and only lastly, tone."

The form of rhythm oldest to the best of our knowledge and dating back to times before Islam (that is, before *ca.* 600 A.D.), was the *saj*. The name denotes a two-line stanza almost in prose, without an actual meter, but with four unmistakable stresses, the whole performed with greatest emphasis and vigorous gestures.[2] Such gestures were probably made in the Biblical world, too.

Of regular forms the oldest was the iambic dimeter *rajaz*. It had a fourfold alternation of weak and stronger units; but some attention was also paid to the length of syllables, especially in the more important second half of a verse. That greater care was bestowed upon the second half of a verse cannot be accepted as an Arabian national trait. We find it a bit everywhere. "The beginning of an iambic verse seems to be a breeding place of bungling." [3] And beyond the iamb, this supranational rule applies to all kinds of verses, in the *Vedas,* in the poetry of Greece, and in that of the Germanic Middle Ages: in all of them "the reins are pulled tighter at the end of a verse than inside." [4]

Since meter was accessory, accent is said to have prevailed. But this is by no means certain. Rhythm, as in the similar case of the *Vedas,* could have been numerical with only accessory accents.

Somewhat later than the iambic *rajaz*—allegedly through Muslem ibn Muhriz (died *ca.* 710 A.D.)—came its counterpart, the trochaic *ramal,* in a fourfold alternation of strong and weak.[5] The newcomer was lively and agitated, so we learn from the life of Abu Yahya Obaj ibn Surayj (died *ca.* 726 A.D. at the age of eighty-five)—just as the trochee was in Greece—while *hazaj,* another

---

[1] Jules Rouanet, *La musique arabe,* in *Encyclopédie de la musique,* ed. A. Lavignac, Part I, Vol. V, 1922, p. 2696.

[2] Gustav Hölscher, *Arabische Metrik,* in *Zeitschrift der Deutschen Morgenländischen Gesellschaft,* Vol. 74, 1920, pp. 359 ff.

[3] Eirik Vandvik, *Rhythmus und Metrum, Akzent und Iktus,* in *Symbolae Osloenses Fasc. Supplet.* VIII, Oslo, 1937, p. 21.

[4] Andreas Heusler, *Deutsche Versgeschichte,* Vol. I, Berlin, 1925 (in *Grundriss der germanischen Philologie,* Vol. 8, i), p. 38, after Gerhard Pohl, *Strophenbau im deutschen Volkslied,* Berlin, 1921, p. 19.

[5] Rouanet, *op. cit.,* p. 2689.

meter, belonged to pieces tender and facile, and *at-taqīl* to slow and serious songs. This means—again as in Greece—the identification of a certain meter with a certain mood and character. Indeed, Abu Muhammad Ishāq ibn Ibrahim (767–850)—who has provided the motto of this chapter—classified all melodies according to their rhythm in the first place and according to tonality only within each rhythmic group.[6] He is also credited with having regularized the terminology of rhythm.

It seems, alas, that terminology was greatly in need of regularization, but also, that regularization did not help too much. For terminology was hardly less confused in the centuries to follow; the traditional names were kept, but their meaning changed all the time—an uncertainty hardly astonishing where most musicians were illiterate and dependent on oral instruction.

The few consistent facts will be enumerated in the following paragraphs.

RHYTHMS SPECIFICALLY MUSICAL, beyond the simple feet and lines of versification, were called *iqā'āt* (sing. *iqā'*). They were allegedly introduced by the earliest man among the otherwise female professional singers of Islam, a virtuoso with the probably not complimentary nickname Ṭuwais, 'the peacock.' His lifetime, from A.D. 632 to 705, coincided partly with the end of the Persian dynasty of the Sassanians (A.D. 652), to which the Iranians attribute elaboration of their own rhythm. It is by no means impossible that Iran, as has been claimed, gave the new principle of supermetrical rhythms to Arabia; [7] but if so, we do not know how much she herself was under Turkish or Indian influence.

Arabian shared with Hellenic theory in the non-poetic concept of *chronos protos*, the 'first time' or time unit from which all patterns derived, as opposed to the metrical short syllable that serves as the unit in poetical rhythms. And it also knew the concept of 'augmentation,' with two, three, and four time units instead of one, somewhat like the *epibatoí* of the Greeks or the duple, triple, quadruple *proportiones* in the later Middle Ages of Europe.

[6] Rouanet, *op. cit.*, p. 2694.
[7] Rouanet, *op. cit.*, p. 2688. The opposite viewpoint is taken by Henry George Farmer in A *history of Arabian music,* London, 1929, p. 49.

Characteristically enough, augmentation was not performed in a proportionate way by multiplying the original values by the same multiplier, as in ancient Greece and the late-medieval *proportiones* of Europe, but in a disproportionate way by adding the same amount to the original values. The eighth note of a so-called fast rhythm became a quarter note in 'light' rhythms, a dotted quarter in 'light-heavy' rhythms, and a half note in 'heavy' rhythms. This could still be interpreted as a multiplication by two, three, and four. Actually, it was addition: an eighth plus an eighth plus an eighth plus an eighth. This shows very clearly in the pattern called Second Disjunct, where the original dactyl, of a quarter note plus two following eighth notes, became, by addition, a dotted plus two undotted quarters, which resulted no longer in a dactyl, but in an epitritic pattern of seven time units. And in the 'light-heavy' version of the same meter, the long became a half note, and the two shorts, dotted quarters, resulting in a ten-unit pattern:

$$2 + 1 + 1 = 4$$
$$3 + 2 + 2 = 7$$
$$4 + 3 + 3 = 10$$

This was an entirely mechanical, antirhythmical procedure.

In a way similar to the doctrine of *ethos* in Greece, the Arabs identified these augmentations with frames of mind: "The heavy rhythms with stretched-out times correspond to depression and mourning, and the light ones with narrow-set notes to joy, violent motion, and openness, and the moderate ones to equanimity." [8]

It is unknown to what extent these and other notions existed in practice. In their double capacity as medieval writers and as Orientals, the great Islamic theoreticians of the ninth and tenth centuries—like Al-Kindi, Al-Farabi, and Ibn Sina—indulged in classification for the sake of classification and, exploiting the remnants of ancient Hellenic theory, availed themselves of Greek ideas, terms, and systems, while the singer-composers, generally illiterate, were hardly impressed by the archaic and foreign wisdom of mathematicians and philosophers—if they knew them at

[8] Al-Kindi (*ca.* 790–*ca.* 874), *Risāla*, ed. Robert Lachmann and Mahmud el-Hefni, Leipzig, 1931, p. 30.

all. In one treatise, of the thirteenth century, Safi al-Din grafted even the delicate Greek concepts of *thesis* and *arsis* on Arabian musical thought.

Actually, the nature of Arabian rhythm points to the northeast and the east rather than westward to Greece. The peculiar spirit and forms of these oriental rhythms have in historical times been common property in the eastern world between Morocco and India, including Persia and Turkey. And although it seemed wiser to deal with Indian rhythm in a special Indian chapter within this book, Islamic rhythm west of India and in India itself should be looked upon as a whole despite insignificant discrepancies in detail.

Which nation should be credited with the original leadership is still a mystery. The only concrete fact is that India already had these oriental rhythms in times that the West calls antiquity, while the world of Islam adopted them only in what we call the Middle Ages. This excludes the Arabs as possible originators. But it leaves unanswered the question whether India or some Turkish or Iranian culture took the earliest step.

Arab rhythm, as we know it today, has little connection with the patterns that the old Islamic theoreticians classify. It will therefore be better to leave their vague and often contradictory surveys and turn to modern practice, which after all must reach far back into the Middle Ages. Just as in India, they crystallize around the drummers' patterns.

DRUM PATTERNS. Most oriental melodies, played or sung, are co-ordinated with one or two coupled drums and, when none is available, at least with clapping or slapping hands. The drum and the hand, however, do not 'accompany' in the western sense of playing a subordinate role. How much the drummer is, on the contrary, the leader in this co-ordination can be gathered from the impressive share of fifty per cent that in earlier days the Moroccan drummer enjoyed in all the earnings of the group, whether small or large.[9]

The melody is sometimes said to be independent of the beats of the drum. This is only a half-truth. Quite seldom, it is true, and only in popular music, does the melody follow the drum in

[9] Jules Rouanet, *La musique arabe dans le Maghreb*, loc. cit., p. 2910.

an almost literal sense. Counteraccents often disguise the basic rhythm, which, however, remains latent and is easily recognized by those who know. One of the most frequent counteraccents is the hemiola, on which this book will have to touch in each of its chapters: the melody and the drum move both in groups of six units; but while the melody organizes them in 6/8 or 2 × 3, the drum beats 3/4 or 3 × 2.[10]

The partners mostly agree at least upon the caesuras and take care that the melodic period is just as long as the drum pattern. But there are a few exceptions. Overlapping of period and pattern is frequent. Indeed, the second line of a melody might shift by half a measure so that corresponding passages of the first and the second line would fall on different drumbeats. This is a procedure curiously related to the so-called isorhythm of France in the later Middle Ages. But the characteristic distortion of the melody in isorhythm is totally absent from the Arabian device because melody and rhythm, given to two different men, keep their identities, while in the Gothic device one singer has to stretch his melody according to the ever shifting rhythmical pattern.

Actually, the melody is never independent of the drum. Though the voice may give itself up to emotion or playful fancy, yet the drummer will mark the rhythm and firmly force melodic freedom into some rigid pattern of meter and accent.

To denote this often fascinating interplay of strict and flexible rhythm one is tempted to speak of heterorhythm. The term is new but possibly useful. Its well-known prototype, heterophony, expresses the simultaneous free and often discordant performance of one melodic line by several voices in keeping with their individual character and with the nature of the performers themselves. The coincident lines can be very different and yet reflect the basic 'idea' without confusing intelligent listeners. One might say they are like a set of variations on a theme that does not appear or even exist except as an ideal configuration. Or one might think of the Doric temples of Greece, which are all individual variations of an idea, not of an existing original.

Heterorhythm, in a similar way, would be the simultaneous ap-

---

[10] F. Salvador Daniel, *La musique arabe*, Algiers, 1863, p. 50. The hemiola is very frequent also in the *siguiriya gitana* form of Orient-inspired flamenco.

pearance of a rhythmic idea both in a melodic line and in a co-operating drum, to allow for greater freedom in the former.

Rhythm appears in patterns recurring all through a piece without a gap, like a *basso ostinato*. Such a pattern is a characteristic sequence of beats, which can be as short as the shortest metrical foot, but is as a rule somewhat longer and may by exception stretch out to as many as ninety-six time units (or twenty-four of our common-time measures).

The beats within a pattern differ in three qualities: (1) distance from each other, (2) strength or accent, and (3) timbre. Some would follow at a distance of a whole note, and others at smaller distances down to that of a sixteenth note; some may carry a heavy, some a light accent, or no accent at all; some, struck near the center of the drumhead, are mellow, some, struck near or on the rim, are dry. The strong and mellow beats are called *tum* or *dum;* the weak and drier beats, *tak,* and beats less weak in between, *tik* or *kā.* When two small kettledrums are used instead of a single goblet drum (under the arm) or a timbrel, the *tum* skin is wetted, and the *tak* skin heated. In the absence of a drum, the fist would strike the *tum* beats on the right thigh; and the open palm, the *tak* beats on the left thigh.

The concurrence of these three qualities of tone—strength, timbre, and time—creates a complex aggregate of meter and accent almost polyrhythmic within every single pattern. It can be —and has been—varied indefinitely, in length, in the distribution of accents and timbres, and in the arrangement of longs and shorts.

As a matter of course, only a restricted number out of these boundless possibilities have remained in general use, hardly more than twenty. In Tunisia, for instance, musicians prefer the smaller patterns of eight, seven, and three units,[11] such as

---

[11] Robert Lachmann, *Die Musik in den tunisischen Städten,* in *Archiv für Musikwissenschaft,* V, 1923, pp. 157 f.

Ex. 27. Tunis, popular song

A note above the line is struck on the rim, a note below the line, on the skin. In Egypt, the most frequent patterns today are *muraba'*, with thirteen, and *sama'i*, with ten units or quarter notes.[12] They read:

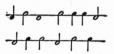

Ex. 28. Egypt, piece for zither and orchestra

Rhythms rarely appear in so bald a form. The drummer is free to fill in the larger values—wholes, halves, and quarters—for which the drumming sound is actually too short. He may even vary the beats within certain limits.

The old experience that the nature of a drum, and particularly the striking angle and distance it imposes on the player's hands, must influence or even determine rhythm finds confirmation in the Islamic world. Lachmann mentions it [13] and quotes von Hornbostel's remark that a drum pattern depends in the first place on motor conditions.

ADDITIVE RHYTHM. Seen from a western viewpoint, all these meters are irregular—indeed, enigmatic. The typical western rhythm, as we understand it, is multiplicative or divisive: a 4/4 measure can be, and actually is, divided into two halves, four quarters, eight eighths, and so on; a 6/8 is twice 3/8, and a 9/8 is three times 3/8 with the principal stress on the first, and lighter stresses on the fourth and the seventh beat. And this is true even if there

[12] Alfred Berner, *Studien zur arabischen Musik*, Leipzig, 1937, p. 37.
[13] Lachmann, *op. cit.*, p. 156.

is a rest or the remainder of a tied-over note where the accent of the divisional caesura should be.

Most oriental patterns—unless influenced by the West—are indivisible and hence non-divisive.

An oriental pattern could have 4/4 or 8/8, like our common time. But eight would not be a multiple of fours or twos. It appears, on the contrary, as a sum of three and three and two, or, by connecting the last two members, of three and five. It is $3 + (3 + 2)$. How wholly natural such pattern is to the East dawned upon the author first in 1930 when he heard in Cairo a group of very unsophisticated street singers persistently call the public's attention with the short melodicle

Ex. 29. Cairo, street musicians

Another case: What we would call a 9/8 is in Turkey a pattern *akçak* in the form

where the two strong accents determine clearly the sum $4 + 5$. And the same would be true of the Turkish *sofian:*

The result is always hovering, playful, light, and entirely different from the pounding monotone of later western rhythms.

The entirely different ideal of oriental rhythm follows from the entirely different character of oriental music. It follows essentially from the total absence of harmony.

Basically, harmony conveys the sense of tension and relaxation, of breathing in and out—in short, of organic motion and life. To achieve this to and fro requires a change from chord to chord; any series of similar chords would mean a cessation of all motion or life.

[14] Raouf Yekta, *La Musique turque,* in *Encyclopédie de la Musique,* ed. Lavignac, Part I, Vol. V, pp. 3024 ff.

In Europe, the concept of supporting the melody by an orderly progression of chords has been driven to extremes. Jean-Philippe Rameau, creator of the modern principles of harmony, boldly affirms in his *Nouveau Système de Musique* of 1726 that "melody stems from harmony"; and though this is nonsense from any historical viewpoint, he is right by the facts of his and later times: many melodies of the eighteenth and nineteenth centuries are triads broken up and adorned with a few passing tones.

Oriental music has no harmony. What harmony means to the West, the almost breathlike change from tension to relaxation, is in the East provided by rhythm. In avoiding the deadly inertia of evenness, rhythm helps an otherwise autonomous melody to breathe in and out [15]—just as harmony does in the West. Harmony, as a vertical configuration—the notes of a chord resounding above one another—is forced to rearrange the spatial distances between its notes from chord to chord, replacing a fourth in the first chord by a third in the following chord. Rhythm, as a concept of horizontal expanse, must rearrange the temporal distances from note to note, giving, say, two units of time to the first, and three to the following note.

This explains the almost total absence of divisive and, more so, of equally divided, 'striding' rhythms in the Near and Middle East. Oriental rhythm is additive. It progresses from a note x time units long to another note y time units long. The sum of x and y forms the metrical pattern to be repeated again and again like the in-and-out of respiration. (There might be three or four such notes in a pattern; but they can easily be reduced to two members, representing, one, tension, and one, relaxation.)

The relation of rhythm and harmony, as interpreted in the preceding paragraph, is confirmed by an irrefutable chronological fact: The transition, inside Europe, from an additive to a divisive rhythm occurred at exactly the time in which the contrapuntal (horizontal) concept of polyphony yielded to the harmonic (vertical) concept. It began essentially around 1400 and had been completed by 1600, with a few predecessors in the fourteenth

[15] To the author's satisfaction, Paul Boepple, too, speaks of the "aesthetic measure of this rhythm" as a "human breathing" (*Theoretisches und Praktisches zur Rhythmik der neuesten Musik*, in *Bericht über den Musikwissenschaftlichen Kongress in Basel*, Leipzig, 1925, p. 81).

century and a few stragglers in the seventeenth. When Pietro Aron in *De institutione harmonica* (1516) described the method of writing the individual voice parts successively as obsolete, while such modern masters as Josquin, Obrecht, and Isaac were considering all the voice parts together—"a very difficult thing that requires long training and practice"—rhythm had already turned to simple, divisive 4/4 patterns.

Additive rhythm has of necessity two aspects; it is metric as well as accentual. It relies on a clear distinction between the two members of which a pattern consists, be they of one, two, three, four, or five time units; and it needs accent in order to keep the two members apart. Obviously, the metrical aspect is more important. Meter is essential, while the accents, often very weak, are accessory as means, and nothing but means, to an end.

'Breathing' rhythms, uneven and additive, are at home in the now preponderantly Muhammedan world between Morocco and India. From there they have spread to essential parts of Europe and Africa. The Moorish conquest of Spain in 711 A.D. carried them to the Iberian peninsula, where they are still alive in the highly emotional *cante jondo* (*hondo*) or *flamenco* of the Andalusian gypsies, and above all in their *peteneras* and *seguiriyas*.[16] More recently, two westward migrations to America—of the Latins and of African Negroes—have freely mixed on this continent and partly returned eastward to the Old World.

In the meantime, a northern flow had taken possession of a vital part of eastern Europe. It will suffice to point to two extremely 'additive' regions. One is Russia, of which a few evidences will be given in the chapters on the nineteenth and twentieth centuries. But closest to the Orient are the almost incredible rhythms of Bulgarian folk music, vocal and instrumental.[17] Most songs and dance melodies appear in asymmetrical groups of smallest units, such as 5/16, 7/16, 9/16, 11/16, 13/16. Seen as meters, a 5/16 is

---

[16] Cf. Donald Duff, *Flamenco*, in *Modern Music*, Vol. XVII, 1939, pp. 214–220. Clemente Cimorra, *El cante jondo*, Buenos Aires, 1943. Columbia Records has just republished eight songs of the finest *flamenco* singer, the late La Niña de los Peines, on long-playing disks.

[17] Stoyan Dzhudzhev, *Rythme et mesure de la musique populaire bulgare*, in *Institut d'études slaves, Travaux*, No. 12, Paris, 1931. Christo Obreschkoff, *Das bulgarische Volkslied*, Bern, 1937.

iambic or trochaic—2 + 3 or 3 + 2; a 7/16 is anapaestic or
dactylic—2 + 2 + 3 or 3 + 2 + 2. Only very few pieces run in
even numbers. But even these have uneven sections in the oriental
way: an 8/16, far from being 2 × 4/16, is actually the sum of
3 + 2 + 3 or 3 + 3 + 2 or 2 + 3 + 3. Moreover, several of these
asymmetrical patterns can be combined to form compound additive sections.

An outstanding parallel from Rumania has found its way to the
concert halls of the West: the fifth of Bartók's *Rumanian Folk
Dances* for orchestra [18] moves in a steady alternation of 3/4, 3/4,
and 2/4, or 3 + 3 + 2. Rumania's northwestern neighbor, Hungary, joins her with rhythms of 5/8, 7/8, 7/4, 5 + 3 eighths,
3 + 2 + 4 quarters, and 4 + 3 + 3 or 10/4.[19]

Ex. 30. Hungarian folksong

Even in western and central Europe, additive rhythms have
played an important role during the sixteenth and seventeenth
centuries and again both in America and in Europe during the
twentieth. This book will come back to them in due time.

On the other hand, these additive rhythms have, no doubt, an
impressive ancestry. Ancient Egypt, poor in drums, nevertheless
shows hand-clapping on a great number of paintings and reliefs,
and her tombs have yielded many hundreds of wooden and ivory
clappers.[20] Indeed, a stele from the eleventh or twelfth dynasty of
the Middle Kingdom (around 2000 B.C.) commits to memory the
names of three professional hand-clapping women [21]—a distinction that the contemporaries would hardly have bestowed upon
subordinate one-two one-two percussionists. The clapperers must
—like the later drummers—have given to melody the intricate pat-

[18] Béla Bartók, *Rumanian folk dances*, Vienna, 1922, pp. 8 f.
[19] Béla Bartók, *Hungarian folk music*, London, 1931.
[20] Cf. Curt Sachs, *Die Musikinstrumente des alten Aegyptens*, Berlin, 1921; Hans
Hickmann, *Instruments de musique*, in *Catalogue général des antiquités égyp-
tiennes*, Cairo, 1949.
[21] Hans Hickmann, *Die ältesten Musikernamen*, in *Musica*, Vol. V, Kassel, 1951,
p. 90.

terns of additive rhythm that the Near and Middle East has preserved through thousands of years to the present.

FREE RHYTHM. Along with all these intricacies of rhythmical
strictness, music in the Near and Middle Orient also knows the
charm of total freedom. Art forms, from solo songs to orchestral
ensembles, have an elaborate introduction, best known under the
Egyptian name *taqsīm* or 'division,' in which the soloist, or all the
melody players one after another, state the characteristic melody
pattern, or *maqām,* of the piece to come in an entirely free, now
meditative, now brilliant, virtuoso-like improvisation, without any
words or a definite rhythm. True, there might be passages sustained by an *ostinato* pedal of even quarter beats. When this occurs the melody must follow somehow, but often breaks loose in
offbeats and syncopations.[22]

This rhapsodic *taqsīm* is an almost exact counterpart of the *alāpa*
before the Indian *rāga,* and of the *bebuka* before the Indonesian
patet.

The present author has even dared suggest that the division of
form into a soloistic, free-rhythmic *taqsīm* and a strict-rhythmic
ensemble *maqām* must have existed in the orchestral practice of
ancient Babylonia that the Biblical book of Daniel describes four
times in greatest detail. Each of the melody instruments—lyre,
harp, pipes, and others—is mentioned as playing individually before the *maqām* proper sets in "with all the instruments together"
(*sumponiāh vkol znē zmārāh* in the Aramaic text).[23]

TEMPO. The Orient seldom speaks of standard tempos. For modern Egypt, the theoretician Kamel el-Kholay [24] has indicated
M.M. 100 to the quarter note. But this is certainly somewhat high-
handed. And then, the average tempo changes in the Arabo-
Islamic world from country to country between Morocco and
Pakistan. Within a piece of strophic character, the tempo often
grows in speed; otherwise it is remarkably constant within a piece
and does not even change in repeated performances.

[22] Cf. Alfred Berner, *Studien zur arabischen Musik*, Leipzig, 1937, pp. 40–56.
[23] Daniel, 3: 5, 7, 10, 15. Curt Sachs, *The history of musical instruments*, New
York, 1940, p. 85.
[24] Kamel el-Kholay, *Kitābu 'l-mūsīqī*, Cairo, 1905.

Tunisian musicians distinguish in general three tempos: slow, lively, very fast. Normally their ratio of speed is 1:2:4—that is, in the terms of Renaissance music, *proportio dupla* and *quadrupla*. But the individual variations and deviations are disconcerting (as doubtless were the ones of the Renaissance). So is the absolute concept of speed: in Robert Lachmann's very reliable transcriptions the allegedly slow pieces span the range from 116 to 162 M.M. for the quarter note.[25] This would be *allegro molto* in our western terminology.

BERBERS AND BEDOUINS. This whole chapter has by no means described 'the' rhythmical concepts of the Near and Middle East, but only those of the cities. In the rural districts and the desert, abodes of the fellahs and Bedouins, all music, including rhythm, is much less sophisticated and hardly metrical. Indeed, the music of the Muhammedan countryside is, in modern terminology, 'primitive' rather than 'oriental.' Its rhythm, far removed from the complicated urban patterns, is very free in solo pieces, and strict-accentual in group and dancing forms. This basic discrepancy does not, of course, exclude an ever repeated exchange between the two realms.

A similar discrepancy exists between the refined music of the Arabian cities and the much simpler musical language of the Berbers, who had been living all over North Africa before the Arabian conquest and still form important contingents in Morocco and Algeria. (Berber music, on the other hand, is very close to the songs of South Arabian Bedouins.) Again, all solo music is free, but group and dancing songs are strict and accentual, mostly

Ex. 31. Moroccan Berbers

in 2/4 and 6/8 with regulating percussion. The 6/8 proceeds sometimes in hemiola with the dancing feet: the feet would organize

[25] Robert Lachmann, *Die Musik in den tunisischen Städten*, in *Archiv für Musikwissenschaft*, Vol. V, 1923, p. 164.

the six eighths in 3/4 with a stamp on the second quarter, which coincides with the third eighth of the percussion.[26]

Metrical patterns, paramount in the Muhammedan world, prove once more to be a later refinement. Did they come from India?

[26] Cf. E. M. von Hornbostel und Robert Lachmann, *Asiatische Parallelen zur Berbermusik*, in *Zeitschrift für vergleichende Musikwissenschaft*, Vol. I, 1933, pp. 4–11. Alexis Chottin, *Instruments, musique et danse chleuhs, loc. cit.*, pp. 11–15. Alexis Chottin, *Musique et danses berbères*, in *Corpus de Musique Marocaine*, fasc. II, Paris, 1933. Alexis Chottin, *Chants et danses berbères*, in *Revue de Musicologie* XX, 1936, pp. 65–69. Brigitte Schiffer, *Die Oase Siwa und ihre Musik*, Diss. Berlin, Bottrop, 1936. Rural Arabs: Béla Bartók, *Die Volksmusik der Araber von Biskra und Umgebung*, in *Zeitschrift für Musikwissenschaft*, Vol. II, 1920, pp. 489–522.

CHAPTER 6

India

The title of this chapter covers the triangular peninsula in the central south of Asia. It includes the modern states of India and Pakistan and the island of Ceylon off its tip. It excludes the Burmese-Siamese-Indochinese peninsula to the east as well as Indonesia beyond the Strait of Malacca.

The distinction between the 'North' and the 'South' of India is geographical as well as linguistic and anthropological; owing to millenniums of conquests from the Indus valley in the northwest, there has been a decisive shift and shuffle of population. The northern part has now a fairer stock with languages related to our own (hence called Indo-European); while the more archaic southern part has peoples with a darker pigmentation and with non-European, 'Dravidian' languages.

Musically, the country has one common idiom, if we except the many native, primitive 'tribes' in secluded parts of the country. But the southern dialect of this idiom, called Carnatic, is as a rule in a slightly better stage of preservation.

VEDIC RHYTHM. Of the numerous Indo-European languages in India, the 'perfect' Sanskrit, India's ancient literary language, developed in the first thousand years B.C. It descended from the tongue in which, sometime after the middle of the second millennium B.C., the Aryan conquerors from the Indus valley had composed the oldest of their holy Books of Wisdom, the *Rigveda*.

The four *Vedas*, in use to this day, are the *Rigveda*, or Book of

Hymns, the *Yajurveda*, a hymnal in prose, the *Samaveda*, an extract for musical use from the *Rig*, and lastly the *Atharvaveda*, the book of curses, spells, and charms.

Those written in verse had a distinct type of rhythm with the following characteristics:

(1) Vedic rhythm is basically numerical, with usually eleven or twelve syllables in a line. Thus it draws very close to the rhythm of the probably somewhat later Bible of the Persian Zoroastrians, the *Avesta*.

(2) Most Vedic stanzas have verses with the same number of syllables.

(3) Within this main numerical principle, Vedic poetry has a definite trend towards a metrical, usually iambic, organization.

(4) Such iambs are nearly strict towards the end of a line but rather vague in the earlier part. This trait is reminiscent of many archaic verses in other civilizations.

(5) Actual stresses are absent.[1]

"Generally the melodies of the *Sāma-Veda* [the 'Veda of melodies'] may be said to illustrate the words no more than the words originate from the spirit of music. In a very archaic way, truly, words and melody go side by side, for which reason the *Sāma-Veda* becomes even more interesting."[2]

SANSKRIT METER. India relies on the metrical aspect of rhythm more than any other country has done, not even excluding Greece.

There are two obvious reasons for such predominance. One is the purely metrical character of the Sanskrit language down to the beginning of our era:[3] long and short syllables were carefully kept apart without any accent in a western sense. The other reason is that verses—metrical verses—were used as the

---

[1] E. Vernon Arnold, *Vedic metre*, Cambridge, 1905. Arthur Anthony Macdonell, *A Vedic grammar*, Oxford, 1916, pp. 436–447. Erwin Felber and Bernhard Geiger, *Die indische Musik der vedischen und der klassischen Zeit*, in *Sitzungsberichte der Kais. Akademie der Wissenschaften in Wien, Phil.Hist.Kl.*, Vol. 170, 1912, No. 7. J. M. van der Hoogt, *The Vedic chant*, Wageningen, 1929.

[2] Van der Hoogt, *op. cit.*, p. 52. Cf. also Friedrich Chrysander, *Ueber die altindische Opfermusik*, in *Vierteljahrsschrift für Musikwissenschaft*, Vol. I, 1885, pp. 21–34.

[3] Arthur A. Macdonell, *A Sanskrit grammar*, London, 1901, p. 11.

idiom, not only of poetry, but also of philosophical, historical, and grammatical treatises: the Hindus failed to develop a literary prose until the nineteenth century; and even today solemn addresses seem to be delivered in verse.

Poetry, unlike conversational language, has kept its metrical character. "When it is recited the accent, so far as it exists in the language, is not obliterated; it falls for the most part on long syllables, but its position in the verse is not determined. . . . It is only a highly developed feeling for *time,* supported by the singsong method of delivery, that brings the metrical law home to the ear." [4]

Though metrical arrangement is common to all the poetry of India, there are two different principles of counting:

(1) The consistent factor in a group is the number of syllables, whether they are long or short. For instance:

$$- - \smile, \text{ or } \smile - \smile, \text{ or } - \smile -, \text{ or } \smile \smile \smile.$$

(2) The consistent factor in a group is the number of time units, notwithstanding the number of resulting syllables. A foot contains of necessity four units, be they $\smile \smile \smile \smile$, or $- -$, or $- \smile \smile$, or $\smile \smile -$.

The epical stanza *śloka,* inherited from Vedic poetry, has a special form: two verses, both in two sections of eight syllables each.

The other kinds of stanzas—the reader will, I hope, not mind being spared their Sanskrit names—have four lines with eleven, twelve, fourteen, fifteen, seventeen, nineteen, or twenty-one syllables each. Twenty-one syllables appear as three even sections of seven syllables; nineteen syllables, as twelve plus seven.[5]

Yamātārājabhānasalagām is the magic word by which the Hindus remember their numerous meters. Its component parts indicate the following single meters of three syllables:

yamātā	$\smile - -$	(Greek: bacchic)
mātārā	$- - -$	(Greek: *molossos*)
tāraja	$- - \smile$	(Greek: antibacchic)

---

[4] E. A. Sonnenschein, *What is rhythm?*, Oxford, 1925, p. 206, quoted from Professor Jacobi of Bonn.

[5] On Sanskrit meters: Albrecht Weber, in *Indische Studien,* Vol. VIII; Theodor Benfey, *Chrestomathie aus Sanskritwerken,* pp. 317 ff.

rājabhā	‒ ◡ ‒	(Greek: cretic)
jabhāna	◡ ‒ ◡	(Greek: amphibrach)
bhānasa	‒ ◡ ◡	(Greek: dactyl)
nasala	◡ ◡ ◡	(Greek: tribrach)
salagām	◡ ◡ ‒	(Greek: anapaest)

In addition, the Hindus have four feet of two syllables, whose names use *la* for the short, and *gā* for the long syllable:

lala	◡ ◡	(Greek: pyrrhic)
lagā	◡ ‒	(Greek: iamb)
gāla	‒ ◡	(Greek: trochee)
gāgā	‒ ‒	(Greek: spondee)

Music, basically vocal and in recitation often running into speech, had to accept the domination of poetical meter; but it did not do so without a challenge.

TĀLAS. Progressing beyond the simple poetic foot, the *lala,* the *gāla,* the *nasala,* the Hindus have developed musical rhythms or *tālas* in the same way as Arabian singers proceeded from merely poetical versification to musical, complicated *īqāʿat.*

The study of these patterns is not easy. A reader can hardly get an adequate idea of Indian rhythm from theoretical sources alone, be they ancient or modern, Indian or English. Their authors suffer from an extreme inability to explain a practice so remote from western concepts; the Indian terms all too often cover more than one idea; and the English words intended to translate them are frequently used in an arbitrary way. The very word *tāla* has at least three different meanings, and our simple and seemingly unmistakable terms 'time unit,' 'beat,' and 'bar' become amazingly ambiguous.

The following paragraphs try to convey the significance and character of Indian rhythm to western readers in the shortest and clearest words at the author's command.

It may be said once more that the musical rhythm of India consists in uninterruptedly recurrent patterns or *tālas* which, being metrical, not accentual, are kept distinct by the different duration of their notes, but (in principle) not by any difference in intensity.

So essential are the rhythmic patterns in India and so intimately connected with, and responsible for, the character of the piece in which they occur that where a Westerner would write 'sonata in C major,' the Indian composer seldom fails to write a double heading: the *rāga* or melodic pattern plus the *tāla* or rhythmic pattern; say, *Bilāval rāga, Tīntāl tāla*.

Within the pattern or *tāla*, the musicians of India distinguish four principal grades of organization:

(1) the time unit or *mātra;*

(2) the 'member' or *anga*, which has the length of one, two, three, four, five, or even seven time units and corresponds to what the syllable in poetry and the individual note in music are;

(3) the 'measure' or *vibāgha*, which corresponds to the poetical verse foot and consists of a number of 'members' or *angas*, one, two, three, or four;

(4) the 'section,' 'period,' or *āvarta*, which corresponds to a whole verse line and consists of several bars or feet, usually four.

Had the Greeks made use of this terminology, they would have called a dactylic tetrapody an *āvarta*, and its four individual feet, *vibāghas;* each dactyl would have had three *angas*, and each *anga*, one or two *mātras*.

Virāmas or rests are admissible.

A musical system so thoroughly metrical as India's cannot create 'divisive' rhythms. A *tāla* like *tīn*, which has 8/8 like our C, is not a square product of two halves or four quarters, but rather the sum of $4 + 2 + 2$. Or 8/8 could be organized in the ubiquitous pattern of the Grecian dochmiac: $3 + 3 + 2$. No Indian pattern can be divided into halves, thirds, or quarters; they all are 'irregular' from our western viewpoint. And while in Greece and other countries a short note had in principle one time unit only, and a long note two, India feels free to allot them any number of units up to seven (and in theory even to nine). A dactyl might appear as the sum, not of $2 + 1 + 1$ (as in Greece) but, for example, of $3 + 2 + 2$ (under the northern name *rūpaka*) or of $7 + 1 + 2$ (under the name of *jhampa*).

According to Sanskrit terminology, the two latter feet have three members or *angas* (like syllables in a verse foot); southern *rūpaka* (to which we would give a 3/4 signature) has only two members: $2 + 1$ or $4 + 2$. There are also meters with only one member (*eka tāla*, 4 units) and others with four members, such as *dhamāra* or *aṭa*: $5 + 5 + 2 + 2$.

In the north more than in the south, the number of accepted meters has essentially gone down since the Middle Ages. The most important theoretical work of that time, the *Saṅgīta Ratnākara* of ca. 1247 A.D., still describes 120 patterns extending from 1 to 19 members.[6] But most of these patterns differ completely from the modern ones. The current rhythms of today are listed in the following survey, in which the letters N and S are added in view of the different and even contradictory terminology used in the north and the south.

Name	*mātras*	
(N) *chautāla* or *chartāla*	$2+2+1+1=6$	
(S) *rūpaka*	$4+2 \qquad =6$	
(N) *rūpaka*, (S) *triputa*	$3+2+2 \quad =7$	
(N) *tīn tāla* or *trivata tāla*	$4+2+2 \quad =8$	
(N) *surphākata*, (S) *maṭhia*	$4+2+4 \qquad =10$	or $2+1+2=5$
(N) *jhāpa*	$2+3+2+3=10$	
(S) *jhampa*	$7+1+2 \quad =10$	
(S) *dhruva*	$4+2+4+4=14$	
(N) *tevra*, (S) *triputa*	$6+4+4 \quad =14$	
(N) *dhamāra*, (S) *aṭa*	$5+5+2+2=14$	

There are also sixteenth rhythms:

trisra	$\frac{1}{2}+1$	$=1\frac{1}{2}$
khanda	$\frac{1}{2}+1+1$	$=2\frac{1}{2}$
misra	$\frac{1}{2}+1+2$	$=3\frac{1}{2}$
sankirna	$\frac{1}{2}+2+2$	$=4\frac{1}{2}$

A charming example of southern *triputa* is the following love song in $3 + 4$ from Malabar (the southwest coast of India) which

Ex. 32. Malabar, piece in *triputa* rhythm

$\downarrow = 142\text{-}184$

[6] Herbert A. Popley, *The music of India*, Calcutta and London, 1921, p. 74.

the men accompany by clapping their hands on the first and the fourth of seven eighths.[7]

Our time signatures may help us to comprehend the organization of these rhythms; but they mislead our judgment. It is characteristic that the Indians call a clear 4/4 rhythm *tīn tāla,* 'three-beat,' and a 3/4 rhythm, *chautāla,* 'four-beat.' The former has indeed only three beats proper and an additional rest; and the latter has four beats proper—two quarter notes and two eighths. Once more: the concepts of India's rhythm are not ours.

Another characteristic fact is the freedom to invert the sequence of members inside a foot: *tīn* can be $4 + 2 + 2$ or $2 + 4 + 2$ or $2 + 2 + 4$ within the same *āvarta* or section. To the Hindu musician dactyls and anapaests or amphibrachs are equivalent, as are also trochees and iambs.

The basic pattern, moreover, can be artfully concealed by subdividing the individual members of a foot into smaller note values,

Ex. 33. South India, piece in *rūpaka* rhythm

sometimes of equal, but oftener of unequal size, like the *fractio modi* of the Gothic time in Europe; it can also be concealed by slurring notes that should be kept apart and by ignoring what in western notation would be the bar lines.

The latter device can be much more complicated than it appears from these few words. In one of the most frequent and difficult forms of Indian music, which is in principle the form of our western rondo with an ever recurring theme and ever changing episodes in between, the episodes or *tānas* very often present themselves as a bewildering, breath-taking array of 6/16, 3/8, 5/8, 2/4, 3/4 bars despite some basic pattern that might be rendered as 4/4 in our notation. But an addition of the time units would show that most of the episodes have exactly the same length—for example,

[7] O. Abraham und E. von Hornbostel, *Phonographierte indische Melodien,* in *Sammelbände der Internationalen Musikgesellschaft,* Vol. V, 1904, pp. 354 f., and in *Sammelbände für Vergleichende Musikwissenschaft,* Vol. I, 1922, p. 257.

128 sixteenths: the motley array marks intricate shifts in grouping but does not affect the structure as a whole. "The effect, to one who is accustomed to this idiom of expression, is that of being hurled through chaos, and then landing right side up on *terra firma* again with no bones broken and a feeling of intense relief." [8]

The landing place is the *sam*, a reference point on which the partners—lest they should make fools of themselves—meet after all their vagaries for a restatement of the theme, only to re-engage in neck-breaking variations in the following *tāna*. And therewith the reader finds himself in the tangle of Indian accompaniment, counterrhythms, and drum patterns.

THE DRUM PATTERNS. The *tālas* apply to all music, whether sung or played on instruments. The word *tāla* itself derives from hand clapping and is in the terminology of instruments reserved to cymbals and certain forms of clappers. But the medium in which the metrical patterns are most fully developed is the drum.

No other civilization is India's equal in drum playing. The Indian drummer is a soloist and a chamber musician. Indeed, India and her eastern neighbor, Burma, have sets of ten or more well-tuned drums in a circular arrangement around the squatting player whose palms and fingertips perform the most astonishing toccatas in strictest melodic and metrical patterns, now in staccato, now in legato or even glissando.[9]

But the usual, almost indispensable role of drums is the sensitive support of vocal or instrumental solo melodies.

This dominant role of Indian drums appears in records of ancient times. Musical scenes depicted on reliefs show that more than two thousand years ago they were just as indispensable as they are today—even in the smallest solo or chamber music; all singers and players were shown with their faithful drummers as early as the second century B.C., when reliefs on the temple of Bharhut initiated the sculptural representation of scenes from Buddha's life

[8] Winthrop Sargent and Sarat Lahiri, *A study in East Indian rhythm,* in *The Musical Quarterly,* Vol. XVII, 1931, p. 434.

[9] Cf. the excellent recording in the Udai Shankar Album. Victor Red Seal M.382, under the title *Tabla taranga.* An illustration from Burma may be found in Curt Sachs, *The rise of music in the ancient world,* New York, 1943. Plate 6 B, opposite p. 161.

on temples and stupas.[10] More than a thousand years later, in 1051 A.D., the Rajarajeśvara temple at Tanjore had no less than 72 drummers among its 157 musicians; and in the sixteenth century, Emperor Akbar's band consisted of one pair of cymbals, twenty-three wind instruments, and forty-two drums.

The early evidences of rhythmical wealth in India mark, not a beginning, but rather an already fixed tradition which may go back to times immemorial. This impression allows us to resume the question asked in the preceding chapter: Where did this stress on rhythmic expression originate, or, at least, where did it grow into a well-wrought system?

The Muhammedan lands to the west of India—Persia, Turkey, the Arab states—are familiar with the rhythmical patterns but have no evidences from times before Islam. Ancient Egypt, so we reasoned, might have used them in the New Kingdom around the middle of the second pre-Christian millennium if not earlier.

One ancient civilization—so far the oldest one explored—has not yet appeared in this context: Mesopotamia, that fertile region between the Euphrates and the Tigris in which the Sumerians and Babylonians lived. Its numerous tablets of clay engraved with cuneiform writing do not speak of rhythm or metrical patterns anywhere, to be sure. But some give information on drums, on their outstanding role and importance—indeed, on the ritualistic veneration that they were granted.[11] No less than a dozen Sumerian names of drums with their Semitic (Akkadian) equivalents have been preserved—a number that seems to preclude any crude boom-boom in the style of our bands.

A close relation between India and Mesopotamia is more than a mere possibility. After the stupendous recent discoveries, "the distance between the Sumerian world and the civilization of the Indus valley tends to diminish, at least spatially. They are no longer two isolated points. The gulf which used to separate them geographically is daily being filled up." [12] To this we might add that

[10] Plates may be found in Curt Sachs, *The history of musical instruments,* New York, 1940, opposite p. 160; Claudie Marcel-Dubois, *Les instruments de musique de l'Inde ancienne,* Paris, 1941; Curt Sachs, *The rise of music in the ancient world,* New York, 1943, opposite p. 176.

[11] Curt Sachs, *The history of musical instruments,* pp. 73–78.

[12] René Grousset, *The civilizations of the east,* Vol. II (*India*), New York, Alfred A. Knopf, 1931, p. 6.

the Akkadian name of the frame drum, *ṭimbūtu,* recurs in the
Tamil or South Indian name of the frame drum: *tambaṭṭam.*

Thus it is possible that Mesopotamia was the cradle of rhythmical drum patterns, and that from there they spread to India, in
the east, and to the Arabo-Muhammedan Orient in the west, with
which she was musically connected in pre-Islamic times through
such educational centers as Al-Hira.[13]

The Indian drummer who accompanies a singer or any other
performer plays either one drum with two heads or else two drums
with one head each. In either case the heads are tuned to different pitches—a fifth or an octave—and hand-beaten (while the
drums of the Near and Middle East, though hand-beaten too, are
not tuned to exact pitches).

Bharata's book on the theatrical arts in India,[14] which was written at a date unknown but certainly not later than 500 A.D., gives
two simple basic forms of drum patterns:

right hand ♩ ♩ ♩.
left hand 𝄽

right hand ♩ ♩
left hand 𝄽 𝄽

It is important that the eight-unit pattern, here as so often elsewhere, amounts to 2 + 3 + 3. Incidentally, Fox Strangways heard
a couple of natives of the Panan tribe of India alternately singing in a four-beat rhythm while a drum and a triangle divided the
beats respectively as 3 + 2 + 3 and 2 + 4 eighths.[15]

But skillful drummers do not rest satisfied with so easy a technique. Often they will show off in complex counterrhythms without upsetting the singer or disturbing his *tāla.*

A favorite but simple counterrhythm uses the same *tāla:* the
right hand plays the pattern in standard tempo while the left

[13] Curt Sachs, *The rise of music in the ancient world,* p. 277.
[14] The Sanskrit text of the Natya-śastra with French translation and commen-
taries, in Jean Grosset, *Contribution à l'étude de la musique hindoue,* in *Bibliothèque de la Faculté des Lettres de Lyon,* Vol. VI, 1888. The English and German
translations are incomplete.
[15] Curt Sachs, *The rise of music in the ancient world,* New York, 1943, p. 47,
ex. 24.

hand augments it in what the later Gothic Age would have called
proportio subdupla:

right:	♪ ♩	♪ ♪ ♩	♪			
	1 2	3 1 2	3			

left:	♩ ♩	♩				
	1 2	3				

or

right:	♩ ♪ ♩	♩ ♪ ♩				
	1 2 3	1 2 3				

left:	♩	♩ ♩				
	1	2 3				

Often, however, the hands play different *tālas,* one in standard
tempo, and the other in augmentation, such as:

right:	♪ ♩ ♪ ♪ ♩ ♪ ♪ ♩ ♪	
	1 2 3 1 2 3 1 2 3	

left:	♩ ♩ ♩ ♩	
	1 2 3 4	

Rhythm, as articulated by the drums, shows in North India an
essential trait which is often only dimly perceptible in the singer's
melody. This is the 'empty' beat or *khāli.* While a short metrical
member or syllable with one time unit or *mātra* is given one beat
only, a member of two units is treated differently. The singer who
slaps his thigh to mark the first beat lifts and turns his hand up
to make the second beat silent or 'empty'; and the drummer who
strikes his right drumhead to mark the first beat strikes the left
one to mark the empty beat in a different color and pitch, as follows:

right:	♪ ♩ ♪ ♪ ♩ ♪
left:	♪ 　 ♪

Symbolizing the syllables of a foot in their natural sequence as
1 2 3, and the empty beats as o,

> *tin tāl* appears as 1 2 o 3
> *tevra* 　　　　as 1 o o 2 o 3 o

In folk and semi-folk dances, the performers take a step backwards on the empty beat: movement, to the Hindus, is arrested on the empty beat.

In cases like these, the drummer actually creates a new *tāla*, because some of the characteristic empty beats are annihilated by a covering full beat in the other voice part. Our second example appears as

$$1\ o\ 2\ 3\ o\ 1\ o\ 2\ 3\ o$$

plus $1\quad o\quad 2\quad 3\quad\quad o$

$$\overline{1\ o\ 2\ 3\ 4\ 5\ 6\ 7\ 8\ o}$$

or:

♩ ♫ ♫ ♫ ♩

The two patterns might even overlap:

♪ ♩   ♪ ♪ ♩   ♪ ♪ ♩   ♪ ♪ ♩   ♪ ♪ ♩   ♪ ♪ ♩   ♪

1 2 o 3 1 2 o 3 1 2 o 3 1 2 o 3 1 2 o 3

♩   ♪ ♩   ♩   ♪ ♩   ♩   ♪ ♩   ♩   ♪ ♩

1 o 2 3 o 1 o 2 3 o 1 o 2 3 o 1 o 2 3 o

Still, all these naked patterns do not give the full story. The drummer, like the singer, feels actually free to improvise elaborate paraphrases in rolls, syncopations, and counteraccents. Indeed, as Fox Strangways relates, "the singer and drummer like to play hide and seek with each other; and the audience watch the contest with amusement." [16]

Before concluding our remarks on drumming, mention should be made of the curious fact that in antiquity the 'audible' slap indicated, not the entry, but the end of a member; for example in *tāla Jhampa:*

♩.			♪ ♩	♩		♪ ♩.				
pattern:	1	2	3	1	1	2	1	2	1	1 2 3
silent gestures:	s	s		s		s		s s		
audible slaps:			A A		A		A A		A	

The audible beat should perhaps not be interpreted as a stress but rather as a warning; it must not be compared to the accented

[16] A. H. Fox Strangways, *The Music of Hindustan.* Oxford, 1914, p. 233.

downbeat of our conductors but rather to the sudden jerk of their arms preparing the downbeat. The shifted emphasis shows once more that Indian rhythm is essentially different from the stressed beats of our western musical style.[17]

But even this conducting interpretation might be too western. Taking a beat at the beginning of a duration for granted might perhaps be altogether inadmissible. Somehow it seems to be more natural to mark the end of a duration or distance or movement. Our clocks strike two when the second hour has gone; on our rulers, the notch marked 2 denotes the end, not the beginning, of a two-inch distance; and the complex movement that we call a step is in our awareness (and terminology) almost identical with its moment, the audible downtread of the sole. Would it not in a way be logical to mark the beginning of a metrical member only when a conscious accent on the first has changed the original concept of mere duration?

TEMPO. The value of the time unit is rather vague. A wise man of old has offered the following recipe, which is poetical although not quite metronomic:

"Take one hundred petals of the lotus flower, place them then one upon the other; and when pierced with a needle, the time in which the point passes through a single petal is called one second; eight such seconds are called one lavâ; eight lavâs one koshtâ; eight koshtâs one nimishâ; eight nimishâs one kalâ; four kalâs one anudruthâ; two anudruthâs one druthâ; two druthâs one lâgu; two lâgus one guru; three lâgus one plutha; four lâgus one kaku-pathâ." [18]

We gain a firmer foothold when D. P. Mukerji [19] gives to the *mātra* or time unit the approximate duration of a second, which would amount to a western quarter note of M.M. 60; or when Bhavánráv A. Pingle [20]—just, once more, as masters in Europe had done in the sixteenth century—recommends counting at mod-

---

[17] Cf. Curt Sachs, *The rise of music in the ancient world*, New York, 1943, pp. 185–191, on patterns and beats.

[18] C. R. Day, *The music and the musical instruments of southern India and the Deccan*, London, 1891, p. 25.

[19] D. P. Mukerji, *Indian music*, Poona, 1945(?), p. 55.

[20] Bhavánráv A. Pingle, *Indian music*, 2nd edition, Bombay, 1898, p. 129.

erate speed: one two three four five, which yields at the very least M.M. 64, but probably a bit more.

Such oversimplifying generalizations are not confirmed in live performances, or in (western) staff notations of Indian music, or even in the rhythmic formulas of theoretical treatises. The absolute speed varies considerably and is, on the average, fast. Of the twenty-nine pieces transcribed by Abraham and von Hornbostel,[21] only five descend to metronomic figures below M.M. 100 for the quarter note, while twenty-four of them keep somewhere between 100 and 192 M.M., with an average of 135 M.M. This is very much reminiscent of tempi in the Near East, as they were discussed in the preceding chapter on the ground of Robert Lachmann's metronomization.

As far as there is a standard tempo in India, it can be halved, doubled, quadrupled, and in exceptional cases even sextupled —if Popley is right; [22] indeed, it can be multiplied by three halves and by five quarters (which, in Renaissance terminology, would be *proportiones sesquialtera* and *sesquiquarta*). Hence—to quote just one example—the reader will find in C. R. Day's book on the music of southern India [23] renditions of the principal triple meter *rūpaka* (in the southern meaning of the term) now in 3/8, now in 3/4, now even in 3/2.

UPBEAT AND DOWNBEAT. Before leaving India and the oriental world for Europe and the West, it might be well to touch upon the concept of upbeat, in which the two branches of civilization are equally interested.

Hugo Riemann [24] and Vincent d'Indy [25] have maintained that, as the latter puts it, "every melody begins with an upbeat whether expressed [or, let us say, real] or simply understood [imaginary]."

The basic idea is obviously that even in a piece of the most outspoken downbeat character such as, say, the *Meistersinger* prelude,

[21] Otto Abraham und Erich M. von Hornbostel, *Phonographierte indische Melodien*, in *Sammelbände der Internationalen Musikgesellschaft*, Vol. V, 1904, pp. 354–380.
[22] Herbert A. Popley, *The music of India*, Calcutta, 1921, p. 73.
[23] *Op. cit.*
[24] Vincent d'Indy, quoting his sentence "No melody starts on a downbeat," fails to indicate his source.
[25] Vincent d'Indy, *Cours de composition musicale*, Paris, 1912, Vol. I, p. 35.

the winds inhale on the preceding imaginary 'four,' the kettle-drummer lifts his arms, and the conductor prepares the entry with an eloquent jerk of his arm, to make the initial 'one' precise and strong. The awareness of a bodily action with which the music is inseparably connected starts before a sound is perceived on the downbeat. Hence, the piece begins on the upbeat, at least physiologically and psychologically.

A confirmation seems to come from Hungarian, Czech, and Slovak folk songs: the compulsory accent on the first syllable in these three languages forces the melody to set it on the downbeat; but as a rule this downbeat is preceded by some meaningless vowel or syllabic sound expressing the nonexistent, merely physiological upbeat.[26]

Yet we are on slippery ground. It is not easy or safe to discuss what other people imagine without saying so—and particularly when these people, as it happens in this book, belong to ages and cultures remote from ours. The musical facts should caution against so sweeping a generalization. The picture that India offers, and later the European Renaissance, is very different and maybe more correct.

While the facts of the Renaissance will duly be discussed in the proper chapter of this book, attention might focus briefly on the situation in India. As a short-cut, the reader may avail himself of the twenty-nine melodies that Otto Abraham and Erich M. v. Hornbostel transcribed half a century ago from Indian recordings.[27] Based on phonograph records and transcribed by two authors of the highest competence, these renditions are particularly trustworthy.

Twenty out of these twenty-nine pieces start on a downbeat; two are doubtful; seven start on an upbeat. Two of these upbeat pieces are expressly marked as dances, one as an instrumental melody, and one as a children's song.

Among the downbeat pieces, Nos. 17 and 18 captivate our attention particularly: the initial note, jumping up to the *finalis* of the mode, has doubtless an upbeat function; and yet it is essen-

[26] Béla Bartók, *Hungarian folk music*, London, 1931, p. 13.

[27] Otto Abraham und Erich M. v. Hornbostel, *Phonographierte indische Melodien*, in *Sammelbände der Internationalen Musikgesellschaft*, Vol. V, 1904, pp. 354–380.

tially lengthened out—in one case to a whole note, in the other one to a half note—so that the melody, somewhat against its nature, is forced to start on a downbeat.

These features are strangely reminiscent of similar traits in the Renaissance. There, too, the majority of melodies start on a down-beat. All polyphonic works do. And there, too, a good many initial notes, which carry unaccented syllables and ought to be upbeats, are lengthened out backwards in order to fill a whole measure and thus to avoid the upbeat. Actual upbeat pieces at that time are either catchy folk songs or instrumental music and, above all, dances. The following chapter will relate how to the Greeks all meters starting on the downbeat, such as dactyls and spondees, were calmer and more dignified than the upbeat meters, as anapaests or iambs.

The duplication of these very elucidating facts shakes the over-all validity of d'Indy's dogma. Granted that all the music of the nineteenth century, safely moored in instrumental grounds and sharing with folk songs and dances an idiom close to regular bodily motion, might easily lend itself to upbeat interpretation. But there is little if any necessity for suggesting nonexistent up-beats in a music remote from bodily motion and accents. And the theory becomes incongruous when the initial note, destined to be an upbeat as the carrier of an unaccented syllable, begins on the first beat instead of the last and thus abjures any allegiance to a compulsory upbeat law.

RHYTHMICAL FREEDOM. The sophisticated strictness of In-dian rhythm is given an ideal contrast and supplement in the free-dom of its preludes, which, even more indispensable than those preceding the fugues of Bach's *Well-tempered Clavier*, seem of late to have increased in length and importance at the cost of the following *rāga* or melody proper. It is the kind of free-rhythmic introduction before the strict-rhythmic piece that we regularly find as the *bebuka* before the Indonesian *patet* or as the *taqsīm* before the Arabian *maqām*.

The soloists, one after another, expound the scale of the *rāga*, its prevailing mood, and its characteristic melody turns in an *ālāpa*, which appears as a more or less elaborate improvisation without a definite rhythm, without words, and almost without accompaniment. Only after all inherent possibilities of the tune to come have been exhausted does the full ensemble strike the *rāga* proper with drums and with the text and hence in the strictest rhythm in a scrupulous observation of the prescribed *tāla*.

The reader will miss such regard for music in its own right when he passes to the chapter on Greece. There he will not meet with rhythmical patterns beyond the versification of poetry, or with an artful polyrhythm of drums; indeed, not even with drums at all except the women's timbrels used at home and in the service of ecstatic rites and mysteries.

CHAPTER 7

Greece and Rome

"All the marvellous principles of Greek thought . . . were established and developed by a regular historical process. And one of the most decisive advances in this process was the new investigation of the structure of music. The knowledge of the true nature of harmony and rhythm produced by that investigation would alone give Greece a permanent position in the history of civilization; for it affects almost every sphere of life."

Werner Jaeger, *Paideia,* translated by Gilbert Highet, New York, Oxford University Press, 1939, p. 163.

Greece, the nation that took its shape about 1000 B.C. around the Aegean Sea, on the Hellenic peninsula, in Thracia, in Asia Minor, and on the numberless isles in between, created a civilization in which the nascent trends of Europe and the maturity of the East were fused to form a peerless flowering of arts, letters, and philosophy.

The arts, despite this fusion, show one common trait all through the history of Greece: the plastic, linear element was infinitely stronger than coloristic tendencies. Not only were the works of sculpture and architecture more important than vases and murals; sculpture, architecture, and painting itself availed themselves of colors only to emphasize their forms and surfaces with energetic contrasts of white and black and red and blue.

Again and again this book will have to stress the fact that all through history rhythm goes with line and plastic form. Any civilization engrossed in sculpture and linear, uncoloristic painting finds rhythm as a strong, maybe the strongest, element of expression in music.

Greece has for this reason been a leading exponent of rhythm—not only in her actual achievements, but in the unparalleled interest that she took in the laws of rhythm, in its classification, and in its terminology. Hellas was the mother of rhythmology.

MUSIC AND POETRY. Ancient Greece was very little interested in the instrumental branch of music, which "did without rhythm and words" [1] and hence, as she deemed, without meaning.

Her spokesmen—theorists, philosophers, scientists—were almost exclusively concerned with vocal music, as the carrier of verses and hence of significant, unequivocal moods and ideas.

In this dependence on poetry, the music of Greece presented the classic example of an almost complete companionship of verse and melody, of the text and its musical setting. For, as Plato states with energy: "Rhythm and harmony [read: melody] are regulated by the words, and not the words by them." [2] Which is exactly what some twenty centuries later Carl Loewe (1796–1869), the famous composer of ballads, meant when he said, "Language is the basic rhythm of music." [3]

So close was the companionship of verses and melody that Greek singers knew the meter of their part from the meter of the words they were singing. Notation indicated pitches; it rarely needed to mark how long the individual notes should be held. Of the dozen Greek vocal pieces and fragments preserved in notation, only one—the charming *skolion* of Seikilos (music example 41) —is written (or, better, carved in stone) with some of the metrical symbols that the Greeks kept in readiness for special cases in which

[1] Cf. Hermann Abert, *Ein ungedruckter Brief des Michael Psellus über die Musik,* in *Sammelbände der Internationalen Musikgesellschaft,* Vol. II, 1901, p. 337.

[2] Plato, *Republic,* III, 400, trans. B. Jowett, New York, 1892.

[3] Karl Anton, *Beiträge zur Biographie Karl Löwes,* Halle, 1912, p. 55.

melodic invention prevailed over metric obedience: a horizontal dash above the pitch sign (—) for the ordinary long (♩), and the angle (⌐) for the dotted long (♩.).[4] This was necessary because, very far from being simple recitation, text and melody of that drinking song are as independent as they would be in a modern song; in one measure as many as three notes fall on a single syllable, and in another one a note is stretched out beyond its normal length in the interest of a well-rounded, symmetrical melody.

THE METERS AND THEIR UNITS OF TIME. Not in this or any similar, music-inspired melody, but in the great majority of vocal music, intended to follow the text as closely as possible, the Greeks accepted the poetical *pous* or verse foot as the elemental pattern of musical meter. Such feet were recurrent groups of two, three, or four syllables, which in a musical setting carried (in principle) one single note each.

Within a foot, the Greeks distinguished only two sizes of syllables: short and long. The latter size was characterized by either a long vowel, as *eta* and *omega,* or else a diphthong, like *ou, ai,* and *au,* or a short vowel like *epsilon* or *iota* if followed by two or more consonants.

The ancient sources at our disposal relate that the lengths of the long and the short were as two to one. (As an exception, the concluding syllables at the end of a line could be stretched to three or even to four units.) The unit in question represents the standard length, albeit only a relative one, of a short syllable; and we learn that Aristoxenos, the greatest Greek rhythmologist, established it in the fourth century B.C. under the name of *chronos protos* or 'primary time.'

Here is Aristoxenos' tidy system:

Duples, *isa* or 'dactyls' (Latin *pares*)

prokeleusmatikós	2 + 2	♫ ♫
dáktylos	2 + 2	♩ ♫

---

[4] Cf. Curt Sachs, *The rise of music in the ancient world,* New York, 1943, Pl. 8, opp. p. 177.

anápaistos	2 + 2	♫♩
spondaiós	2 + 2	♩ ♩

Triples, *diplasia* or 'iambs' (Latin *duplices*)

trochaios, choreios	2 + 1	♩ ♪
tribrachýs	1 + 2 or 2 + 1	♫♪
iambos	1 + 2	♪♩

Quintuples, *hemiolia* or 'paeons' [Paeonia was a state in the extreme north of Greece] (Latin *sescuplices*)

bákcheios	3 + 2	♪♩ ♩
kretikós, amphímakros	3 + 2	♩ ♪♩
antibákcheios, palim- *bákcheios*	2 + 3	♩ ♩ ♪

Septuples, *epítrita*

first	3 + 4	♪♩ ♩ ♩
second	3 + 4	♩ ♪♩ ♩
third	4 + 3	♩ ♩ ♪♩
fourth	4 + 3	♩ ♩ ♩ ♪

By the end of antiquity, around 400 A.D., the number of foot names and feet had been increased, obviously in order to have a proper meter ready for every word of the Latin language up to four syllables. The *Musica* of St. Augustine (354–430 A.D.) mentions— in addition to the already quoted feet—about a dozen more:

two units

pyrrhic	1 + 1	♫

four units

amphibrach	1 + 3 3 + 1	♪♩ ♪

five units

first paeon	2 + 3	♩ ♫♫
second paeon	3 + 2	♪♩ ♫
third paeon	2 + 3	♫♩ ♪
fourth paeon	3 + 2	♫♫ ♩

six units

ionic *a minore* [5]	2 + 4	♫♩ ♩
ionic *a maiore* [5]	4 + 2	♩ ♩ ♫
choriamb	3 + 3	♩ ♫♩
diiamb	3 + 3	♪♩ ♪♩
ditrochee	3 + 3	♩ ♪♩ ♪
antispast	3 + 3	♪♩ ♩ ♪

eight units

dispondee	4 + 4	♩ ♩ ♩ ♩

Another detailed enumeration and classification of feet can be found in the *De ratione metrorum commentarius* by Maximus Victorinus.[6]

All meters, some theoreticians taught, could be varied,
  (1) by changing the length of certain syllables (*ancipes,* 'ambiguous') from long to short or from short to long, particularly at the end of a line;
  (2) by resolving a long into two shorts;
  (3) by contracting two shorts into one long;
  (4) by 'syncopating' or suppressing a short syllable;
  (5) by adding a second short to an otherwise single short.

But these licenses must not be generalized, for (2) and (3) would destroy the identities of dactyls and spondees. St. Augustine, on the other hand, a metrist with actual words in mind, presents the four paeons with one long resolved by means of (2) under names other than the customary bacchic, cretic, and anti-bacchic, that is indeed, as independent meters.[7]

Iambs, trochees, and anapaests, obviously too short or too fast, existed only in reduplication; thus an iambic dimeter had four iambs, not two.

In principle feet could be enlarged to twice and four times their

---

[5] These epithets mean: beginning with the smaller or the larger element of the foot—the pyrrhic or the spondee. The Greek terms were *ap'elássonos* and *apò meízonos.*

[6] Reprinted in Heinrich Keil, *Grammatici latini,* Vol. VI, Leipzig, 1874, pp. 207 f.

[7] Aurelius Augustinus, *Musik,* German translation by C. J. Perl, Strassburg, 1937, p. 68.

original length by substituting—to speak in modern language—quarters and even halves for eighth notes. Such an enlarged foot was called *epibatós* or 'apt to be ascended.' Some enlarged feet had, however, names of their own: the double trochee became a choriamb; the quadruple trochee, a *semantós;* the quadruple iamb, an *orthios.*

The reason for formal augmentation is obvious. Music, as an integral part of Greek 'orchestics'—the organic aggregate of poetry, music, and rhythmical gesture—had to adjust itself to the needs of prosody, marching, and dances. In pieces of a more solemn character, any slowing down in the arbitrary way of modern music was unfeasible: it would have led to awkward marching steps in slow motion. The best and maybe the only way out of the difficulty was a strict multiplication of the time unit, which allowed the marchers to take exactly two or four instead of one of their regular steps on the *longa* of a pattern.

A CRITICAL COMMENT on the historical place and the meaning of Aristoxenian and later men's principles cannot be avoided.

Aristoxenos has in the first place been credited with introducing the time unit or *chronos protos* instead of the vaguer concept of a 'short' syllable.[8] This is not quite convincing. Several hundred years before Aristoxenos the Greeks had sung in choruses; and much of this choral music was done to the regular steps of dances or marching processions. How could it have been possible to sing in ensembles and in unison with the body without a well-established ratio from step to step, from note to note, from syllable to syllable? Aristoxenos, who lived a century after the so-called Classical Age, was hardly the first to codify numerical ratios.

Still, as a faithful pupil of the greatest classifier, Aristotle, Aristoxenos may well have been the first to unify and simplify such ratios and to squeeze them into a comprehensive over-all pattern.

Such was unmistakably the trend of the time. In the fourth century, too, melodists, under the leadership of the mathematician Euclid, squeezed the various incompatible Greek scales into a

---

[8] Rudolf Westphal (*Die Aristoxenische Rhythmuslehre,* in *Vierteljahrsschrift für Musikwissenschaft,* Vol. VII, 1891, pp. 78 ff.) thinks that Aristoxenos must have spoken about the difference between syllables and primary time units in the first, unfortunately lost, part of his Elements of Rhythm.

unified, simplified 'Perfect System,' [9] which in the interest of uni-
formity did not hesitate to violate the intrinsic structure of at least
a part of the scales.

Indeed, Aristoxenos himself, as the only theoretician, did not
hesitate to yoke the melodic genera of Greece in a single team
against their very nature. He developed a system of equal temperament or at least of temperament, which equalized the two smaller
steps in the various tetrachords, while all the other writers recognized and codified the unequal 'shades' that the practice of singers
and players provided.[10] His 'enharmonic' genera had (in modern
terms)

$$400 + 50 + 50 \text{ cents};$$

he allowed for three different 'chromatic' genera, of

$$366 + 67 + 67 \text{ cents},$$
$$350 + 75 + 75 \text{ cents},$$
$$300 + 100 + 100 \text{ cents};$$

and for two 'diatonic' genera, of

$$250 + 150 + 150 \text{ cents},$$
$$300 + 100 + 100 \text{ cents}.$$

By the same token, the ratio of 2:1 for long and breve in all
the meters of Greece is highly suspect. It is artificial and too good
to be true. A restriction to just two sizes and the allotment of
the uniform ratio 2:1 are rather unrealistic and oversimplified.
They cannot have had the backing of actual speech, either in
ordinary talk or in formal recitation. A famous physiologist in
Vienna, Ernst W. Brücke, found with the help of a kymograph or
recorder of sound waves that in the New High German language
"the syllables have very different lengths, and that their classification as long and short syllables is very crude. . . . The longest
syllables are far more than twice as long as the shortest, while there
is no exact borderline between long and short syllables." [11] For
English poetry, modern laboratory tests have shown that the

[9] Cf. Curt Sachs, *The rise of music in the ancient world,* New York, 1943, pp.
222 ff.

[10] *Ibid.,* pp. 211–215.

[11] E. Brücke, *Die physiologischen Grundlagen der neuhochdeutschen Verskunst,*
1875, p. 29.

ratio, far from being 2:1, is extraordinarily variable. It keeps as an average to a ratio around 3:2, but would go up to 8.66:1.

It is quite possible and even probable that the Greeks were aware of this variability; a sensitive ear perceives them without any modern laboratory equipment. Ignoring these shades in vocal music would have meant a violation of the supreme principle that the melody should follow the versification of the text.

The survival of other, less rigid forms is indeed implied in the somewhat embarrassed mention, though not description, of (doubtless older) 'alogical' meters, which refused to be squeezed into the neat but stiff enumeration of 1:1, 2:1, 3:2, and 4:3 feet. Furthermore: if de Groot is right in saying that the average ratio between a long and a short is in speech 3:2 rather than 2:1,[12] the epitrite would be at bottom a dactyl or an anapaest more fluent and natural than the drawling Aristoxenian form of two and one and one. And in a similar way, the paeonic, quintuple forms would be better trochees and iambs than those which were denoted as such in the metrical system of Aristoxenos. Could they be thought of as the older patterns still kept along with later simplifications? After all, the later iambs and trochees, as well as the anapaests, did not exist as individual feet, but only in pairs, as diiambs, ditrochees, choriambs, and antispasts. Both the quintuple- and the septuple-time meters have survived in Hellenic folk music down to this

Ex. 34. Modern Greek folk song

day.[13] But they were relinquished in art music not too long after Aristoxenos.

This discussion would in its turn entail another reflection. Of fourteen Aristoxenian meters, four were *isa* or binary; and two more, the iambs and the trochees, though by nature *diplasia* or ternary, were actually *isa* since they had to be coupled in pairs (6/8 or 6/4). This brings the number of divisive, binary rhythms to almost a half of all the meters in common use, while the other

[12] A. W. de Groot, *Der Rhythmus*, in *Neophilologus*, Vol. XVII, 1932, pp. 83 f.
[13] Cf. S. Baud-Bovy, *La chanson populaire grecque du Dodécanèse*, Paris, 1935.

half were additive. The neat bipartition is unique and is a challenge to interpretation.

Such interpretation must be based on the fateful position of Greece and on that of the fourth pre-Christian century. Both geographically and culturally, the Greek world lay on the threshold between the East and the West, between the Ionian, Phrygian, Lydian parts of Asia Minor and the south of Italy or *Magna Graecia* (of which Aristoxenos himself was a native). She welded elements from the Orient and from the Occident. And as in all such welding processes, the elements came alternately to the fore. An excellent musical example is the competition between the Asiatic pipes and the European lyre, with a continuous shift in importance from one to the other instrument.

Rhythm must then be supposed to have followed similar laws. If later times imposed on European music divisive, binary rhythms as a particular Mediterranean, non-Nordic trait, as later chapters of this book will show, would not this Mediterranean trait have existed in ancient Greece and Italy as the European element against the additive rhythms of Asia?

And again: If Greece availed itself of binary, divisive rhythms and of additive meters, would it not be natural that these two forms had the lead now here, now there, now at this, now at another time according to the trends of regions and generations? If so—and the fact can hardly be denied—the fourth century, in which the Italian, Aristoxenos, lived, should have favored divisive, binary rhythms, since it offered the nearest parallels to the binary Italian Renaissance. They have so many things in common: the endless wars between city-states with ever changing federations in the political field; psychologically, an ever growing individualism; philosophically, a factual, nature-minded empiricism. But more important is an ardent struggle for realism in the arts, indeed for illusion. Well known is the story of the two competing painters Zeuxis and Parrhasios, where Zeuxis' canvas deceives the picking birds, and that of Parrhasios, his gazing fellow artist. But the main point of agreement between the two ages—the one that concerns the rhythmic problem directly—is the endeavor of painters and sculptors to render nature in a convincing three-dimensional style with the help of perspective: as later chapters will show, all perspective ages have fostered divisive, binary rhythm at the cost of additive trends.

ETHOS. Aristides Quintilianus, outstanding theorist of the period around 100 A.D., reports that the individual meters—like the individual melody patterns (Dorian, Phrygian, Lydian)—had a different *ethos* or effect on man's behavior and character. Meters starting on the downbeat, such as dactyls and spondees, were calmer and more dignified than the upbeat meters, as anapaests or iambs. Those with two sections of equal length, as dactyls and spondees, were calmer than those in 3:2 or 2:1 ratios. But the meters with nothing but shorts—though in equal lengths—such as pyrrhics and proceleusmatics, did not share in the soothing quality of the *isa*. They were "ugly, indecent." Iambs and, despite their downbeat form, the trochees—just as in the Near and Middle East—were hot-blooded and dancelike, and the paeons, violent and enthusiastic (in the Hellenic sense of the world: fanatically rapt).[14]

Half a thousand years before Aristides, Plato had already said that "more than anything else rhythm and melody find their way to the inmost soul and take strongest hold upon it." [15] Rhythms, he said, were "imitations of good and evil characters in men." [16] But he himself referred in the *ethos* question to the authority of an older man:

"We must take Damon into our counsels; and he will tell us what rhythms are expressive of meanness, or insolence, or fury, or other unworthiness, and what are to be reserved for the expression of opposite feelings. And I think that I have an indistinct recollection of his mentioning a complex cretic rhythm, also a dactylic or heroic, and he arranged them in some manner which I do not quite understand, making the rhythms equal in the rise and fall of the foot, long and short alternating. . . ." [17]

Aristotle, Plato's greatest pupil, was no less convinced of rhythmical *ethos*: "Rhythms and melodies contain representations of

[14] *Aristeides Quintilianus,* translated into German by Rudolf Schaefke, Berlin, 1937, pp. 291 ff.
[15] Cf. Oliver Strunk, *Source readings in music history,* New York, 1950 p. 8.
[16] Plato, *Laws,* VII, 798, Jowett transl., Vol. II, p. 554.
[17] Plato, *Republic,* III, 400, Jowett transl., Vol. I, p. 664.

anger and mildness, and also of courage and temperance and all their opposites and the other moral qualities that most closely correspond to the true natures of these qualities." Of the rhythms, "some have a more stable and others a more emotional character, and of the latter some are more vulgar in their emotional effects and others more liberal. . . . We seem to have a certain affinity with . . . rhythms." [18]

That the Greeks themselves described a number of their meters as skittish, insolent, furious, hot-blooded, violent, enthusiastic, belies the oversimplifying statement of Thrasybulos Georgiades [19] that quantitative rhythm, as opposed to accentual rhythm, was meditative or introspective (*beschaulich*). In the face of Hellenic testimony, this is simply erroneous.

As to the tempo, the sources agree upon the desirability of a moderate speed.

THE CRETIC. Two meters, the cretic and the anapaest, deserve our special attention.

The cretic, long–short–long in $3 + 2$ (and probably any paeonic, five-time foot), was a meter for jumping dances.[20] In Baud-Bovy's collection of modern Hellenic folk songs [21] we find an impressive amount of cretic dance melodies right *in situ*.

Ex. 35. Modern Greek folk song

But when the late philologist, Ulrich v. Wilamowitz-Moellendorff, calls the cretic a five-time 'variety' of the allegedly normal four-time measure,[22] he falls a victim to the typically nineteenth-century weakness of accepting historical facts only when they are 'plausible' according to modern western standards and concepts.

[18] *The Politics* [VIII, 5 ff.], translated by H. Rackham, London, 1932, and reprinted by Oliver Strunk, *op. cit.*, pp. 18, 19.
[19] Thrasybulos Georgiades, *Der griechische Rhythmus*, Hamburg, 1949, pp. 32 ff.
[20] Cf. the quotations in Wilhelm Christ, *Metrik der Griechen und Römer*, Leipzig, 1874, p. 416.
[21] Baud-Bovy, *op. cit.*
[22] Ulrich v. Wilamowitz-Moellendorff, *Griechische Verskunst*, Berlin, 1921, p. 234, and in *Göttingische Gelehrte Anzeigen*, Vol. 160, ii, 1898, p. 149.

Not even Hugo Riemann, who, as a music historian, should have known better, was able to grasp the normalcy and incomparable beauty of paeonic rhythms: in studying the Delphic hymns, he

Ex. 36. First Delphic hymn

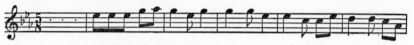

conceded that the bar "would have" five time units; "but we [!] can hardly conceive of such a thing" (eleven years after Tchaikovsky's Pathetic Symphony!). "The piece is essentially simpler [!] and more convincing . . . if one gives up the five-time meter"; and he had indeed, let us say, the courage to falsify the archaic, light-footed five-time into a heavy, banal 6/4.[23]

To add a folklorist to a music historian: Ilmari Krohn, a Finlander himself, deemed it advisable to believe that the preponderantly quintuple rhythms of Finnish folk songs originated as extensions of the third beat in common time.[24]

The hypothesis of an abnormal 'variety' is quite unwarranted. Five-time meters, not as varieties but in their own right, exist all over the world; Finns, Tatars, Turks, Hungarians, Russians, and, above all, the Basques in northern Spain are fond of them, and the Balkan peoples, including modern Greece, dance to this day in cretic and antibacchic rhythms.[25]

Ex. 37. Hungarian folk song

Ex. 38. Basque folk song

Lento

[23] Hugo Riemann, *Handbuch der Musikgeschichte*, Vol. I, i, Leipzig, 1904, pp. 240–242. Cf. also his *Musikalische Dynamik und Agogik*, Hamburg, 1884, pp. 56 f.

[24] Ilmari Krohn, *De la mesure à 5 temps dans la musique populaire finnoise*, in *Sammelbände der Internationalen Musikgesellschaft*, Vol. II, 1901/02, pp. 142–146.

[25] Cf. Stoyan Dzhudzhev, *Rythme et mesure de la musique populaire bulgare*, in *Institut d'études slaves, Travaux*, No. 12, Paris, 1931. Christo Obreschkoff, *Das bulgarische Volkslied*, Bern, 1937. Baud-Bovy, *op. cit.*

THE ANAPAEST. The anapaestic meters served for marching songs or *embateria*, particularly, with the admixture of spondees, in the earlier Spartan form called *messeniaca* by Victorinus: [26]

♫ ♩ ♩ ♩ ♫ ♩ ♩ ♩ ♫ ♩ ♩

—a rhythm familiar to us from the second (C minor) fugue in the *Well-tempered Clavier*, Part I.

One of the latest metrologists, Amy M. Dale, has doubted the possibility of marching to anapaests: one step on a short would be too fast, one step on a long would be too slow.[27] The statement would be acceptable if the anapaest were just an inverted 'heroic' dactyl as it looks on paper. The difficulty is probably removed when we presume that the anapaest was a considerably faster meter, in which a step with the left foot and a step with the right coincided with one entire anapaest each. We have the most exact parallels in two of the world's outstanding military marches: the Hungarian *Rákoczy March*, generally known from the powerful version that Berlioz gave it in his "dramatic legend" *La Damnation de Faust* (1846), and the irresistibly stirring *Radetzky March* of the Imperial Austrian army, composed by the elder Johann Strauss

Ex. 39. Johann Strauss the Elder, *Radetzky March*

in *alla breve*. It seems indeed necessary to give the anapaest a much faster tempo. Not always, but definitely in march music, the Greeks saw in it a mere half-foot, for an actual foot consisted of two anapaests; and an anapaestic dimeter consisted of four, not of two, anapaests.

The best-known anapaestic processional song among the relics of Grecian music, Mesomedes' *Hymn to the Sun,* would indeed be more convincing in a faster tempo, even in a tempo twice as fast, both poetically and musically. And could the early Christian Church have adopted this hymn as an *Alleluia Jubilus* for Pentecost, had it not been brisk and driving?

[26] Wilhelm Christ, *Metrik der Griechen und Römer*, Leipzig, 1874, pp. 244, 665.
[27] A. M. Dale, *The lyric metres of Greek drama*, Cambridge (England), 1948, p. 47.

One must not refuse to accept a faster tempo for the anapaest for fear that it would be incompatible with a uniform *chronos protos*. This musical time unit was nothing but a relative, theoretical concept. Otherwise, Aristides Quintilianus could not have called the trochee *epítrochos*, 'quick,' [28] and Horace the iamb a *citus pes*, 'a rapid foot.' [29]

THESIS AND ARSIS. A metrical foot was understood to be composed of two, and only two, sections, even when it had three or more notes or syllables. Feet of two and of four time units, like the proceleusmatic or the dactyl, had two such sections of equal length (2 + 2) and hence were called 'equals'—*isa* in Greek, *pares* in Latin. Feet of three, five, or seven units, like the trochee, the cretic, or the epitrite, had two sections of unequal length (2 + 1, 3 + 2, 4 + 3).

Of the two sections in every metrical foot, one had a strong and one a weaker weight, however such weight may have been realized or simply suggested. The ticklish question of the nature of this weight will be discussed in a later paragraph on stress.

The Greeks called the stronger of these weights the *thesis* or *basis*, 'downtread,' or simply *kato*, 'down,' because the chorus conductors marked it with a stamp of the foot. The weaker weight, coinciding with the lift of the stamping foot, was called *arsis*, 'lifting,' or simply *ano*, 'up.' Accordingly, the earlier Romans spoke of *positio* and *sublatio*.

In meters like iambs, trochees, and anapaests, which were not allowed to stand alone but had to be paired in order to form acceptable feet, the functions of *thesis* and *arsis* were not given to the two parts of one single foot, but to the two feet: in the iamb short–long short–long, the first two syllables were the *arsis*, and the second two, the *thesis*.

Alas, the later phase of antiquity, reaching into the Christian era, failed to understand this pair of terms and confused their meanings. The Romans, estranged from the once indivisible unity of poetry, music, gestures, and orchestic steps, hardly marked their accents with the noise of stamping feet. The orator, Fabius

[28] *Aristeides Quintilianus, op. cit.,* p. 222; ed. Meibom, p. 38.
[29] Horatius Flaccus, *Ars poetica,* 252.

Quintilianus (35–95 A.D.), to be sure, still speaks of time-beating feet.[30] But a hundred years before, Horace (65–8 B.C.) had in his Fourth Ode already invited the maidens and youths to obey the Lesbian meter and the snapping thumb.

Meaningless and yet still used, the original terminology of *thesis* and *arsis* shifted in a quite natural development from the pounding feet to the singing or reciting voice and thus completely reversed its connotations.

Nothing could be more characteristic than the perplexing *thesis-arsis* discussion in Marius Victorinus' *Ars grammatica*.[31] He begins with the correct statement that "*arsis* and *thesis*, as the Greeks say, or *sublatio* and *positio* [as the Romans say] denote the movement of the foot. For *arsis* is the *sublatio* of the foot without a sound," and so forth. But later in the same paragraph, he attributes *sublatio*, the allegedly soundless lifting of the foot, to the long syllables, and *positio*, the allegedly noisy stamp, to the short ones, which is exactly the contrary. "In the dactyl the long is lifted, and the two shorts put down"; in ternary feet, the "*sublatio* is twice as long as the *positio*." This is manifestly impossible if the two terms still refer to stamping feet.

The other Romans of imperial times confirm that the second of Victorinus' statements was then valid. Atilius Fortunatianus gives an irrefutable example: he takes the first dactyl of Virgil's *Aeneid* and explains that in *Arma vi* (*rumque cano*) the two time units of *ar-* form the *sublatio*, and the two time units of the shorts, *ma vi-*, the positio.[32]

The process of terminological inversion is completed when later, in the fifth century A.D., the African encyclopedist, Martianus Capella, defines *arsis* as lifting, not the foot, but the voice, and *thesis*, accordingly, as letting it down: [33] *Arsis est elevatio; thesis depositio vocis ac remissio.*"

[30] Rudolf Westphal, *Die Aristoxenische Rhythmuslehre*, in *Vierteljahrsschrift für Musikwissenschaft*, Vol. VII, 1891, p. 100, stresses the fact that Quintilianus speaks of the feet *and*, not *or*, the fingers. He ventures the explanation that the feet marked the principal, and the fingers, the subordinate accents of a polypody.

[31] Marius Victorinus, *Ars grammatica*, in Heinrich Keil, *Grammatici latini*, Vol. VI, Leipzig, 1874, p. 40.

[32] Atilius Fortunatianus, *Ars*, in Keil, *op. cit.*, p. 281.

[33] *Martiani Capelle de Nuptiis philologiae & Mercurij libri duo*, Vicenza, 1499, fol. u ii v; *De musica lib.* IX, in Marcus Meibomius, *Antiquae musicae auctores septem*, Amsterdam, 1652, Vol. II, p. 191.

St. Isidore of Seville followed him early in the seventh century.[34] There are exact parallels in the modern English use of the two Greek words and in the terms *Hebung* and *Senkung* in German versification.

Any reversal in semantics implies a period of indecision and doubt, such as the quiet minutes before the turn of the tide. The reversal of *thesis* and *arsis* was indeed prepared when certain ancient authors made "arsis the first part of every foot and thesis the second part"[35] and therewith ended the original connection of thesis and stress. How great the confusion was appears from the curious fact that the Romans had two ways of accenting their iambic trimeters: one school stressed the odd-numbered feet, and the other school the even ones,[36] so that the same syllables were *theses* in one case, and *arses* in the other:

$$. \mid \ldots \mid \ldots \mid \ldots$$
$$\text{or} \ldots \mid \ldots \mid \ldots \mid$$

Grammarians of the Middle Ages, and even of the later ages well down into the twentieth century, followed the postclassic misuse. This is bad enough in itself. But when modern historians, such as Rudolph Westphal, use the later terminology in their own words, and the original terminology in quotations from Aristoxenos, the reader finds himself in a hardly bearable mess.

This is why we should avoid the two ambiguous terms as much as possible.

E. A. Sonnenschein,[37] fully aware of the embarrassing confusion in the use of *thesis* and *arsis*, has replaced them by 'rise' and 'fall,' and the two words seem to have been widely accepted. But this is not an ideal solution either. In the first place, they are exact translations of German *Hebung* and *Senkung*, which Sonnenschein himself deems inadequate. In the second place, 'rise' and 'fall' express movements upwards and downwards, but not parts of a verse. They also collide with our common terms 'upbeat' and 'downbeat,' since the rise would be a downbeat, and the fall an

[34] Isidorus, *Etymologiarum liber* III § 20. Cf. Oliver Strunk, *Source readings in music history*, New York, 1950, p. 96.

[35] Dale, *op. cit.*, p. 202.

[36] Christ, *op. cit.*, pp. 68 f.

[37] E. A. Sonnenschein, *What is rhythm?*, Oxford, 1925, p. 9.

upbeat. Indeed, rhythmical discussions, in English and other languages, have used these words to mark those rhythms which
'ascend' from short or stressless syllables to the length or stress,
such as iambs and anapaests, while trochees and dactyls are 'falling' rhythms.

The modern terms 'downbeat' and 'upbeat,' just mentioned, are
probably best for our purpose: *thesis* is indeed a downbeat, both
in name and in fact, and *arsis,* an upbeat. And so are two other,
synonymous terms in the treatise of Aristoxenos: *kata chronos*
and *ano chronos,* 'down time' and 'up time.'

It must be understood that *arsis* and *thesis* could only fall upon
an entering note and under no circumstances after the note has
set in. Thus an amphibrach, ♪ ♩ ♪, was not deemed a foot proper
—there was no place for an *arsis.* On the second note, it would
have created a ratio of 1:3, and on the third note a ratio of 3:1.
Such a dotted group was to the Greeks 'arhythmic' and hence un-
acceptable. Placing the *arsis* in the middle of the foot and thus
creating an acceptable 2:2 ratio was, on the other hand, impossible
because the *longa* could not be halved without destroying the identity of the foot.[38]

In this strict indivisibility of the sounding note we have probably the most essential contrast to divisive rhythms. The introductory chapter of this book has stated that in accentual rhythm "all
accents, indeed all notes, may fall between the beats; and, ignoring the conductor's gesture, the composer might place a rest or
else let die the fading remainder of a previous note tied over the bar
line where properly the strongest beat should be." All metrical
rhythm is, on the contrary, perceptual. No beat can interfere with
the pattern; no beat can be heard, seen, or even felt while a note is
still sounding. As in India, a ternary foot, say an iamb ♩ ♩, has "two
beats," not three.

Additive rhythm must not and cannot be gauged by the standards of divisive rhythm. The two classes, additive and divisive,
are essentially different, as the preceding chapter has shown.
Thrasybulos Georgiades opposes them as 'static' and 'dynamic' and
correlates the static meters to a certain staticism in Hellenic grammar, mechanics, and other fields. He thinks that a long–short pat-

[38] Aurelius Augustinus, *op. cit.,* p. 68.

tern rests in itself without leading anywhere. This is probably true to a certain extent; no such pattern is actually dynamic.

But elsewhere Georgiades says that a metrical element behaves like a "monad [an individual elementary being] without windows or doors." This, however, is more than doubtful. Quite a number of metrical feet were never allowed to stand alone—the trochee and the anapaest, for instance. A foot, even when single, was in any case only a part of a *kôlon* or a period. Indeed, the fact that any polypody had a *thesis* and an *arsis* of its own, superimposed on those of the component feet, proves that the metrical foot, as an organic part of a greater whole, could hardly have been "without windows or doors."

Did the Greeks accent the first note of a foot whether or not it was long, or did they stress the long wherever it stood in the foot? The dozen relics of Greek music [39] convey the following information:

Dactyls, as in the fragment from Euripides' *Orestes* and in the Second Berlin Fragment, stress the long and start on the downbeat.

Anapaests, as in the hymns to Helios and to Nemesis, stress the long, too, and start on the upbeat (although there are exceptions).

Cretics, as in the two Delphic hymns, stress the first long and start on the downbeat.

Trochees must have started on the downbeat. Otherwise they would have become iambs.

Iambs, however, were ambiguous: the stress is on the long in Mesomedes' hymn to the Muse, but on the breve in the *skolion* of Seikilos. Aristoxenos confirms this optional stress. In all three-unit feet, he says, the long could fall on the downbeat, and the breve on the upbeat; or else, the other way round, the breve on the downbeat, and the long on the upbeat. Incidentally, the *skolion* of Seikilos is not strictly metrical.

The downbeat iamb seems to prevail in the folk song of modern Greece.[40]

[39] Curt Sachs, *The rise of music in the ancient world,* New York, 1943, pp. 239–247.
[40] Cf. Baud-Bovy, *op. cit.,* No. 3, p. 11.

HOMOGENEOUS POLYPODIES. Single feet (and the afore-mentioned iambic, trochaic, and anapaestic double feet) were nothing but the building elements of poetic or musical compositions without a life of their own. They needed crystallization into larger organisms, for which the Greeks had, above all, three concepts and names:

syzygía, a dipody or pair of feet;
kôlon, a longer unit containing less than three complete dipodies;
períodos, a complete line, composed of several *kôla*.[41]

(These concepts and names applied also when the polypodies were heterogeneous.)

The well-known *skolion* or drinking song of Seikilos, for instance, has in its sixteen ternary measures two periods with two *kôla* each.

In Roman times the terms were not used in a quite consistent way. Atilius Fortunatianus reserved the term *colon* (in its Latin spelling) for a group with the last foot complete, like the three trochees of an ithyphallic, while a group is called a *comma* when the last foot is incomplete or catalectic, such as in the first verse of the Aeneid: *Arma vi-|rumque ca-|no*,[42] or ‿‿‿‿‿‿‿(‿‿).

Crystallizations such as *syzygiai, kôla, commata, periodoi* appeared as

dimeters or dipodies of two feet or double feet,
trimeters or tripodies of three feet,
tetrameters or tetrapodies of four feet,
pentameters or pentapodies of five feet,
hexameters or hexapodies of six feet.

Thus, the Greeks would speak of a
dactylic trimeter: ♩ ♫ ♩ ♫ ♩ ♫
dactylic tetrameter: ♩ ♫ ♩ ♫ ♩ ♫ ♩ ♫

And so on.

The end of a line could be made more definitive, masculine, and

[41] Cf. E. A. Sophocles, *Greek lexicon of the Roman and Byzantine periods*, Boston, 1870; H. G. Liddell, *A Greek-English lexicon*, Oxford, 1925, *s.v.*
[42] Atilius Fortunatianus, *loc. cit.*, pp. 282, 293.

even solemn by dropping the last syllable or the last two syllables (or, rather, by replacing them with an equivalent rest) in order to conclude on a long syllable—which again is reminiscent of the Gothic *ordines*. Such a clipped verse (which we found in Virgil's half-verse or *comma*) was called 'catalectic.'

Any polypody, such as the single or double foot, was organized in two sections, one with a strong, and one with a weaker accent. Again, these sections formed ratios of length comparable to those of the single foot: any dipody was by nature an *ison* or 'dactyl'; any tripody, a *diplasion* or 'iamb'; any tetrapody, again a dactyl; any pentapody, a *hemiolion*.

The result was a superimposition of two equal or unequal metrical patterns. A trochaic dimeter (twice two feet) would be organized as a greater spondee:

♩ ♪♩ ♪♩ ♪♩ ♪
𝅗𝅥. 𝅗𝅥.

And a dactylic pentapody might be organized in any of the following forms:

greater bacchic:	𝅗𝅥	○		○
greater cretic:	○		𝅗𝅥	○
greater antibacchic:	○		○		𝅗𝅥

so that the accents of the greater pattern overshadowed those of the individual feet.

From the viewpoint of style the polypodic principle has supreme importance. No single foot is more than a mere structural element. Several of them must grow together in order to create a living whole. It is in this point that the ancient polypody differed essentially from the simple, additive seriations of feet in Gothic *ordines*. In superimposing an *arsis* and a *thesis* of its own on those of the individual meters, the polypody became a higher form, in which the structural elements yielded their identity. Polypodies in Greece were integrated organisms.

Hexapodies or hexameters were organized in iambic form; there was a definite caesura within the third foot, either after the first short, as in the first line of Homer's *Odyssey—Andra moi ennepe*

Mousa—or after the long, as in the first line of Virgil's *Aeneid*—
Arma virumque cano, thus creating two sections in the ratios 11:24
or 5:12. The caesura was necessary lest the number of time units
should grow too large for ready perception. (Modern psychology
has observed that twelve seconds is "the maximum filled duration
of which we can be both distinctly and immediately aware.") [43]

It should be made clear, however, that this conception of superimposed over-all rhythms did not apply to actual time-beating.
In the case of a single dactylic foot, the Greek would take a right
and a left step to each dactyl. A dactylic hexameter (which, as we
saw, was organized in an iambic ratio) should have followed two
beats as well: a shorter one, covering two feet or eight units, and
a longer beat, covering four feet or sixteen units. This longer, slow-
motion beat would have amounted to a tempo of about M.M. 5
or even M.M. 4, which was impossible, both physiologically and
psychologically.

In keeping with this fact the sources [44] speak exclusively of one-
foot and two-foot beats. Despite the silence of these sources, there
is even a possibility that two-foot beats occurred only in faster
tempi (in the way *proportio dupla* was treated in the Renaissance,
and *alla breve* in our time). Even within such one-foot or two-foot
beating it would not have been difficult to mark the over-all *thesis*
of a whole polypody with a stronger accent.

Incidentally, the so-called hexameter had only five true dactyls.
The sixth was replaced by a broadening spondee.

HETEROGENEOUS POLYPODIES. The irregularity just mentioned shifts this discussion from uniform, homogeneous polypodies made up of similar feet to the so-called synthetic, heterogeneous polypodies built of different feet. Homer's broadening
spondee formed with the preceding dactyl a synthetic dipody
known to Greek metrologists as the

adonios ⏤ ⏑⏑ ⏤⏤

(the meter of the slow movement in Beethoven's Seventh Symphony, music example No. 2).

[43] William James, *The principles of psychology*, New York, 1896, Vol. I, p. 613,
after Dietze, in *Philosophische Studien*, Vol. II, p. 362.

[44] Cf. Rudolf Westphal, *Die aristoxenische Rhythmuslehre*, in *Vierteljahrsschrift
für Musikwissenschaft*, Vol. VII, 1891, pp. 83 ff., 93 ff.

On the whole, such compound meters were much more frequent than uniform lines. A few of the most important were

ionic *a maiore*	— — ⏑ ⏑
ionic *a minore*	⏑ ⏑ — —
choriamb	— ⏑ ⏑ —
antispast	⏑ — — ⏑

There are fine examples of antispasts and choriambs in modern Greece.[45]

Choriamb and ionic could be combined in the dimeter

— ⏑⏑ — ⏑⏑ — —

Other, frequent compounds went by the name of dochmiac or 'oblique' meter, commonest in the forms

⏑⏑⏑ — ⏑ —

⏑ — ⏑⏑⏑ —

which is nothing but the ubiquitous additive rhythm $3 + 3 + 2$.[46]

In Hellenistic times the number of twenty-six units was reached in the so-called greater asclepiadean:

— — — ⏑⏑ — — ⏑⏑ — — ⏑⏑ — — —

which seems to be symmetrical.

But there are more complicated cases. The iambo-anapaest, for example, runs

⏑ ⏑ — ⏑ ⏑ — ⏑ — ⏑ — ⏑ — —

or, at its face value,

2/4 ♫|♩ ♫|♩ 3/8 ♪|♩ ♪|♩ ♪ 2/4 ♩ ♩

which is not exactly impossible to sing or even to dance, but so sophisticated that without further confirmation it must be ruled out.

There is no such confirmation. The facts point the opposite way: with the freedom from the strict 2:1 ratio of 'meter' granted by the 'rhythmical' conception, ternary groups surrounded by quater-

---

[45] Cf. Baud-Bovy, *La chanson populaire grecque du Dodécanèse*, Paris, 1936, No. 9, p. 36, and No. 3, p. 12.

[46] For a modern Greek parallel, cf. Baud-Bovy, *op, cit.*, No. 73 f., and Seidler, *De versibus dochmiacis tragicorum graecorum*.

nary groups, as in the iambo-anapaest, and vice versa, could be adjusted to their environment by means of extension or shrinking. If the iamb was given a 'trisematic' long of three units or, in our language, if the quarter note was dotted, the iambs, too, formed 2/4 bars:

2/4 ♪|♩ ♪|♩. ♪|♩ ♪|♩. ♪|♩ ♩|

According to the ninth fragment of the Byzantine, Michael Psellos (eleventh century), Aristoxenos had expressly admitted *triplásioi* (dotted) iambs and trochees, although only when they were mingled with other meters, not in *kôla* of their own.[47]

Quaternary feet surrounded by ternary groups, on the other hand, could be shortened in different ways. The first possibility was 'rational': replacing the two shorts with extra-shorts in a so-called choreic dactyl (♩ ♬ instead of ♩ ♪♪). The second possibility was 'irrational' or, in Greek terminology, *álogos*. An irrational value [48] was, in the definition of Bakchios the Elder (fourth century A.D.), longer than the short and shorter than the long or, in modern words, about a dotted short—like the expanded iambs and trochees mentioned in the preceding paragraphs. Keeping the general dactylic pattern long–short–short, the singer might have given to the three-unit duration some free articulation independent of the original dactyl, such as the 'cyclic' form ♩. ♪ ♩ .

The whole field of alogical rhythms looks like the confirmation of an idea voiced above: that the system of Aristoxenos might be an attempt, like the so-called Perfect System of scales, to pigeonhole a motley heritage from various tribes and ages into one single, consistent array, even at the cost of spoiling the very nature of some of the patterns. Within such an artificial array, built on the convenient but all too simple ratio 2:1, a dactyl of different sizes of shorts, albeit more flowing and natural, was 'alogical' indeed or, literally, 'beyond description.' And just for this reason, it seems to antedate the standardized and somewhat lifeless dactyl in Aristoxenos' system.

Heterogeneous polypodies with such cyclic dactyls were called logaoedic or 'prose-poetic.' The most outstanding example is the

[47] Thomas D. Goodell, *Chapters on Greek metric*, New York and London, 1901, pp. 209 f.
[48] But cf. Sonnenschein, *op. cit.*, pp. 53–56.

sapphic verse—a pentapody of four trochees and, in the middle, a cyclic dactyl split by the caesura:

$$-\cup \ -\cup \ -\cup\cup \ -\cup \ -\cup$$

Three such lines, concluded by an *adonios* ($-\cup\cup--$) formed the sapphic strophe.

(The *Fragmenta Bobiensa* [49] give the *sapphicus* a paeon of the second form, a choriamb, and a bacchic or an amphibrach:

$$\cup-\cup\cup \ -\cup\cup- \ \cup-\bar{\cup}.)$$

Another logaoedic meter was the glyconic verse, usually ending on a 'catalectic' long and consisting of three trochees and one dactyl. The latter could take the first, the second, or the third place.

(Here, too, the *Fragmenta Bobiensa* dissent: their *glyconius* has a spondee, a choriamb, and, as the last foot, a pyrrhic or an iamb.)

METRICISTS AND RHYTHMICISTS. The explanation of these and other differences is found in the ancient dualism of metricists and rhythmicists, of which Dionysios of Halikarnassos the Elder has given the earliest account. This dualism, again, can only be understood if one knows that the ancients distinguished between meter and rhythm in a way quite different from the definitions in this book or, rather, in many contradictory ways.[50] Fortunately, we are in a much better position when it comes to telling rhythmicists from metricists.

The *metrikoí* were orators, grammarians, and poets, concerned with syllables, words, and verses to be spoken correctly; the *rhythmikoí* were musicians, concerned with verses to be sung or even to be danced.

The metricists based their systems essentially on the unit of length provided by a short syllable. In doing so, they ignored as immaterial those finer shades of length that any correct recitation entails and stuck to the fundamental rules (1) that all the shorts were equal in length (which they actually are not) and (2) that every long syllable (except at the end of a line) had the duration of two such equal shorts.

[49] *Fragmenta Bobiensa*, in Heinrich Keil, *Grammatici latini*, Vol. VI, Leipzig, 1874, p. 629.
[50] Cf. Ernst Graf, *Rythmus und Metrum*, Marburg, 1891.

The rhythmicists, on the contrary, based their systems on the *chronos prōtos* or standard time unit of Aristoxenos (uncertain as it was in an absolute sense) and recognized the possibility and existence of still shorter shorts—our sixteenths—and still longer longs—our dotted quarters—to comply with musical requirements without regard for a neat division by feet.

Practically all Roman grammarians outline the difference between the two viewpoints. Probably the most detailed treatment is the long discussion by the orator, Marius Victorinus, who lived around the middle of the fourth century A.D.[51] "Between metricists and musicians there is quite some dissension about the durations of syllables. Musicians [think] that not all the longs or breves have the same *mensura*, since syllables can be shorter than short and longer than long." And so forth.[52]

More tersely, Servius said: "Rhythmicists accommodate their syllables to time; the metricists accommodate time to their syllables." [53] And Atilius Fortunatianus: "The difference between meter and rhythm is that meter deals with the division of feet, but rhythm with sound." [54]

The difference shows graphically in the comparison of two of the best-preserved relics of ancient music, the *Hymn to the Sun* by Mesomedes (second century A.D.) and the *Skolion* by Seikilos (*ca.* 100 B.C.). Mesomedes, the later of the two composers, keeps close to the metricists. His hymn is notated without any rhythmical symbols, and the melody follows easily the light-footed anapaests

Ex. 40. Mesomedes, *Hymn to the Sun*

of the poem. Seikilos, on the contrary, is a true rhythmicist. The notation of his drinking song includes rhythmical symbols throughout; and it must do so because the melody is independent of

[51] William Smith, *Dictionary of Greek and Roman biography*, 1856, Vol. III, p. 1258.

[52] Marius Victorinus, *Ars grammatica*, in Keil, *op. cit.*, p. 39.

[53] Servius, *De accentis*, quoted from Rudolf Westphal, *Fragmente und Lehrsätze der griechischen Rhythmiker*, Leipzig, 1888/89, p. 43.

[54] Atilius Fortunatianus, *Ars*, in Keil, *op. cit.*, p. 282.

the meter of the poem. By stretching out a syllable over two or three units here and there, it adapts an irregular text to a symmetrical, possibly pre-existent melody, whose rhythm cannot be expressed by any metrical term, as iambic, trochaic, or otherwise, but only by a musical time signature—3/8 or 3/4.

Ex. 41. Seikilos, *Skolion*

As a true representative of the 'new' school, which kept the concepts of metrics and rhythmics (in the Greek sense) carefully apart, Aristides Quintilianus defines the rhythm of musicians or 'rhythmicists' as an alternation of *thesis* and *arsis*—even when the syllables (but not the meters) are equal.[55]

This means unmistakably the decline of meter and the ascendancy of accent.

Therewith we are caught in the crossfire of those who believe in, and those who deny, the existence of stress in Hellenic music.

STRESS. It has been an age-old problem whether or not the Greeks knew stress in addition to meter.[56] Since ancient writers seem not to mention any such concept, most philologists are agreed on the total absence of accent in ancient Greece.

Still, the case is not yet closed. At least one material witness, though often heard, has hardly been listened to: the coryphee (*koryphaios*) or chorus leader, who held his men together with the obtrusive noise of the *kroúpalon* (Latin *scabellum*). This odd contraption was, in the words of the present author,[57] "a kind of thick sandal, tied to the right foot and consisting of a block of wood cut out to form an upper and an under board, fastened together at the heel. Each board had a kind of castanet inside. In

[55] Aristeides Quintilianus, *op. cit.*, p. 90; ed. M. Meibom, p. 49.
[56] Cf. the discussion in Goodell, *op. cit.*, pp. 158 ff.
[57] Curt Sachs, *The history of musical instruments,* New York, 1940, p. 149.

stamping, the boards with the castanets were clapped together with a sharp cracking sound." The coryphee marked the *thesis*, quite as its name implies, by a noisy downtread, and the *arsis*, by a silent lift. Aristides Quintilianus, indeed, describes the *thesis* as 'noise' or *psophos*, and the *arsis* as 'silence' or *eremía*.[58] Other Greeks called the sound of the *thesis* a *krotos* or 'rap,' and the Romans, *ictus* and *percussio*. Even notation marked particular stresses by a dot above the note (*stigmé*) or, probably for a stronger accent, a double dot. And very late, in the eleventh century A.D., Michael Psellos, the Byzantine apologist of Grecian music, still said that "at wedding ceremonies songs, eurhythmical striding and handclapping accompanied the first cohabitation of woman and man to procreate children." [59]

How can one, in the face of these unmistakable testimonies, assert that the concepts of *thesis* and *arsis* had nothing to do with stress?

The coryphee, it is true, functioned in choral music only. He cannot testify to solo music, where every interference of a conductor would have been obnoxious. But then, if *thesis* and *arsis* were distinguished by noise and silence in one case, there is hardly a justification for denying that they marked a stress, or even for saying that accent was unknown to the Greeks.

The very concept of stress, on the other hand, seems to be overdone, in the Greek question as elsewhere. All the music of the last two hundred years in the West is built on stress; and yet any good musician would carefully avoid a pedantic *ONE*, two, *three*, four pattern unless the composer had added sforzato symbols. Our melodic themes, extending over a number of bars and having high and low points of their own, preclude such mechanical procedure; and the same is true of our many long *crescendo* and *decrescendo* episodes, in which an allegedly stressed *ONE* is often weaker than the preceding, allegedly unstressed fourth beat. Still, the four beats are conceived of and omnipresent; and omnipresent is, with them, the unwavering suggestion of stressed and unstressed quarters, provided that the ear is given a clue once in a while.

[58] Aristeides Quintilianus, *op. cit.*, p. 210.
[59] Hermann Abert, *Ein ungedruckter Brief des Michael Psellus über die Musik*, in *Sammelbände der Internationalen Musikgesellschaft*, Vol. II, 1901, p. 339.

Something of this kind may have occurred in Greek solo singing: the suggestion of stress without an outspoken reinforcement.
Such suggestion did not need any special study; it would hardly
have been a conscious experience. Why, then, should the old
theoreticians have mentioned it?

There is one more consideration. The Greeks distinguished
'meter' and 'rhythm'—meter being in words, and rhythm in the
motion of bodies. How, then, can meter be the sole characteristic of either one? The musicians, we read, counted not syllables
but time units: a normal dactyl, to them, had not three syllables
but four time units. Thus they were in the same situation as their
modern colleagues: to make organization in equal groups of motor
units audible, be it by actual or by suggested stresses.

And a final point. Goodell has tried to make clear that all meters
can be rendered perfectly well on an organ, where actual stresses
do not exist. This proves, he says, that meter can live without stress.
He is right to a certain extent. But what about polypodies, which
as we have seen, were always organized in two sections, *arsis* and
thesis, to be superimposed upon the *arses* and *theses* of the individual feet? I am afraid no organist will be able to render these
conflicting stresses without—stresses.

On reading a recent German book on the rhythm of Greece by
Thrasybulos Georgiades,[60] I enjoyed our agreement on this important point: that metrical rhythm is not necessarily unstressed,
and that, on the other hand, accentual rhythm can be metrical.
(His terminology, however, differs from mine.) The decisive
fact that keeps them apart is that an accentual configuration—
one–two–three, *one*–two–three—cannot be affected by any internal arrangement of longs and shorts; nor can a metrical configuration be affected by an accent. He gives as an example the foot
⌣⌣⌣ ⏤, which may be taken as ⌣⌣⌣ ⏤́ or else as ⌣́⌣⌣ ⏤ without
losing its metrical identity. Incidentally, this is the case with Beethoven's Fifth Symphony, as this book will show at the proper
place: in the first movement, the master uses the meter with the
stress on the last syllable, and in the scherzo, with the stress on
the first of the shorts.

Finally, it should be mentioned again that both poetry and

60 Georgiades, *op. cit.*, p. 49.

music offer a contradictory rhythmical picture. As essential parts of orchestics, they were inseparably connected with the stride of man; but as basically metrical structures, they were 'breathing' rather than 'striding.' As a consequence, one half of the meters were divisive and binary, and the other half, additive and measured by an odd number of beats. Only additive trends can have created paeonic and epitritic meters; only additive trends can have avoided the halving of even-footed polypodies and preferred their odd articulation—as, for instance, that of the dactylic hexameter in the surprising ratio 5:7, with a caesura right in the middle of the third dactyl. Only divisive trends, on the other hand, could give such prominence to the *isa*, as in pyrrhics, proceleusmatics, dactyls, anapaests, and spondees; only divisive trends could destroy the ternary character of iambs and trochees by pairing them and thus replacing a limping, odd 3/8 by an even, binary 6/8.

It may be correct to attribute feeble stresses to additive meter. But it is hardly avoidable to postulate accents for divisive rhythms, albeit not as sforzatos.

EVOLUTION. Ulrich von Wilamowitz-Moellendorff [61] thought that there had been an *Ur-Vers* or oldest meter with four stresses and often a masculine ending. From this four-stressed verse, he said, derived a dimeter, in which (as in Arabian poetry) the first *metron* kept a certain freedom while the second appeared in a well-settled form as a choriamb, iamb, trochee, or otherwise.

The general assumption has, however, been that the oldest historical meter of the Greeks was the dactyl. The epic age, with Homer and Hesiod as the central figures, seems to have used it exclusively; and until prose for scientific writing began to appear in the sixth century B.C., the dactylic hexameter served this purpose, too. There is hardly any evidence of specifically musical rhythms in those early times.

But the seventh century B.C. seems to be responsible for the rhythmical riches of Greece, since almost every choral song was written on a novel metrical pattern; the *nomos Athenas*, a piece that Plutarch ascribed to the somewhat legendary Olympos around

[61] Ulrich von Wilamowitz-Moellendorff, *Griechische Verskunst*, Berlin, 1921, pp. 612 f.

the year 700 B.C., began in the *paión epíbatos* (5/4) but changed
to trochees (3/8). The seventh century also witnessed the entry,
from the Orient, of the popular, 'naturalistic' iamb, the meter
nearest to speech, as Aristotle said. Finally, it created the subjective solo art song.[62] Dionysios of Halikarnassos (first century B.C.)
relates that the "older melic poets," as Alkaios and Sappho—both
born late in the seventh century B.C.—made their *periódous* small,
while Stesichoros (who in fact was just as old) and, later, Pindar
(*ca.* 500 B.C.) lengthened them out.

In the second half of the fifth century, when music under the
radical composers Phrynis and Timotheos turned to a revolutionary 'modern' style, rhythm, too, took liberties unknown before.
In a famous passage of one of his comedies, *The Frogs*, Aristopha-
nes caricatured the progressive style of his great contemporary,
the tragedian Euripides, by introducing a length of six units—like
our dotted half note—beyond the accepted maximum of five
units.[63]

Aristotle's pupil, Aristoxenos, who lived in the later part of the
fourth century B.C., is wrongly credited with the concept of a unit
of time independent of poetical syllables and hence with liberat-
ing musical rhythm from the meters of verses.

But it is not necessary to entangle the reader in the confusing
network of rhythmical chronology; the less so, as every source
feels free to mingle concepts contemporary and concepts of prior
centuries. It might suffice to quote a general statement from the
twenty-first chapter of *Perì mousikês*, the most important musical
work from around 100 A.D. Its author, Plutarch, speaks of the
motley patchwork (*poikilía*) in the rhythm of 'older' music (that
is, probably, before 400 B.C.), especially in instrumental parts. The
later masters, he says, abandoned rhythmic complication and
turned to melodic emphasis. Indeed, he contrasts the two groups
as the older 'rhythmophiles' and the subsequent 'melophiles.'

It is quite true that in the times of Kallimachos, who lived approximately between 310 and 240 B.C., the poets used a few meters
only. On the other hand, they would not have been sons of the
restive, 'baroque' Hellenistic age, had they not delighted in novel,

[62] Cf. Goodell, *op. cit.*, p. 194.
[63] Line 1313.

complicated, and lengthy meters, such as the already mentioned asclepiadean, the phalac,[64] or the simiac,[65] which amounted to four measures of six time units each, with, in the last one, a change of arrangement. Simmias and his group are known as those notorious poets who wrote their poems in the visual forms of a hatchet, a wing, or an egg.[66]

But the theoreticians of Alexandrian times, strictly metricistic and exclusively concerned with speech enunciation, ignored the claims of music and dancing and even of poetry. Only in the time of Heliodoros (ca. 100 A.D.) did the rhythmicists again come to the fore.

Heliodoros himself was no longer able to grasp paeonic meters.[67] The sense of meter, the respect for syllabic duration, was more and more decaying.

Instead, the third century B.C. had already begun to give a role to accent at the cost of duration.

THE ROMAN PHASE is still controversial. But a few facts seem to be certain.

The Romans completed what the Hellenistic Greeks had partly started: they allowed the natural accents of the words, once independent from the *ictus* of the meters, to coincide with the outstanding metrical syllables, to ignore the delicate balance of long and short, and to kill the feet eventually.[68]

Ennius, the Greek-born tragedian, and Plautus, the creator of Roman comedy, are considered to have imposed the Greek meters on the unmetrical poetry of Rome. But even in this process, the older Hellenic principle of ignoring the accents of the words in favor of the *ictus* of feet was not wholeheartedly forced upon Latin. The successors of Ennius and Plautus, Virgil and Terentius, tried

---

[64] The phalac consists of one spondee, one dactyl, and three trochees (*Fragmenta Bobiensa*, in Heinrich Keil, *Grammatici latini*, Vol. VI, Leipzig, 1874, p. 629):

$$-- \;\; -\cup\cup \;\; -\cup \;\; -\cup \;\; -\cup$$

[65] The simiac, named after Simmias of Rhodes, consists of a *kôlon* of three antispasts and one diiamb:

$$\cup--\cup \;\; \cup--\cup \;\; \cup--\cup \;\; \cup-\cup-$$

[66] Christ, *op. cit.*, p. 607.

[67] Cf. Ernst Graf, *op. cit.*, pp. 74 ff.; also Eirik Vandvik, *Rhythmus und Metrum*, in *Symbolae Osloenses*, Fasc. Supplet. VII, Oslo, 1937, *passim*.

[68] Cf. Edmond Bouvy, *Poètes et mélodes*, Nîmes, 1886, *passim*.

at least in the second *kôla* of their verses to make the natural accents and the *ictus* of the verses agree.[69] Already, the accents must have been more vital than they were in Greek.

The final victory of the natural accents over the arty meters implied a victory of divisive over additive rhythm. Marius Victorinus [70] said outright that the best meters have an *arsis-thesis* ratio of 1:1, and that, hence, the ionic, as a ternary foot, was no meter proper. This meant a radical shift toward divisive binary rhythm.[71]

From the viewpoint of musical tempo in Roman times it might be interesting that Quintilianus, the orator, gives as one of the principal rules in reciting verses that the student must learn where to hasten or to slow down, where to be excited or to calm down (*quid lentius celerius, concitatius lentius dicendum*).[72] With the ideal of animating simple recitation by changing the outer and the inner tempo, it is hardly conceivable that singing should have been rigid.

Scarce as these data are, they throw some light on the early Middle Ages, which, at least in the music of the Church, were the heirs of Rome.

[69] Cf. Vandvik, *op. cit., passim.* Christ, *op. cit.,* p. 4.

[70] Marius Victorinus, *op. cit.,* 2:8, 20.

[71] Cf. also Vollmer, in Gercke and Norden, *Einleitung in die Altertumswissenschaft,* 3rd edition, 1923, Heft 8.

[72] Fabius Quintilianus, *Institutio oratoria,* 1:8:1.

CHAPTER 8

The Early and High Middle Ages

DIVISION OF THE MIDDLE AGES. The so-called Middle Ages reach from the end of Roman antiquity to the advent of the Italian Renaissance. Exact dates cannot be given because the countries of Europe necessarily differed in chronology. The nations whose general character was at bottom opposed to medieval ideologies were eager and early to drop them as quickly as possible; those whose character agreed with the spirit of the Middle Ages were reluctant to adopt the novel trends of the Renaissance. This is why the Middle Ages lingered in the North about two hundred years or more after they had been brought to an end in Italy. But we can approximately lay the beginnings of the Middle Ages in the fourth century, and the end in the fifteenth or sixteenth, which would cover a span of eleven or twelve hundred years.

The subdivision of the earlier Middle Ages during the first millennium A.D., dependent on similar national conflicts, is highly controversial and in the context of this book irrelevant. At least from 1000 A.D. on, we speak of the Romanesque Age, which in France yielded to the Gothic Age during the twelfth century, while it lasted a century longer in Germany.

LACK OF INTEREST IN RHYTHM. In early times Europe seems to have been little interested in rhythm. No drum or other tool of rhythm appears in ancient sources. At most, the ancient Britons, Gauls, and Germans might have seen the shallow timbrel from Semitic countries which itinerant jugglers carried occasionally on their tours along the highways of the Roman Empire. The Middle Ages, ceaselessly in contact with the Orient through trade, crusades, and conquests, keep the use of this Asiatic timbrel alive down to the sixteenth century, but the subtle rhythmical patterns played on it in many regions of the East are no longer present. A few drums in barrel or cylinder form and eventually even kettledrums followed the timbrel on its way from Asia to Europe. But they were exclusively struck with sticks, and not with fingers or palms—an unmistakable clue that their rhythmical scope was limited.

When Thoinot Arbeau at last notated percussion in his epochal manual of the dance of 1588,[1] he had not much to write beyond the primitive dactyls and anapaests into which a drummer likes to subdivide his quarter beats. Seven years before Arbeau, Orlando di Lasso's well-known serenade *O Matona* of 1581 had imitated a military drum rhythm in the singing voices:

2/4 ♪♩ ♩ ♫♫ ♪ ♩ ♪ ♩
don don don diridiri don don don don

This sounds much richer. But must the riches be credited to an actual army model or rather to an ingenious composer?

The earlier Middle Ages were no more interested in rhythm than northern antiquity had been. Unlike Greece, Rome, and parts of the Orient, the Middle Ages, hopelessly absorbed in problems of scales and counterpoint, did not give birth to a single writer in rhythmics. All our knowledge must derive from scattered words and facts.

Medieval music belongs to two very different realms: one the secular song, of both the courts and the commoners, and the other the chant of the Christian Church. Disregarding the Orthodox liturgy of the East and the Southeast of Europe as well as the regional liturgies in the west (as Gallican and Mozarabic), the chant is divided into the (earlier) Ambrosian or the (later) Gregorian plainsong.

Secular music was never written down before the tenth cen-

[1] Thoinot Arbeau, *Orchésographie*, Paris, 1588. Reprints and translations into both English and German.

tury; and in five more centuries it was, when written down, notated without indication of rhythm. Most of our very sketchy
knowledge comes from the little that we dare infer from later
folk songs; and this is not much. But we know at least one fact
of utmost importance: None of the languages in Europe, including the post-Roman Latin of scholars and priests, based its verses
on the metric alternation of syllables long and short. Whether
Romance or Germanic, Slavonic or Finno-Ugric, the tongues con-
trasted accents and unaccented syllables, with the accent often
on a short syllable, just as in the *vers syllabiques* of later France.
This fact does not exclude a careful alternation of longer and
shorter notes; but it excludes recurrent metrical patterns in the
secular music of medieval Europe.

We know much more, though little enough, of the rhythms in
medieval Church music.

HYMNS AND SEQUENCES. In the music of the Church, we
must separate (i) the melodies of hymns and sequences on strictly
versified poems from (ii) the ordinary chant or cantillation on
mostly Biblical prose in Masses and daily Offices.

The hymns and the sequences are popular, congregational melodies on non-Scriptural poems in honor of God. They were of Jewish origin, found their way into the liturgy of the Syrian Christians under St. Ephraim (A.D. 306–373), and were transplanted
into the western, Roman liturgy by St. Hilary of Poitiers in France
(died 366 A.D.). But it was a slightly younger man, St. Ambrose,
Bishop of Milan (died 397 A.D.), who gave them a prominent position in the Catholic service.

At present, hymns and sequences are sung in even strong–weak
patterns, as seems to have been customary for more than a thousand years. In St. Ambrose's time, however, they are supposed to
have followed the long–short patterns of ancient Hellenic poetry.

This was hardly the case. Even as merely literary products, the
hymns of St. Ambrose are as a rule not only metrical, but accentual, too.[2] This means that the poet took care to write in regular short–long patterns, which would have been an unnecessary

[2] Cf. A. S. Walpole, *Early Latin hymns*, Cambridge, 1922; E. A. Sonnenschein,
What is rhythm?, Oxford, 1925, pp. 86–90.

bother if only the accents, not the durations, mattered. Indeed, he often dissolved a long into two shorts—a device very common in metrical versification, but entirely opposed to a merely accentual concept with no difference between long and short.

On the other hand, St. Ambrose arranged his patterns so that the tonal accents coincided with the lengths—as was often done in imperial Rome. Meter and accent were equivalent.

But even St. Ambrose's hymns do not fully comply with the rules of either accent or meter. Any such deviation makes it almost certain that there is a third form of rhythmical pattern involved, in which neither the length nor the stress of syllables counts, but only their number.

Still, this is only the poetical side of the coin. The scholarly hymn poets, educated in classic traditions, reflect the meters of Greece, the accents of Rome, and the numerical rhythms of all late antiquity. But they were responsible for the words only, not for their melody. There is no reason why the composers, summoned to find unsophisticated melodies for congregational use, should have tried to render all the highbrow subtleties of the clerical poets. The Syrian models, derived from the sacred song of the Jews, had been based on the Hebrew principle of accentuation. One cannot well believe that the non-metrical West should have Hellenized and metricized a Semitic accentual form at a time when even in the countries of classical antiquity the long–short principle was already yielding to the strong–weak principle of the Middle Ages—only to resume after a short while the strong–weak principle, which was at once Semitic and native transalpine.[3] It is so much the more unbelievable as the hymn, meant to be congregational and therefore popular, had no reason to revert to a particularly highbrow style.

The oldest hymns, strictly syllabic with one single note to a syllable, followed the pattern of iambic dimeters: *Vení Redémptor géntiúm.*[4] Somewhat later, trochaic patterns were admitted: *Crúx*

[3] Jacques Handschin, too, is skeptical about long–short hymns (*Acta Musicologica*, X, 1938, pp. 17 f.). Wilhelm Christ, in *Metrik der Griechen und Römer*, Leipzig, 1874, p. 4, does not even question the purely accentual character of hymns and sequences.

[4] Cf. Peter Wagner, *Einführung in die gregorianischen Melodien*, 3d edition, Leipzig, 1910, vol. I, p. 44 ff.; Guido Adler, *Handbuch der Musikgeschichte*, 2d edition, vol. I, pp. 111 ff.

fidélis ínter ómnes. Finally, the learned poets went back to more sophisticated patterns. There were also sapphic strophes out of a sapphic and an adonic line:

$$- \smile - \smile - \smile\smile - \smile - \smile$$
$$- \smile\smile - \smile$$

of which the famous hymn of the eighth century, *Út queánt laxís resonáre fíbris* by Paul the Deacon, is an outstanding example; and there are asclepiadean strophes out of an asclepius and a glyconic verse, such as *Inventór rutilís dúx bone lúminís:*

$$- \smile - \smile\smile - - \smile\smile - \smile -$$
$$- \smile - \smile\smile - \smile -$$

This sophistication heralds the later trend to exclude congregational participation as much as possible. The syllabic character, in the same spirit, was marred more and more.

Strict strong–weak rhythm under similar conditions has applied to the strophic sequences as well. The *Stabat mater dolorosa* is one of the best-known examples.

But the *Stabat mater* is a ripe fruit of the thirteenth century, and its qualities do not apply to the early stage of sequence composition. Those of the ninth century from the abbey of St. Gall on the Lake of Constance, whether or not Brother Notker Balbulus, the Stammerer, was their author, were unmistakably written in numerical rhythms: except the first and last verse of a piece, every two lines formed pairs in a kind of *parallelismus membrorum—* the second and the third, the fourth and the fifth, the sixth and the seventh, and so forth. The two lines of a pair had the same number of syllables; but this number changed from pair to pair. There is no trace of accent patterns or meters in the texts.

This numerical plan was abandoned no later than the eleventh century. At the time of Adam de St. Victor, the poet (died 1192), the sequence already had its final strophic form and accentual rhythms.

THE CHANT. Less simple is the case of the 'chant' or 'cantillation' on prose texts from the Latin translation of the Scriptures.

How much the opinions about Gregorian rhythm have differed

—today and in earlier centuries—is a well-known fact. Shelves of controversial volumes have been written on this subject, and all the manuals on medieval music devote whole chapters to recapitulating the opposed viewpoints, evidences, and conclusions.[5] The interested reader may consult them and excuse the present author from reporting the valiant jousts of the 'mensuralists' and the 'accentualists.' Let us rather see what medieval sources yield.[6]

The outstanding trait of Gregorian cantillation, mentioned all through the Middle Ages, though neglected today, is the mingling of short and longer notes; the contemporary writers insist again and again on a careful distinction between the two values. Guido of Arezzo (995–ca. 1050), among others, even likens the component note groups of the chant to dactyls, spondees, and iambs and reports that such meters can be read from notation unless the copy at hand is poor.[7]

The notation in Guido's mind, predecessor of the plainsong notation used in Catholic service books to this day and also of our modern notation, was 'neumatic.' Symbols or 'neumes' above the text—such as dots and dashes, hooks and crooks, and their contractions—rendered either single notes or, oftener, under the name of ligatures, whole groups of notes to be sung in one breath on one syllable. After the abandonment of this tradition, beginning around 1000 A.D., the neumes were as a rule interpreted as signs devoid of metrical qualities. Hence, in our time the authoritative versions of the Benedictine monks of Solesmes, and accordingly the official editions of the Vatican, ignore the alternation of longs and shorts almost entirely.

In the realm of Gregorian scholarship matters have changed a great deal. Even Peter Wagner, once a staunch accentualist, decided in his later years for the metrical cause.[8] Eventually he was

[5] E.g., Gustave Reese, *Music in the middle ages,* New York, 1940, pp. 140–148.

[6] A valuable survey can be found in J. G. Schmidt, *Haupttexte der gregorianischen Autoren,* Düsseldorf, 1921 (English translation, *Principal texts of the Gregorian authors concerning rhythm,* Buffalo, 1928). Cf. also Alexander Fleury, *Ueber Choralrhythmus,* Leipzig, 1907, in *Beihefte der Internationalen Musikgesellschaft,* II Folge, Heft 5.

[7] Cf. also Oliver Strunk, *Source readings in music history,* New York, 1950, p. 120.

[8] Peter Wagner, in Guido Adler, *Handbuch der Musikgeschichte,* 2nd edition, Berlin, 1930, Vol. I, pp. 92 f. Cf. also Seelgen, *Zur Frage des mittelalterlichen Choralrhythmus,* in *Kirchenmusikalisches Jahrbuch,* 1935, and Ewald Jammers, *Der*

convinced that the two single neumes, the dash or *virg(ul)a* and the dot or *punctum,* denoted a long and a breve respectively, and that the group symbols or ligatures in their various forms had definite metrical values:

flexa, clivis	trochee	♩ ♪
pes, podatus	iamb	♪♩
climacus	dactyl	♩ ♫
scandicus	anapaest	♫ ♩
torculus	amphibrach	♪♩ ♪
flexa resupina	cretic	♩ ♪♪

An additional symbol for length, to be found in manuscripts of the ninth and tenth centuries, is the *episema* or 'sign [written] above,' a little dash on top of a neume.

It would, however, be wrong to think of metrics in the sense of the Greeks. The chant, composed on texts in Latin prose, had no recurrent meters and hence no metrical plan. Nor did its meter depend upon the meter of the text: even a writer as close to metrical concepts as St. Augustine (354/55–430 A.D.), who was born in antiquity (though as a Semitic Carthaginian), said expressly that musicians were free to set long notes to short syllables and vice versa.

The contradictions begin with questions of tempo. A treatise of the tenth century, the *Commemoratio brevis de tonis et psalmis modulandis* [9] insists on an even tempo without accelerando or ritardando. Some manuscripts, on the other hand, mark individual groups of notes with letter symbols such as *c* (*celeriter*, 'swiftly'), *m* (*mediocriter*, 'moderately'), *t* (*trahere*, 'to drag'), *x* (*expectare*, 'to linger'), and others.[10] In a similar way, Guido of Arezzo says in the first half of the eleventh century that the singers could learn from the very shape of the notes "which ones are retarded and tremulous, and which hastened." [11]

But all deviations from normal were possibly local and tem-

---

gregorianische Rhythmus, Strasbourg, 1937. Above all: Dom André Mocquereau, *Le nombre musical grégorien,* Rome-Tournay, 1908.

[9] Printed in Gerbert, *Scriptores,* Vol. I.

[10] Cf. Gustave Reese, *Music in the middle ages,* New York, 1940, pp. 142 f.

[11] Guido of Arezzo, *Prologus antiphonarii sui,* in Gerbert, *Scriptores,* Vol. II, quoted from Strunk, *op. cit.,* p. 120.

porary forms of expression and must not be used as a basis for generalizations. Their local character is the more probable as three different sources of three centuries, the ninth, tenth, and eleventh, report a steady tempo in chant, to be beaten with the hand, the foot, or otherwise.

Wherever tempo is beaten, the difference between breve and long cannot be irrational. Thus Alcuin, an English educator and scholar (died 804) who lived at Charlemagne's court, and other writers of the time, indicate a definite 1:2 as the compulsory ratio. All longs should be evenly long, all shorts evenly short.

This rule was, however, not valid for concluding notes. Guido of Arezzo explains that they must be lengthened out according to the importance of the section to be ended: *in syllaba quantuluscunque*, 'just a bit at [the end of] a group of notes'; more, *in parte;* and *diutissima*, 'longest,' at the end of a *distinctio*, or phrase. These different lengths were probably irrational. No mensuration was indicated.

Guido's century, the eleventh, appears, however, to have seen a good deal of metric disintegration. Nothing shows this better than the *Musica seu prologus in tonarium* by Berno, Abbot of Reichenau (died 1048),[12] who insists energetically upon the careful distinction of longs and breves and warns his singers against the men who spurn such distinction as an irrelevant sophistication. There must have been a powerful antimetrical current.

In the second half of the same century, the eleventh, the Franco-German, Aribo Scholasticus (died 1078), made a unique, classicistic, and evidently futile suggestion: he demanded a balance of neume groups. When there were two groups, one, say, of two, and one of four notes, the notes of the shorter one should be given double values in order to create complete symmetry.[13]

This abandonment of tradition has often been attributed to the growth of polyphony, which either destroyed the original meters in the endless pedal notes of the *tenor* or else adjusted them to the exigencies of neighboring voice parts. This cannot be true. In the first place, there was no polyphony until the twelfth century except the early, two-part organum; and in the second place, the organum

[12] M. Gerbert, *Scriptores*, Vol. II.
[13] *Ibid.*

was certainly confined to a very small part of the liturgy and to a smaller part of the large cathedrals and abbeys—either way a part small enough to acquit the organum of the charge of having undermined the chant. The actual reason for the collapse of tradition was the fact that the quasi-metrical chant stood alone in a foreign surrounding of non-metrical language and poetry and was eventually influenced by them.

Two hundred years after these early signs of disintegration, probably little before 1250, the *Tractatus de Musica* of a Dominican friar, Jerome of Moravia,[14] provided the only actual guide for a metrical performance of the chant. At the same time, this learned monk averred, among the earliest writers, that the notes were in principle even and short. There should, however, be a few exceptions to this rule. The initial note of a phrase, for instance, must be twice as long as the breves, but only if it is the *finalis* or principal tone of the mode. The last note has two, three, or four time units and must exceed the following rest by at least one unit.

Ligatures have their own rules in Jerome's treatise. Of two or three notes, the second should be long—against the rules of mensural notation. But larger ligatures read differently. Those of four notes are performed in a rhythm of 3 × 3 units:

$$♩ ♪ ♩. ♩.$$

or

$$♪ ♩ ♩. ♩.$$

Five notes have an extra-short or semibreve in the middle, which seems to dot the preceding note:

$$♪ ♩ ♪♩. ♩.$$

Six notes appear with four extra-shorts at the beginning, possibly in a quadruplet:

$$\underset{4}{♪♪♪♪} ♩. ♩.$$

More than six notes in a ligature follow the pattern of four-note ligatures with as many extra-shorts as needed in the middle, evidently to constitute a perfect long, that is, a dotted quarter:

[14] P. Simon M. Cserba, *Hieronymus de Moravia O.P., Tractatus de musica*, in *Freiburger Studien zur Musikwissenschaft* No. 2, Regensburg, 1935.

♪ ♩ ♪ . . . . . ♩. ♩.

The Moravian's rules contain a few convincing facts. Two traits, well known from older sources, are confirmed: the preponderance of even breves and the widening of some of them to longs and extra-longs. Two other traits are probably also true of earlier times: that in ordinary ligatures the notes are breve and long, and that only the longest ligatures have a few shorter passing notes.

But on the whole, Jerome's codification must doubtless be taken, not with a grain, but with quite a cellar of salt. For Johannes de Grocheo, little younger and a Parisian at that, emphasized expressly that Gregorian plainsong was—'not quite precisely measured.' [15] And before him, the influential teacher, Franco of Cologne, had clearly divorced the chant from mensuration, when he said, around 1260, that plainsong preceded mensurable music "as the principal of the subaltern." [16] And again, he remarked: "I say 'mensurable,' because in plainsong this kind of measure is not present." [17]

Jerome's opposite interpretation, probably wishful rather than factual, is illogical, nay, unthinkable, at a time midway between the first symptoms of equalization in even values during the eleventh century and its final recognition in Franchino Gafori's *Practica musicae* of 1496.

To understand Jerome's position, one should realize that he wrote in the thirteenth century, and probably in Paris, at a time and place where rhythm underwent one of its most radical revolutions; where 'mensuration' and compulsory metrical *modi* for polyphonic music became imperative in the minds of musicians; where units of time were carefully counted, and the *longa* was forced into the ideal of ternary 'perfection.'

It is this new conception of rhythm that the following paragraphs are going to discuss.

POLYPHONY. Be it repeated: the Middle Ages comprise two principal stages, the first being the Romanesque Age, and the sec-

[15] Johannes Wolf, *Die Musiklehre des Johannes de Grocheo,* in *Sammelbände der Internationalen Musikgesellschaft,* Vol. I, 1899, p. 84.

[16] *Ars cantus mensurabilis,* translated in Strunk, *op. cit.,* p. 140.

[17] *Ibid.*

ond, beginning with the later twelfth century, the Gothic Age.

The two names, coined at first for architectural styles, and later expanded to cover all the arts, letters, philosophy, indeed, the whole mentality of their times, apply to music almost better than to architecture. For Romanesque music is dominated by Latin ideals, by the chant of Milan and of Rome and the secular songs of southern France. And the Gothic Age, shaped by northern needs and anti-Latin, withdraws attention from homophonic melody and finds its characteristic expression in the skillful, often bewildering, even confusing coexistence of two or three or four melodic lines superimposed, both in church and in secular music. The Gothic Age has the stamp of polyphony.

In the preceding Romanesque Age, the only form of polyphony had been a redundant homophony rather than actual part singing: in the early organum, an evenly progressing liturgical melody was accompanied note-against-note by another, consonant voice, and each of these twin notes was sustained indefinitely like the notes of the old Confucian hymn in China. "Slowly and deliberately," says the *Musica enchiriadis* around 800 A.D. When the organum had freed itself from this rigid, heavy note-against-note style during the eleventh century, the counterpointing upper voice, written down in rhythmically noncommittal notes, was more or less florid. We had assumed for many decades that it flowed in a completely free-rhythmic rhapsody, without organization in meter or time. Willi Apel attacked this old assumption in 1949 [18] after re-examining the focal treatises written in the thirteenth century at a time when the practice of the preceding century had hardly been forgotten. He made it clear that there was a strict distinction between *longa* and *brevis*. But instead of forming recurrent metrical feet, they adjusted themselves to the march of counterpoint: any note in consonance with the *tenor* or *cantus firmus* was, he said, a *longa* or quarter note, and any note in dissonance, a *brevis* or eighth note. Consonances at that time were unison, octave, fifth, fourth, and third; dissonances were seconds, sixths, and sevenths.

There is no doubt that this principle is sound. It can be doubted,

[18] Willi Apel, *From St. Martial to Notre Dame*, in *Journal of the American Musicological Society*, Vol. II, 1949, pp. 145–158.

however, that the solo singer arrayed his notes pedantically in longs and breves in the ratio of 2:1. There was after all no need for adaptation, since the singer of the *tenor,* his only accompanist, waited patiently until the first voice had finished its phrase and only then moved to another note. For what reason should the soloist have deprived himself of the freedom due to his role? And would not such careful, regular scanning in 2:1 have spoiled the contrasting effect of the well-disciplined, strictly metrical *clausula* episodes that interrupted the more rhapsodic flow of the organum? The truth perhaps lies somewhere between the two extremes: the singer may have lengthened the consonant notes and shortened the dissonances; but in doing so, he may have been as free in rhythm as any soloist.

If such freedom is accepted, Apel's idea can easily be reconciled with the older concept of a contrast—in Handschin's words—between a 'naturalistic' liberty in the time of Leonin and a 'rationalistic restraint' in Perotin's age.[19]

The singer certainly lost the remainder of his freedom in the strictly measured three- and four-part organa of Leonin's successor Perotin the Great and in the two other polyphonic forms of the time around 1200: the almost chordal conductus and the versatile motet. Here, the carefully timed coexistence of two, three, or four contrapuntal voice parts forced the composers to achieve a mutual adaptation in virtue of some binding organization.

This organization was ruled by three concepts, all rather foreign to modern ideas: *perfectio, modus,* and mensuration. The latter two were more or less included in the notion *perfectio.*

'PERFECTION' was ternary organization, as opposed to the 'imperfection' of binary time. It appeared in two closely related aspects: any group of notes, corresponding to what we call a measure, or rather half a measure, was supposed to follow triple time (as a rule in 3/8 of modern values); and since such a measure or half-measure was determined by the length of a *longa* note, this latter was given the duration of three ordinary breves. In other

[19] Jacques Handschin, *Was brachte die Notre-Dame-Schule Neues?,* in *Zeitschrift für Musikwissenschaft,* Vol. VI, 1924, p. 550, and Vol. VII, 1925, p. 386.

words, a perfect long (and later any other 'perfect' note value) would in modern notation be dotted.

The concept is strange, and a modern reader has difficulty in understanding the rather dogmatic words of Magister Lambertus, thirteenth-century author of the so-called pseudo-Aristotelian treatise: [20] "Nobody is able to sing a succession of pure imperfect longs." Which, however, did not hinder the *tenor* part of one of the motets in the Codex Montpellier, a most important thirteenth-century collection of motets, to proceed in just such a succession of imperfect longs—right in Lambert's age, during or near his lifetime.[21]

The ideal of ternary organization was alive from the later twelfth to the fifteenth century. It coincided exactly with the Gothic Age. In name, at least, *perfectio* survived in theoretical works of the sixteenth century. Otherwise, the post-Gothic Renaissance preferred binary organization.

Nor had perfection existed in Romanesque, pre-Gothic times: the highly respected British author around 1300, Walter Odington, reports in his *Speculatio musicae* that earlier organum composers had only known the imperfect long of two breves.[22]

He was certainly right. For before musicians spoke of perfection and imperfection, they had called the long of two time units *recta* or 'normal,' and the (future perfect) long of three time units (called 'perfect' in the thirteenth century) *ultra mensuram* or exceeding the (normal) two-beat length.

Lastly, the conductus, a processional, chordal polyphony of the thirteenth century with one text and one meter, almost certainly admitted binary rhythm.[23]

Earlier generations, from Franco of Cologne in the thirteenth century to the present day, have tirelessly relayed from age to age the time-honored explanation that ternary perfection derived from the Holy Trinity in its common possession with the latter of

[20] Charles-Edmond-Henri Coussemaker, *Scriptores de musica series*, Vol. I, 1864, p. 271a.
[21] Yvonne Rockseth, *Polyphonies du XIIIe siècle*, Paris 1936–1939, No. 164. Willi Apel, *The notation of polyphonic music*, Cambridge, Mass., 1945, p. 292.
[22] Coussemaker, *op. cit.*, p. 235.
[23] Jacques Handschin, *Was brachte die Notre-Dame-Schule Neues?*, in *Zeitschrift für Musikwissenschaft*, Vol. VI, 1924, p. 553.

the sacred number three. Modern historians can no longer rest satisfied with this truly Gothic theological explanation. If there is any explanation at all, it must come from the specific character of ternary rhythm itself and from its fitness to answer the needs of the Gothic age. An attempt will be made in the section on additive and divisive rhythm.

MODI. The meters discussed in the preceding section were codified towards the end of the twelfth century in the momentous generation of Perotin the Great in Paris, who continued Leonin's work and led the organum to its peak. This codification was first described in the anonymous *Discantus positio vulgaris* [24] of about 1230–1240 as six metrical feet of classical standing, although they were hardly meant to follow classical models:

First	mode:	long–short	trochee
Second	mode:	short–long	iamb
Third	mode:	long–short–short	dactyl
Fourth	mode:	short–short–long	anapaest
Fifth	mode:	long–long (–long)	*molossos*
Sixth	mode:	short–short–short	tribrach

The fourth was unusual.

(Contemporaries established various numbers of modes, from five to nine. And some considered the long–long mode the first.)

The long–short organization of the *modi* is poetic, not musical. What notes or time values had to be used in order to realize the poetical patterns?

The key to answering this question is: *perfectio.* As was said in the preceding section, any group of notes was supposed to follow triple time (as a rule in 3/8) and to have the duration of three ordinary breves. All the modes had to follow perfection, equaling a perfect long or, if this was not possible, two of them, and sacrificing, if necessary, the perfection of *longae* within.

The compulsory form of trochees and iambs met the requirements of 'perfection' in any case: the first two *modi* were of necessity ternary: ♩♪ and ♪♩ .

The third and the fourth *modus* would in the mind of an un-

[24] Coussemaker, *op. cit.,* Vol. I.

prepared modern musician be quadruple: ♩ ♫ and ♫ ♩. But this they were not and truly could not be. The long was necessarily perfect, ♩. ; therefore, the two shorts, equaling the long, had to share in another ♩. or ♫♪ . Since halving was impossible, the first short was given the duration of a breve or eighth note, and the second, that of two breves. The dactyl became 6/8 ♩. | ♪ ♩, and the anapaest, 6/8 ♪ ♩ |♩. . In these forms, the two modes could easily coexist with two iambs, two trochees, two tribrachs, and one *molossos:*

♩ ♪♩ ♪

♪♩ ♪♩

♩. ♪♩

♪♩ ♩.

♩. ♩.

♫♪ ♫♪

POLYMODALITY AND *ORDINES.* Such coincidence of the *modi* was indeed realized in the polyphonic forms of the thirteenth century, above all in the motet. Growing out of the modal *clausula* episodes of the organum, then at the peak of its development, the motet presents the earliest examples of true polyrhythm (if we neglect the polyrhythmic audacities of oriental drums). Since the two-, three-, or four-voice parts of a motet were meant to be, within the aesthetic limits of the thirteenth century, individual, independent elements of a unified whole, they had different texts (sometimes even in different languages), different melodies, and different meters. Thus the upper voice or *triplum* might proceed in the hasty sixth mode of uniform triplets, the middle voice or *motetus* in the flowing, trochaic first mode, and the lowest voice or *tenor* in the sedate longs of the fifth or *molossos.* The unification of the whole was despite this difference safeguarded by the homogeneous 6/8 co-ordination of the modal system:

6th   ♫♪ ♫♪
1st   ♩ ♪ ♩ ♪
5th   ♩.   ♩.

Polyrhythm was still in the bud.

Although the various voice parts of a polyphonic piece could move in different meters, meter was consistent within an individual voice part; the mode, first, second, third, or otherwise, repeated itself from measure to measure. Still, articulation was possible by uniting a number of feet in a section or *ordo*.

An *ordo* consisted of any number of homogeneous feet and was rounded off by a resumption of the initial time value and a subsequent rest. An ordinal number indicated how many single feet the *ordo* comprised: first ordo was the unrepeated foot or monopody; second ordo, a foot repeated once, or dipody; third ordo, a foot repeated twice, or tripody; and so on. For example:

First Mode, fourth ordo:
Second Mode, third ordo:
Third Mode, second ordo:
Fifth Mode, first ordo:

Such *ordo* allowed for an occasional *extensio modi*, that is, contracting a one-unit and a two-unit note into a three-unit note (♩. instead of ♩ ♪); or, the other way around, for a *fractio modi*, in which a two-unit note was split into one-unit notes (♫ instead of ♩). The whole concept of sections out of repeated feet or bars is reminiscent, not only of the Greek polypodies, but also of the Indian *āvartas* and similar groupings in the Near and Middle East.

EMERGENCE AND DECLINE OF THE *MODI*. The emergence of the *modi* poses a momentous problem. Long–short patterns seem to have been dead for seven or eight hundred years. What spiritual force could conjure them up?

Julián Ribera's claim that the French *modi* were shaped after Arabian patterns [25] is hardly valid. The Arabs, it is true, had quite similar patterns—just as did premodal Europe. But had they any classification close enough to the *modi* to justify a derivation from Arabian practice or theory?

Again: what spiritual force could lead to the *modi?* The prob-

[25] Julián Ribera, *Historia de la música árabe medieval*, Madrid, 1927, pp. 122 f.; *Music in ancient Arabia and Spain*, Stanford, 1929, pp. 194 ff. Cf. also Eric Werner and Isaiah Sonne, *The philosophy and theory of music in Judaeo-Arabic literature*, in *Hebrew Union College Annual*, Vol. XVI, 1941, pp. 300–303.

lem is actually dual: (1) What created the metrical feet, and (2) what brought the *ordines?*

In the first place it should be emphasized that the times around 1200 had a strong rationalistic trend despite their faith and theology, indeed, hand in hand with them. Thomas Aquinas himself, the greatest thinker and scholasticist of the thirteenth century (1225–1275) claimed that music proceeded "from principles known through arithmetic." [26]

As a consequence of such mathematical concepts, rhythm, too, was meant to obey arithmetical ratios.

Another motivation of the seeming revival of Greek poetic concepts might be found in the strange rebirth of classical learning, which has led to the age being called the "Renaissance of the twelfth century" and in the curious Hellenization that makes it hard sometimes to tell the statues of the early thirteenth century in France and Germany from sculptures of ancient Greece.

The idea of metrical feet was apparently still alive in the clusters of notes or 'ligatures' of the chant. Here and there at least, the one called *flexa* or *clivis* must still have been trochaic, the *pes* or *podatus* iambic, the *climacus* dactylic, the *scandicus* anapaestic; a set of *virgae* formed a *molossos,* and a set of *puncta* a tribrach. Metrical feet, probably foreign to secular music, must have existed all the time in the chant and the organum. This can be proved to be true. Alcuin in the ninth century, Guido and Berno in the eleventh, Jerome in the thirteenth century testify unmistakably to the long–short organization of the plainsong; and Willi Apel has warmly spoken in favor of such an organization in the organum of the twelfth century. There cannot be any doubt that metrical tradition had been kept alive in the Church despite a tendency here and there to measure *non ita praecise,* of which we hear from the eleventh century on.

The *ordines* made their appearance together with the Gothic style and with its typical musical forms, the *clausula* of the organum and its offshoot, the motet. Translated into very general terms, this meant the ideal of strictness, staticism, and orderly form.

In rhythm, too, a thorough change took place. The *modi* began

[26] Henry Osborn Taylor, *The mediaeval mind,* London, 1930, p. 321.

to degenerate as early as the second quarter of the thirteenth century. Built upon the contrast of long and breve, they were vitally affected when a still shorter value, the diamond-shaped *semibrevis*, was introduced. The newcomer dimmed the basic contrast and slowed the older values.

Friedrich Ludwig and his former pupil Heinrich Besseler have dwelt in detail on the revolutionary changes in rhythm during the decay of the *modi*. They describe how the French avoided more and more the unadulterated *longa* (which, shifted to about M.M. 44, had lost the striding quality of a motor unit) and broke it up into pulsating breves.[27] Despite contradictory accents in the text, two semibreves would replace the first breve in the sixth mode; rhythmic patterns became dashing and catchy; and in the fourteenth century, in Philippe de Vitry's *tripla* or melodic upper voices, pattering passages alternated with long sustained notes which, in Friedrich Ludwig's words, led at last to "complete rhythmical anarchy." [28]

Heinrich Besseler also hints at a decay of the old iambic meters and a progress of smoother, flowing trochees [29] (although even as outstanding a theorist of the time as Marchettus of Padua [30] insists upon the necessity of placing the shorter breve before the longer one). We today are indeed inclined to call the trochee less rugged and bumpy than the iamb in its medieval downbeat form. It would be dangerous, though, to lend such subjective epithets to alien civilizations. But then, the Greeks, too, gave the trochee an *ethos* or emotional quality calmer than that of the iamb; and so we are probably on safe ground. If rhythm thus shifted in the second half of the thirteenth century from ruggedness to smoothness, it is well in keeping with the general style of the arts at that time. To cite just one example: in churches, as in the slender cathedral at Beauvais in France, the columns, without capitals, were united with the ribs and rose in a single sweep to the bosses in the vaults of the roof.

[27] Heinrich Besseler, *Studien zur Musik des Mittelalters*, in *Archiv für Musikwissenschaft*, Vol. VIII, 1926, p. 150.

[28] *Ibid.*, p. 152.

[29] *Ibid.*, p. 160.

[30] Marchettus de Padua, *Brevis compilatio*, in Coussemaker, *Scriptores*, Vol. III, p. 2.

MODAL AND MENSURAL NOTATION. The straitjacket of the modes and of polyphonic coincidence forced musicians around 1200 to develop the old neumes to a notation of greater precision. The two simplex signs, the longer *virga* and the shorter *punctum*, were solidified in squares with or without a stem. And in a similar way, most of the old flourishes were transformed into somehow connected squares so that each note was duly accommodated on a staff line or in a space in between. The concept had begun to shift from a purely dynamic script of melodic motion to a more static script of individual, albeit still connected, notes.

These ligatures, as they were called, had inherited definite (relative) time values from the ancestral neumes. Tacitly, some of them were meant to express the ratio short–long; others betrayed by their writing arrangement the sequence long–short–long; still others, the sequence short–long–short.

Such distinctions sufficed to indicate the mode of a piece without a possible doubt:

A long–short–long ligature at the beginning of a piece denoted the first mode (long–short, trochaic);
a short–long ligature denoted the second (iambic) mode;
a single long, followed by a short–short–long ligature, denoted the third (dactylic) mode.

Around 1225, this square or 'modal' notation began to yield to the so-called mensural notation. Its purpose was to rid notation of modal bonds at a time when the metrical *modi* were loosening their grip.

The symbols did not change much; the long and the breve were still the same; and the ligatures were similar to those of the modal script. New features were the diamond-shaped semibreve as a still shorter value, and the addition of vertical strokes to the ligatures, upward or downward, to give them metrical meanings that they had not had in modal times. Here are a few of them.

Two-note ligatures
    Descending, with a left-side stroke
        downward from the first note: long–breve
    Descending, without the stroke: long–long

Descending, with the stroke upward:	semibreve–semibreve
Descending in an oblique beam:	long–breve
Descending in an oblique beam with a left-side stroke downward:	breve–breve
Descending in an oblique beam with a left-side stroke upward:	semibreve–semibreve
Ascending, with a right-side stroke downward from the final note:	breve–long
Ascending, with a right-side stroke downward from either side:	long–long
Ascending, without a stroke:	breve–breve
Ascending, with a right-side stroke from the first note:	long–breve
Ascending, with a left-side stroke upward from the first note, or the same in an oblique beam:	semibreve–semibreve

Three-note ligatures

The two outer notes keep the values just recorded. The middle note, as a rule, is a breve.

The mensural terms *cum* or *sine proprietate* and *cum* or *sine perfectione* given to the various stemmed or stemless forms of ligatures need not detain us for the moment.

Mensural notation, in its beginnings early in the thirteenth century, was very far from the principles that we follow today.

Our modern script—although derived from mensural notation —expresses all relations between time values with unambiguous, unmistakable symbols: every beginning musician knows at a glance that the group ♩ ♩. ♪ means the values of 4, 3, 1 eighth notes; and, in the case of irregular changes within, a figure 3 above a group makes it a triplet instead of a duplet.

Mensural notation, on the contrary, betrays at first sight very little besides the sequence of pitches. It requires elaborate parsing —often from the tail-end backward—before the symbols can be correctly decoded and grouped. For the long and the breve, as the section on *modi* has shown, were poetical concepts, taken from syllables, not from time units. In musical rendition, the long could be imperfect, with two time units, or perfect, with three time units. And the breve could be *recta*, with one time unit, or *altera*, with two time units, exactly like the imperfect long. And yet, notation had only one symbol for the two longs, and one for the two breves. Which one it meant depended on the context, and on nothing but the context, sometimes on a dot as a punctuation mark, sometimes on the number of breves before or after a long.

The basic principle was that a piece consisted of ternary measures, each comprising either one note of three time units, or three notes of one unit each, or two notes in a 2 + 1 or a 1 + 2 arrangement. Hence the following rules:

(1) Any long before another long was of necessity perfect. The second long could not provide the one-unit complement that an imperfect long would have required to fit in a perfect measure.

(2) Any long before a single breve was, on the contrary, imperfect; the two notes provided a natural 2 + 1 arrangement.

(3) Any long before two breves was perfect, since the two breves, the first consisting of one unit, and the second of two, formed a ternary perfection of their own, and could not complement the preceding long.

(4) Any long before three breves was perfect, too; the three breves, each of one unit, formed a perfection in the arrangement 1 + 1 + 1.

(5) Any long before four breves, again, was imperfect. No more than three breves could form a perfection. The first one, in excess, was excluded from the company of its peers and allotted a third of the preceding measure at the cost of the long.

(6) Exceptions were marked by a dot or a little dash indicating *divisio* between two perfections.

All this is bewildering, to say the least. No modern musician can be expected to grasp why composers, singers, and theorists preferred ambiguous to unequivocal meaning. But he should here, as elsewhere, refrain from shrugging his shoulders and resigning himself to the somewhat complacent thought that the fellows of old were not yet clever enough to find a safe and unmistakable notational method.

In the first place, we should consider their place in history. Mensural notation was a stair within a consistent flight from analysis to synthesis, from depicting a whole group of notes to depicting individual notes out of which a group could be composed. This was true in a melodic, but also in a metrical, sense. The *modi* show that in the thirteenth century the group that we call meter or foot was a whole with precedence over the individual note. It presented a certain arrangement of long and short syllables, but not of definite time values. It was up to the musician to 'realize' these meters, musically vague in themselves. It was up to him to allot unmistakable values to their members without ever forgetting that they were functionally longs and breves, whether he gave them one, two, or three units—even when a breve happened to become as long as an actual *longa*.

Ours is a mechanically counting notation; the mensural script was functional.

All these explanations have dealt with the relation of *longa* and *brevis*. Similar rules apply to the perfection and imperfection of the breve, that is, the relation of breve and semibreve; and later, to the relation of semibreve and minim. Not to count a host of exceptions and restrictions. At that, the reader must not forget that bar lines did not yet exist.

ADDITIVE AND DIVISIVE RHYTHMS. Perfection, *modi*, mensuration, cannot be fully understood unless the relation of additive and divisive rhythms in the Gothic Age is clear. This applies above all to the concept of perfection.

The general character of ternary rhythm has been established in previous chapters of this book. At first sight, it looks divisive: 3/8, 3/4, and 3/2 are familiar time signatures within our modern rhythmical framework. But its triple time does not allow for that halving so dear to purely accent-minded societies: orthodox 'divisive' civilizations, like those in the East of Asia, cling to binary, square arrays and more or less exclude all ternary groupings. These latter, on the contrary, must be organized either as tribrachs (3×1), or as iambs $(1 + 2)$, or else as trochees $(2 + 1)$. The tribrachs could be interpreted as divisive, unless (which is the rule) they are disguised iambs or trochees; however, these two are beyond doubt metric and additive. Thus the 3/8, 3/4, and 3/2 live midway between divisive and additive rhythms. Their physiological character is 'breathing' rather than 'striding'; and seen from this angle, a binary group, without the breathing-out excess of the longer over the shorter member, must needs seem imperfect.

This also explains why in the first four *modi* the shorter breve precedes the longer one, as it actually does in the vast majority of cases in Greece, in the western Orient, and in India. The Thomism of the time or other theologico-philosophical systems must not be made responsible. If really some spiritual law had prescribed the precedence of the shorter value, the time would not have tolerated the trochaic pattern, and still less in the capacity of the first *modus*. This precedence, on the other hand, is easily explained by analogy: the long was the standard note, whence the *molossos* ranged before the tribrach, the dactyl before the anapaest, and, consequently, the trochee before the iamb. By the same token, some contemporaries called the long–long mode the first.

Does additive character answer the needs of the Gothic Age?

It can hardly be overlooked that the Gothic style was in many, if not in most, of its expressions strongly 'additive.'

The most impressive symbol of this additive character in Gothic times is the cathedral. These structures were seldom conceived and finished in a single lifetime—if finished at all; work was resumed again and again by subsequent generations, not in the spirit of the original plan, but in a different concept and form—so much so that some of the most pre-eminent churches, as in Chartres, have the two towers built in styles many hundreds of years apart; or, as in Paris, they present the three porches of a façade in different sizes.

In the Paris front, as more or less on all cathedrals, we behold the myriad statues in the *voussures* of the portals placed in rows which the French so aptly call *registres* side by side in niches of their own. And the same is true of the Gallery of the Kings of Judah all across the façade above the porches. They all add up to sets and rows.

In a similar spirit, the painters, far from conceiving a unity of time, action, and space to be seen as a well-integrated whole, would gather within one picture scenes occurring at different times in different places; nor would they hesitate to draw their figures, houses, trees, on different scales, some people taller than others, and all the stage properties too small as compared with man. And speaking of stage properties: on the medieval mystery stage, the various *mansions* used one after the other from the stable at Bethlehem or Mary Magdalene's perfumery shop to the Tomb were aligned from left to right, and the actors had to move accordingly. Nowhere was integration intended; the ruling concept was x + y + z.

Music behaved in a similar way. Polyphonic voice parts, far from being conceived as components of a unified, simultaneous perception, were composed one at a time, first the *cantus firmus* or *tenor*, next the *duplum*, and at last the *triplum* or even a *quadruplum;* in fact, a part could be added or dropped or replaced without doing harm to the whole. In the frequent and important counterpoint improvised from the *cantus firmus* written in the book (*supra librum*), a voice part was actually expected to be in orderly consonance with this *cantus* only, but not necessarily with the other parts.[31] No integration was required.

Even in monophonic music preference was given to purely additive structures—most strikingly in the omnipresent form that is sometimes named after the secular *lai*, sometimes after the sacred sequence, sometimes after the danced *estampie:* a different melody to every two lines or phrases—which we express in the graphic symbols: *AA BB CC DD EE . . . .* And poetry, melody, and the dance allowed freely for *additamenta.*[32]

Gothic rhythm, too, proceeded in an additive way: a piece would consist of an *ordo* plus an *ordo* plus an *ordo;* and an *ordo,* of a foot plus a foot plus a foot. Indeed, Heinrich Besseler has called the whole principle of metrical *modi* a 'serial' rhythm, a *Reihenrhythmik.*[33]

To what extent the Gothic *ordo* was additive in nature appears best in its striking contrast to similar traits in the rhythms of ancient Greece. The Hellenic polypodies, somewhat related to the *ordines,* had had an *arsis* and a *thesis* of their own, prevailing over

---

[31] Johannes Tinctoris, *Liber de arte contrapuncti,* in C. E. H. de Coussemaker, *Scriptores,* Vol. IV, pp. 129 f. Cf. also Ernest Ferand, *"Sodaine and unexpected"* music in the Renaissance, in *The Musical Quarterly,* Vol. XXVII, 1951, pp. 9–27.

[32] Cf. Curt Sachs, *World history of the dance,* New York, 1937, p. 289.

[33] Heinrich Besseler, *op. cit.,* p. 149.

those of the individual feet; the constituent members were organically integrated. But the medieval feet, their *ordines*, and even the isorhythmic *taleae* (to be discussed in the next chapter) formed mere unintegrated sequences. They were additive.

Still, there is one more question unanswered: If the Gothic age had an additive mentality and hence preferred an additive rhythm, which in turn demanded unequal lengths of *theses* and *arses*, why did the period confine itself to only one of them? Why did it accept ternary rhythm, but not the paeonic meter $3 + 2$, or the epitritic $4 + 3$, or any of the complicated oriental meters?

The next and natural answer must be: because, despite his additive leanings, medieval man was after all neither a Greek nor an Oriental. This banal statement implies two important facts: (1) medieval man spoke an accentual language and heard accentual verses, as against the meters, in principle nonaccentual, of the Greeks and the Hindus; and (2), never inclined towards preponderantly rhythmic expression, he was just then, in the Gothic Age, building up the third dimension of music in a coincident counterpoint, indeed, in the roots of harmony, so much so that his rhythm could not win the prominent position as a functional quality of melodic expression that it had of necessity in the two-dimensional music of Greece and the East.

It is thus merely a half-truth to speak of additive rhythm. Actually, Gothic rhythm had a dual character, similar to that of Greece. Belonging in a world of additive art, it turned to the ideal of odd-numbered time units. Belonging in a world of accentual language and poetry as well as of a nascent harmony, it did not carry its odd-numbered time units beyond three, which was the logical combination of additive, metrical, and divisive, accentual rhythm. Indeed, it accepted outright binary organization by linking every two, not three, such ternary groups in a 'divisive' group of six time units (6/8), for which a third note value was created: ¬ , the *duplex longa*—not a *triplex longa*.

It is hardly necessary to emphasize that the dance forms of the time—like the *estampie* and later the basse danse—also linked their ternary groups in binary over-all rhythms of $4 \times 3/8$ or 12/8.

Have we not on the whole exaggerated the concept of ternary organization? Are we not once more the victims of an illogical and hence misleading transliteration of mensural values? Those to whom the sight of a *longa* suggests a long-drawn-out note in a modern sense—over four or six measures—are necessarily lost in this question. And so are those who timorously reduce these forbidding lengths by some quite arbitrary divisor. But those who know that early in the thirteenth century a long had only the value of a moderate quarter note with or without a dot must realize that, representing the motor unit, it left the breves as mere subdivisions without any rhythmic importance.[34]

A living, archaic parallel is the old stock of dance songs in the Faeroes north of Scotland, a group of islands Danish in nationality and arrested in a medieval stage of dance and song development. In Hjalmar Thuren's publication,[35] most of the songs appear in 3/4 time and trochaic meter. But there again we are victims of modern misnotation. With a few exceptions, metronome numbers between M.M. 100 and 126 cover whole 3/4 measures. This gives the quarter notes excessive M.M. numbers between 300 and 378, as against their normal speed of about M.M. 60–80. In other words, the unit of motion is Thuren's dotted half note (which should accordingly be replaced by a dotted quarter note). Thuren confirms that this is the unit of motion when he says that the dancers "take always one step on every accented syllable. . . . The fourteen accents correspond to fourteen dancing steps and to fourteen bars." [36] The triple time is a mere subdivision, which in itself is so unimportant that more recent dances in the Faeroes have simplified the ternary into binary groups without much affecting the melodies.

On the Continent, ternary rhythm became momentous and obtrusive only when the continuous shift of time values and motor standards had divested the perfect long of its position as the motor unit and lengthened it out to the duration of a modern dotted half note.

This shift has been thoroughly studied in Heinrich Besseler's paper repeatedly quoted above.[37] The chart that he gathers from

[34] Curt Sachs, *Some remarks about old notation*, in *The Musical Quarterly*, Vol. 34, 1948, pp. 365–370.

[35] Hjalmar Thuren, *Tanz, Dichtung und Gesang auf den Färöern*, in *Sammelbände der Internationalen Musikgesellschaft*, Vol. III, 1901/02, pp. 222–269.

[36] *Ibid.*, p. 246.

[37] Besseler, *Studien*, pp. 213 f.

musical and notational traits gives essentially the following three metronome figures:

About 1200, the long had *ca.* 80 M.M.
About 1250, the long had *ca.* 44 M.M.
About 1280, the breve had *ca.* 54 M.M.

If he is right, then the quarter note—our motor unit—should be allotted around 1200 to the long; around 1250, to the breve; around 1280, to the breve or to the semibreve according to the musical character of the piece.

It is, however, misleading to call this steady shift of tempo a slowing down. Only the time values connected with the individual notational symbols become slower. The tempo itself may change within certain limits, but it reverts again and again to the constant physiological standard. This will be explained in detail in a subsequent chapter.

SECULAR SONGS. The knowledge of the six metrical *modi* has had a catastrophic effect on the modern interpretation of secular music written down in neumes or plainsong squares, be they goliard, minstrel, troubadour, trouvère, minnesinger songs, or even dances. They were all supposed to follow one of the *modi,* and since these had triple time, so the scholars reasoned, all medieval music must have been ternary. As a result of this bewildering deduction, all extant melodies were transcribed in a limping, tedious ternary time, whether they were French or Italian, tenth or fourteenth century, religious or secular, polyphonic or monophonic.

There is the curious case of the *chanson historique* in Paris, *Bibliothèque Nationale, mscr.français* 846 fol.45 r°—an unaccompanied melody written in the twelfth century with an unmistakable distinction of stemless breves and stemmed longs. Each two longs are separated by two breves in a doubtless dactylic meter. Hence, Pierre Aubry, the French scholar who published the piece in 1905,[38] assumed boldly that it followed the third of the metrical modes: ♩. |♪ ♩. Anybody less convinced of the all-embracing validity of the *modi* and aware of the fact that they only applied

[38] Pierre Aubry, *Les plus anciens monuments de la musique française,* Paris, 1905, p. 11, Pl. XI.

to polyphonic music, might just as boldly have written ♩ ♫ . But this would not necessarily be correct either. In view of metric alteration in the Middle Ages and later, the two breves could just as well be different, though possibly in an irrational relation rather than in the pedantic 1:2 ratio that is implied by the *modus tertius*.

The metrical question has been particularly imperative in the field of courtly singing. Many hundreds of melodies have been preserved, but in the rhythmically often noncommittal plainsong notation. Hugo Riemann tried unconvincingly to squeeze the Provençal and northern French verses into a fantastic scheme of square rhythm or *Vierhebigkeit*—four beats to a measure, four measures to a phrase—and this at times by hook or by crook, with arbitrary lengthenings where the verses were too short.[39]

The French rightly refused to accept this wholly unsupported theory. Thus it came to pass than in 1907 and 1908 two eminent scholars on the other side of the Rhine, the Frenchman Pierre Aubry and the Alsatian Jean-Baptiste Beck, ventured another solution, enthusiastically accepted at the beginning but in the long run just as unconvincing as Hugo Riemann's. The German scholar had at least been aware that the *modi,* as a general principle, did not apply to secular monodies. The French, misled by a few deceptive modal notations of the thirteenth century, did not hesitate, on the other hand, to squeeze all secular monodies into the straitjacket of ternary modes—even those occurring long before the time of modes and *ternalitas*. They gave a length to every more or less accented syllable and made every unaccented syllable short, with the result that the melodies, mostly trochaic, limped along in an intolerable, dragging, obtrusive triple time—long–short, long–short, long–short.[40]

Rather late, in 1927—almost thirty years after Johannes Wolf had published and translated Johannes de Grocheo's decisive

[39] Hugo Riemann, *Handbuch der Musikgeschichte*, Vol. I, ii, Leipzig, 1905, Chapter 15, §§ 46, 50.
[40] Pierre Aubry, *La rythmique musicale des troubadours et des trouvères*, Paris, 1907. Jean-Baptiste Beck, *Die Melodien* der Troubadours, Strasbourg 1908. Reply: Hugo Riemann, *Die Beck-Aubry'sche "modale Interpretation" der Troubadourmelodien,* in *Sammelbände der Internationalen Musikgesellschaft*, Vol. XI, 1910, pp. 569–589.

treatise [41]—Jean-Baptiste Beck recanted his original opinion and admitted other possibilities even for his special wards, the songs of the troubadours in the south and of the trouvères in the north of France. Perhaps we should say, not 'recanted,' but only 'liberalized.' For he still believed that one outstanding manuscript, the *Chansonnier* frç.846 in the *Bibliothèque Nationale* in Paris, testified to ternary organization in the first three metrical *modi*.[42] Most of its notations follow the general custom of indicating the pitches in rhythmically noncommittal squares; but once in a while, and quite irregularly, the noncommittal square notation yields to definite mensural notation.

The fact is correct, but probably not the interpretation. If the composers wanted a definite rhythm and had a definite script to notate it, why did they not use it throughout? Or, the other way round, if the rhythm was supposed to be modal and ternary anyway, why did the composers make the quite futile effort to guide the performer just in a few instances? This section will in a few moments turn to an exact parallel: the basse danse notations of the fifteenth century. There, too, almost the whole book is written in noncommittal square notation, and only here and there is a mensural episode intermingled. The solution is simply that these episodes mark exceptions from an accepted rule; they accompany incidents of free, pantomimic dancing where the performers could not rely on routine.[43] In a similar way, the few mensural episodes in the *Chansonnier* cannot but indicate that by exception a special rhythm, not used otherwise, was required and could not be expected to be known to the performer without a special notational guidance.

If modal and maybe ternary rhythm were just exceptions, we would all too easily be ready to assume that the only possible alternative to triple time was regular duple time. But this would be a wrong conclusion. Is not a rhythm without our modern time signatures the better choice?

Even dance music did without our strict 2/4 or 3/4. One of its

[41] Johannes Wolf, *Die Musiklehre des Johannes de Grocheo,* in *Sammelbände der Internationalen Musikgesellschaft,* Vol. I, 1899, pp. 65–130.
[42] Friedrich Ludwig, in Guido Adler's *Handbuch der Musikgeschichte,* 2nd edition, Berlin, Heinrich Keller, 1930, Vol. I, p. 193, follows Beck's misinterpretation.
[43] Curt Sachs, *World history of the dance,* New York, 1937, pp. 319 ff.

forms, the *ductia*, was *decenti percussione mensuratus*, and its *ictus* determined the movements of the dancers. But the *stantipes* must do without the *percussio* that the *ductia* had.[44] The word *ictus* makes irrelevant whether or not the *ductia* availed itself of percussion instruments; in the first place, *percussio* must mean a strict, accentual rhythm.

As to vocal music, should we not realize that in the secular monody of the French the words were more important than the tune? And would not the next step be to realize that French versification is neither metric nor accentual, but simply numerical? And that, as a consequence, we must not impose upon these melodies patterns of either meters or accents?

Indeed, when we recur once more to the most important theoretical source of the time, there is not a single allusion to either binary or ternary time in Grocheo's lengthy treatise. What this keen observer states is, on the contrary, that musica mensurata *comprises exclusively polyphonic works like conducts and motets but neither Gregorian chant nor any monophonic secular music,* and that the latter type, a *musica non ita praecise mensurata,* is sung *totaliter ad libitum.*[45]

Does this leave any doubt?

Monophonic music, far from being subject to the *modi,* had the privilege of free rhythm.

Once more, our one-sided education in formalized written music has been responsible for the unrealistic assumption that a piece of music necessarily has a time signature—written or unwritten—and that the performer obeys it strictly. But any Mediterranean folk singer, in the vineyards and fields, shows how expressive, how beautiful and convincing a song can be without pedantic beats or uniform ratios of length from step to step.

DANCE MUSIC, to be sure, needs strictness at least in those principal beats which are meant to coincide with the basic steps. But even there, an elasticity not often known in formal modern music allowed (and forced) musicians and dancers to perform a given melody in whatever rhythms the dance required. To serve a

[44] Wolf, *op. cit.,* pp. 97, 98.
[45] Wolf, *op. cit.,* p. 84.

processional dance in couples, a piece might appear in moderate duple time; but played for the subsequent leaping dance, the same piece would be faster and ternary. The French of the Renaissance called such pieces *à double emploi*. But at that time, selective rhythm to be imposed on the same melody was almost certainly no beginning but rather a written leftover from the unwritten music of the Middle Ages.

If, then, rhythm was not an integral part of a melody even in the limited field of the dance, we can safely revise the famous story of the *troubadour* Raimbaut de Vaqueiras (*ca.* 1195), who, having heard two jugglers from France play a novel *estampida* to the court of Montferrat in northern Italy, repeated the melody with improvised verses in honor of the margrave's sister. But did he sing it in the rhythm he had just heard? In face of the elasticity (and unimportance) of rhythm in the Middle Ages, it is hardly admissible to impose the well-known 12/8 of the *estampida* upon the noncommittal plainsong notation of Raimbaut's song.

But even dance music shows an almost complete separation of rhythm and melody. The most eloquent, though essentially later witness is the precious basse danse manuscript of the late fifteenth century in the Royal Library at Brussels [46] and its subsequent printed version, of which one single copy has been found in the Royal College of Physicians at London.[47] It contains almost sixty pieces of dance music on single staves. Only two of them are written entirely, and three partly, in mensural notes, while all the others are rendered in the noncommittal squares of plainsong notation. Modern music historians—Hugo Riemann,[48] Ernest Closson in Brussels,[49] Friedrich Blume [50] tried in vain to deduce the

[46] Facsimile, ed. Ernest Closson, Bruxelles, *Société des Bibliophiles et Iconophiles de Belgique*, 1912. Cf. Curt Sachs, *World history of the dance*, New York, 1937, pp. 311–322.

[47] *L'art et instruction de bien dancer*, Paris (before 1496) facsimile, London, 1936. Cf. also: Manfred Bukofzer, *Studies in medieval and renaissance music*, New York, 1950, chapter VI, pp. 190–216.

[48] Hugo Riemann, *Die rhythmische Struktur der Basses danses der Handschrift 9085 der Brüsseler Kgl. Bibliothek*, in *Sammelbände der Internationalen Musikgesellschaft*, Vol. XIV, 1912/13, pp. 349–368.

[49] Ernest Closson, *La structure rythmique des basses danses du mst. 9085 de la Bibliothèque royale de Bruxelles*, in the same volume, pp. 567–578.

[50] Friedrich Blume, *Studien zur Vorgeschichte der Orchestersuite im 15. und 16. Jahrhundert*, Leipzig, 1925.

still uncertain rhythm of the basse danse from the few mensural passages. They could not but fail. The mensural episodes meant just the contrary. They covered the exceptional sections where, as so often in the courtly dances of the fifteenth century, the formal basse danse was interrupted by episodes of freer dancing in an imitative, pantomimic character. This appears clearly from scenic directions like *Eux deux ensemble font ce cy* ("The two together perform this") or *Lomme se part de la femme* ("The man leaves the woman"), and others, added in the mensural sections but never during the ordinary plainsong notation. While the musicians needed a definite rhythmical lead to accompany in these panto-mimic episodes, they could in the usual basse danses easily rely on their traditional skill and experience to interpret and accom-pany the melody according to the number and sequence of steps in any individual basse danse, of which they found the well-known symbols below the notes.

Altogether, only freedom and changeability of rhythm—except where a doubt is excluded in any case—can account for the other-wise inexplicable fact that composers wrote all monophonic music in noncommittal signs of plainsong notation, although they pos-sessed from the thirteenth century on in mensural notation a per-fect means of indicating time in general and the length of each individual note.

And on the other hand:

In the western world, the use of a rhythmically noncommittal notation in times when a metrical script was available indicates a free or optional rhythm.

CHAPTER 9

The Later Middle Ages

THE FOURTEENTH CENTURY, revolutionary in Italy, did not change the basic national concepts of France, which still adhered to the Gothic ideals that she had created. Even in the over-decorated, luxuriant forms of the so-called Flamboyant or Perpendicular, which took shape in the last quarter of the century, she stuck to, and overdid, the structural ideology of the preceding age.

The arts of the Middle Ages—all of them—had a very limited field outside the churches, convents, and monasteries. Sculpture, painting, metalworking, wood carving, glass staining, were almost entirely confined to the needs of ecclesiastical buildings. And the church building itself presented basically a problem of structure. The architect was in the first place an engineer. He would speak of thrust and counterthrust, of staticism and elasticity; more rarely, of symbolism; and hardly ever of beauty, of religious messages, of mystic oneness with God and Christ. These latter concepts existed, of course; but they were so much part and parcel of the time that they eluded the architects' discussion and possibly even awareness. They did not interfere with structural problems; indeed, they allowed the architect to freely expose the support of his flying buttresses and the skeleton of his ribs and piers, although none of them were either religious or mystical or even pleasant. In the absence of such very human qualities, the great cathedrals were dehumanized and carried away from petty, personal sentimentalism far up into the realm of superhuman, superpersonal ex-

179

perience. And in the boldness, logic, and mathematical orderliness of their structures, they conveyed to mortals the awesome image of cosmic coherence in which the faithful found their God.

Every piece of sacred music from Gothic times shows how much stronger the ideal of musical engineering was than that of musical imagination in a romantic sense. It shows to what extent even music was basically structural.

This is borne out by the following striking words in Gombosi's excellent paper on the Mass of Machaut, which, he correctly says, is to a great extent "entirely outside of the sensuous. It concerns itself with the higher order of metric units and lines by bringing them into a complex system of symmetries. It transgresses the proper limits and limitations of music as a perceptible order of tones, and acquires an abstract spatial quality. It mirrors a world outlook that is idealistic and transcendental, mystic and hieratic, Gothic and scholastic. It is other-worldly.

"On this level, linking of music with architecture and the minor arts of the time becomes imperative. Though another medium, music shows the same basic attitude towards complex symmetry of in themselves asymmetrical elements, the same feeling for space and form, the same reverence for and the same disdain of matter. Spiritualization and abstraction of tone or stone under the sign of abstract number are expressive of the same ideal order of things." [1]

Musical engineering shows particularly in the so-called canonic artifices of the fourteenth century, where, obeying some enigmatic prescription added to the notes, singers developed whole polyphonic movements out of tiny stretches of melody in the weirdest combinations of straight, or crab, or mirror canons in standard tempo, diminution, or augmentation. It shows above all in the sophisticated device of isorhythm, which the following section will discuss.

ISORHYTHM was probably the strongest, most evident musical expression of late medieval trends in search of audacious structure rather than of sensuous satisfaction or emotive experience. Allegedly we owe this principle to the famous French composer,

[1] Otto Gombosi, *Machaut's Messe Notre-Dame*, in *The Musical Quarterly*, Vol. XXXVI, 1950, pp. 204–224.

Philippe de Vitry, who flourished in the fourteenth century. Actually, isorhythm was considerably older: Heinrich Besseler has found it in French motets of the later thirteenth century.[2] Indeed, this book has offered non-European, surprisingly early instances in the music of North American Indians.

Isorhythm or 'equal' rhythm sprang, no doubt, from the *ordines* of the earlier thirteenth century; but the individual patterns to be repeated were no longer merely simple, modal feet of shortest duration with tiny rests in between. Isorhythmic members, often much longer, were separated by quite a number of silent measures, so that in a good many cases the principle was hardly able (or intended) to reach the audience via their ears.

In its elementary form, isorhythm was a characteristic pattern of equal or unequal note values, appearing as a rule in the *tenor* or 'sustaining,' principal voice, although not necessarily so: sometimes both the *tenor* and the *contratenor* are isorhythmic, and sometimes even all the voice parts. Ever recurring from the beginning to the end of a piece, the pattern reappeared in each melodic phrase of the isorhythmic voice part or parts. There were different notes in the new phrase, to be sure; but these notes were forced into a Procrustean bed: in their time values they had to fit the durations that their counterparts had had in the initial phrase. In other words, the first note in the new phrase was just as long as the first note in the initial phrase, whatever its pitch; the second was as long as the second initial phrase; and so forth. By way of comparison, the national anthem of the United States is truly isorhythmic, since the composer has forced the metrical pattern ♫♩ ♩ ♩ ♩ on its melody from phrase to phrase.

An unusually concise example of the fourteenth century is the *tenor* part or backbone in the *Agnus Dei* of Machaut's famous Mass: ♩. ♩ ♩ ♩. .[3]

Not only were there patterns of much greater length. There was also a much more complicated form of isorhythm, in which the melodic pattern or *color* and the metrical pattern or *talea* over-

---

[2] Heinrich Besseler, *Studien zur Musik des Mittelalters,* in *Archiv für Musikwissenschaft,* Vol. VIII, 1926, p. 167. Richard H. Hoppin, *Rhythm as a structural device in the motet around 1400,* abstract of a paper read in Austin, Texas, 1949, in *Journal of the American Musicological Society,* Vol. III, 1950, pp. 157 f.

[3] Cf. also Gombosi, *op. cit.*

lapped. The *color* might be a little or essentially longer than the *talea*, and to be complete, it might reach over several repetitions of the *talea*, say two and a half. Its last note would then be somewhere in the middle of the third appearance of the *talea*; and without a break, the initial note of the repeating melody would adapt its length, not to that which it had had the first time, but to the value following in the metrical pattern. Thus the melody, as an abstract sequence of pitches, was not affected. But its individual notes would shrink or expand according to their ever changing places in the pattern.

It should be repeated that this conflict and change did not mean one melodic part against another, metrical part. The two patterns, of melody and of rhythm, materialized in the same voice at once. One might think of a façade whose appearance depends at the same time on two often conflicting principles: the immutable design of the stones and the fleeting play of lights and of shadows. This, to be sure, is not meant to be a specific comparison.

An excellent example of overlapping isorhythm is Philippe de Vitry's motet *Colla jugo subdere*.[4] The metrical pattern of the *tenor* (and we are concerned with the *tenor* only) is ◦ □ ◦ ◦, repeated over and over, although the initial whole note is missing in the first statement. The melodic line of the same *tenor* extends

Ex. 42. Philippe de Vitry, isorhythmic tenor

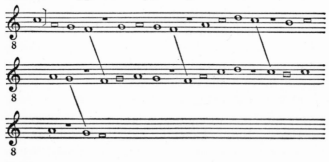

over three *talea* episodes and ends in the middle of the fourth. Its repetition sets in at once. The starting note A appears this time on the third note of the pattern and has consequently the value of a

4 Printed in Heinrich Besseler, *Studien zur Musik des Mittelalters*, in *Archiv für Musikwissenschaft*, Vol. VIII, 1926, pp. 247 ff.

whole note only (instead of a breve, as before), and in a similar way, the whole melody or series of pitches is shifted by one note value to the right against the metrical pattern. If there were another repetition of the *color*, it would be shifted by two digits to the right against the metrical pattern. And so on.

Guillaume de Machaut's first ballade, *S'amours*,[5] illustrates, not exactly isorhythm, but in principle a similar structural device of greatest strictness and consistency. Excepting the refrain, there are four lines of text, but only two lines of melody, so that the third and fourth repeat the melody of the first and second. But the two musical lines, although melodically different, follow scrupulously the same rhythmical pattern of seven measures. The following refrain has three lines of text and three lines of music, which are melodically different, but once more rhythmically identical. So far we have analyzed the upper voice only. The *tenor* has rhythmical patterns of its own; but they repeat or change whenever the *cantus* repeats or changes its rhythm.

NEW NOTATIONAL SYMBOLS. While isorhythm, rooted in the preceding century, shows the engineering interests of France in the Gothic Age, the creation of two shorter notes beyond the four existing values of *duplex longa, longa, brevis,* and *semibrevis* is characteristic of the greater refinement and, at once, of the flickering restlessness of the fourteenth century. Around 1300, "somebody in Navarra" introduced a *minima* next below the semibreve and gave it the diamond symbol of the latter plus an upward stem ($\downarrow$). Not much later, Philippe de Vitry (born 1291) added a flagged semiminim (λ) half as long as the minim.[6]

But the two latter values, minim and semiminim, were still very far from being common property. A more important innovation, for the time being, was the general recognition of binary 'imperfect' rhythms together with the ternary 'perfect' values to which the preceding thirteenth century had granted a monopoly. In the fourteenth, each value could be either 'perfect' or, in our language and notation, dotted; or else it could be 'imperfect,' that is,

[5] Printed in Guillaume de Machaut, *Musikalische Werke*, ed. Friedrich Ludwig, Vol. I, Leipzig, 1926, p. 1.

[6] Johannes Wolf, *Geschichte der Mensural-Notation*, Leipzig, 1904, Vol. I, pp. 76 f.

undotted. An exception was the minim, which, being too short, never held more than two semiminims.

PERFECTION AND IMPERFECTION. The equal rights that the fourteenth century gave to the perfection and the imperfection of most values led to the following concepts.

Modus maior expressed the length of the largest note value or maxim; if 'perfect,' the maxim comprised three, if 'imperfect,' only two longs.

Modus minor expressed the length of the long; if perfect, it comprised three, if imperfect, only two breves.

Tempus expressed the length of the breve; if perfect, it comprised three, if imperfect, only two semibreves.

Prolatio expressed the length of the semibreve; if perfect, it comprised three, if imperfect, only two minims.

Graphically:

	perfect		imperfect	
modus maior:	▟ ▟ ▟	○ ○ ○	▟ ▟	○ ○
modus minor:	▪ ▪ ▪	○·	▪ ▪	○
tempus:	◆ ◆ ◆	♩·	◆ ◆	♩
prolatio:	♦ ♦ ♦	♩·	♦ ♦	♩

A perfect, ternary value corresponded to what we today call dotted; it was *not* a triplet with the duration of an imperfect duplet.

As a consequence of alternative perfection and imperfection on almost all levels, 'time' represented a product of four numbers, each of which was either two or three. It could be, say, perfect major mode, perfect minor mode, perfect tempus, and minor (or imperfect) prolation, which would amount to $3 \times 3 \times 3 \times 2$ minims, or any other combination of twos and/or threes.

TIME SIGNATURES OF THE FOURTEENTH CENTURY. The complication of a musical 'time' in which the maxim, the long, the breve, the semibreve could each be either ternary or binary, faced the performer with a reading problem beyond his power; some unmistakable signature on the staff became imperative in order to make the time structure evident without too much parsing of the still barless script.

Owing to the complex concept of time as a combination of *modus maior, modus minor, tempus,* and *prolatio,* the symbols that the composers devised were not comprehensive either, but consisted of separate signs for each note value, for the long, the breve, the semibreve, etc., so that some signatures comprised no less than four symbols.

It would be confusing rather than elucidating to enumerate here all the divergent and often contradictory signatures devised in the fourteenth and fifteenth centuries. Only the principal symbols will be explained.

The history of time signatures begins with two names, one of a Frenchman, one of an Italian, both apparently belonging to the same generation. They are Philippe de Vitry and Marchettus of Padua. The Italian's *Pomerium,* a treatise recently dated 1318,[7] uses, as a timid beginning, the figures 3 and 2 for perfect and imperfect *tempus:*

$$3 = \ \blacklozenge \ \blacklozenge \ \blacklozenge \quad \text{in a breve,}$$
$$2 = \quad \blacklozenge \ \blacklozenge \quad \text{in a breve.}$$

Philippe de Vitry's famous *Ars nova* of about 1316–1325, which has given its title to a whole century of music, was the first work to combine in a single time signature a symbol for *modus* and another one for *tempus:* that for *modus* (*minor*) was a square with either three or only two vertical dashes through the upper half; that for *tempus* was a full circle, if perfect, or a semicircle, if imperfect:

In another work, the *Ars perfecta,* Philippe de Vitry, or whoever the author was, indicated prolation by dots; contrary to later use, however, he used three dots and two:

---

[7] Oliver Strunk, *Intorno a Marchetto da Padua,* in *Rassegna musicale,* October, 1950.

This, then, was the essential contribution of the fourteenth century to the development of time signatures.

DIVISIONES. The lively, flickering style of the time could not rest satisfied with the subdivision of the long and the subdivision of the breve (*tempus*). It needed the subdivision of the semibreve, but did not yet have notational symbols beyond the semibreve. Out of this lack of adequate signs, musicians had recourse to what they called *divisiones* of the breve in the following way.

Tempus imperfectum, meaning a division of the breve into two semibreves, yielded the *divisio binaria;* and *tempus perfectum*, meaning a division of the breve into three semibreves, yielded the *divisio ternaria*. A subdivision into minor and major prolation would add to the *binaria* a *quaternaria* (2×2 units) and a *senaria* (3×2 units); and to the *ternaria*, it would add another *senaria* (2×3 units) and a *novenaria* (3×3 units). Again, an *octonaria* would subdivide the *quaternaria*, and the *duodenaria* would subdivide a *senaria*. The two *senariae* were distinguished as *senaria perfecta* (3×2) and *senaria imperfecta* (2×3).

Only the *binaria* was unequivocal; it had two semibreves of half a breve each. All the other divisions had fewer semibreves than the name of the division seemed to require, and in the majority of cases, these semibreves had different time values. A *ternaria* had, not three, but only two semibreves with the values of one and two units; a *quaternaria*, two ($2 + 2$, $1 + 3$), or three ($1 + 1 + 2$); a *duodenaria*, two ($6 + 6$, $4 + 8$) or three ($4 + 4 + 4$), and many more combinations. All figures could be inverted—as $2 + 1$ instead of $1 + 2$—although the smaller semibreves were usually put before the longer ones.

Except for a few patterns, like $1 + 1$, $2 + 2$, $3 + 3 + 3$, etc., which are obviously multiplicative (2×1, 2×2, 3×3), all the patterns were purely additive.

The question arises: Were the breves kept in a standard tempo, while the semibreves varied in duration according to their greater or lesser number within a breve? Or was the semibreve kept in a standard tempo, while the breves grew longer or shorter according to the number of semibreves that they contained?

Johannes Verulus, whose exact lifetime we do not know, seems to have given an unmistakable answer.[8] Having established the value of an *uncia* as the eighth part of a minute, he states: "From this ounce the musician derives *tempus rectum* and *perfectum*, not the *maius* or the *minus tempus*, but the mean *tempus*, [which is represented] in a quadrangular shape in the image of the four parts of the world. [Verulus uses the word *tempus* as a synonym of *brevis*.] And this *tempus* is divided into three parts in the image of the Trinity and is called *tempus perfectum medium*."

Specifically, the (perfect) breve in a *duodenaria* lasted a sixth of a minute (our M.M. 6); in an *octonaria*, M.M. 9; in a *quaternaria*, M.M. 18. In other words, the semibreve had a standard of M.M. 72, and the breve lasted from M.M. 6 in the *duodenaria* to M.M. 36 in the *binaria*.

As far as the regular prolations, major and minor, are concerned, the semibreve of 72 M.M. is not only convincing but also in agreement with the deductions of Besseler. While the motor unit, according to Besseler,[9] was an imperfect breve of M.M. 60 around 1315, the same author indicates the semibreve as a new motor unit for the latter part of the century and gives

M.M. 84 to the perfect semibreve around 1325,
M.M. 60 to the perfect semibreve around 1350,
M.M. 66 to the perfect semibreve around 1400.

But with the subsequent statements of Verulus we run into serious difficulties. Marchettus of Padua [10] says expressly that the French already called the semibreve of one time unit a minim (and the note was indeed written with the upward stem characteristic of the minim). Must we then conclude that in Verulus's time the minim was the motor unit, to be rendered by a modern quarter note? This is not possible; the minim shifted to the rank of motor

[8] *Johannis Veruli de Anagnia liber de musica*, in E. de Coussemaker, *Scriptorum de musica medii aevi*, Vol. III, Paris, 1869, p. 130.

[9] Heinrich Besseler, *Studien zur Musik des Mittelalters*, in *Archiv für Musikwissenschaft*, Vol. VIII, 1926, p. 214.

[10] Cf. Oliver Strunk, *Source readings in music history*, New York, 1951, p. 168.

unit in the fifteenth century only. The answer, if any, must come
from actual music of the time.

Let us confine ourselves to a piece with *divisio novenaria:*
Machaut's motet *Amara valde—Quant en moy.*[11] Without over-

Ex. 43. Guillaume de Machaut, motet, *Amara valde*

stretching it or, on the other hand, without making a satisfactory
enunciation of the text impossible, the tempo would be 72–80 M.M.
for the perfect semibreve and 24–27 M.M. for the perfect breve.
The minim would then be 216–240 M.M., one-third as long as that
of Verulus. Any similar piece gives the same answer. Verulus must
have been mistaken.

DOTTING. A study of Italian pieces from the *trecento* and the
quattrocento conveys the impression that in those centuries the
Italians favored 'imperfection' or duple, binary time to a degree
unknown and unwanted in France.

Within the duple time, subdivisions were greatly done in the
French, medieval way, that is, by triplets in the ratio 2:1. But
often the subdivision, too, was binary; and in this case, there
could, though seldom, be a surprise in store: the appearance of
the dotted figure ♪♪ instead of the less energetic ♩♪. At least

from Prosdocimus on, in the early fifteenth century, this figure was
written in the form of a *semibrevis* diamond with a slanted up-
stroke, followed by a minim.[12]

---

[11] Johannes Wolf, *Geschichte der Mensuralnotation,* Leipzig, 1904, Vol. II, p.
16; Vol. III, p. 28.

[12] Details in Johannes Wolf, *op. cit.,* Vol. I, pp. 275 ff.

The Greeks had somewhat reluctantly used such dotting in
'alogical' meters, but as an exception only and against their general
principle that from an oratorical viewpoint the ratio 3:1 was not
properly rhythmical, since the longer syllable became too long
and the short one too short. The early and high Middle Ages seem
to have followed the same dogma; and so did the subsequent
centuries as far as the leading, vocal music was concerned.

As a consequence of vocal idiosyncrasy, the brisk and springy
♪♪ was for hundreds of years almost exclusively instrumental:
a rhythm for bowing, drumming, and tonguing. And it is just as
natural that the dotted group emerged in the dance, where instrumental music gained its first maturity. Johannes Wolf, himself unaware of this fact, has published the earliest instances of
dottings in his essay on the dances of the Middle Ages.[13] The
dance tunes of the thirteenth century, in the opening section of
the paper, have not a single dotted figure. But those of the fourteenth century teem with dots—most beautifully the melody
called *Il lamento di Tristano* (when the notational symbols are
properly shortened) and, on the same page, *La Manfredina*.[14] Also

Ex. 44. Anonymous 'ballo,' *Il lamento di Tristano*

many of the *istampite* or *estampies,* the courtly striding dances of
the time, have here and there a dotted eighth with a resilient sixteenth.

Is it a mere accident that all these dances have titles in Italian
language? Certainly not. For the earliest reference to dotting is
in theory the *Pomerium* of the Italian, Marchettus of Padua. There
we learn expressly that the Italians would in *divisio quaternaria*
give three units to the first semibreve, and only one to the second.
This is dotting in the ratio 3:1.[15]

The ultimate victory of Italy in all the arts, presaged in this

[13] Johannes Wolf, *Die Tänze des Mittelalters,* in *Archiv für Musikwissenschaft,*
Vol. I, 1918, pp. 10–42.
[14] *Ibid.,* p. 41.
[15] Translated in Strunk, *op. cit.,* p. 167.

often so-called Proto-Renaissance of the fourteenth century, belongs in the following Renaissance proper, which took its name from the rebirth of Mediterranean classicism.

METRIC ALTERATIONS. The frequent term 'hemiola' did not mean at that time what it had meant in Greek metrology: a paeonic five-time pattern. It covered the twofold character given to a group of six units, which might occur either alternatingly within the same voice part or simultaneously in two contrapuntal voice parts. One of these characters showed in the organization of the six units—say, eighths—as two triplets or 6/8; the other one, as three pairs or 3/4:

$$6/8 \quad \text{♪♪♪♪♪♪}$$
$$3/4 \quad \text{♩♩♩♩♩♩}$$

Since there was hardly an actual stress and hence no stumbling caused by unforeseen irregular accents, music derived a particularly light and easy character from the hemiola. But it has been used all the way through to the present although we have an outright accentual rhythm.

Another form of changing rhythm—this time affecting the values themselves—was the process of coloration, ascribed to Philippe de Vitry (1291–1361).[16] When composers wanted to transform triplets into episodic duplets, or duplets into triplets, without changing the time signature, they altered the color of the notes in question: during the period of black notation—as late as the middle of the fifteenth century, and even longer in England—the changes were indicated by making the notes red or white; in the subsequent era of white notation—after the middle of the fifteenth century—the notes were reddened or blackened.

To make this quite clear: There are two different cases. (1) Within an imperfect, binary *tempus,* coloration creates triplets instead of duplets, that is, *proportio sesquialtera.* (2) Within a perfect, ternary *tempus,* coloration creates three imperfect values instead of two perfect ones, that is, 3×2 instead of 2×3 units, otherwise called a hemiola.

[16] Johannes Wolf, *Mensuralnotation,* Vol. I, pp. 65, 66.

This is probably clearer than Georg Rhaw's description in the sixteenth century [17] that coloring takes away one-third of a perfect figure, and a quarter from an imperfect figure.

Maybe the so-called *minor color* should be appended here: A pair of colored lozenges, the first without, the second with a stem, indicated originally a triplet but changed later into a dotted group. This symbol survived beyond the end of mensural notation; it appears as late as the end of the seventeenth century.

This discussion should not close without touching upon the astonishing reappearance of the three–three–two meter within an eight-beat rhythm. This was discussed in the chapters on Near Eastern and Indian rhythm, and, under the name of dochmiac, in that on Grecian rhythm. It will once more have an important place in the chapters on the Renaissance and on the twentieth century.

The three–three–two is not frequent in the fourteenth century. But it occurs in the works of the greatest French master, Guillaume de Machaut—for instance, at the beginning of the *cantus* part in

Ex. 45. Guillaume de Machaut, ballade, *On s'amours*

his ballade *On s'amours*.[18] On the Italian side, it opens the middle voice in Filipoctus de Caserta's *Par les bons Gedeons*.[19]

Ex. 46. Filipoctus de Caserta, *Par les bons Gedeons*

Why and how this curious oriental pattern suddenly emerged on the soil of Europe is not easy to say. That it is due to an Arabian influence via Spain is not outright impossible but it is hardly probable, especially in view of the vital importance that the

[17] Georg Rhaw, *Enchiridion utriusque musice*, Wittenberg, 1546, fol. Hij.
[18] Guillaume de Machaut, *Musikalische Werke*, ed. Friedrich Ludwig, Vol. I, 1926, No. 1.
[19] Johannes Wolf, *Mensuralnotation*, Vols. II and III, No. 66.

three–three–two was given in the Renaissance. Rather, it may have existed long ago in European folk music, of which we have no rhythmical record.

GOTHIC RESTIVENESS, the greater array of available time values, and the means of alteration caused composers of France sometime before 1300 to dissolve their melodies in confusing concoctions of notes and rhythms. Continually changing from sixteenths all the way through to dotted half notes and from normal grouping to irregular triplets, quintuplets, septuplets, they ignored the steadfastness of accented principal beats in frequent ties over (our) bar lines and indulged in offbeats and awkward rubato syncopations.

In 1324, Pope John XXII intervened. "A few adherents of the new school," he stormed in his famous bull against contemporary music, "focus their attention on novel notes and mensuration. . . . They sing the melodies of the Church in semibreves and minims and dissolve them in smallest time values. They slice the melodies in hockets.[20] . . . They run and do not rest, inebriate the ear and do not soothe it. . . ." This was not only the aggressive opposition of an older man who represented a bygone generation, but also the protest of an Italian exile in Avignon exposed to the restiveness and complexity of the latest style of France.

But opposition was strong even in the North. It found a fervent, almost fanatical spokesman in Jacob de Liége, who wrote sometime in the second quarter of the fourteenth century a *Speculum musicae* as an apology of the 'despised' *ars antiqua* and an eloquent condemnation of the 'lascivious' *ars nova,* where "the words are lost, the harmony of consonances is diminished, the value of the notes is changed, perfection is brought low, imperfection is exalted, and measure is confounded." [21]

But neither the conservative musicians nor the papal bull could change the destined course of art.

This course, prescribed by the nervous restlessness and sophistication of the Flamboyant Age, led in music to the weirdest poly-

---

[20] 'Hiccup,' a kind of openwork writing in which, in rapid alternation, a scrap of melody in one of the voices concurred with a rest in the other one.

[21] Coussemaker, *op. cit.,* Vol. II, pp. 193–433. Transl. in Strunk, *op. cit.,* p. 190.

rhythm, to an unprecedented independence of the three voice parts of which a normal polyphonic work consisted. Not many pieces could in this respect outdo the daring rondeau by Baude Cordier, *Belle Dame*, of about 1400, whose upper voice starts in

Ex. 47. Baude Cordier, rondeau, *Belle dame*

9/8, but changes to 3/4 duplets in the second, and to 2/4 in the fourth measure, while the middle voice passes from 9/8 to 6/8, and the lower voice hastens from 6/8 to 3/8, 3/4, and 2/4.[22]

Quite recently, Dr. Willi Apel has considerably deepened our sketchy knowledge and understanding of this dazzling phase of France's secular music in the late fourteenth century. The splendid publication of his monograph is due to the Mediaeval Academy in Cambridge.[23]

Apel's analysis distinguishes three subsequent styles: the style of Machaut, the manneristic style, and the modern style, of which the modern style, sedate and harmonically oriented, bridges the gap between the manneristic style around 1400 and the fifteenth-century styles of Dunstable and Dufay.

The manneristic style is probably the all-time climax of rhythmic complication and over-refinement, with a constant alternation and opposition of duple and triple meters, extended rubatos, and polyrhythms that often result in so complete an independence of

---

[22] The extraordinary piece is printed in Willi Apel, *Notation of polyphonic music*, Cambridge (Mass.), 1943, p. 175; in his *Harvard Dictionary of music*, Cambridge (Mass.), 1944, p. 594; and in Davison-Apel, *Historical anthology of music*, Cambridge (Mass.), 1946, Vol. I, No. 48, pp. 51 f.

[23] Willi Apel, *French secular music of the late fourteenth century*, Cambridge (Mass.), 1950.

the three voice parts that for several measures not a single note
of one part coincides with any note of the two other parts. Our
example of such utter freedom comes from Matteo da Perusio—
Italian composer of French music—who was the most eminent

Ex. 48. Matteo da Perusio, *Ballata*

master of the manneristic style but subsequently showed the way
to the modern style and became its main representative.

The reader should also compare a few examples from the book
of Johannes Wolf quoted above: particularly No. 63, by Master

Ex. 49. Filipoctus de Caserta, *Par les bons Gedeons*

Zacharias; No. 66, by Filipoctus de Caserta; and No. 68, by
Bartolommeo da Bologna, all Italians and all from the early fifteenth century.

THE ITALIANS VERSUS THE FRENCH. The fundamental
difference between the French and the Italian way of interpreting
shows clearest in their performance of the *divisiones,* of which

Marchetto of Padua has left us the most detailed account. Suppose the composer writes three semibreves per breve in binary time, neither French nor Italian performers would make them uniform in length; the Italians would render them with the values $1 + 1 + 2$, but the French, still in the vein of *perfectio*, as $3 + 2 + 1$. If the composer writes four semibreves per breve, the Italians would render them as four notes of equal value, but the French as two trochaic triplets, $(2 + 1) + (2 + 1)$. If the composer writes eight semibreves per breve, the Italians would render them as eight notes of equal value, but the French, as four trochaic triplets, $(2 + 1) + (2 + 1) + (2 + 1) + (2 + 1)$. The confusion of the two national interpretations was so great that Marchettus insisted on adding the letters G or Y according to whether the passage should be read in the 'Gallic' style or in that of the 'Ytalians.' [24]

The gist of this comparison is: in the first half of the fourteenth century, the Italians turned energetically towards a thoroughly binary, divisive idiom, while the French, more conservative, adhered to the additive idiom and tried to smuggle in a perfection wherever it was feasible. Imperfection was in France still an object of discrimination.

ITALIAN ART reacted strongly against the Gothic spirit of the North. Unconcerned with structural interests and opposed to bewildering complexity and overdecoration, Italy wanted simplicity, noble moderation, and appeal to the senses, to the ear and the eye. Hers was the world of Giotto, Orcagna, and the painters of Siena; hers the world of Dante, Boccaccio, Petrarch. It was a world of poets in colors, lines, and words, not of engineers. Even the churches, though built in the outer forms of Gothic style, were meant to be seen while the merely structural elements were reduced to a bare minimum.

Music, focused on the noble forms of *ballata* and madrigal and the life-enjoying realism of the *caccia,* kept very far from the fidgety restlessness of the North. On the whole, they were serene and simple; they often let the voice parts march in even steps and dwelt long on higher notes to display the singer's vocal charms.

[24] Marchettus of Padua, *Pomerium*, 1318, transl. in Strunk, *op. cit.*, pp. 166 ff.

To be sure, composers did not fail to pay their tribute to the time. They availed themselves of hemiolas and syncopations, of intermingled triplets and changing signatures, and at times produced an outright rough and rugged melody.

Only for a short moment, around 1420, did the Italians join the Gothic Flamboyant of France. Just before the Renaissance began, Italian sculpture lapsed into Gothic concepts and forms: Nanni di Banco in Florence and Jacopo della Quercia in Bologna swerved from their austere, classicistic beginnings and created impressive statues in ecstatic motion, with floating gowns and wildly jerking folds in an overdecorated and lambent architecture.

In a strict parallel, a school of Italian composers, too, grew Gothic around 1420 and tried their hands at polyrhythmic complication.

We find a characteristic example of this un-Italian and somewhat anachronistic Gothicism in the *Sumite* by the papal singer Zacharias as No. 70 in Johannes Wolf's *Geschichte der Mensural-*

Ex. 50. Magister Zacharias, *Sumite carissimi*

Notation of 1904. Wolf's transcription, in the third and final volume, unfortunately gives a uniform 6/2 signature to all the three-voice parts as a kind of common denominator and conceals therewith the essential, almost unbelievable complication of the piece. Actually, one ternary, one binary, and one compound rhythm—3/4, 2/4, and 12/16—contend from the very beginning. They change rapidly from bar to bar or stand against each other in counterpoint: at the end of the first section, the *contra* or middle voice performs in 9/8 against the 6/8 of the upper voice or *cantus* and against the 3/4 of the *tenor*. But this conflict still does not give the whole picture. Whatever transparency might be left in the texture is dimmed in weirdest syncopations.

CHAPTER 10

The Renaissance: Concepts
of Rhythm and Tempo

The Renaissance—rebirth of the classical spirit—was the definitive reaction of the Latin spirit against the spirit of the Gothic North from around 1430 on. No country except Italy ever had a Renaissance in the true sense of the word. Early in the sixteenth century, England, France, the Netherlands, Germany, Spain, imported Italian artists and adopted many details and even a few of the ideals that Italy professed—in painting, sculpture, and architecture. But all these so-called Renaissances—German, French, or otherwise—were in fact very doubtful attempts to graft the new fashion somehow on domestic traditions of a preponderantly Gothic character. A French or a German town of the sixteenth century might show some classical pediments, friezes, and columns, but not for a moment could it be mistaken for an Italian town. This is why the word 'Renaissance' covers to a certain degree a period rather than a trend.

The musical situation complicates matters still further. The Italians had a bewildering dearth of creative musicians of the first rank all through the Renaissance, between Landino and Palestrina. Hence, reversing the position found in the visual arts, they imported a host of northern musicians, especially Burgundian, French, and Flemish, from the early fifteenth century in the days of Guillaume Dufay to the middle of the sixteenth century in the time of Lassus.

198

The curious consequence of this almost unique situation was a long carry-over on the very soil of Italy of a powerful Gothic thought and attitude in music. The imported Burgundians and Flemings held their own against the demands of Italian taste, but could not entirely escape a stylistic transformation under the influence of the Italian Renaissance. For a long time they abode by the musical language of the North, but with definite changes in accent, grammar, and vocabulary. They brought polyrhythmic structures and queer enigma canons along, but smoothed their native angular melodies, simplified their complex forms, and sacrificed the intellectual, engineering approach of the Gothic Age to the enjoyment of sound.

It thus happened that the musical Renaissance became a fascinating struggle between the northern Gothic and a classicistic Italian spirit. The latter was eventually victor. But for reasons of a general nature the Gothic side proved unusually powerful: music always thrives best in the atmosphere of ending, ripened cycles, and worst in the climate of nascent cycles that are still trying to assert themselves.[1]

We will behold the rhythmic aspect of the Renaissance at first from the older, Gothic angle, whether or not the acting personalities were Italians or men from the North. And in doing so, we will deal with mere technicalities first.

TIME SIGNATURES OF THE FIFTEENTH CENTURY. In 1408, Prosdocimus de Beldemandis of Padua related that 'one' gave a time signature even to the maxim. It consisted in the squares with two and three half-dashes that the preceding century had used for the long, perfect and imperfect; but, in keeping with the broadened form of the maxim symbol, the squares proper were stretched out to prone rectangles:

$$▥ = ⊓ \ ⊓ \ ⊓$$
$$▤ = ⊓ \ ⊓$$

(During the fifteenth century the notes, once filled black, became white.)

[1] Curt Sachs, *The commonwealth of art*, New York, W. W. Norton, 1946.

Prosdocimus also reported that "a few moderns" reduced the prolation dots inside the circle or semicircle to one and none: [2]

$$\odot = \quad ♦ \quad ♦ \quad ♦$$
$$\bigcirc = \quad ♦ \quad ♦$$

After Prosdocimus, the short *Regule* of the Carmelite monk Weyts [3] expressed in figures both the *modus* (here, the quality of the long) and the *tempus* (quality of the breve): 33 meant the perfection of both, and 22, their imperfection; 32 made them perfect—imperfect, and 23, imperfect—perfect.

Another account of the customary time signatures of the time is given by the Hispano-Italian, Ramis de Pareia (1482).[3a] Some *esoterici* or 'initiated' people, he said, were using the squares with dashes inside, while others preferred fractions, such as ⅔, where the numerator indicated prolation, and the denominator, *tempus*. But the common rule was to represent the *modus* by a circle, the *tempus* by a figure, and the *prolatio* by a dot.

A contemporary Fleming, Johannes Tinctoris (1446–1511), seems to have been responsible for introducing *longa* rests to characterize *modus:* three rests written as a time signature indicate perfect maxims; two rests, imperfect maxims; one rest, neglect of maxim values. Particularly,

3 three-space rests mean perfect maxims, perfect longs;
2   "   "   "   " imperfect   "   "   "
3 two-space   rests   " perfect   " imperfect   "
2   "   "   "   " imperfect   "   "   "

TEMPO, STANDARD AND STRICT. Right in Tinctoris' time, the relation of such concepts as *modus, tempus, prolatio* to living music was changing essentially, as their note values, *longa, brevis, semibrevis,* though keeping their ratios, became ever longer in duration and therefore less vital for all the music moving along in an almost immutable tempo. A similar shift in values against a

[2] Prosdocimi de Beldemandis *Tractatus de musica mensurabili,* in E. de Coussemaker, *Scriptores de musica medii aevi,* Paris, 1869, Vol. III, pp. 214 f.

[3] Coussemaker, *op. cit.,* p. 262.

[3a] Ramis de Pareia, *Musica practica,* ed. by Johannes Wolf, in *Beihefte der Internationalen Musikgesellschaft,* Vol. II, Leipzig, 1901.

normal tempo was discussed in the preceding chapter on the Later Middle Ages.

Indeed, from the High Middle Ages on, a growing emancipation from the mere long–short alternation of metrical poetry, as it appeared in the metrical *modi* of the thirteenth century, had led to the unavoidable introduction of shorter and ever shorter time values. Mensural notation, once devised to keep the poetical values *longa* and *brevis* apart, had gradually added the symbols for a *duplex longa* or *maxima* above, and a *semibrevis*, a *minima*, a *semiminima* below, and had eventually proceeded to the *fusa* and the *semifusa*.

The obvious modern assumption would be that a newly added value must have taken just a half or even a third of the note till then considered to be the shortest. This, however, is not justified, for reasons both technical and psychological. The recent note, for whose unwonted speed performers and listeners are not yet fully prepared, will necessarily turn out to be less fast than its theoretical value. As a consequence, it must slow down the whole array of older standing in order to maintain the correct relations of longs and breves, of semibreves and minims, of semiminims, fuses, and semifuses. This is the reason why a long, originally the motor unit equivalent of a modern quarter note, would today (if it still existed) be from sixteen to twenty-four times slower.

This process of gradual elongation would have been simple and continual but for the fact that tempo (when not considered from a psychological viewpoint) depends upon a human, physiological motor unit, from which it cannot deviate too much without losing its kinetic power and musical usefulness. True, the slowing-down movement affected the motor unit. It might start from, say, M.M. 80 and subsequently slacken to less than M.M. 60 under the pressure of recent smaller values. But it could hardly drop too far below M.M. 60. For if it did so, say, to M.M. 53, the next-smaller time-value, then at 106 M.M., would draw closer to the physiologically established starting point of M.M. 80 and succeed automatically to the rank of motor unit. This is why within a few centuries the long inevitably yielded its position to the breve, the breve to the semibreve, the semibreve to the minim, the minim to the semiminim. Graphically,

M.M.	4	8	16	32	64	128
					ꟼ	ꟼ
				ꟼ	□	◇
			ꟼ	□	◇	♩
		ꟼ	□	◇	♩	♩
	ꟼ	□	◇	♩	♩	♪

(The M.M. numbers have been chosen here as convenient powers of 2, and the notes, including the few black ones, follow the forms of the later, so-called white, notation, although the upper lines belong in times of black notation.)

Around 1500, the role of motor unit had devolved upon the minim (♩) which consequently must be transcribed by a quarter note in modern editions.

The concept of a normal motor unit, of a *tempo giusto* independent of personal interpretation, has been foreign to us and our ancestors in the nineteenth century. From a romantic, subjective, self-expressive age we have inherited an almost absolute freedom of tempo, of an exaggeratedly fine gradation, indeed, a gliding gamut of tempo shades between the extremes of prestissimo and molto adagio—only to fight bitterly over the "correct" tempo in which Opus Such and Such should have been, but was not, played in last night's recital.

Non-romantic civilizations, on the contrary, prefer a well-established normalcy, with a few lawful deviations which, felt as such, confirm the *tempo giusto*. Recipes for a normal tempo, like that of Johannes Verulus discussed in the preceding chapter, were, however, exceptions in the Middle Ages—probably because the tempo did not need support from theory.

When later the critical clash of Gothic and Renaissance, of northern and southern ideals, posed the question of tempo among its many problems, the motor unit was taken from the innate physiological rhythm of man: either from his leisurely stride—as in Johann Buchner's *Fundamentbuch* for organ [4] early in the six-

---

[4] Carl Paesler, *Fundamentbuch von Hans von Constanz*, in *Vierteljahrsschrift für Musikwissenschaft*, Vol. V, 1889, p. 28: ". . . *quantum temporis inter duos gressus viri mediocriter incedentis intercurrit.*"

teenth century—or, oftener, from the regular pulse of a man with quiet respiration.[5] The heart has indeed provided the principal standard, from Ramis de Pareia's *Tractatus de musica* of 1482 all the way through to Johann Joachim Quantz's *Versuch einer Anweisung die Flöte traversiere zu spielen* (Berlin, 1752). The metronomical value of both these motor units, the stride and the heartbeat, lies between M.M. 60 and M.M. 80.

Less accurate was the occasional practice of counting syllables. Two Germans, Hans Gerle (1532)[6] and Hans Neusiedler (1536)[7] recommended counting *fein gemach* or 'gently' *eins zwey drey vier*. And so did, in the following century, the two Englishmen, Christopher Simpson[8] and Henry Purcell:[9] the player may pronounce *One Two Three Four* "in an equal length as you would (leisurely) read them." Such counting yields about M.M. 64. Simpson wanted the syllables *One Two* to be "pronounced with the Hand Down," and *Three Four* "with it Up." That is, each two of these syllables formed a motor unit—a fact that the reader will fully understand on reading the section on *Tactus*.

In 1619, Michael Praetorius fixed the tempo at "a good moderate speed": 160 *tempora* should be played in a quarter of an hour.[10] Since *tempus* represented the value of a breve, there would be 320 semibreves, 640 minims, and 1280 semiminims, which at that time were the motor units or quarter notes. Divided by 15, the number of minutes in a quarter of an hour, the result would be $\downarrow$ = M.M. 85.

The existence of such a norm, or any other, must not mislead. Variants were always taken for granted as the inevitable consequences of individual and national temperaments, of technical difficulties, and of the particular character of the pieces performed.

It is unnecessary to clarify the differences of individual temperaments and their effects on tempo. Evidence of national tempera-

[5] Ramis de Pareia, *Tractatus de musica*, 1482, ed. J. Wolf, p. 77; Gafurius, *Practica musica*, Mediolani, 1496, Book III, Ch. iv, fol. dd iij; Giovanni Maria Lanfranco, *Scintille di musica*, Brescia, 1533, p. 67.

[6] Hans Gerle, *Musica teutsch*, Nürnberg, 1532, fol. B III, v.

[7] Hans Newsidler, *Ein newgeordent Lautenbuch*, Nürnberg, 1536, fol. B. III, v.

[8] Christopher Simpson, *The principles of practical musick*, London, 1665, § 4.

[9] Henry Purcell, *A choice collection of lessons for the harpsichord or spinnet*, London, 1696 (p. 4).

[10] *Syntagma musicum*, Vol. III, Wolffenbüttel, 1619, p. 88.

ments can be found in the seventeenth chapter of Quantz's above-mentioned *Versuch;* and they can also be gathered from the different, highly characteristic tempi of military marches in various countries. Sir John Hawkins writes in 1776 in his *General History of Music:* [11] "It seems that the old English march of the foot was formerly in high estimation, as well abroad as with us; its characteristic is dignity and gravity, in which respect it differs greatly from the French, which, as it is given by Mersennus, is brisk and alert." We also know that in Queen Elizabeth's time the march drums were "slow, heavy, sluggish." It should, however, not be passed over in silence "that the solemn measures of the Continent became quicker and brighter when naturalized" in England.[12]

That technical difficulties often force us to slow the tempo down is almost a truism; and every musician knows that a hymn in bare half notes invites to a faster tempo than a contrapuntal, flowing Bach chorale suggests.

But there have of course been outspoken differences in tempo within the same age, the same country, and the same degree of difficulty. As a rule the sources are rather reticent. But once, at least, we get unmistakable, straight information about such differences: from Antonio Cornazano's *Libro dell'arte del danzare* of 1455 [13] we learn that the mid-century had four principal dances and that their tempi were not the same; compared with the ceremonious, courtly *bassadanza,* the livelier *quaternaria* was as 5:6, the brisk *saltarello* as 5:8, and the full-speed *piva* as 1:2. If, as it seems, the *bassa,* with its gliding, dignified steps, had a moderate striding tempo with the motor unit, say, M.M. 60, we would get this table:

bassadanza	*ca.*	60 M.M.
quaternaria	*ca.*	72 M.M.
saltarello	*ca.*	96 M.M.
piva	*ca.*	120 M.M.

Cornazano could have said—as anybody without a metronome would do today—that the *piva* was about twice as fast, and that

[11] Hawkins, re-ed. London, J. A. Novello, 1853, Vol. I, p. 229.
[12] Jeffrey Pulver, *The dances of Shakespeare's England,* in *Sammelbände der Internationalen Musikgesellschaft,* Vol. XV, 1913, pp. 99, 100.
[13] Cornazano, ed. C. Mazzi, in *La Bibliofilia,* Vol. XVII (1915/16), pp. 185–209.

the remaining two dances were in between, the *quaternaria* closer to the *bassa,* and the *saltarello* closer to the *piva.* But he expressed the difference in algebraic values, with an exactness that actual performance can hardly have achieved. In doing so, he complied with the current concept and practice of the time: to accept a standard tempo—even if imaginary—and to derive from it all other tempi under the form and name of *proportiones.*

PROPORTIONS. As early as 1409, the Italian, Prosdocimus de Beldemandis, had presented a complete, indeed, an over-complete list of all possible tempo proportions in a special treatise, the *Brevis summula proportionum.*[14] The authenticated date 1409, so close to the preceding fourteenth century, suggests that the latter might already have had full knowledge and practice of proportional tempi.

Prosdocimus classified them in five categories. Most important among them were the

> *Multiplex* proportions, in which the tempo was
>> doubled (*dupla*),
>> trebled (*tripla*),
>> quadrupled (*quadrupla*).

Next in importance were the

> *Superparticulares* proportions, in which the faster tempo exceeded standard tempo by some aliquot part, such as
>> *sesquialtera,* 3:2,
>> *sesquitertia,* 4:3,
>> *sesquiquarta,* 5:4.

More or less theoretical were the

> *Superpartientes* proportions, in which the faster tempo exceeded standard tempo by a non-aliquot or 'aliquant' part, such as
>> *superbipartiens:* 5:3 or 7:5 or 9:7,
>> *supertripartiens:* 7:4 or 8:5 or 10:7,
>> *superquadripartiens:* 9:5 or 11:7 or 13:9.

The following last two categories contained proportions in

[14] C. E. H. Coussemaker, *Scriptorum de musica medii aevi nova series,* Vol. III, Paris, pp. 258–261.

which the faster tempo held the aliquot or non-aliquot part in addition to at least twice the standard tempo. Examples are in

>*Multiplices superparticulares* the
>>*dupla superparticularis,* such as 7:3,

and in

>*Multiplices superpartientes* the
>>*dupla superbipartiens,* such as 8:3.

Sad experience in class makes a few arithmetical remarks advisable. An aliquot part divides a whole without a remainder: 1 is such a part of any integer. In *multiplex* proportions, 2:1 or 3:1, the faster tempo, being a simple multiple of standard, can always be divided by the standard without a remainder. The same is true of the *superparticulares:* the excess of 1, as in 3:2, is necessarily an aliquot part of standard. But in the *superpartientes,* as in 5:3, the excess of 2 is not an aliquot part of either 3 or 5 or 7; the exesss of 3, in the following line, is not an aliquot part of either 4 or 5 or 7; nor is the excess of 4 an aliquot part of either 5 or 7 or 9. In the last two categories, the awkward *multiplices super* . . . , 7 is 2 × 3 plus the aliquot 1; and 8 is 2 × 3 plus the non-aliquot 2.

All these *proportiones* are 'diminutions.' What such diminution actually is and how it works can be easily seen from its only remnant in modern times, the *alla breve* or, as the fifteenth century would have called it, *proportio dupla.* Its two beats are represented in the form of half notes; but the real value of either half note is only that of a quarter note in a 2/4 measure. In *alla breve,* the time values are halved or diminished in the ratio 2:1. Generally speaking, diminution is the allotment to notational symbols of time values less than standard.

Guilielmus Monachus or Monk William, who seems to have lived close to 1480, mentions, besides diminution, also its opposite: proportional augmentation of time values, denoted by the prefix *sub,* as in *subdupla, subtripla, subquadrupla.* Augmentation is the allotment to notational symbols of time values proportionally greater than standard.

Within a voice part, any augmentation subsequent to diminution re-establishes the *status quo ante*. It does not refer to standard tempo. And vice-versa.

Most proportions outside the *multiplices* and the *sesquialtera* were certainly rare. But they must not be thought of as the pallid brain-children of thorough theorists and their age-old mania for completeness. A work so fully practical as Ganassi's method for the flute, the *Fontegara* of 1535,[15] teaches diminution or embellishment by rules, the first of which dissolves a semibreve into four semiminims; the second, into five; the third, into six; the fourth, into seven semiminims. The four and the five semiminims are in the ratio of a *sesquiquarta;* the four and the seven, of a *supertripartiens;* the five and the six, of a *sesquiquinta;* the five and the seven, of a *superbipartiens;* the six and the seven, of a *sesquisexta.*

None of Ganassi's followers in the art of diminution went into such weird proportional intricacies. But then, the tempo ratios indicated by Cornazano had been distinctly *proportio sesquiquinta* for the *quaternaria* dance, *supertripartiens* for the *saltarello,* and *dupla* for the *piva.*

PROPORTIONAL SIGNATURES have found their most complete and comprehensible survey in the treatise written sometime in the second half of the fifteenth century by Monk William. This survey is reproduced below in its entirety but—for the sake of shortness and clarity—only in minor prolation, that is, with two minims to the semibreve. The prolation dot would simply change from 2 to 3 the last of the four figures that indicate the sizes of maxims, longs, breves, and semibreves.

(1) A circle alone at the beginning of a piece or section of a piece denotes perfection of the breve, while the other values are binary:

O = 2 longs, each of two breves, each of three semibreves, each of two minims, or, in abbreviation: 2 2 3 2 .

[15] Sylvestro di Ganassi, *Opera intitulata Fontegara*, Venice 1535, facs. Milan 1934, Ch. IX ff.; examples in Imogene Horsley, *Improvised embellishment*, in *Journal of the American Musicological Society*, Vol. IV, 1951, p. 7.

(2) A circle in front of a single figure expresses perfect longs, while the following figure, either 3 or 2, indicates the value of the breve. Maxims remain imperfect:

O 3 = 2 3 3 2,
O 2 = 2 3 2 2.

(3) A circle with two figures indicates maxims (circle), longs (first figure), and breves (second figure):

O 33 = 3 3 3 2,
O 22 = 3 2 2 2.

(4) [Particularly important:] A semicircle alone, open to the right, indicates binary organization *throughout*:

C = 2 2 2 2

(5) A semicircle before a single figure expresses the imperfection of the long, while the figure indicates the value of the breve:

C 3 = 2 2 3 2
C 2 = 2 2 2 2

(6) A semicircle before two figures indicates maxims of two longs each, while the figures express the values of the long and the breve:

C 33 = 2 3 3 2
C 22 = 2 2 2 2

(7) A lone semicircle open to the left expresses *proportio dupla* against C; each figure must be shifted by one place to the left, since semibreves become breves; breves, longs; and longs, maxims:

Ɔ　　 = 2 2 2 —
Ɔ 3　= 2 3 2 —
Ɔ 2　= 2 2 2 —
Ɔ 33 = 3 3 2 —
Ɔ 22 = 2 2 2 —

(8) A dash through the full circle or the semicircle has the same purpose of shifting all values one place to the left:

ϕ = 2 3 2 —   ¢   = 2 2 2 —

ϕ 3 = 3 3 2 —   ¢ 3 = 2 3 2 —

ϕ 2 = 3 2 2 —   ¢ 2 = 2 2 2 —

ϕ 33 = 3 3 2 —   ¢ 33 = 3 3 2 —

¢ 22 = 2 2 2 —   ¢ 22 = 2 2 2 —

(9) A dash through the inverted semicircle halves once more the values already halved; semibreves become longs, and breves maxims; or better, the other way around, the symbol for the long represents in fact only the value of a semibreve, and that for the maxim, the value of a breve:

♭   = 2 2 — —

♭ 3 = 3 2 — —

♭ 2 = 2 2 — —

♭ 33 = 3 2 — —

♭ 22 = 2 2 — —

To sum up, the value of a semibreve appears as

◇   in standard tempo,

▫   in diminution,

♩   in augmentation.

Musicians found a certain difficulty in the different situations presented by perfection and imperfection. In thorough imperfection, every long had two breves, every breve two semibreves, every semibreve two minims—altogether eight minims. A thorough imperfection in diminution would require a maxim of two longs, a long of two breves, a breve of two semibreves, a semibreve of two minims—altogether sixteen minims. In other words, the diminution followed the ratio 2:1. But in thorough perfection, every long had three breves, every breve three semibreves, every semibreve three minims—altogether twenty-seven minims. A thorough perfection in diminution would then require a maxim of three longs, a long of three breves, a breve of three semibreves, a semibreve of three minims—altogether no less than eighty-one minims, as against sixteen in imperfection. In other words: the diminution followed the ratio 3:1.

Theoreticians, eager to have a complete Latin terminology for all events, confined the word *diminutio* to the 3:1 reduction. The 2:1 reduction, to them, was a *semiditas*. Even as late an author as Glareanus emphasized that *semiditas* existed only in *tempus imperfectum*.[16]

Monk William's survey, strangely enough, does not give any special symbol for the other proportions, not even for the current ternary proportions *tripla* and *sesquialtera*. But outside the survey proper, a remark in the same treatise appears to answer this question: "The figure 3 denotes sometimes ternary semibreves [*ternalitatem minimarum*] and sometimes ternary breves [*ternalitatem semibrevium*]."

Does this *ternalitas* mean a subdivision of the minim into three semiminims or of the semibreve into three minims? Or does it mean that the next higher values, semibreves or breves, are divided by three? The first possibility must be answered in the negative, because any subdivision of the minim appears to be beyond the scope of William's system. In *ternalitas*, then, three minims equal one semibreve, or, in a similar way, three semibreves equal one breve.

But there again are two possibilities: is *ternalitas* meant as a dotting, which does, or as a tripling of the smaller value, which does not, add to the greater value? In the first case, however, William would speak of perfection, not of *ternalitas*. For the perfection of the semibreve, the Monk had the common name *prolatio maior* and the common symbol of a dot with the full or open circle. This leaves no doubt that William's *ternalitas* refers to a triplet. But triplets of minims form *proportio sesquialtera*.

This unavoidable conclusion answers the question why William's time signatures cover *integer valor* as well as duple and quadruple proportions, but neither of the two ternary proportions. Again, he would probably not offer a symbol for the *sesquialtera* and ignore the *tripla*. But since triple proportion is actually a triplet of semibreves, is not the Monk's statement meant to indicate that either form of ternary proportion can be symbolized by the figure 3—without the later distinction of $\frac{3}{2}$ for the *sesquialtera*?

16 Glareanus, *Dodecachordon*, Basel, 1547, III, viii.

If such is the case, we face here, in the earliest stage of proportional signatures, an ambiguous use of figure 3, denoting now
tempus perfectum, now ternary proportion.

This is the more probable as the figure 2 seems to have been in
a similar position. The symbol O 2, says William elsewhere, stands
for the rhythmic configuration 2 × 3 × 2 × 2, or for two longs,
each divided into three breves, with the breve composed of two
semibreves, and the semibreve, of two minims. But he adds: "Many
singers take this sign *per medium,*" which is his term for duple
proportion in imperfect *tempus.* Thus figure 2 means both *tempus
imperfectum* and *proportio dupla.* We will see that *tempus imperfectum* usually stood in diminution.

The complexity of this system, and the redundance of its symbols, is, to say the least, bewildering. In the first place, there are a
number of confusing synonyms:

ɔ and ¢
O and C 3
O 3 and C 33
O 2 and ¢ 33
O 22 and ¢ 2
C 2, C, C 22, ϕ 22, ♭, ♭ 22, ¢ 22.

The situation becomes somewhat clearer when we learn from
Georg Rhaw [17] that symbols with a figure after the circle or semicircle were used only within a voice part as actual proportions,
while *symbols without figures stood as time signatures at the beginning and had no proportional significance.*

To understand the practice as a whole, one must comprehend
one point of utmost importance: the individual symbol had a
permanent meaning only within the combination of signs in which
it stood, and not in itself. In chapters seven and eight of his lucid
Practica musicae of 1496, Franchino Gafori makes it perfectly clear
—without saying so expressly—that there are three different cases:

(1) Any single symbol indicates the nature of *tempus:* a full
circle makes it perfect, a semicircle, imperfect.

(2) In a signature of two symbols, the circle indicates *modus,*

[17] Georg Rhaw, *Enchiridion musices,* Leipzig, 1518, quoted after the edition of
1546.

and the figure, *tempus*. The full circle stands for longs of three breves, and the semicircle, for longs of two breves. Three semibreves per breve are shown by a figure 3, and two, by a figure 2.

(3) In a signature of three symbols (a circle and two figures) the circle or semicircle stands for the perfection or imperfection of *modus maior,* that is, for the subdivision of maxims; the first figure, for the perfection or imperfection of *modus minor* (subdivision of the longs); and the second figure, for the perfection or imperfection of the breve.

In graphic form:

O 33	three longs	three breves	three semibreves
O 32	three longs	three breves	two semibreves
O 23	three longs	two breves	three semibreves
C 32	two longs	three breves	two semibreves
C 23	two longs	two breves	three semibreves
O 3		three breves	three semibreves
O 2		three breves	two semibreves
C 3		two breves	three semibreves
C 2		two breves	two semibreves
O			three semibreves
C			two semibreves

Since around 1500 the minim had the value of a modern quarter note, the equivalents of these rhythms were:

O 33: $3 \times 3 \times 3/4$
O 32: $3 \times 3 \times 2/4$
O 23: $3 \times 2 \times 3/4$
C 32: $2 \times 3 \times 3/4$
C 23: $2 \times 2 \times 3/4$
O 3 : $\quad 3 \times 3/4$
O 2 : $\quad 3 \times 2/4$
C 3 : $\quad 2 \times 3/4$
C 2 : $\quad 2 \times 3/4$ [but mostly in duple proportion]
O : $\quad\quad 3/4$
C : $\quad\quad 2/4$

In major prolation (with a dot inside the circle or semicircle), 3/4 must be replaced by 9/8, and 2/4 by 6/8.

But this generally accepted meaning of the dot cannot pass without due allowance either. Confusingly enough, the dot could also mean augmentation: each of the three symbols in Adam of Fulda's *alla minima* group has it inside the circle or semicircle. Ornithoparchus confirms this use in his *Micrologus* of 1517: in 'augmentation,' a minim takes the place of a semibreve, and its symbol is "a point in the Signe of time."

It will suffice to add a second confirmation: Glarean's *Dodecachordon* of 1547. Better than Ornithoparchus has done, Glarean explains in Book III, Chapter VIII, that the dot means augmentation when it occurs in one voice part only. Otherwise, it is a prolation dot.

Glareanus adds that the augmentation dot gives to a minim the value of a semibreve, and to a semibreve the value of a dotted breve. This different rate of augmentation clarifies the strange table of symbols "according to more recent music" in Sebald Heyden's *Ars canendi* (Nürnberg, 1540). The dots in half of them can hardly mean prolation: the dotted symbols are allotted three times more semibreves than the undotted ones—C 2 (two breves, two semibreves) stands for 4 semibreves, but ℂ 2 for 12; O 3 stands for 27 semibreves, but ☉ 3 for 81; and so throughout.

To complicate matters further, in Adam of Fulda's *Musica* of 1490 the inverted semicircle—known from Monk William's treatise as the symbol of *proportio dupla*—indicates *proportio sesquitertia* or 4:3; with a dot inside, it stands for *sesquiquarta* or 5:4; with a dash, for *proportio superbipartiens* or 5:3; with dot and dash, for *dupla bipartiens* or 8:3; with a figure 8 below, for *sesquioctava* or 9:8.[18]

At the end of the sixteenth century, the Englishman, Thomas Morley,[19] summarized the essential symbols of the age as

O 3	three longs to a maxim
C 3	two longs to a maxim
O 2	three breves to a long

[18] Gerbert, *Scriptores*, 1784, III, p. 379.
[19] Thomas Morley, *A plaine and easie introduction to practicall musicke*, 1597.

C 2	two breves to a long
O	three semibreves to a breve, two breves to a long
2	two semibreves to a breve, two breves to a long

THE MEANING OF PROPORTIONAL WRITING, so far from all our modern concepts, requires some explanation.

Musicians of today might argue that reading the score would be simpler if a semibreve were always a semibreve instead of having half or double this value in one or two of the parts. But musicians around 1500 had no scores and consequently did not care about the easy reading of a polyphonic texture as a whole. It was the individual voice part that they wanted to read as easily as possible. In doing so, they seem to have felt, curiously enough, that in order to facilitate visual perception the notes should not go beyond the semiminim (♩) as the smallest written symbol. Quite obviously they had a *horror fusae*, a reluctance to write and read the flagged *fusa* and, more so, the double-flagged *semifusa*, whose outer forms have led to modern eighth and sixteenth notes.

That the *horror fusae* is not a bold historian's fancy may be gathered from a source almost two hundred years after the heyday of *proportio*: Georg Muffat admonishes his performers not to be terrified by the sight of double *fusae* or sixteenths! [20]

A voice part with such a dreaded *fusa* in standard or *integer valor* was simply sung in diminution so that the *fusa* value appeared under the next higher graphic form of a semiminim. This did no practical harm, since—as just stated—compositions were written, printed, and read in individual voice parts without comprehensive scores.

It might be a psychological help to think of those curious wind parts in orchestral scores of the nineteenth century where the French horns would change suddenly from *F* to *E* or *B* in order to avoid accidentals, although to the best of the author's knowledge no horn player with valves has ever been afraid of reading a *b* flat or an *f* sharp or, for that matter, has ever actually changed crooks. Musical notation, it seems, has in all times examples of unnecessary complication under the disguise of alleged simplification.

[20] Georg Muffat, *Florilegium Secundum*, Passau 1698, repr. in *Denkmäler der Tonkunst in Oesterreich*, Vol. II, 2, p. 24.

It was a particular advantage of proportional writing that it allowed one to avoid ambiguous mensural symbols at a time when a new generation had outgrown the cumbersome, more and more unnecessary intricacies of mensuration. In one of these cases, the *perfectio* under the signature O, two sizes of breves, binary and ternary, would stand side by side without any visible difference —the same square would indicate either one. A transcription of the passage by way of diminution could remove the difficulty: the signature would be ₵, the *brevis* symbols were replaced by *longa* signs, which, as a consequence of the now perfect *mensura*, had to be dotted when ternary. Thus the alleged imperfection under ₵ stood in fact for a ternary rhythm.[21]

Very soon, the circle of perfection yielded almost completely to ₵.

Often enough, proportion was used where it did not serve any musical purpose. Isaac would write some recurrent passage in two or three different forms of proportional notation after one another—probably from sheer Gothic delight in enigmas. Again, Isaac (or his publisher Formschneider) added a *resolutio* to a certain cryptic bass line in his Mass *Confessoris*.[22] Two generations later, Jacobus Gallus wrote a piece with exactly the same movement in several voice parts, one note to the *tactus*, and yet he gave a different proportion and hence a different symbol to each, whether he wanted to look profound or—much more probably—to ridicule the outmoded unnecessary complication.

THE LIMITATIONS OF PROPORTIONAL PRACTICE. Proportional time signatures appear under three different circumstances:

(1) in a polyphonic piece in which at least two of the voice parts follow different signatures, throughout or temporarily;

(2) in a piece, monophonic or polyphonic, in which the different signatures are used one after another without (in polyphonic pieces) a conflict in the parts;

[21] Sebald Heyden, *Musica, id est ars canendi*, Nuremberg, 1537, p. 63. Cf. also Arnold Schering, *Takt und Sinngliederung in der Musik des 16. Jahrhunderts*, in *Archiv für Musikwissenschaft*, Vol. II, 1920, pp. 465 f.

[22] Heinrich Isaac's *Choralis Constantinus Book III*, ed. Louise Cuyler, Ann Arbor, 1950, pp. 26, 226. Cf. the preceding note.

(3) a piece, monophonic or polyphonic, with no change of signature within it.

The first of these three cases is the only one with compulsory proportional reading.

In the second case, where two or more signatures were used one after another in all the voice parts simultaneously, exact proportion was mostly *but not always* required.

Glareanus complains in a significant passage on ternary time: [23] Today the common run of singers call this "august, magnificent" rhythm *tripla*. This, he says, is quite improper, since proportion cannot take place where all four voices stride along with uniform steps. In other words: *Actual proportion applies only to poly-rhythmic webs.*

Still less is proportion exacted when, as in the third case, there is no change of signature within a piece:

A time signature, valid all through a voice part and nowhere in conflict with another signature, cannot be, and is not, proportional.

The most important example—as a subsequent section of this book will show—is the indiscriminate use of C and ₵ for the same piece in different manuscripts: the two signatures, in separate pieces of notation, do not imply the theoretical proportion of 2:1.

Proportiones were greatly a matter of pen and ink.

The sixteenth century knew tempo changes from piece to piece or within a piece without proportional strings, even where a changing signature suggested obedience to a definite ratio. One proof of this is Glarean's recommendation to change the tempo within a piece from section to section in order to avoid fatigue. Another proof is the tempo indications in the tablatures of Spanish vihuela players. In the first place, they emphasize that within a piece more florid passages should be altogether faster than chordal episodes. In the second place, they anticipate the later tempo marks: in the collections from 1536 to 1547, of Luis Milán, Narvaez, Mudarra, and Valderrabano, we find the indications *a priesa*, 'swiftly,' and *a espacio*, 'leisurely.' In a similar way, Milán's contemporary and countryman, Luis de Narvaez, in his *Delphín de música* of 1538, wanted the players of his third variation on O

[23] Glareanus, *Dodecachordon*, Basel, 1547, III, viii.

Gloriosa Domina to *levar muy apriesa el compás que paresca bien,* 'to take the tempo much faster in the interest of a good presentation.' And yet the vihuelists availed themselves of proportional time signatures to indicate these doubtless arbitrary tempi.

BINARY TACTUS. The concept of proportional reading entailed the concept of proportional beating. In choral ensembles, the standard tempo and its proportional derivatives were made coercive, visible, and often audible, through a uniform, moderate up-and-down or down-and-up movement of the conducting hand or foot. This up-and-down was known under the Latin name *tactus*, literally 'touching' or 'beating.'

Organized conducting had been known in some form in the Orient as well as in ancient Greece and Rome, be it with the foot or the hand or the finger. It also seems to have been practiced all during the Middle Ages: medieval writings mention it once in a while, and some paintings of the later Middle Ages show it. To be sure, all medieval descriptions refer to unaccompanied Gregorian chant and speak of 'depicting' the melody [24] in what is known as cheironomy. But Gothic polyphony from Perotinus to Dufay cannot have been ruled with the melody-drawing hand of Gregorian cheironomy. There must have been a predecessor of the *tactus* or actual time beating which appears for the first time in Ramis de Pareia's *Tractatus de musica* of 1482.

Far from beating out the constituent elements of a measure in the sense of modern conducting, as one–two–three or one–two–three–four, the *tactus* was always composed of two beats only, one up, one down.

Modern musicians take the sequence down-and-up for granted. But sixteenth-century men disagree (without giving any importance to this disagreement): some describe the movement as down-and-up, and some as up-and-down.[25] This proves once more

---

[24] Cf. Ambrosius Kienle, *Notizen über das Dirigiren mittelalterlicher Gesangschöre,* in *Vierteljahrsschrift für Musikwissenschaft,* Vol. I, 1885, pp. 158–169.

[25] Down-up:

Martin Agricola, *Musica figuralis deudsch,* 1532
Pierre Davantes, *Nouvelle et facile méthode pour chanter,* 1560
Oratio Tigrini, *Il compendio della musica,* 1588
Girolamo Diruta, *Il transilvano,* 1597
Michael Praetorius, *Syntagma musicum,* 1619

that the two beats were quite even without any stress on the first note, although the beat "which strikes up high does not have anything to hit against, as that which strikes below. . . . Both of them are struck with equality, that is, the low *golpe* [beat] is not struck more forcefully than the high, nor vice versa." [26]

To this statement, Sancta Maria adds that all the *tactus* "go measured and equal to the measure of the first *compás*" or *tactus;* tempo was constant. No source mentions *accelerando* or *rallentando.* Not even at the end of a piece or a section is there any trace of that *ritenuto* so dear to modern performers of older music. Instead, there is sometimes virtual *rallentando* in the progress of the music itself. Arcadelt, at the end of his famous, often-sung madrigal *Il bianco e dolce cigno,* sustains the soprano for four entire measures on the same tied-over note g', stops the move-

Ex. 51. Arcadelt, madrigal, *Il bianco e dolce cigno,* end

ment in eighths of the other three voices with the last but two and leads them in the penultimate measure from quarter notes to quiet halves. The music as such dies down; any additional *ritardando* would be distortion and redundancy. Another exam-

Marin Mersenne, *L'harmonie universelle,* 1636
Christopher Simpson, *The principles of practical music,* 1665

Up-down:
Giovanni Lanfranco, *Scintille di musica,* 1533
Luis de Milán, *El Maestro,* 1536
Angelo da Picitono, *Fior angelico,* 1547
Vincentio Lusitano, *Introduttione,* 1561
Tomás de Sancta Maria, *Arte de tañer,* 1565
Francisco de Salinas, *De musica,* 1577
Tans'ur, *Grammar,* 1746
Leopold Mozart, *Violinschule,* 1756

(Georg Schünemann, quoting an earlier edition of Lusitano's [1553], which the present author has not seen, attributes to him the inverse order, rightly or wrongly.)

[26] Tomás Sancta Maria, *El arte de tañer,* Valladolid, 1565, quoted from John Ward's doctoral dissertation. Georg Schünemann's translation in his paper is not correct.

ple, Tomás Luis de Victoria's motet *O vos omnes*, broadens its last measure to 6/4 after a consistent 4/4. Such pieces prove that the ritardando was a matter of rhythm, not of tempo, and that, where it was needed, the composer, not the performer, took care of it.

Whether up-and-down or down-and-up, the *tactus* had two beats in opposite direction, each one measuring between M.M. 60 and 80. There was only one such binary *tactus*—but it could denote three different tempi.

The normal, standard *tactus*, often called *maior* or *integer*, represented the two beats by minims and hence comprised a semibreve (♦ + ♦ =˙ ⬦). Thus it was also called the *tactus alla semibreve*.

Proportio dupla or *diminutio* by two, derived from the standard *tactus maior* by a duplication of all values: the two beats—again of M.M. 60–80—were written as semibreves, and the value of the full *tactus* became a breve (⬦ + ⬦ = ◻). Hence its name —still in use—*tactus alla breve*.

Proportio subdupla, or *augmentatio* by two, derived from the standard *tactus maior* by halving all values: the two beats—again at M.M. 60–80—were written as semiminims, and the value of the full *tactus* became a minim (♦ + ♦ = ♦). Hence its name *tactus alla minima* or *tactus minor* (English *lesser tact*, German *halber Takt*).

Altogether:

augmented:	♦ + ♦ = ♦	(*alla minima*)
standard:	♦ + ♦ = ⬦	(*alla semibreve*)
diminished:	⬦ + ⬦ = ◻	(*alla breve*),

in which each of the symbols on the left side of the equation has a speed of M.M. 60–80.

This basic tripartition is authoritatively stated in as early a source as the *Musica* of Adam of Fulda, dated 1490.[27] Adam, himself a composer, arranges nine time signatures in three groups. In the first group, he says, *tactum facit minima* ("the minim forms a *tactus*"); in the second, *tactum facit semibrevis*; in the third, *tactum facit brevis*.

---

[27] Adam de Fulda, *De musica*, printed in Martin Gerbert, *Scriptores ecclesiastici de musica*, 1784, Vol. III.—Facsimile edition, 1931.

Nothing could be clearer than this statement. Still, drowned in the superabundance of sources, neither the contemporary writers nor their modern commentators have always seen how easy, consistent, and logical the *tactus* situation was.

Most theoreticians of the sixteenth century distinguish a *tactus maior* and a *tactus minor*. Both appear under various vernacular names, as, in Germany, *ganzer* and *halber tactus*. Some call *maior* the *alla breve,* some the *alla semibreve;* some call *minor* the *alla breve,* some the *alla semibreve,* some the *alla minima*. Obviously this contradiction is due to the confusing fact that longer note values are given shorter time values, and vice versa.

Sometimes the contradiction is hopelessly bewildering. Georg Schünemann [28] quotes Hermann Finck's *Practica musica* (1556) as alleged evidence that after 1550 the *alla breve* had become *tactus maior,* and the *alla semibreve* had taken its place as *tactus minor*. This is not correct. In Finck's music examples, the *tactus maior,* ruled by a O, is characterized by *tempus perfectum;* and the *minor,* ruled by a C, represents *tempus imperfectum*. Finck adds: "This is the common division of tactus, accepted in schools." This is indeed the key to understanding all these archaisms: here and elsewhere we find the stuff inherited from generations ago and rechewed over and over again for the benefit of the school. It has nothing whatsoever to do with the live practice of 1556. It even contradicts, in its definition, the *alla breve* reading of the binary, imperfect rhythm.

There are a few more misunderstandings in Schünemann's monograph.

One mistake concerns a passage in the sixth chapter in Martin Agricola's *Musica figuralis deudsch.*[29] It says: "*Item / das nidderschlagen und das auffheben zu hauff / macht allzeit einen Tact / Und wird der Halbe noch so risch / als der gantz Tact / geschlagen.*" It means: "Furthermore, a downbeat and an upbeat together form always one *tactus,* and the lesser *tactus* is beaten *noch so risch als* the major *tactus.*" The four critical words *noch so risch als* are rendered in Schünemann's interpretation as "twice as fast." Actually, they mean, in the archaic language of the six-

[28] Georg Schünemann, *Zur Frage des Taktschlagens in der Mensuralmusik,* in *Sammelbände der Internationalen Musikgesellschaft,* Vol. X, 1908–1909, pp. 73–114.
[29] Wittenberg, 1532.

teenth century, "just as fast." The *tactus* could not go "twice as fast." It remained the same whether the notes indicated *alla breve*, *alla semibreve*, or *alla minima*.

Also misinterpreted is a significant passage in F. Salina's *De musica libri* of 1577: "In the time that it takes to sing a breve, the hand goes up and down either once, in the *tactus maior;* or else twice, in the *tactus minor.*" Schünemann understands this as a choice between beating the same value once or twice. He is mistaken. As every source repeats or implies, *one, and only one,* up and down forms a *tactus*, never two. Actually, Salinas means this: the breve requires only one up and down in a *tactus alla breve;* but in a lesser *tactus*, the same notational symbol stands for two *tactus alla semibreve* and, hence, is represented by beating up and down twice.

In a third misstatement, Schünemann implies that the recognition of the *alla breve* came only around the middle of the sixteenth century. This is not, and cannot be, true. The *alla breve* was in fact essentially older than the *alla semibreve*, since, after the long, the breve had preceded the semibreve as the motor unit. Besides, one of those who lived in the middle of the sixteenth century—Glareanus—said expressly that the *alla breve* was the older one and still enjoyed popularity in a large part of Germany.[30]

But such mistakes can hardly be avoided; contemporary sources all too often elude comprehension. In the face of this confusion, modern historians had better avoid as much as possible such ambiguous terms as *major* and *minor* with their vernacular counterparts and stick to the three unmistakable characterizations *alla breve, alla semibreve, alla minima.*

The theoreticians say very little about the three *tactus* in actual performance. But we can easily learn about them from the explanatory surveys that the writers give to their signatures. For it was customary not to indicate how many longs were in a maxim, or breves in a long, but to assign to each value its number of *tactus* without saying so expressly. The Spaniard, Francisco de Montanos, for example, does not say that in O 3 the maxim has three longs, and the long two breves, but says instead that in O 3 the maxim has six, the long two, the breve one *tactus;* thus it is an

[30] Glareanus, *Dodecachordon*, Basel, 1547, III, vii.

alla breve rhythm. Wherever, on the contrary, the figure 1 is given to the semibreve or to the minim, there is *alla semibreve* or *alla minima* rhythm. Arranged accordingly, Montanos' survey reads: [31]

		⊏	⊏	◻	◇	◊		
alla breve:	O 3	6	2	1			or	3 × 2
	¢	4	2	1				2 × 2
		4	2	1				2 × 2
	¢ 3	4	2	1				2 × 2
	C 2	4	2	1				2 × 2
alla semibreve:	O 2	12	6	2	1			2 × 3 × 2
	O	12	6	3	1			2 × 2 × 3
	⊙ 3	12	4	2	1			3 × 2 × 2
	ℂ 3	8	4	2	1			2 × 2 × 2
	C 3	8	4	2	1			2 × 2 × 2
	C	8	4	2	1			2 × 2 × 2
alla minima:	ℂ	24	12	6	3	1		2 × 2 × 2 × 3
	⊙ 2	36	18	6	3	1		2 × 3 × 2 × 3
	⊙	36	18	9	3	1		2 × 2 × 3 × 3

It is certainly more important, even from the practical viewpoint of modern performance, to find out what the signature ¢ actually meant.

Nothing could be more bewildering than the contradictory statements of contemporaries:

(1) that ¢ was half as long as C;

(2) that ¢ was just as long as C;

(3) that ¢ was slower than C;

(4) that ¢ was faster than C.

This is pretty hard to swallow. And yet each statement is correct.

Once more, the essential point is to distinguish between proportion and non-proportion. ¢ meant *proportio dupla* ("half as long as C") only where it clashed with C in another voice part. Otherwise, its relation with C was vague or nonexistent.

As a rule, the non-proportional ¢ was slightly faster than C.

[31] Francisco de Montanos, *Arte de musica,* Valladolid, 1592.

Georg Rhaw (*Enchiridion musices,* 1518), Michael Koswick (*Compendiaria musices artis,* 1514), and Johannes Cocleus (*Tetrachordum musices,* 1512) were correct in stating that ¢ required faster playing (*velocius tangi debent*). But nothing could be more elucidating than what Glarean says in *lib.* III, *cap.* viii: when musicians are afraid the audience might get tired, they hasten the *tactus* by crossing the circle or semicircle and calling it a diminution. Actually, they do not diminish the value or the number of notes; they just quicken the beat, *quod tactus fiat velocior.* Thus the three sections of the *Kyrie* in a Mass (Kyrie I, Christe, Kyrie II) are often signed O ¢ ◐ to avoid boredom.

This statement can hardly be mistaken: such change of tempo was not a proportional diminution. It did not, as it should, affect the values of notes and make an *alla breve* out of an *alla semibreve.* While *proportio dupla* was in fact a duplication of note values without giving the feeling of a faster tempo, this pseudo-diminution affected the tempo of beating. Instead of doubling the tempo, it was just *festinandum* and *velocior;* it speeded up.

One sees that a good amount of freedom was granted despite the official standardization of tempo, and the crossed symbol took care of it.

In order to get this quite straight, let us skip a hundred years and glance at the picture of binary *tactus* that Michael Praetorius has given in the third volume of his *Syntagma musicum* of 1619 (*lib.* III, *cap.* vii).

Praetorius speaks of C and ¢ *tactus.* But nowhere is there any mention of duple proportion between them. C is *tardior* or a bit slower—*etwas langsamer und gravitetischer.* Madrigals and similar songs are given a C because they teem with black notes. ¢ is faster (*celerior*); it is given to the whiter motets.

This explains why around 1550—apparently for the first time in the printer Scotto's collection of 1549—Italian madrigals were characterized on their title pages as *a note negre* or *a note bianche,* "with black notes" or "with white notes." Those with black notes (semiminims, *fusae,* and *semifusae*) have the plain C, and those with white notes, the crossed ¢.

It is evident that the situation has completely changed. The old *alla breve* in its capacity of duple proportion had once been prescribed for faster pieces with black notes because it transformed the undesirable *fusae* into semiminims, and semiminims into minims. In Praetorius' time, however, the proportions have practically gone and, with them, the possibility of replacing unwelcome note values with preferred ones. Now, pieces are signed as C or ₵, and nobody can tell the difference by the notes—*unnd kan man gleichwol an den Noten oder gantzem Gesange keinen unterscheid erkennen*. C and ₵ are shades of the same standard tempo—if they differ at all. Actually, there are often no differences: Giovanni Gabrieli (1557–1612)—so Praetorius relates— has dropped C entirely; Claudio Monteverdi (1567–1643) writes C when there are more black than white notes; and Ludovico Viadana (*ca.* 1564–1645) reserves C for instrumental and ₵ for vocal pieces. Thus music had arrived at a practical equalization of C and ₵.

But partially such equalization had existed as early as 1500. A good example—out of many—is the anonymous chanson *Fortuna desperata*,[32] which supplements the tenth volume of Josquin's *Complete Works* in three different versions—two under a crossed semicircle, and one, in a manuscript of the British Museum, under an uncrossed semicircle. But all have the same note values: the ₵ has no proportional meaning whatsoever.

We can now understand why Sebald Heyden said that musicians would often sing a minim as if it were a semibreve: the same piece could appear now under C, now under ₵, and yet preserve its tempo and character.

Nor are other statements about the uncertain relationship of the two signatures mysterious. Georg Rhaw alleged around 1518 that the C *tactus* was still the most widespread—*volgatissimus* —and in a similar spirit, Henricus Faber (*Ad musicam introductio,* 1550) thought he should champion the old C as the only "true and proper" measure. Actually, the masters around 1500 had already abandoned the C *tactus* almost entirely. In Smijers' complete edition of the works of Josquin des Prés only one among thirty-one motets has a C *instead* of a ₵, and among thirty-seven *chansons,* not one. Thus Josquin's contemporary, Ornithoparchus (1517), was certainly not right when he said that the ₵ *tactus* was "al-

---

[32] According to Dr. Catherine V. Brooks, the composer is Antoine Busnois.

lowed of onely by the unlearned," [33] the less so as Glareanus stated in 1547 that the *tactus alla semibreve* was "doubtless easier on the students."

After all this uncertainty, the relation of the two keys began around 1600 to change towards the modern conception. The French organist, Jean Titelouze (1563–1633), warns in his *Hymnes de l'église* of 1623: "The half-circle without a bar that I have placed in front means to slacken the time and meter by half, which is also a way to play the most difficult things." [34]

And yet, this was no permanent settlement.

The merely graphic distinction between C and ₵ lasted down to the times of Bach: the master does not allot a *proportio dupla* to ₵, except once in the Goldberg Variations, where he adds *alla breve*.[35] Indeed, every Beethoven player has faced the dilemma between obeying the time signature and obeying the master's unmistakable intention.[36]

THE DIMINUTION AND CONSISTENCY OF BINARY RHYTHM. A very strange detail of measuring appears much more clearly than elsewhere in Sebald Heyden's *Ars canendi* of 1540. In his complex arrays of full circles and semicircles, figures and dots, the full circle indicates three longs in a maxim; the semicircle, two longs in a maxim; the figure 3, three breves in a long; the figure 2, two breves in a long; and a dot, for a last tripartition. This would be quite normal. For it applies to ternary rhythm only. In *modus minor*, says Heyden, the signs are always *diminuta*: whenever the long is imperfect, the tempo must be *alla breve*. In other words, the figure 3 indicates triple time *alla semibreve;* but the figure 2 means duple time *alla breve.*

This is not the sole distinction of binary rhythm. Another one, already stated in Monk William's comprehensive survey, is the important fact that C marks not only binary breves, but binary

[33] All quotations from Ornithoparch's *Micrologus* follow John Dowland's belated translation, London, 1609.

[34] Quoted from Eugene Belt, *Three seventeenth century French organ composers,* New York University master's thesis, 1951, p. 47.

[35] Var. XXII, *Bach-Gesellschaft,* Vol. III, p. 293. Also Edward Dannreuther, *Musical ornamentation,* London (1893–1895), Part I, p. 193.

[36] Cf. also Hans Gál, *The right tempo,* in *Monthly Musical Record,* Vol. LIX, 1939, pp. 176 f.

organization throughout. Under the signature C, "a maxim equals eight semibreves, a long four, a breve two semibreves; and a semibreve, again, holds two minims," as in the following graph.

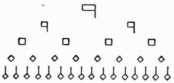

This square division under C must have been general. The German priest-musician Sebastian Virdung made in his *Musica getutscht* of 1511 the similar statement that a crossed semicircle indicated a rhythm *de tempore imperfecto,* in which every maxim held [two longs or] four breves, every long two breves, every breve two semibreves, every semibreve two minims, every minim two semiminims, every semiminim two *fusae,* and every 'fusele'—in his South German idiom—two *semifusae.*[37] In other words, the *alla breve* sign stood for a binary organization throughout from the maxim to the *semifusa.*

Virdung's statement is reiterated in another German source of the time, Martin Agricola's *Musica instrumentalis deudsch* of 1528, where the only time signatures mentioned—¢ and C 2— stands likewise for a binary organization throughout from top to bottom.[38]

Extending the imperfection of one single symbol up and downward to all other symbols was an important step away from the complex mixture of perfect and imperfect values towards the modern concept of a normally square organization.

THE ADVANCE OF DUPLE TIME. The growing trend towards square organization brings home the fact that, against the complexity of French proportions, the Italians, always fond of simple, static, symmetrical form, were winners in one battle in the eternal tug-of-war between the two elementary trends: they imposed the clean-cut duple time upon the music of all countries.

It is safe to assume that the Italians had written in duple time as

[37] Sebastian Virdung, *Musica getutscht,* Basel 1511, fol. H ij v° to H iij r°; facsimile edition by Robert Eitner, Berlin, Gesellschaft für Musikforschung, 1882.

[38] Martin Agricola, *Musica instrumentalis deudsch,* Wittemberg, 1528, fol. xxij r° and v°; reprint by Robert Eitner, Leipzig, Breitkopf & Härtel, 1896.

early as the Middle Ages. There is little Italian music of the thirteenth century extant, to be sure. But in the first half of the fourteenth century—judging from the works of Giovanni da Cascia, Jacopo da Bologna, Bartolino da Padua, and others—duple time was indeed more used in Italy than anywhere else. And as we have seen earlier, the Italians were leading when, not many years after 1300, theorists began to recognize and codify what they still called by the derogatory name of imperfection: the binary organization of longs, breves, semibreves, and minims.

But despite its disparaging name, imperfection was soon not only admitted to the rights of perfection: it grew stronger and stronger, gained victory eventually, and tolerated short triple-time episodes only for the sake of contrast in the middle or at the end of a piece. And far from being 'perfect,' these episodes were, on the contrary, incomplete diminutions of duple time, as the reader has seen in the section on proportion and will once more see in the section on ternary *tactus*.

A statistical survey of some music in the fifteenth and sixteenth centuries shows that pieces in the old perfect triple time make up

100% of the German *Locheimer Liederbuch* (1455–60) [39]
97% of Paumann's *Fundamentum organisandi* (1452) [40]
95% of Guillaume Dufay's works (d.1474) [41]
93% of a collection of English music before 1418 [42]
93% of John Dunstable's works (d.1453) [43]
79% of Burgundian works 1420–1467 [44]
79% of all the Trent codices (later 15th century) [45]
79% of Johannes Ockeghem's works (d.1495) [46]
46% of various French works copied *ca.* 1470 [47]

[39] *Locheimer Liederbuch,* ed. Konrad Ameln, Augsburg, 1925.
[40] Conrad Paumann, *Fundamentum organisandi,* in *Jahrbuch für musikalische Wissenschaft,* Leipzig, 1867, Vol. II, pp. 177–224.
[41] *Denkmäler der Tonkunst in Oesterreich,* Vol. VII, XI i, XIX i, XXVII i, XXXI, XL.
[42] *Music, cantilenas, songs, etc., from an early fifteenth century manuscript.* London, 1906.
[43] Cf. note 41.
[44] Jeanne Marix, *Les musiciens de la cour de Bourgogne au XVe siècle,* Paris, 1937.
[45] Cf. note 41.
[46] Ed. Dragan Plamenac, Vol. I, Leipzig, 1927, Vol. II, New York, 1947.
[47] [Eugénie Droz], *Trois chansonniers français du XVe siècle,* Paris, 1927.

44% of the *Schedelsche Liederbuch* (1461–1467) [48]
37% of the *Copenhagen Chansonnier* (1470–1480) [49]
37% of Spanish works around 1500 [50]
27% of the *Glogauer Liederbuch* (*ca.* 1480) [51]
12% of Senfl's works (1534) [52]
7% of the *Odhecaton* (1501) [53]
6% of Italian madrigals all through the 16th century [54]
5% of Isaac's works (d. 1517)
4% of French motets 1534/35 [55]
3% of Finck's works (d. 1527)
2% of Willaert's motets [56]
Less than 1% of
    Obrecht's works (d. 1505)
    Josquin's works (d. 1521)
    Italian organ music *ca.* 1520
    Palestrina's works (d. 1594)
    Lasso's works (the present author found only three ternary pieces among a total of 579 examined)

This survey is impressive but nevertheless misleading. The progress of binary rhythm under the pressure of Renaissance ideals is an incontestable fact. But another, just as important, fact is—as the following chapter will show in detail—that the binary signature does basically reflect a binary *tactus* but not necessarily a binary rhythm, since the practice of the time allowed for beating any ternary rhythm in an even two-time up and down.

TERNARY TACTUS. Besides the three binary *tactus* forms—*alla breve, alla semibreve, alla minima*—the sixteenth and seventeenth centuries had two ternary *tactus*, which, confusingly enough, ap-

[48] *Das Schedelsche Liederbuch*, ed. A. Rosenberg, Kassel [1933].
[49] Knud Jeppesen, *Der Kopenhagener Chansonnier*, Kopenhagen-Leipzig, 1927.
[50] Higino Anglés, *La música en la corte de los reyes católicos*, Barcelona, 1941–47.
[51] *Das Glogauer Liederbuch*, ed. Ringmann, Kassel, 1927.
[52] Ludwig Senfl, *Deutsche Lieder*, Vol. II, in *Das Erbe deutscher Musik*, Kassel, 1940.
[53] *Harmonice musices odhecaton*, ed. Helen Hewitt, Cambridge (Mass.), 1946.
[54] Alfred Einstein, *The Italian madrigal*, Vol. III, Princeton, 1949.
[55] *Treize livres de motets*, ed. A. Smijers, Paris [1934–1936].
[56] Adriaen Willaert, *Sämtliche Werke*, ed. Hermann Zenck, Vol. I, in *Publikationen älterer Musik*, Vol. IX, Leipzig, 1937.

pear under three names—*triplus, sesquialter, and proportionatus*
—and not even consistently.

The *triplus* was nothing but the old *proportio tripla:* under its
signature, one beat of the hand, instead of commanding one single
minim, now regulated three minims; the tempo became three
times as fast.

The *sesquialter* was only one and a half times as fast as standard:
three minims were given the duration of two standard minims.
In other words, triplets appeared where there had been duplets.

The name *proportionatus,* being noncommittal as to the amount
of proportion, was indiscriminately given to both the *triplus* and
the *sesquialter.* To make things worse, Michael Praetorius [57] called
tactus proportionatus any *multiplex* proportion, such as the *dupla,*
the *subdupla,* and the *quadrupla.*

Ordinarily, the *triplus* was indicated by a figure 3 or by 3 over 1
on the staff; and the *sesquialter,* by 3 over 2.

These unwonted signatures have been a pitfall for many an
uninformed modern editor of Renaissance and Baroque music.
Mistaking 3 over 1, and 3, for a three-one time, they have transcribed the briskest episodes in sixteenth- and seventeenth-century
music in an incredibly sleepy tempo three times as slow as common
time and up to nine times as slow as they should be.

Nor does 3 over 2 mean three half notes in a measure, but rather
triplets where there had been duplets before.

While the actual *triplus* did not pose any problem to the beating
hand, the *sesquialter* was curiously at odds with the rigidly duple
quality of *tactus* beating. When the hand went down on the first
and up on the second semibreve, it had to go down again on the
third semibreve. To be sure, this was not as bad as it would be
today where the downbeat suggests stress. Still, it was a confusing
discrepancy between the beaten and the musical measure, between
gesture and meaning.

But there was also another practice, similar to that of the Greeks
and closer to our modern concept: singing two thirds of the measure on the first beat and the last one on the (obviously shortened)
second beat. Agricola shows it in a graph,[58] and Vincentio Lusitano

---

[57] Michael Praetorius, *Syntagma musicum,* Vol. III, Wolffenbüttel, 1619, p. 49.
[58] Martin Agricola, *Musica figuralis deudsch,* Wittenberg, 1532, Ch. VI.

says unmistakably in the chapter *Della battuta* of his *Introduttione:* "*In tripla e sesquialtera . . . le due* [figure] *si mettranno* ['will be put'] *nella prima testa* ['beat'], *& una nella seconda.*"[59] Orazio Tigrini, apparently with Lusitano's booklet on his writing desk, makes a quite similar statement.[60] And so does Father Mersenne.[61]

Indeed, Michel L'Affillard,[62] whose editions extend from the end of the seventeenth century to late in the eighteenth, still says: "The minuet has three very light beats or else two unequal beats."

The practice is most clearly expressed by Simpson:[63] "In these two sorts of Tripla, we count or imagine these two words [*One, Two*] with the Hand *down*, and this word [Three] with it *up*." Not only do we learn that at least the English used the 1½ beat, but—more important—that the "two sorts of Tripla" were of equal speed: "the more *Common Tripla*" with three minims to a measure, and another one, 'sometimes,' with three semibreves to a measure. The name *sesquialtera* has disappeared, and also the original concept of *tripla* as triple proportion. There is little doubt that Simpson's "common *tripla*" was the old *sesquialtera* in standard tempo, and his other *tripla* a *sesquialtera* in *alla breve*.

In one of the confusing inconsistencies of the time, *proportio tripla* was actually only a *sesquialtera* whenever the signature 3 appeared in all the voice parts. Martin Agricola[64] says expressly that the *sesquialtera* is used "in *proportione tripla / hemiola /* when all the voice parts have it / and thus they always sing a semibreve instead of a minim." *Hemiola*—not to be confused with the name for an exchange of 3/4 and 6/8—was a frequent misnomer for *sesquialtera*.

An important example easily accessible in Otto Kade's supplement volume to the music history of Ambros[65] is the motet *Stabat mater dolorosa* by Josquin des Prés. In measure 71, the time signa-

[59] Vincentio Lusitano, *Introduttione facilissima*, Venezia, 1558, fol. 9v.

[60] Orazio Tigrini, *Il compendio*, Venezia, 1588 (1602), p. 123.

[61] Marin Mersenne, *L'harmonie universelle*, Paris, 1636.

[62] Michel L'Affillard, *Principes très-faciles pour bien apprendre la musique*, Paris, 7th edition, p. 100.

[63] Christopher Simpson, *The principles of practical musick*, London, 1665, p. 34.

[64] Martin Agricola, *op. cit.*

[65] August Wilhelm Ambros, *Geschichte der Musik*, 3rd edition, Leipzig, 1889, Vol. V (ed. Otto Kade), p. 76. Recorded in *L'Anthologie Sonore*, No. 73.

Ex. 52. Josquin des Prés, Motet *Stabat mater dolorosa*

ture changes to the figure 3 in two of the voice parts. But this does not and cannot mean a *tripla*. For the three semibreves in these voices coincide with one of the weighty breves in the *cantus firmus*, while there had been only two per breve in the section before the signature 3. Consequently, 3 indicates the ratio 3:2, not 3:1—*sesquialtera*, not *tripla*.

The figure 3, however, denoted not only *tripla* and *sesquialtera*, but at times the *hemiola* as well, that is, a measure of 6/8 instead of 3/4. An outstanding case is the well-known *ritornello* of *Vi recorda* in the second act of Monteverdi's drama *Orfeo* (1607). The rhythmic interpretation of this beautiful piece has not been easy since the figure 3's are often misplaced or left out altogether (just as the printers of the time were careless with sharps and flats and naturals). The difficulties show in the often tragicomical failure of all the Monteverdi editors from Robert Eitner on, until Peter Epstein gave the only correct and convincing transcription as a hemiolic alternation from bar to bar, that is, as a change between three quarters and six eighths.[66]

Ex. 53. Monteverdi, opera, *Orfeo*

PROPORTZ—DOUBLE EMPLOI—VARIATION SUITE. Long, long before Monteverdi, the *tactus proportionatus* together with its scholarly names had glided into the least scholarly field of practical music: the dance. The basic form of all social dancing, both in the Middle Ages and the Renaissance, was a striding couple dance, to be followed without interruption by a brisker treading

[66] Peter Epstein, *Zur Rhythmisierung eines Ritornells von Monteverdi*, in *Archiv für Musikwissenschaft*, Vol. VIII, 1926, pp. 416–419.

and hopping dance.[67] While the Italians and the French had different names for the two, such as *bassadanza* and *saltarello*, or *pavane* and *gaillarde*, the Germans spoke of *Vortanz* and *Nachtanz* or, oftener of *Tanz* and *Proportz*. They took the first one of each such pair in a dignified standard tempo, and the second one in *proportione sesquialtera*, that is, in triplets where there had been duplets before.

In the seventeenth century, the name *Proportz* was as a rule replaced by the name of the other *proportionatus:* the *tripla*. The preceding section has shown that the names and their notational symbols were freely exchanged even outside the dance.

In an attempt at stylistic unification, the *Proportz or Nachtanz* often—though by no means always—shared its melodic material with the *Vortanz*, from which it necessarily differed in its ternary rhythm. Such 'amphirhythmical' melodies, as one might call them, or *à double emploi*, as the French said, first appeared in German prints of the sixteenth century,[68] but had almost certainly been improvised a long time before.

Double emploi of dance melodies extended to three movements —*pavana, saltarello, piva*, or *passamezzo, gagliarda, padovana*— in a number of sixteenth-century collections, especially in the lute tablatures of Dalza (1508) and Rotta (1546) and, during the second half of the century, in those of Gorzani (1463), Waisselius (1573), and Hadrianus (Adriaenssen, 1584).[69]

The amphirhythmic principle reached a climax later on in the seventeenth century when the concept of unification had taken possession of the new suite of four or more contrasting dances to be played one after another in sequence. These so-called variation suites consisted in a number of movements, like *pavane, gaillarde, courante, allemande*, or *allemande, courante, sarabande, gigue*, whose melodic material was practically the same, but appeared bent and distorted to fit the characteristic tempi and rhythms of the individual dance forms, now in ¢, now in 3, now in 6/4. The

[67] Curt Sachs, *World history of the dance*, New York, 1937, pp. 324 and later.
[68] Cf. Hugo Riemann, *Tänze des 16. Jahrhunderts à double emploi*, in *Die Musik*, Vol. VI, 1906, No. 3; Wilhelm Merian, *Der Tanz in den deutschen Tabulaturbüchern*, Leipzig, 1927, p. 77.
[69] Cf. Tobias Norlind, *Zur Geschichte der Suite*, in *Sammelbände der Internationalen Musikgesellschaft*, Vol. VII, 1905/06, pp. 174–182.

melody as such was shapeless and meaningless; it accepted the rule of rhythm and made it autonomous.

This final, consistent suite, inaugurated in the *Neue Paduan* by the Austrian Paul Peurl (1611), was brought to a peak in Hermann Schein's *Banchetto musicale* of 1617, and continued down to Johann Neubauer's *Neue Pavanen, Galliarden, Balletten,* etc., of 1649. It declined in the second half of the century with the keyboard suites of Johann Jacob Froberger.

The mingling of various tempi within a piece or set of pieces was, after all, the reason for the existence of the proportions.

✿ ✿ ✿ ✿ ✿ ✿ ✿ ✿ ✿ ✿ ✿ ✿ ✿

CHAPTER 11

The Renaissance: Rhythmical Styles

THE EARLY RENAISSANCE. The momentous first generation of foreigners from Burgundy in the North that filled the courtly chapels of Italy between 1425 and 1460 did not find much native music of rank to guide their Gothic taste and technique. What they found were just the over-all ideals of the Italian Renaissance which, materializing first in architecture, applied inevitably to music as well as to the other arts: simple, sober clarity versus complex involution and dimness; free, creative imagination versus the engineering spirit and delight in technical feats; and satisfaction to the eyes and the ears against satisfaction to reason and reckoning.

The Burgundians in Italy were not yet able to yield to the new environment wholeheartedly. With one foot in the Gothic North and one in the anti-Gothic South, they indulged now in bizarre, belated isorhythmic structures, now, on the contrary, in rhythms of bodily inspiration, in well-shaped, sensuous melodies, and in a smiling, warm serenity.

In the sensory atmosphere of Italy, the Burgundian masters knew those sheer, unadulterated chords that the restive, hasty Gothic melody had never known. Again and again the Italians poured forth their ecstasy in timeless chains of fermatas at the beginning or the end of a piece. Cristoforo da Feltre's solemn, long-drawn-out fermatas on *Patrem omnipotentem* in his *Sanctus* [1] is a striking example from the early years of the fifteenth century.

[1] Printed in Johannes Wolf, *Geschichte der Mensuralnotation,* Leipzig, 1904, No. 71.

Ex. 54. Cristoforo da Feltre, Sanctus

Probably less than a hundred years later, an anonymous lauda—
Ave panis angelorum—had seventeen bars of consecutive fermatas
in some thirty measures altogether.[2] The beatific twenty-two quasi-
fermata bars at the end of Guillaume Dufay's motet *Alma Redemp-
toris Mater* [3] are Italian-born.

Nowhere could one feel more clearly that strict rhythm, as
Karl Bücher has said, is a driving force from without, not from
music proper. Nowhere does one better see that music can exist
without a restless rush from beat to beat. Nowhere could one
realize more strongly that measured rhythm can and does interfere—as much as anxious glances at a watch would do—with aban-
doning oneself to blissful devotion and to the delight of motionless
and undiluted sound.

Modern musicians know this pulseless quiescence from the tonic-
dominant fermatas in the third act of Wagner's *Parsifal* (full score
No. 254) when the pilgrimage through darkness has reached its
end and redemption dawns.

Ex. 55. Wagner, *Parsifal*

All these time-arresting fermatas recall to the author's mind the
words of a classical philologist, Thomas D. Goodell:

"Obviously tune in itself has no content of alien nature, that
limits in any way the duration of the single note; an essential qual-

---

[2] Knud Jeppesen, *Die mehrstimmige italienische Laude*, Leipzig-Copenhagen,
1935, p. 15.
[3] *Denkmäler der Tonkunst in Oesterreich*, XXVII, i (= Vol. 53); recorded in
L'Anthologie Sonore No. 34.

ity of purely musical sound is that it be prolongable at pleasure, within the capacity of the instrument." [4]

FLAMBOYANT POLYRHYTHM. After the simplification of the Early Renaissance, the last third of the fifteenth century—inside and out of Italy—relapsed into a motley restlessness which here and there assumed the traits of a new, belated Flamboyant (or 'Perpendicular'). "In architecture the Flamboyant of the French came to a last peak with the florid open work of the Palace of Justice in Rouen (1493–1499). Of Germany, too, Wilhelm Pinder could say that the last part of the fifteenth century was more Gothic than the beginning had been." [5] Art delighted in complication rather than in simplicity, in confusion rather than in clarity, in restlessness rather than in serenity or quiet.

This was true of music as it was of the visual arts. Dividing, articulating cadences were concealed; notes at the far end of a measure often reached over to the following bar; voice parts re-entered on the 'weak' beats; triplet groups intruded on common, and duplets, on ternary time; duple and triple time coincided in the polyphonic web. In short, the rhythmic organization of the earlier age, too static and sober, yielded to an ever moving, often confusing texture.

The simplest and most frequent case was the old hemiola, such as we find it in Ockeghem's *Missa cuiusvis toni:* though all four parts are marked with the symbol for perfect time, there is a steady counteraction of *tempus perfectum cum prolatione minori* and *tempus imperfectum cum prolationi maiori* or, to put it in easier modern terms, of 3/4 and 6/8.

Often, as in Ockeghem's *Missa sine nomine*,[6] the individual voice parts lapse from 3/4 to 6/8 almost measure by measure with so much ease that, there too, the composer did not see any reason for giving up the symbol for 'perfect' time.

A more exciting example of polyrhythm is Ockeghem's *Missa prolationum*, which indicates in its very title the structural, typically Gothic interests of its composer.[7] The first of its four voice

[4] Thomas D. Goodell, *Chapters on Greek metric,* New York and London, 1901, p. 69.

[5] Curt Sachs, *The commonwealth of art,* New York, W. W. Norton, 1946, p. 109.

[6] The two Masses in the first volume of Ockeghem's *Complete works,* ed. Dragan Plamenac.

[7] *Ibid.*

parts has common time with imperfect *tempus* and minor prolation—2/4 in modern terms; the second, under the signature of a full circle with 3 over 1 written below, has perfect *tempus* and minor prolation—3/4 in modern terms; the third, under the unusual signature of 6 over 2 and 3 over 1 under a dotted semicircle, is imperfect in its *tempus* and major in its prolation—6/8 in modern terms (but with an occasional hemiolic shift to 3/4); and the fourth voice, introduced with the fraction 9 over 2 under a dotted full circle, proceeds in *perfect tempus* and major prolation—modern 9/8. Since the figures 4, 6, and 9 meet for the first time in the product 36, the four voice parts reach a common bar line (speaking in modern concepts) only after nine *tempora* of the first voice, when the second and third parts have completed six *tempora,* and the fourth voice merely four.

The *Agnus Dei* in the *Missa L'Homme armé* of Josquin des Prés (*ca.* 1450–1521) is written for three voice parts. But each of them avails itself of the same musical text notated on one single staff. Three different time signatures at the head of this staff give the voices their individual cues as to reading and performing the text each in its own way. They are ₵3, C, and ₵. This means that the middle voice proceeds in standard tempo (C), which equals the semibreve to a modern half note; the lower voice, in ₵, is twice as fast, its semibreve equaling a quarter note only; and the upper voice, in ₵3, follows a *sesquialtera* tempo, with each three of its semibreves forming triplets against the duplets of the lower voice.[8]

The most impressive array of time signatures—no less than twenty-seven—can be found in Isaac's motet *Conceptio Mariae Virginis:* [9]

Discantus:	⊙	Ȼ	O	O 2	C	C 2	$\frac{3}{1}$
Altus:	O 2	C	₵	$\frac{3}{1}$	₵ 2	$\frac{4}{1}$	
Tenor:	Ȼ	O	O 2	C	₵	3	$\frac{2}{1}$
Bassus:	O	O 2	C 2	$\frac{3}{1}$	₵	Ɔ	$\frac{4}{1}$

[8] Transcription in Davison-Apel's *Anthology,* Vol. I, No. 89, p. 92.
[9] Sebald Heyden, *De arte canendi,* Nuremberg, 1540, pp. 114/115.

Even as late a man as the Austrian, Jacobus Handl or Gallus (d. 1591), wrote a four-part motet, *Deus meus,* with twelve different proportional symbols.[10]

Another form of proportional sophistication within the framework of the "canonic artifices" of the Netherlanders was what we might call progressive diminution. In each section of his Mass *Si dedero,* Jacob Obrecht gives to the tenor nothing but a short melodic stretch that the singer is expected to repeat in diminution after an interim of rests and, after a second interim, in another diminution twice as fast. His written part contains just this one passage; but the cluster of three or four time signatures amassed in front of the passage gives the singer his cue. Thus the group

$$\mathsf{C} \quad \mathsf{C} \quad \mathsf{\phi}$$

would indicate that the passage occurs three times—in *subdupla* or augmentation, standard, and *dupla* or diminution, or 4:2:1; and the group

$$\mathsf{O} \quad \mathsf{C} \quad \mathsf{\phi}$$

would require perfect *tempus,* imperfect *tempus,* and *dupla,* or 3:2:1.

A similar example is the *Credo in* Brumel's Mass *Ut re mi fa sol,* which Petrucci printed in 1503.[11]

Jacob Obrecht went even further in the *Credo* of his Mass *Je ne demande:* the time signature in the section *Et in spiritum sanctum* has no less than five different symbols,

$$\mathsf{O} \quad \mathsf{C} \quad \mathsf{O} \quad \mathsf{C} \quad \mathsf{\phi}$$

inviting the tenor to perform (1) *in tempore perfecto,* (2) *in tempore imperfecto,* (3) again *in tempore perfecto,* (4) once more *in tempore imperfecto,* (5) *in proportione dupla.* This amounts to 3:2:3:2:1.

Much later—the printing date is 1570—Palestrina resumed this almost forgotten Gothicism in a Mass on *L'homme armé:* the

---

[10] Printed in Michael Praetorius, *Syntagma musicum,* Vol. III, Wolffenbüttel, 1619, pp. 57–69; modern reprint by Bernoulli, pp. 214–226, 230–235.

[11] Communication by Mr. Lloyd Biggle, Ann Arbor, August, 1950.

soprano of the *Pleni sunt coeli* in the *Sanctus* appears in a belated progressive diminution under the three symbols

$$\mathbb{C} \quad C \quad \mathbb{¢}$$

or 4:2:1.

Progressive diminution had had some early forerunners in the fourteenth century. In *Douce playsence*,[12] a French motet written by Philippe de Vitry (1291–1361) as a young man, the first section of the isorhythmic tenor appeared four times in perfect longs and four more times in perfect breves.

THE HIGH RENAISSANCE. When Petrucci was printing Brumel's Mass, taste had once more essentially changed. The motley rhythms, polyrhythms, and structural 'artifices' of the Gothic ages were forsaken. Looking back, Zarlino sneers at "the speculations put forward by certain idle theorists of that day," who "treat of nothing but circles and semicircles, with and without points, whole or divided not only once but two and three times, and in them one sees so many points, pauses, colors, ciphers, signs, numbers against numbers, and other strange things that they sometimes appear to be the books of a bewildered merchant." [13]

The new ideal, known as the High Renaissance, was an almost puristic classicism.

This reversal of 1500—or, more exactly, of 1498—affected the visual arts: Leonardo da Vinci, Bramante, Raphael, and the lesser masters turned to noble simplicity, to static symmetry, to dignified serenity.[14]

Heinrich Wölfflin, the late historian of art, seems to have been the first to draw attention to the slowness with which the people move in paintings of the early sixteenth century. Compared with the flurry of the later fifteenth, figures on the canvases of Fra Bartolommeo, Raphael, or Pontormo stride and act in *andante maestoso*.[15]

[12] Printed in Heinrich Besseler, *Studien zur Musik des Mittelalters*, in *Archiv für Musikwissenschaft*, Vol. VII, 1925, pp. 249 ff.

[13] Gioseffe Zarlino, *Istituzioni armoniche*, Venice, 1558, liber III, § 71, quoted from O. Strunk, *Source Readings in Music History*, New York, W. W. Norton, 1950, p. 251.

[14] Cf. Curt Sachs, *The commonwealth of art*, New York, 1946, pp. 112–119.

[15] Heinrich Wölfflin, *Die klassische Kunst*, München, first edition 1899.

The musical relics of the time do not allow for any such sweeping statement. But it seems permissible to mention that the leading dance in the first third of the century, the *pavane*, "was intended to express, not charm and lightness, but ceremonial dignity. In its step and rhythm princes walked. The piper played a *pavane* when a bride of good family proceeded to the church, or when priests, or masters and members of important corporations, were to be escorted in dignified procession." [16] There are many pavans preserved—most beautiful among them those by the Spaniard Luis Milán of 1536. As far as it is at all possible to gauge the 'correct' time of such old pieces, it seems that these pavans make sense only at a tempo of about 80 M.M. without losing their dignity and without sinking below the limit of well-connected steps.

It is characteristic that exactly at the end of the dignified High Renaissance the pavan passed into disuse. In 1536—the year of Milán's *pavanas*—comes the earliest mention of its successor, the *passamezzo*, a lighter and somewhat more lively *pavane* of Italian origin to be danced by younger people. The High Renaissance was dead; another generation had taken over and restored a faster tempo.

The number of gayer dances increased tremendously. Never were so many lively, excited dances performed. The galliard was done tumultuously and stormily; Shakespeare, in *Henry V*, called the *courante* 'swift'; the *danse des Canaries* was possible only for people with much practice and very agile feet; the *bergamasca* and, at that time, the *sarabande*, were quick, the *volta* impetuous, the *branle de Montirandé* very rapid, the *branle de Bourgoigne* light and quick, and the *branle du Haut Barrois*, according to Arbeau, "good to dance in winter to make oneself warm."

The reversal of 1500 affected rhythm with equal strength. Those of the northern composers in (and partly outside) Italy who lived to see the sixteenth century, like the Dutchman Obrecht and the Flemings Isaac and Josquin des Prés, chimed in with the visual arts and led the way to the classicistic ideals of clarity and symmetry in one of the most impressive apostasies in the history of music.

[16] Curt Sachs, *World history of the dance*, New York, W. W. Norton, 1937, p. 356.

The models of calmness, unaffected severity, unsophisticated simpleness that Italy held in readiness to show the invited Flemings the goal required were the religious *laude* with which the

Ex. 56. *Vengo a te, Madre Maria,* Lauda

guilds and fraternities worshiped their patron saints and the courtly secular *frottole* out of which the later madrigal developed.

Ex. 57. Fogliano, frottola, *Tua volsi essere*

Both forms proceeded, wherever possible, in even coincident beats within the frame of a binary *tactus.*

Outside the *laude* and *frottole,* the coincidence of *tactus* and rhythm shows particularly well in French *chansons* and the earlier Italian madrigals. Two examples, one early, one later, are the chanson *Autant en emporte le vent* by Pierre de la Rue (d. 1518),

Ex. 58. Pierre de la Rue, chanson, *Autant en emporte le vent*

and, on the very soil of Italy in a typically Italian form, Jacob Arcadelt's famous madrigal *Il bianco e dolce cigno* (1539):

Ex. 59. Arcadelt, madrigal, *Il bianco e dolce cigno,* beginning

THE PITFALLS OF TIME SIGNATURES. Alas, the coincidence of *tactus* and rhythm must not be taken for granted. Neither

is the time signature in itself an indication of the actual rhythm since it is a graphic symbol of the *tactus* and of nothing else.

To men of our time, a 4/4 signature denotes a neat organization in groups of two times two quarter notes with perceptible or at least suggested accents, a stronger one on the first, and a weaker one on the third quarter. But to men of the sixteenth century, the 4/4 or 2/4 did nothing but reflect the steady up-and-down of the *tactus*-beating hand without the slightest rhythmic or accentual implication. And since even triple time was as a rule regulated by the same steady up-and-down or down-and-up, with the first, accented quarter falling now on a downbeat, now on an upbeat. any outright ternary rhythm could hide under the guise of C or ₵.

How meaningless the *tactus* was from a musical viewpoint is implicit in a curious passage to be found in the introduction to a collection of French dances, published in 1612 under the title *Terpsichore* by Michael Praetorius.[17] The passage admits us to the workshop of a conductor around 1600 under the guidance of one of the great conductors of the time. The master discusses at some length what to do with a certain round dance, the *bransle gay.* Should it be beaten in *tripla,* in *sesquialtera,* or *alla breve?* In the first case, it would be ternary and would start on a downbeat; in the second case, it would also be ternary but would start on an upbeat; in the third case, on the contrary, it would be binary. To us, the result, in each of the three cases, means a complete change of rhythm as our ears and eyes perceive it. We see a rhythmic variation and transformation where the composer and conductor of 1600 saw a mere variety in *tactus* beating and notating. The whole question whether it might be more advantageous and to the point to count one, or three, or two, and to make or not to make an upbeat is thinkable only where the *tactus* was completely independent of rhythm and accent.

Let us underscore this fact: the *tactus* was wholly unconcerned with the actual rhythm, with grouping or accent. It just maintained the even pulsation of units, and nothing else. As Father Mersenne said later, in the seventeenth century: "Time beating is nothing but lowering and lifting the hand to indicate the duration of every note"—the duration, not its function or intensity.

[17] Michael Praetorius, *Gesamtausgabe,* Vol. XV, Wolffenbüttel, 1929, p. xiii.

As a consequence, the time signature, reflecting the *tactus,* does not, and cannot, reflect the rhythm of a piece.

The simplest case of clash of rhythm and time signature is ternary rhythm under the disguise of binary notation. As the preceding chapter has shown, the usual procedure in the face of ternary rhythm was beating, so to speak, in a *hemiola* way: two three-four bars were beaten as if they were three two-four bars, although this meant for the quarters of the second measure a downbeat where there had been an upbeat in the first measure:

1 2 3   1 2 3
u d u   d u d

This did not deceive the contemporaries, because they found in the conductor's beat as little rhythmic suggestion as we find in the clicks of a metronome. But it misleads our modern editors and performers who take their cues from bar lines and signatures.

A convincing example is Cipriano de Rore's madrigal *Quando lieta sperai,* which, though written *in alla breve,* is an unmistakable 3/4 piece and appears completely distorted in Schering's transliteration:

Ex. 60 / 61. Cipriano de Rore, madrigal, *Quando lieta sperai*

Analysis is much harder where a voice part is not simply ternary under a binary signature, but proceeds—and often in the same measure—now in binary, now in ternary groups, be it because a uniform *tactus* organization is not intended or for the sake of a more adequate rendition of the text.

The funeral motet *Ecce quomodo moritur justus* by the Austrian, Jacob Handl or Gallus (1550–1591), to quote one famous example, would run in even four-four measures if the time signature were what we think it to be.

All modern transcriptions follow suit.

The actual rhythm of this beautiful motet is entirely different.

Far from complying with the seeming, artificial evenness, **it** smoothly takes its rule from the words; and not only from their natural accent and meter, but also from their importance within the text. *Ecce,* 'behold,' the broad gesture inviting attention, stands out in square, sustained notes; *quomodo,* 'how,' being just an adverb of manner, forms a normal 3/4 dactyl; *moritur,* 'dies,' as the essential theme of the poem, proceeds in a dactyl twice as wide (3/2); and *justus,* 'a righteous man,' as the essential subject, concludes the line in the square, sustained notes of *Ecce.*

Ex. 62. Handl (Gallus), motet, *Ecce quomodo moritur justus*

It seems to be characteristic of the time, and particularly of German masters down to Schütz, to underscore the heading of a composition in what amounts to musical boldface capitals. Heinrich Schütz wrote his spiritual concerto for two tenors, *Die Furcht des Herren* ("The Fear of the Lord"), under the general signature

Ex. 63. Schütz, spiritual concerto, *Die Furcht des Herren*

C, which only at times yields to the *tripla* 3 over 1. But on closer analysis, the four initial words, as they appear at the beginning and later in the middle of the piece as well, stand out in a broadening 3/2 that the *tactus* signature 4/4 ignores.

German rhythm was at that time particularly independent of any square-cut norm. The *Lieder* often change from bar to bar, now counting 4/4, now 6/8, 3/4, and 6/4.[18] In one short and simple lied, *Bist du der Hensel Schütze,*[19] the Fleming, Mattheus Le Maistre (d. 1577) could pass from 4/2, to 3/2, 6/4, 3/2, 6/4 in the first five measures. This is truly Stravinskian.

[18] Hundreds of examples may be found in Franz M. Böhme, *Altdeutsches Liederbuch,* Leipzig, 1877, *e.g.* pp. 1, 38, 67, 73, 77.
[19] Reprinted in Arnold Schering, *Geschichte der Musik in Beispielen,* Leipzig, 1931.

Ex. 64. Le Maistre, lied, *Bist du der Hensel*

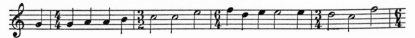

The free combination of binary and ternary groups within the same measure is actually an almost general characteristic of the polyphonic style in the Renaissance—of Masses and motets, madrigals, *teutsche liedlein*,[20] and keyboard forms.

Nowhere is this combination more striking and evident than in the older forms of Lutheran chorales. Nowhere has it been more misunderstood. The rhythmical form in which they appear in the earliest hymn books has seemed incomprehensible to the modern mind. How could a simple-minded congregation have been able to sing a melody quite awkwardly patched together of long and a few shorter notes which made no sense from the viewpoint of symmetrical accents? Modern hymnologists, at a loss to understand these notations, put the cart before the horse and reluctantly concluded that the clumsy melodies must simply have been taken from previous polyphonic settings—*tenores* or theme-holding voices cut off from their fellow parts, not homophonic melodies in their own right. One of the strongest arguments in favor of this assumption was that often the musical notation began with a rest, which, they said, could have a meaning only within a voice of part music.[21]

The present author cannot quite agree with this interpretation. Certainly, we today would not write initial rests, because, with our bar lines, we make unmistakably clear whether the first note is an upbeat or a downbeat. Luther's contemporaries were in a different position. They did not use bar lines in vocal music, nor were they acquainted with upbeats in sacred melodies. The only possible symbol at hand was to replace the missing downbeat of the first *tactus* by a rest, thus allotting the initial note to the second beat. We know these downbeat rests from dance prints of the time, say, the *Neuf basses danses* that Pierre Attaingnant in Paris pub-

[20] Cf. also Robert Geutebrück, *Ueber Form und Rhythmus des älteren deutschen Volksgesanges*, in *Archiv für Musikwissenschaft*, Vol. VII, 1925, p. 354.

[21] Friedrich Blume, *Evangelische Kirchenmusik*, in Ernst Bücken, *Handbuch der Musikwissenschaft*, p. 38.

lished in 1530, or his *Basse danse, Tourdion,* etc., of 1547.[22] Any upbeat is marked by a preceding rest.

Ex. 65. Attaingnant, *Basse danse*

This function of the rest is, however, not the only answer to the question of the queer chorale rhythms.

As a short cut, the reader may look up the nine versions of *Ein' feste burg ist unser Gott* from 1569 to 1610 in Friedrich Blume's work on Protestant church music[23] and add three more versions from the seventeenth century (by Schütz, Schein, Scheidt) in Manfred Bukofzer's Baroque book.[24] In all of them the second measure, on the words *Burg ist unser,* appears quite oddly as

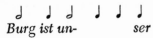

and the same is true of *Wehr und Waf-* in the fourth measure.

It would not be hard to come across a hundred similar examples. Going at random through an early volume of *Geystliche Lieder,* printed in Leipzig under Luther's supervision in 1545, we would find in the chorale *Mit Fried und Freud ich fahr dahin* the characteristic group

Ex. 66. Geistliches Lied, *Mit Fried und Freud fahr ich dahin*

or, in Psalm 130,

Ex. 67. Geistliches Lied, Psalm 140

and numberless similar passages.

---

[22] Not in Eitner's *Bibliographie der Musik-Sammelwerke.* This author has recorded the *basse danse* as No. 6 of his *Anthologie Sonore,* 1934.

[23] Friedrich Blume, *Evangelische Kirchenmusik, loc. cit.,* pp. 66 f., 76.

[24] Manfred Bukofzer, *Music in the Baroque era,* New York, 1947, p. 82.

Late and beautiful samples of this supple, versatile rhythm are the settings of the chorales *Wenn mein Stündlein vorhanden ist* [25] and of *Vater unser im Himmelreich* [26] by Hans Leo Hassler (1564–1612):

Ex. 68. Hassler, Chorale, *Wenn mein Stündlein vorhanden ist*

Ex. 69. Hassler, Chorale, *Vater unser im Himmelreich*

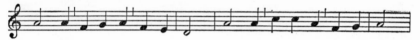

Seen from the limited viewpoint of the nineteenth century, these 'irregular' rhythms are quite unintelligible. You cannot subdivide them into either two or three or four equal parts. Small wonder that historians and church musicians have dismissed them with an embarrassed shake of the head as completely disagreeing with the rules of even accents.

Still, the allegedly 'irregular' rhythms become convincing and quite natural when interpreted in terms of eastern music or of the Greek *dochmiac* as the lawful grouping of eight units in 3 + 3 + 2.

Very slowly did the modern concept of equal half notes replace 'irregular' chorale meters, and not before the second half of the seventeenth century was the process completed. But these ultimate equal half notes were not unprecedented. Polyphonic settings of chorales had often evened out the melody of the *cantus firmus* as early as Luther's time.

Lutheran chorales are the most conspicuous, but by no means the only, examples of additive rhythms. Similar patterns had occurred in the fourteenth century; and in a treatise of the mid-fifteenth, *De musica mensurabilis,* written by Brother Theodoric de Campo, we read how the *veteres* or 'old' musicians parceled out the shortest notes squeezed in between the longs and breves: if

---

[25] Recorded in the author's *Anthologie Sonore,* No. 72.
[26] Hans Leo Hassler, *Kirchengesäng,* 1608, repr. Augsburg, 1927, No. 25.

there are eight, he says, they are organized in *tres et tres et due* [*minime*].[27]

The pattern is rather frequent in polyphonic music around 1500. Witness the works of Ockeghem, Isaac, Josquin, and Hayne, of

Ex. 70. Ockeghem, Mass *mi-mi*, Credo

Ex. 71. Isaac, lied, *Zwischen Berg und tiefem Tal*

Ex. 72. Josquin des Prés, Mass, *Pangue lingua*, Incarnatus

ex Ma - ri - a ver - gi - ne

Ex. 73. Hayne, *À l'audience*

Ex. 74. Forster, *Teutsches Liedlein*

Ex. 75. Finck, lied, *Ach herzigs Herz*

Ex. 76. Adam von Fulda, *In principio erat*

[27] Coussemaker, *Scriptores de musica medii aevi*, Vol. III, p. 155.

Ex. 77. Senfl, *Ave rosa sine spinis*

Ex. 78. Goudimel, Psalm 42, *Ainsi qu'on oit le cerf bruire*

Forster, Finck, Adam von Fulda, and Ludwig Senfl. The most fascinating three-three-two rhythms occur in Goudimel's psalms, like the forty-second, "As the hart panteth after the water brooks" (1565).

In the seventeenth century, examples outside Germany are rare. Carissimi presents a few, for instance in one chorus of his oratorio *Jephte* from about 1645.

But the works of Heinrich Schütz, the leading German master, are a true mine of this form of additive rhythm in three-three-two. The reader who has his *Complete Works* at hand will find the following three examples from the *Musicalische Exequien* in their proper context on pages 62, 70, and 77 of Volume XII: [28]

Ex. 79

Sie - he das ist Got - tes lamm

Ex. 80

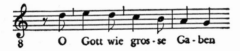

O Gott wie gros - se Ga - ben

Ex. 81

Sein Wort, sein Tauf, sein Nacht - mahl

The three-three-two interpretation, supported by poetical and musical logics as well as by parallels in all ages and countries, re-

[28] These three examples were kindly provided by Arthur Mendel.

moves most of the tedious offbeats and tie-overs with which our current modern editions teem. There is no syncopation, no "deliberate upsetting of the normal pulse of meter, accent, and rhythm," where there is "a regularly recurrent accent on the first beat of each group," and "a disturbance or contradiction between the underlying (normal) pulse and the accentual (abnormal) rhythm." [29] In vocal polyphony, 'norms' and 'regularly recurrent accents on the first beats' were almost nonexistent, and hence any 'abnormal' syncopation as well. The truth is that Renaissance polyphony, very far from our normalcy and recurrent accents, relies on an unrestrained polyrhythmic writing, on a continual, almost erratic change from binary to ternary groupings, with or against the other parts, with or against the time signature. Often, it appears only in the cadences, but oftener throughout a piece. [30]

VERS MESURÉS AND HUMANISM. All these additive rhythms appear to have an intimate, causal connection with one of the most important elements of the Renaissance: the revival of classical studies, known as humanism, in all European civilizations, its philological methods, and, hence, the deferential esteem bestowed upon the individual word in its meaning and sound.

The learned movement affected music in two ways, one specific and the other one general.

The specific and all too literal way, a curious and somewhat artificial afterglow of Greek and Latin metrology, revived the ancient practice of giving uniformly a short note to a short syllable, and one twice its length to a long syllable. The century of these metrical experiments began in 1507 with the *Melopoiae secundum naturam et tempora syllabarum et pedum* [31] or 'melodies according to the nature and durations of syllables and feet.' The texts were Horace's odes, and the composer, one Petrus Tritonius, whom the scholarly circles around the Bavarian humanist, Conrad Celtis,

---

[29] Willi Apel, *Harvard dictionary of music*, Cambridge, Harvard University Press, 1944, *Syncopation*, p. 726.

[30] Cf. also Otto Gombosi, in *The Musical Quarterly*, Vol. XXXVIII, 1952, pp. 163–167.

[31] R. von Liliencron, *Die Horazischen Metren in deutschen Kompositionen des 16. Jahrhunderts*, in *Vierteljahrsschrift für Musikwissenschaft*, Vol. III, 1887, pp. 26–91.

had inspired in the 1490's. Our example, the first ode, *Maecenas atavis edite regibus* ('Maecenas, who haileth from kingly ancestors') follows the lesser asclepiadean meter—spondee, choriamb,

Ex. 82. Tritonius, ode, *Maecenas atavis edite regibus*

dactyl, dactyl—which would not yield any regular time pattern in a musical sense. The voice part rendered here is the tenor; the other three parts help in reproducing the meter in the strictest note-against-note.

Not only were the odes of Tritonius reprinted in a second edition of 1532; new solutions of the same problem were presented by Germany's two greatest musicians: by Ludwig Senfl in the *Varia carminum genera* of 1534 and by Paulus Hofhaimer in the *Harmoniae poeticae* of 1539.

Then the movement shifted to France. Poetically prepared since the end of the fifteenth century (as in Germany), it continued and ended in the shadow of Jean-Antoine Baïf's *Académie de Poésie et de Musique* [32] with sacred and secular works by the greatest French composer of the time, Claude Lejeune: with his psalms (*Pseaumes en vers mezurez mis en musique*) with from two to eight voice parts and with a collection of songs under the title *Printemps* or *Spring*, both published after he had died in 1600.[33]

Most of the metrical songs between 1500 and 1600 are strictly note-against-note and syllabic with their longs and shorts in the regular ratio 2:1. Evenly recurring stresses or uniform measures are not at all considered, as they belong to a different rhythmical concept and can easily be in disagreement with mingled meters of three or four or five units. The result, unavoidable even in the works of eminent masters, is pedantic artificiality against nature, mechanical translation against imaginative re-creation. The hu-

[32] Cf. also Julien Tiersot, *Ronsard et la musique de son temps*, in *Sammelbände der Internationalen Musikgesellschaft*, Vol. IV, 1902, pp. 70–142.
[33] 'In' 1600 according to an oral communication by Mr. Kenneth J. Levy in the Music Department of Princeton University. Hitherto the date has been uncertain.

manistic composers appeal to learning and reason, not to the soul
or the senses. But above all, they did not understand the very laws
they wanted to impose on music. They show completest ignorance
of the important Greek distinction between 'logical' and 'alogical'
meters, between poetic and musical patterns, between the fields
of 'metricism' and 'rhythmicism.' The humanists did not yet see
that the theoretical ratio 2:1 of *longa* and *brevis* had applied to
recited poetry and its musical kin but not to the more independent
vocal music, such as the *skolion* of Seikilos.

Lejeune had been the last composer of *vers mesurés*. But a generation later the French still toyed with the idea. Their greatest
musical scholar in the seventeenth century, Marin Mersenne, did
reverence to the rhythms of Greece as a matter of scholarly
courtesy. But his real allegiance went to the metricists of the sixteenth century, to Baïf and Mauduit, although he rejected recurrent metrical patterns as an undesirable straitjacket. Indeed, he
admitted such additive groupings as in five, seven, or nine units
on the two beats of a *tactus*, in three and two, in four and three,
in five and four. But in all his dependence on language, he
occasionally allowed a short syllable to fall on a longer note, and
vice versa. For he was well aware of the intricacies of accent in
French. He knew that there was an *accent logique*, an *accent
oratoire*, an *accent tonique*, indeed 'all sorts of accents,' which
music was hardly able to render.[34]

A hundred and fifty years later, the *vers mesurés* had a curious
afterglow in Gluck's musical settings of Klopstock's *Oden und
Lieder beym Clavier zu singen* (1787): not only did the composer
follow the poet's very strong and personal meters to the letter,
but in a number of cases he also added Klopstock's meter in graphic
form above the music to show how faithfully he had heeded the
poet's intentions.

The *vers mesurés* were the specific humanist means of influenc-
ing melody. And, let us add, they were the classicistic means, since
they modeled music after the outer, metrical appearance of the
words, not after their meaning or weight.

The general way in which humanism affected music was an unwonted emphasis on the meaning and enunciation of the text. No

[34] Marin Mersenne, *Harmonie universelle*, Paris, 1636, p. 366.

longer were composers allowed to leave the distribution of the text to the discretion of the singers. In place of such music *with* a text, they were expected to compose music *to* a text and to give the words their proper meters and accents. This new respect for speech and poetry is the essential secret behind the cryptic 'irregular' rhythms.

The earliest steps in this direction had been taken before 1500. The mere presence of the sacred words, still satisfactory to the medieval mind, no longer sufficed: the appeal to the senses characteristic of the Renaissance and the claims of philology—in the original sense of the word—required an easily understandable text and therefore a careful, adequate setting to longer and shorter notes, even if the meter was not pedantically rendered in 2:1 ratios.

Although this new ideal was not fully accepted in the first half of the century, except by Josquin des Prés and the masters around him, it became essentially part and parcel of the currents in the second half: By 1552, when the Fleming Adriaen Petit Coclicus was publishing his often quoted *Musica reservata*, it had become a serious prerequisite of decent writing to apply the text to its proper place and to avoid setting a long note to a short syllable or vice versa; 'for music has much in common with poetry.'

Only six years later, Gioseffe Zarlino warns composers to "adapt the words of the speech to the musical figures in such a way and with such rhythms that nothing barbarous is heard, not making short syllables long and long syllables short as is done every day in innumerable compositions, a truly shameful thing. . . . Thus over and over again we hear length given to the penultimate syllables of such words as *Dominus, Angelus, Filius, miraculum, gloria,* and many others, syllables which are properly short and fleeting. . . . And the listener does not know what to do and remains thoroughly bewildered and confused." [36]

Again a few years later, the Council of Trent, eager to restore the dignity of church music, and the subsequent meetings of a Vatican-appointed Roman commitee on musical reforms insisted on a careful treatment of the texts.

[36] Gioseffe Zarlino, *Le Istitutioni armoniche*, 1558, *liber* IV §§ 32, 33; quoted from Strunk, *op. cit.*, pp. 258, 259.

At the end of the century, Thomas Morley said in *A Plaine and Easie Introduction to Practicall Musicke* (1597): "We must also have a care so to applie the notes to the wordes as in singing there be no barbarisme committed: that is, that we cause no syllable that is by nature short, to be expressed by many notes, or one long note, nor so long a syllable to be expressed with a short note." [37]

In a similar vein, William Byrd had his *Psalmes, Songs, and Sonnets* of 1611 "framed to the life of the words."

A correct analysis of all this irregular grouping will help the modern editor with the often thorny problem of *Textunterlegung* or putting the right syllables of the text under the right notes. We need no longer blame all the 'incorrect,' 'inconsistent,' or 'contradictory' placing of the words in Renaissance polyphony on negligence. In many—although not in all—cases it becomes correct and consistent once the inner rhythm of a piece is bared beyond the fictitious rhythm that the signature deceivingly suggests.

MUSIC TO WORDS OR MUSIC WITH WORDS? The picture of Renaissance polyphony, so far, is rather confusing: rhythm in agreement with *tactus* and time signature or, at least, with modern bar lines; mingled rhythms against a unifying time signature; rhythms subservient to the words of the text; rhythms against correct pronunciation. Was polyphony written with words or actually upon the words of the texts?

Small wonder that modern scholars have been confused. Anxious to get at the truth, they took sides and engaged in fiery battles to decide whether the sixteenth century was 'accentual' or 'textual.' The accentualists believe in the supremacy of purely musical logics in the polyphony of the sixteenth century—logics to which the words had more or less to bow. The textualists believe in the supremacy of the words, to which the musical lines were forced to yield the musical logics. The first group interpret the polyphonic works of that time as regular sequences of *theses* and *arses*, of ups and downs, to which the words were adapted, cost what it might. The latter are ready to sacrifice the normal, regular musical rhythm to the proper enunciation of the text. The former group admit the

[37] Cf. also: Bruce Pattison, *Music and poetry of the English Renaissance*, London (1948).

insertion of modern bar lines as the symbols of musical organization. The latter taboo them as artificial dams arresting the free,
allegedly non-accentual stream of polyphony.

The cause of the accentualists is most strongly represented in a
temperamental paper by Arnold Schering.[38]

On reading these controversies, the author cannot help thinking
of Wilhelm Kaulbach's gigantic mural in Berlin's New Museum
and of Liszt's symphonic poem that it inspired: the "Battle of the
Huns." The field is covered with corpses; the fighting has come to
an end. But above, in the skies, the ghosts of the slain still charge;
the fight goes on with lances and swords. The battle of music and
words was fought in the sixteenth century. Shall we be the ghosts
and challenge what has been decided? Would anybody stop to
argue whether the nineteenth century insisted on the prerogatives
of music by quoting the many misaccentuations in the *Lieder* of
Brahms or else, by pointing at the *Lieder* of Hugo Wolf, that the
century was primarily devoted to the words and their correct inflections?

There is no need for arguments, but only for a sound discretion.
For there is no either–or.

The polyphony of the sixteenth century covered the whole expanse from musical to textual supremacy. It should suffice to recall
to the reader's mind a few of the quotations in the preceding section. There was a need for Coclicus' insisting, in his *Musica reservata,* on "setting a long note to a short syllable or vice versa";
Zarlino had to warn against the 'barbarous' practice of 'shamefully'
misplacing the accents of words, "as is done every day in innumerable compositions"; and, to quote from the chapter to come, Caccini and his contemporaries around 1600 disavowed polyphony
wholesale because it "stretched out or on the contrary compressed
the syllables for the sake of counterpoint and thus destroyed meter
and words."

Purely musical considerations prevailed "in innumerable compositions."

[38] Arnold Schering, *Musikalischer Organismus oder Deklamations-Rhythmik,* in
Zeitschrift für Musikwissenschaft, Vol. XI (1928/29), pp. 212–221. See also Arnold
Schering, *Takt und Sinngliederung in der Musik des 16. Jahrhunderts,* in *Archiv für
Musikwissenschaft,* Vol. II, 1920, pp. 465–498; Karl Gustav Fellerer, *Die Deklama-
tions-Rhythmik in der vokalen Polyphonie des 16. Jahrhunderts,* Düsseldorf, 1928.

These criticisms, on the other hand, prove that there existed an important party concerned with the rights of the words in vocal music. That they were backed by creative musicians all over Europe, can be read from the polyphonic scores from Josquin through a hundred years to William Byrd, who "framed" his vocal music "to the life of the words." And during the same one hundred years some of the greatest masters went to extremes in their *vers mesurés,* which forced the musical settings to a complete subordination to the victorious words.

This, then, was the situation. The sixteenth century, linking the Middle Ages with the Baroque, was given the task of leading from the music-firsters of the Middle Ages to the poem-firsters of the Baroque. This mission could not but give it a dual stamp. Stragglers kept a good deal of textual unconcern, while the pioneers anticipated much of the devotion to correct enunciation characteristic of the early seventeenth. But careful as the progressive masters from Josquin to Byrd and Lejeune were to pay their tribute to the words of their texts, they were not willing to sacrifice the noble flow of their melodic lines to mere declamation. Thus we do not face the alternative Musical Organism *or* Declamatory Rhythmics, as the title of Schering's essay makes us believe. There was Musical Organism in all cases, and often it was Musical Organism *and* Declamatory Rhythmics. This is why lutanists and vihuela players of the time were able and eager to render so much sacred and secular polyphony on their instruments even when the pieces had been meant to express particular texts in faithful rendition.

In a similar way, the question of accent must not be given a rigid, exclusive answer. That the polyphony of the sixteenth century did not know accentuation is a pious legend. This book has sufficiently shown that meter does not and cannot exist without at least a suggestion of stresses. Even where the stresses are weak, the mere entrance of a new voice part has the effect of a decided accent. To be sure, these and other unavoidable stresses must not be confused with intentional sforzatos.

There is no doubt, on the other hand, that the strength of good beats, as they were already called in the Renaissance, varied considerably according to the nature of a piece. But performers and listeners were hardly aware of these minute shades and had no reason for mentioning them.

Whatever their nature and strength, the accents were quite certainly not always the ones that the treacherous time signature suggests to the reader. They were, rather, the delicate stresses that the grouping by twos and threes within or against the *tactus* necessitated.

The relation of accent, *tactus,* and time signature draws our attention to the troublesome question of the bar line.

BAR LINES are intimately connected with vertical hearing and score arrangement. Based on an exact one-below-the-other array, the score is meant to show the notes to be played and heard at the same moment and to facilitate the simultaneous reading by means of bar lines cutting through the staffs. As a consequence, such lines could have no place in scoreless polyphony, where every concurrent singer did his own individual part without a share in the accentual patterns of his fellow-performers. Separating lines had a meaning only where a single performer played a piece in all its voice parts together, be they in chords or in counterpoint. Hence bar lines and scores (very often as fingering tablatures) were offered to lutanists and to the players of organs, clavichords, and virginals, as early as the fourteenth century.[39]

The early vertical lines were actually orientation marks only, but not yet bars to delineate the accentual patterns; they would quite arbitrarily separate sections of different length. In a timid way, however, the sixteenth century began to connect the originally unrelated concepts of bar and *tactus.* Lutanists and Spanish vihuela players often reached the modern way by coupling two *tactus* between two bar lines and thus creating complete 4/4.

Indeed, the ever growing divisive rhythm, main condition of bar lines, was inseparable from the fast-developing idiomatic instrumental music which, often connected with dancing or marching and thoroughly free from any regard for texts, poetical feet, or speech inflections, was naturally opposed to the erratic flow

[39] Cf. Dragan Plamenac, *Keyboard music of the 14th century,* in *Journal of the American Musicological Society,* Vol. IV, 1951, p. 186 and facsimiles.

of vocal polyphony. With the exception of those polyphonic forms that instrumental ensembles derived from vocal models—such as the Italian *canzone da sonare*—and of free improvisational forms like toccatas and dirges (*tombeaux*), instrumental music adopted rhythmical strictness with an alternation of stressed and unstressed beats.

The very vocal polyphony could no longer stay aloof. The earliest known score in print is, to be sure, more instrumental than vocal: the printer Gardano in Venice published in 1577 *tutti madrigali di Cipriano de Rore a 4 voci*, "scored [*spartiti et accomodati*] to be played on all kinds of instruments."

As to vocal polyphony in its original form, the German, Michael Praetorius (1571–1621), still averse to actual bar lines, adopted at least short vertical dashes outside the staff as orientation marks. Orazio Benevoli's beautifully written giant score of the Salzburg Inauguration Mass of 1628, however, is already barred in the modern way; [40] the synchronization of many vocal and instrumental choruses with soloists and organs made a unifying arrangement imperative. But not before the later part of the seventeenth century was the ultimate function of the bar line assured: to precede the first and strongest beat of a measure.

A particular, intricate problem arises when we publish modern editions of Renaissance music and find ourselves presented with the complex question as to whether, where, and how we should facilitate their reading by the addition of bar lines. One modern school of musical philologists execrates the bar line as something that, foreign to the spirit of old polyphonic music, suggests a pedantic *ONE*-two-*three*-four without attention to the inner life of the voice parts and forces the singer to place accents where there are none. This argument would apply to most of our modern music, too, without anybody wanting to deprive it of bar lines. The said philologists, too, must compromise. The very fact that they publish their music in anachronistic scores, against the concept and practice of the Renaissance, shows the inadequacy of all attempts to save the soul of polyphony by notational means. As the score

---

[40] Reprinted in *Denkmäler der Tonkunst in Oesterreich*, Vol. (*Jahrgang*) X, i; a facsimile in Robert Haas, *Musik des Barocks*, in Bücken's *Handbuch der Musikwissenschaft*, pl. V, opp. p. 80.

invites vertical reading, it is incomprehensible without the orientation of vertical separating lines. Their compromise consists in a
little trick: if bar lines are unavoidable, let us at least pretend that
they are not real bar lines, either by dotting them or by drawing
them from staff to staff without crossing the staffs themselves.
Thus, they are bar lines; and again, they are not bar lines.

A reader who misinterprets the inner life of a score is after all
a victim of insufficient education rather than of bar lines. We
should not shift the responsibility.

If we decide for good and honest bar lines in principle, we have
to face the further question of where to put them. When the
actual rhythm seems to go against the beat, as so often happens in
Renaissance polyphony, shall a modern edition place the bar lines
as if such metrical intricacies did not exist, or shall it, on the other
hand, bar every single meter so that, for instance, a three-three-two
rhythm would appear as three measures: 3/8, 3/8, and 2/8?

Since our bar lines are not in the original, but are in form and
meaning taken from modern music, the answer should be taken
from modern scores. There have been two ways of notating rhythmic deviations: either keeping a uniform barring and conducting
pattern throughout, with the finer intricacies of group formation
left to the reader and the performer, or else freely changing the
time signatures and the conducting gestures wherever the groups
are organized against the original signature.

The composer will change the signature where the listener is
meant to feel at ease in the new rhythm and accept it as something
in its own right. He will not do so when a passage is definitely offbeat, when it antagonizes the original signature and wants to
convey this self-willed opposition beyond any doubt. The whipping offbeats in the *Eroica* (music example 113) would completely
lose their unyielding, obstinate character if they were accommodated in a frictionless 2/4 episode. The resistance should be perceived with the eyes as well as with the ears and hence become visible against the bars and the conductor's beat.

One thing is certain: the modern bar line, wherever the composer
chooses to place it, goes through from top to bottom, even at the
risk of disturbing the group arrangement in one of the voice parts.
It may occasionally be interrupted in cases as simple as a 3/2 in

one voice part against two 3/4 in the other parts. But even such insignificant alterations are exceptional.

All these remarks apply to older music, too. The only difference is that there the signature regulates the even ups and downs of the *tactus,* but not the basic rhythmical pattern. It is therefore illogical and distorting to place our modern bar lines, which do have rhythmic significance, in one–two sequences where the music is quite definitely in ternary rhythm (cf. music example 61). This is true also of cases in which the modern transliteration ties all voice parts across the bar line. Such tying falsifies the immanent organization of the passage.

In considering how far we should go in denoting the finer intricacies of rhythmical grouping, we must not forget that notation is not analysis. The ideal parsing of a composition is thorough; its ideal notation must not sacrifice visual clearness to the tangles of interpretation.

The following suggestions might be acceptable.

(1) The modern bar line is independent of, and often opposed to, the original time signature and the *tactus* that it entails.

(2) The editor places his bar lines according to the modern signature that the piece requires—3/2, 4/4, 3/4, or whatever it may be. He ignores the medieval *tempus* and the post-medieval *tactus* and establishes 'measures.'

(3) He changes signatures and bars wherever the rhythm actually changes.

(4) A regrouping in a single voice part or in all of them can best be notated by omitting one bar line. Two examples may suffice. The *hemiola* of 3/2 within (and over) a 3/4 arrangement can best be shown by drawing the bar line between the two 3/4 but interrupting it inside the 3/2 in order to avoid the offbeat-suggesting ties across the bar line. The frequent $3 + 3 + 2$ within an otherwise 4/4 piece can stand unmarked when this group consists of eighths and hence coincides with an ordinary measure; it should be written without the one disturbing bar line when it consists of quarters and hence coincides with two ordinary measures.

(5) Small orientation marks through the uppermost line of the staff might be welcome in the two latter cases.

(6) Individual cases differ so much that a good deal of freedom

must be granted to the editor, even where some re-editing society imposes uniform rules of transliteration upon its editors.

(7) Upbeats must clearly appear as such. This follows directly from suggestion (2). Otherwise, the reader is forced to parse the score, as he is, for example, in the medieval dance notations by Johannes Wolf.[41]

UPBEATS. We might look over hundreds and hundreds of polyphonic pieces from the Middle Ages and the Renaissance and never find an upbeat. They have, as metricists would say, a falling rhythm, with the initial note on the first beat, or downbeat, of the measure. Even where an iambic or anapaestic text seems to make an 'upbeat' on the last note before (our) bar line imperative, the masters of those times had an easy way out: they extended the initial short and stressless syllable backward so that it began on a first beat and filled a whole measure. One impressive example out of many is the beginning of a typical madrigal, *O begl'anni dell'oro,* by Francesco Corteccia (d. 1571).[42] That so curious a

Ex. 83. Corteccia, madrigal, *O begl'anni dell'oro*

circumvention was at all possible and acceptable may have been partly in virtue of the often observed rule that iambic meters enjoy a certain freedom at the beginning of a verse.

An actual upbeat—like winding up for a throw—prepares a stress; it is necessarily four–ONE. It was out of place in the polyphonic forms which depended, on the whole, upon an even, little-stressed flow. It was a logical trait, on the contrary, wherever catchy songs and dances were meant to convey an irresistible motor impulse.

Among the very few exceptions seems to be Dufay's strictly iambic hymn *Ad coenam agni.*[43] But maybe it is not an exception

[41] Johannes Wolf, *Die Tänze des Mittelalters,* in *Archiv für Musikwissenschaft,* Vol. I, 1918, pp. 19–42.
[42] Printed in Arnold Schering, *Geschichte der Musik in Beispielen,* Leipzig, 1931, No. 99.
[43] *Denkmäler der Tonkunst in Oesterreich,* Vol. 7, 1900, p. 159.

at all. For as a hymn it probably should be classified as popular and even catchy. In all the other iambic hymns of the master that the *Oesterreichische Denkmäler* reprint the upbeat is stretched out to a full measure.

The actual field of upbeats was dancing. The leading dances of the fourteenth and the fifteenth century, *estampie* and *basse danse*, had upbeats as a rule; they began *in lo vuodo*, on the empty time. And a good number of the *saltarelli* and the *balli* were of the same kind.[44]

THE LATE RENAISSANCE, Michelangelo's and Lasso's age, reverting to a taste less calm and simple than the preceding High Renaissance had had, once more gave attention to the Gothic problems of rhythmic complication. Indeed, it refilled for a little while the prescriptions of flamboyant polyrhythm, although the dosage came out essentially weaker than it had been at the ends of the fourteenth and fifteenth centuries.

A lovely example of simple counterrhythm in three against two in the Late Renaissance is Cipriano de Rore's madrigal *Vergine pura* of 1548, where the two upper voices move in an unmistakable 3/4, while the third voice proceeds just as unmistakably in 2/4. Arnold Schering's reprint [45] conceals this contrast when it squeezes both rhythms into the same 2/4 measures.

Ex. 84. Cipriano de Rore, madrigal, *Vergine pura*

This delicate piece illustrates at once the necessity of beating a binary *tactus* and of adapting the 3/4 to its contradictory one–two, one–two in the curious way described above: with the third quarter falling now on an upbeat, now on a downbeat.

[44] Curt Sachs, *World history of the dance*, New York, 1937, pp. 292 ff., 318 ff.
[45] Arnold Schering, *Musikgeschichte in Beispielen*, Leipzig, 1931, No. 106, p. 103.

That even Palestrina, allegedly the 'purest' of all the masters in the century, could at times quite heartily delight in Flemish-Gothic 'artifices' and *proportiones* of the past has been shown in a characteristic quotation from his *Missa L'homme armé.*

Thomas Morley reprints a curious madrigal by Alessandro Striggio (died 1587), where "the Treble contayneth *diminution* in the *quadrupla* proportion. The second Treble or sextus hath Tripla prickt all in blacke notes: your Altus or Meane contayneth *diminution* in Dupla proportion. The Tenor goeth through with his Tripla (which was begonne before) to the ende. The *Quintus* is *sesquialtra* to the *breefe* which hath this signe $\mathbb{C} \frac{3}{2}$ set before it: But if the signe were away, then would three *minyms* make a whole stroke, where as nowe three *semibriefes* make but one stroke[.] The Base is the ordinary Moode, wherein is no difficulty as you may see." [46]

Actually, each bar has one semibreve in the bass, one breve in the third voice (*dupla*), one long in the first soprano (*quadrupla*), one black dotted semibreve in the second soprano (*tripla*); the fourth part proceeds equally in *tripla,* and the fifth in *sesquialtera.* All signs are different; all values are the same. This hodgepodge, however, is nothing but a meaningless toying around with an already outmoded practice.

But the time for such bewildering concoctions had gone for good. "There are many examples of difficult singing," said the Netherlander, Adrian Petit Coclicus, in 1552,[47] "where one voice part proceeds in a *triplus,* while another one has a duple-time signature or no signature at all. Such practice does not lead to lucid singing, but rather to deception and vexation."

Since, as a rule, we are unable to handle a style that we dislike (and vice versa), the generation of Coclicus needed and used a somewhat clumsy simplification. Instead of combining duple and triple time, says Henricus Faber in his *Introductio* of 1550, one should sing as if all voice parts had the same signature, "until practice frees you from this annoyance [*molestia*]." Hermann Finck's *Practica musica* (1556) is even more specific: "When three notes [of similar speed—*simili celeritate*] devolve on one *tactus,* the first

---

[46] Thomas Morley, *A plaine and easie introduction to practicall Musicke,* 1597.
[47] Adrian Petit Coclicus, *Compendium musicum,* Nürnberg, 1552, fol. H II v°.

note takes one half, and the two others, the second half, as ♩ ♫."

But then, the Gothic polyphony had not been problematic in times of 'horizontal' conception, where the singer followed his own melodic line with little interdependence with those of his partners. In a time of 'vertical' conception—as in the sixteenth century— where the composer as well as the singer proceeded from beat to beat in closest connection with the other parts, counterrhythms offered essential difficulties.

A typically vertical impulse emanated late in the century, the 1580's and 1590's, from the homestead of vertical writing, from Italy. The impulse materialized in brisk and catchy songs that their fathers called *canzonette* and *balletti*, the English, *ayres*, and the French musicians, *airs de cour*. All of them were part songs with or without the participation of instruments, limpid, concise, symmetrical in structure, and syllabic in the treatment of their texts. Moreover, the majority of them were written in a strict 4/4 with only a few enlivening eighths which never veiled the clean-cut two-beat *tactus* of the piece. Coming on the threshold of the Baroque, this vertical concept was part and parcel of the general renunciation of polyphonic ideals.

CHAPTER 12

The Baroque

The so-called Baroque stretched from about 1550 to about 1750. (The usual date 1600 is convenient but erroneous.)

It seems still necessary to emphasize that this span of two hundred years was by no means what its nickname unfortunately suggests to laymen: a crazy age of irregular forms and grotesques, of distortion and extravagance. Very few phases of that venerable style have indulged in such excesses, and hardly a land but Germany, Italy, Spain, and Latin America.

Countries like England, North America, France, on the contrary, followed ideals of an often severe classicism, of noble simplicity, strictest symmetry, and mathematical orderliness. "Thus Christopher Wren, the builder of St. Paul's in London, could say that in art always the true test is natural or geometrical beauty; the painter Charles Lebrun, chief decorator of the palace of Versailles, demanded that painting be founded upon geometry; and Father Mersenne, the greatest musicologist of the seventeenth century, distrusted imagination, [merely] sensuous perception, and any judgment based on them, and averred again and again that music was a mere part of mathematics." [1]

By the same token, the generations that, one after another, formed the Baroque alternated in their attitudes. The most impressive reversal occurred in the 1630's, when in all the arts the high spirits of the early Baroque, its naturalistic trends and un-

[1] Curt Sachs, *The commonwealth of art, a lecture*, Washington, D.C., The Library of Congress, 1950, p. 10.

restrained passion, yielded to restraint and strictness,[2] and when in music the free, emotional monody left its domineering position to the well-wrought tripartite form of the *da capo* aria.

Above all these contradictory attitudes—simplicity against extravagance, symmetry against irregularity, orderliness against distortion—the Baroque had a few conceptions common to all its phases in every habitat. Three of them seem to have been especially important in shaping rhythmical aspects: the opening of space, three-dimensionalism, and expressiveness.

The first two of these qualities look so exclusively visual that the reader can hardly be expected to see their connection with rhythm.

In many respects, the Baroque aimed at the infinite as opposed to the finite of the Renaissance. Spinoza's pantheistic conception of the 'infinite' perfection of the 'infinite' attributes of God is more than a symbol.

In the Baroque, the frames of paintings often did not bound self-sufficient scenes or landscapes, but cut through bodies, houses, trees, and thus suggested that the picture was nothing but an accidental segment from a boundless space. Its statues would jut forth from their niches with an arm or a leg, breaking out of an all too narrow prison. And buildings seemed to merge with neighboring houses or blend with their parks. Inside, they opened up into adjacent halls or stairs in endless vistas.

Music followed this urge for reaching out into the infinite in its frequent entries off the beat. Instead of beginning a piece with the initial note of a measure, composers often started quite informally after a rest or empty beat, and the listener experiences a lack of actual opening, indeed, a seeming continuation of a music that might have been going on for a long time, or, to speak in modern terms, before you take up the receiver. At least at one end, such music is unbounded.

This procedure is diametrically opposed to that of the Renaissance, where even upbeats were lengthened backward to fill a whole measure in order to start on a downbeat and thus avoid an open beginning.

The delayed, 'procatalectic' entry of the theme after a down-

Ex. 85. Bach, B minor Mass, *Dona nobis pacem*

beat rest, such as the weighty *Dona nobis pacem* at the end of the
B minor Mass, has a very strong driving quality, a vigorous tendency to reach the nearest downbeat, a tension and *dynamis* that no
downbeat could achieve.

Precursors appear at prominent places in the sixteenth century;
indeed, there is an example in Palestrina's well-known Mass for
Pope Marcellus (1555).

Ex. 86. Palestrina, *Missa Papae Marcelli*, Crucifixus

Characteristically enough, the majority of examples, in both the
sixteenth and the seventeenth century, have exactly the same very
simple motive: a stepwise ascension from the dominant to the octave—just as in the *Dona nobis pacem*. An earlier parallel is the
beginning of the second part of Frescobaldi's *Partita sopra l'aria*

Ex. 87. Frescobaldi, *Partita sopra la Romanesca*

della Romanesca. A later parallel is the entry of the basses in the
Wartburg march of *Tannhäuser* (1845).

Ex. 88. Wagner, *Tannhäuser*, Wartburg march

The next of the common qualities of all Baroque was its striving
for depth. In the visual arts, this striving appeared as a delight in

achieving an almost palpable reality, indeed, the illusion of nature and life. Not only was the individual object given an all-round bodiliness, but by means of perspective, the artists treated every person and object as a part of space.

The present author has shown elsewhere [3] that the musical third dimension is harmony, which conveys a feeling of depth and space completely absent from oriental music—just as perspective is absent from oriental painting. It is unnecessary to repeat the discussion. Suffice it to restate that harmony proper coincided chronologically and geographically with perspective: it existed exclusively in the West between the fifteenth and twentieth centuries. Even in our own civilization, it did not exist before the Renaissance and it has been discarded in our time—just like 'school' perspective.

Harmony, in its turn, is closely connected with rhythm. Nobody denies that harmony and rhythm are interrelated. Consonance and dissonance, the basic concepts of harmony, are reflected in the concept of 'good' and 'bad' beats, of accented and unaccented beats, whether passing dissonances require unaccented 'passing' beats, or whether dissonances demand a strong accent, to be resolved on a stressless beat. Harmony and rhythm share in the alternation of tension and relaxation which are the essence of our music.

The words 'accent' and 'stress' in the preceding paragraph imply that any rhythm related to harmony must be of the accentual, divisive kind. Additive rhythm belongs to civilizations without harmony.

Therewith, the equation of perspective and harmony repeats itself. Throughout history, divisive rhythm has replaced additive rhythm whenever and wherever two-dimensionalism has yielded to perspective and all-round reality. In the East, divisive rhythm as a binding principle exists only in the Far Orient, where painting draws quite near to spatial concepts. In the West, divisive rhythm blooms in the age of perspective and harmony between 1400 and 1900, but not in the Middle Ages, characterized by counterpoint and lack of perspective, or in the somewhat similar age after 1900.

(Greco-Roman art took an important turn to perspective, im-

[3] Sachs, *The commonwealth of art*, New York, 1946, pp. 271 ff.

perfect, it is true, at the beginning of the Common Era, as evidenced in the paintings of Pompeii and Herculaneum. There is a strong possibility that the change from meter to accentual rhythm in later antiquity was a kindred phenomenon.)

This, then, seems to be the result: if visual perspective implies harmonic function, and harmony implies divisive rhythm, perspective belongs necessarily to divisive rhythm whatever the physio-psychological connection may be. The Baroque, an age of spatial illusion and functional harmony, was also an age in which divisive rhythm ruled almost exclusively.

The third of the common qualities of the entire Baroque, but particularly of the earlier Baroque, is its highly emotional, passionate expressiveness. In discussing its repercussions on rhythm, we will proceed from the negative side, that is, from the dying past that it was meant to replace.

DECLINE OF THE PROPORTIONS. The new emotionalism, the urge to overwhelm the listener and make his nerves vibrate—an urge so strong in the works of the early monodists around 1600 that a weeping audience seemed to be the vital aim of composing —excluded rhythmic devices born of sheer delight in purely rational structures without emotional values. The Gothic *proportiones* had to go.

The polyphony of the sixteenth century, both vocal and instrumental, burdened as it was with the structure-ridden heritage of the Middle Ages, had found in the intricacies of proportions and *tactus* an adequate, orderly, mathematical means of ruling its rhythms and counterrhythms. But we saw that even in polyphony the laws of proportion had applied only to simultaneous counterrhythms. These laws were relaxed or even completely repealed when all the voice parts moved together from tempo to tempo within a piece.

The end of polyphonic leadership around 1600 entailed the final collapse of the proportions.

Seen from without, the system of the proportions seems to climax at the end of the sixteenth century in Thomas Morley's pyramidal graph, reproduced in Grove's *Dictionary of Music* under the heading 'Proportion.' To find the proportion that "any one number hath to another, finde out the two numbers in the Table, then looke upwarde to the triangle inclosing those numbers, and in the angle of concourse, that is, where your two lynes meete togither, there is the proportion of your two numbers written: as for example, let your two numbers be 18 and 24. Looke upward, and in the top of the tryangle covering the two lynes which inclose those numbers, you find written *sesquitertia*, so likewise 24. and 42. you finde in the Angle of concourse written *super tripartiens quartas*, and so of others." [4]

But Philomathes, the otherwise intelligent, polite, and willing interlocutor of the 'Master' in the dialogue of Morley's *Plaine and Easie Introduction*, gets impatient: "Heere is a Table in deede contayning more than ever I meane to beate my brayns about. As for musick, the principal thing we seek in it, is to delight the eare, which cannot so perfectly be done in these hard proportions, as otherwise, therefore proceede to the rest of your musicke. . . ."

Another day was dawning.

Morley himself concedes elsewhere: "Although there be no proportion so harde but might be made in Musicke, but the hardnesse of singing them, hath caused them to be left out, and therefore there be but five in most common use with us: *Dupla, Tripla, Quadrupla, Sesquialtera,* and *Sesquitertia*." [5]

The change is possibly most obvious in Germany. From the *Compendium musicae*, written by Sethus Calvisius (1556–1615), [6] one of Bach's distinguished predecessors at St. Thomas' in Leipzig, such outmoded concepts as *modus* and *prolatio*, alteration and imperfection, have disappeared. The age-honored, scholarly name *sesquialtera*, it is true, still haunts the first edition of 1594 or 1595, but it is conspicuously absent from the later edition that Calvisius published in 1612 under the new title *Musicae praecepta*. The usual time signature, a crossed semicircle, indicates the "normal" *alla breve*. The dotted semicircle stands for the slower *alla semibreve* (the dot then being already divorced from the abolished

---

[4] Thomas Morley, *A plaine and easie introduction to practicall musicke*, London, 1597, pp. 33 f.

[5] *Ibid.*, p. 27.

[6] Cf. Kurt Benndorf, *Sethus Calvisius*, in *Vierteljahrsschrift für Musikwissenschaft*, Vol. X, 1894, p. 430.

prolation). And the crossed semicircle with the figure 3 denotes the *tripla*. But it was no longer the tempo three times as fast that the name had implied a hundred years before. The *tripla* held three semibreves to the *tactus alla semibreve* and stood consequently in 3:2 or sesquialter proportion with the then normal *alla breve*.

At the end of the century, Henry Purcell declared unmistakably that every *tactus* consisted in a semibreve, and that the three usual (and once proportional) signatures indicated different tempi and nothing else: C "is a very slow movement," ₵ "a little faster," and ₵ a "brisk & airry time." [7]

It was a meaningless bow to the past when Lully's faithful German disciple, Georg Muffat, spoke of proportions as late as 1698.[8]

MODERN TEMPI. On the threshold of the century, the German, Michael Praetorius (1571–1621), more a son of the sixteenth century than of the seventeenth, found the mingling of different tempi within a piece particularly *lieblich* or 'lovely.' He himself delighted in jumping from solemn sustentions to impatient *stretti* and back. A perfect example is the Latin psalm *Beati omnes qui timent Dominum*, printed in the tenth volume of his *Complete Works* [9] and recorded on No. 72 of the present author's *Anthologie Sonore*. Although the score, as the eye perceives it, seems to change between duple and ternary time only, some of the binary sections move in awe-inspiring wholes and halves, and others, in quarters, eighths, and nervous sixteenths. In other words, modern notation takes care of changing tempi that would have been written in the previous century as standard time interspersed with sections in *proportio dupla, subdupla, quadrupla*, and so forth. Still, the proportions are present, albeit without a change of signature.

While the rest of Europe was still wrestling with the remainders of standard tempo and proportions, progressive Italy—although she had had her predecessors in the sixteenth century—began to

---

[7] Henry Purcell, *A choice collection of lessons for the harpsichord or spinnet*, London, 1696.

[8] Georg Muffat, *Suavioris harmoniae florilegium secundum*, Passau, 1698, reprinted in *Denkmäler der Tonkunst in Oesterreich*, Vol. II, 2, Vienna, 1895, p. 24.

[9] Michael Praetorius, *Musarum Sioniarum motecti et psalmi latini* (1607), *Gesamtausgabe*, Wolffenbüttel, 1931, Vol. X, pp. 112–117. The note values of this reprint should be halved.

concentrate on free, unmathematical changes of tempo; indeed, she gave them a privileged place in music. Most of the leading instrumental forms were composed of episodes in different, contrasting tempi: sonatas, concertos, Venetian orchestral *canzoni* (hence nicknamed the "patchwork *canzoni*"), and the so-called Italian overture, fast–slow–fast. Outside of Italy, there were the German suites of dances, the French overtures, slow–fast–slow, and numerous other forms.

With the general recognition of free-chosen tempi, the Italians began to introduce the modern speed indications that we have kept in their original Italian forms, although they partly express a mood rather than an actual tempo, such as *adagio,* 'with leisure,' *allegro,* 'gaily.' Adriano Banchieri's organ repertory *L'organo suonarino* of 1611 already presents *adagio, allegro, veloce, presto, più presto, prestissimo.*

Around the middle of the century, suites by the Bavarian, Matthias Kelz—*Primitiae musicales* (1658)—already carried the Latin and Italian tempo marks: *animose, lente, agiliter, fuso* ('melting'), *tardo, largo, presto,* indeed, *nervose.* In the preface of his *Neuer Clavier Ubung Erster Theil* (1689),[10] Johann Kuhnau—another predecessor of Bach at St. Thomas' in Leipzig—used the German words *etwas hurtig* ('rather swift') for *gigues* and minuets, and *langsam* ('slow') for sarabands and *airs.*

It must not be overlooked that Kuhnau's indications are partly at variance with those of other masters. Early in the century, in Michael Praetorius' collection of dances in the French taste (*Terpsichore,* 1612), the saraband is listed as a species of *courante.* He calls it *courrant sarabande* and adds elsewhere that the *courante* is *gar geschwind* or 'very fast.' [11] On reading the scores, one arrives at a tempo of about 150 M.M. for each of the three beats, or 50 M.M. for the whole measure. At the end of the century, J. A. Schmicerer, composer of suites (*Zodiacus musicus,* 1698), wanted, on the contrary, the saraband taken *adagio e staccato.*

In spite of all these shades, the concept of a standard *tempo giusto* was still alive. It was what it had been before and what it will be in later chapters: Father Mersenne, author of the *Har-*

[10] Reprinted in *Denkmäler Deutscher Tonkunst,* Vol. IV, p. (3).

[11] Michael Praetorius, *Gesamtausgabe,* Wolffenbüttel, 1929, Vol. XV, pp. XIII and 75 f.

monie universelle (1636/37) equated the *tactus* beat with a pulse beat—downward with the contraction of the heart, and upward with its dilation or diastole. But as this was not precise enough in the face of differences from person to person and from hour to hour, many contemporaries, he said, preferred the duration of a second on the dial for the semibreve or motor unit, which amounts to M.M. 60 for the quarter note. Incidentally, the sensible difference between the two standards shows once more that the pulse beat measures tempo, but does not determine it.

THE EXPRESSIVENESS of the Baroque Age was much less introvert in a romantic sense than it was extrovert, indeed, rhetorical. The *Oxford Dictionary* defines rhetoric as "language designed to persuade or impress"; and this is indeed what all the arts, including architecture, were then meant to do. Whether visual or auditory, they aimed at a public that willingly followed and reacted. René François describes in 1621 how an Italian lutanist can do "what he will with men," and Father Mersenne says in his *Harmonie Universelle* of 1636 that modern music forces its way into the listener's soul to appropriate and lead it whither the composer wishes. Indeed, he thinks that a singer's performance should have the convincing power of a well-made speech. For speech is every man's medium. In his speech, he betrays education, character, taste, intelligence; in his speech he might ascend to art in the finest sense of this word before even reaching the level of poetry. No wonder that all through the seventeenth century wording and speech were given a place of honor. In its two forms, enunciation and eloquence, they were in the van of human expression. No wonder that in the seventeenth century an orator and preacher like Bishop Bossuet in France could attain a fame no less than that of the immortals in art and in science.

Singing, bound to words, could not evade the domination of speech. Even the greatest composer of the century, Claudio Monteverdi, pronounced that "speech be the master, not the servant of music." Mersenne, its greatest theorist, insisted on language as the model for melody. And Lully modeled his operatic tunes after the inflection and accents of the greatest actors, whom he used to study in the *Comédie Française.*

The hundred years from the 1580's to the 1680's achieved the subordination of music to the word in their new melodic style: the so-called *stile recitativo e rappresentativo* concentrated on a speechlike melody to express emotion and passion in the most direct way. Taking possession of most of the music outside and inside the newly invented opera or *dramma per musica*, it was meant to draw as near as possible to natural diction with all its irrational lengths of syllables and ever changing shades of tempo. The old polyphonic style was unable to comply with this modern ideal. It had, in the weighty words of Caccini (died 1618), "stretched out or on the contrary compressed the syllables for the sake of counterpoint and thus destroyed meter and words." With this style discredited and gone, melodic inspiration, freed from the tight-fitting fetters of orthodox part-writing, no longer needed to adjust itself to the orderly progress of fellow voices.

"I call that the noble manner of singing which is used without tying a man's self to the ordinary measure of time, making many times the value of the notes less by half, and sometimes more, according to the conceit of the words, whence proceeds that excellent kind of singing with a graceful neglect, whereof I have spoken before." [12]

These significant words are taken from the foreword to Giulio Caccini's epochal collection of monodic art songs, *Le nuove musiche* (1602). And indeed, somewhere in the middle of one of these songs, we find the prescription *senza misura, quasi favellando con sprezzatura,* or "without a regular rhythm, as if pattering leisurely." Similarly, Monteverdi's lengthy monody *Lettera amorosa,* of 1614, is marked *senza battuta.* This expression cannot be mistaken. But not so *sprezzatura,* which recurs in other scores as well. Recently, Dr. Manfred Bukofzer in Berkeley interpreted it as tempo rubato,[13] without, however, defining whether he meant this much-misused term in the correct sense. If so, it would conflict with the indication *senza misura,* which implies a free, not a basically strict tempo. If not, it would run against the literal translation 'disdain,' 'neglect,' 'artlessness,' which points toward free

[12] Transl. Oliver Strunk, *Source Readings in Music History,* New York, W. W. Norton, 1950, p. 391.

[13] Manfred Bukofzer, *Music in the Baroque era,* New York, W. W. Norton, 1947, p. 28.

tempo rather than a rhythmical shift within the strictest tempo.
A memorable illustration of the clash between strictness and
freedom is found in Monteverdi's *Madrigali guerrieri* of 1638: The
three-voice piece *Non havea Febo ancora*, printed in separate
parts, must be sung *al tempo della mano*, that is, in the rigid *tactus*
of the conducting hand. But the subsequent four-voice piece
Lamento della ninfa, printed in score, should be performed *a
tempo del'affetto del animo e non a quello della mano*, 'in a tempo
(dictated by) emotion, not by hand.'

As a matter of fact, the *tempo dell'affetto del animo* against that
della mano had existed in the early days of the Baroque. In 1555,
the priest-musician, Nicola Vicentino, insisted in one of his endless
sentences [14] that the accents of a melody should conform "to the
pronunciation of the words." It would be impossible to notate
compositions "as they are" or, better, as they must be played, "with
their piano and forte, presto and *tardo*, and in keeping with the
words." He wanted a free change of tempo (*muovere la misura*) "to
evidence the passions [expressed in] the words and the harmony."
Such change of tempo *nelle cose volgari*, that is, in madrigals, will
"gratify the listeners more than a steady tempo would do." Following the meaning of the words, the movement should be slower or
faster. And so on ad infinitum.

Even where freedom proper was not granted, a characteristic
means of avoiding the mechanization of strictness when the words
required particular emphasis was what we might call emphatic
offbeats. They were a typically monodic device.

The monody had hardly conquered the stage when Jacopo Peri
and Claudio Monteverdi, its greatest promoters, made the offbeat
stress an outstanding means of expression. When the bereaved
Orfeo—both in Peri's opera *Euridice* (1600) and in Monteverdi's
opera *Orfeo* (1607)—laments in deeply moving outbursts, *O mio*

Ex. 89. Peri, Opera *Euridice*, Act I

O   mio · co- re

[14] Nicola Vicentino, *L'antica musica*, Roma 1555, libro IV, cap. 42, on f. 94ᵛ
(actually misnumbered 88). Dr. Edward Lowinsky was kind enough to draw my attention to this passage.

core, 'Oh my heart,' and *Tu se' morta,* 'thou art dead,' Peri's *O* and Monteverdi's *Tu,* both placed on offbeats, have an expressive power that could never have been achieved on a regular strong beat.

Beyond the Alps, Heinrich Schütz, in the wake of these pioneers and most probably inspired by them, would often lay emotional stresses on offbeats as an essential trait of his passionate *stile oratorio,* as he called his monody. Those who know the author's *Anthologie Sonore* [15] may recall the beginning of a *Geistliches Konzert* or psalm of 1636, *Eile mich Gott zu erretten,* with its emphatic offbeat on the subsequent *Herr* or 'Lord.' Another example, just as powerful, is the desperate appeal, *Vater, Vater, Vater* in the *Seven Words of Christ* (*Sieben Worte Christi,* 1645).

Ex. 90. Schütz, *Sieben Worte Christi*

In the same year, 1645, the father of the modern oratorio, Giacomo Carissimi in Rome, wrote the Italian counterpart in his *Jephte,* where twice the doomed daughter sings her *Pater mi* on the second quarter.

One generation later, Carissimi's greatest pupil, the Frenchman, Marc-Antoine Charpentier (1634–1704), followed the master's practice in Magdalen's words *Hei hei* in the oratorio *Le reniement*

Ex. 91. Charpentier, Oratorio *Le reniement de Saint-Pierre*

de Saint Pierre. And, to add an example from Germany, in a cantata, *Herr, wenn ich nur dich hab,* Dietrich Buxtehude (1637–1707) underscored the invocation *Herr* in forceful entries off the beat.[16]

Here as elsewhere—even in certain forms of Japanese drumming

[15] *Anthologie Sonore,* Vol. III, no. 28.
[16] Cf. Buxtehude's works in the Ugrino edition, Vol. I, p. 35.

—a rest on the downbeat seems to imply a silent 'power-stroke' provided by the active tension of the body and a bated breath,

Ex. 92. Buxtehude, Cantata, *Herr, wenn ich dich nur hab*

Herr, Herr.

while the audible discharge on the unaccented beat is in fact a relaxation. Ilmari Krohn calls such rests 'pathetic.' [17]

INSTRUMENTAL FREEDOM. Created for vocal music and its emphasis on the words to be sung, the expressive freedom of tempo soon took possession of instrumental music, too.

Girolamo Frescobaldi (1583–1643), the most famous organist at St. Peter's in Rome, demanded that his earlier *Toccate e partite* for harpsichord (1614) and again his *Fiori musicali* for organ (1635) be played in a tempo as free "as singers used to perform the modern madrigals" (those of Prince Gesualdo or Monteverdi).

The preface to the *Toccate* says expressly:

"1. Correctly played, these pieces do not proceed in even beats. Rather should they follow the style of performing modern madrigals, which, though difficult, can be facilitated by tempo changes, singing now languishingly, now fast, and once in a while letting a tone hang in the air when the meaning and affect of the word suggest it.

"3. The beginning of a toccata should be *adagio* and *arpeggiando*. . . .

"4. The last note of a trill and of a passage that progresses leapwise or stepwise should be held back a little by an eighth or sixteenth or otherwise in order to distinguish it from the following note values. This *ritenuto* keeps a *passaggio* from flowing into the next one.

"5. Cadences, even when written in rapid notes, must slow down very much, and so must gradually the notes preparing them.

"8. When both hands play sixteenth passages, the notes pre-

[17] Ilmari Krohn, *Der metrische Taktfuss in der modernen Musik,* in *Archiv für Musikwissenschaft,* Vol. IV (1922), p. 103.

ceding them—even if they are written as short notes—must be held a little to better show the agility of the hands in the energetic delivery of the passage.

"9. *Passaggi* and expressive sections in toccatas and partitas must be played in slow tempo, while the other sections can be played somewhat *allegro*. The player's taste and judgment should be the arbiters. It is upon the correct tempo that the spirit and perfection of this style depends."

In the original edition, the last paragraph is printed in boldface; it must have carried particular weight—indeed, it must have been something unwonted at the time.

Once more, in the preface of his *Capricci fatti sopra diversi soggetti* (1624), Frescobaldi insists on the freedom of tempo: "The beginning should be adagio, to give more zest and liveliness to the following part. The cadences should be well held back [!] before the subsequent section begins." And he adds: "Sections in ternary rhythm must be taken adagio when the values are great, but faster when the values are smaller, still more so in 3/4, and allegro, in 6/4."

Frescobaldi's greatest pupil, Johann Jacob Froberger (1616–1667), the leading German keyboard player of the time, performed certain of his pieces in a similarly free expression. In the year of his death, his protectress, Duchess Sibylla of Württemberg, wrote to the Dutch poet, composer, and scholar, Constantijn Huygens in the Hague, that one could hardly play his pieces from the written music, but had to study them "from his hand, note by note. Unless one has learned the things from him, the late Mr. Froberger, one cannot play them with the right discretion as he did." [18]

À (or *avec*) *discrétion* is indeed the word that the publishers added to some of his pieces—*gigues* and *lamentations*—and once, in the *Tombeau sur la mort de Monsieur Blancheroche* (about 1655), they even went to the length of prescribing *fort lentement à la discrétion sans observer aucune mesure.*[19]

Across the Channel, Thomas Mace [20] voiced a similar viewpoint:

[18] Edmund Schebek, *Zwei Briefe über Johann Jacob Froberger,* Vienna, 1874, p. 22.

[19] *Denkmäler der Tonkunst in Oesterreich,* Vol. XIII, pp. 38, 59; Vol. XXI, pp. 110, 114.

[20] Thomas Mace, *Musick's monument,* London, 1676, p. 81.

"When we come to be Masters, so that we can command all manner of Time, at our Pleasures; we Then take Liberty . . . to Break Time; sometimes Faster and sometimes Slower, as we perceive the Nature of the Thing Requires, which often adds, much Grace, and Luster, to the Performance."

It should be understood that Mace's "broken time," Froberger's *discrétion*, and particularly Frescobaldi's *ritenuto* cadences were completely at variance with Georg Muffat's contradictory prohibition of 1698, only a few decades later: "One must take care," Muffat says, "*not* to dwell longer or less on cadences than the notes imply." Muffat insists, indeed, on maintaining a uniform tempo throughout a piece. And he also pillories the abuse of playing a piece indiscriminately, the first time slowly, the second time faster, and the third time very fast.

Whether these discrepancies were a matter of difference between ages, nations, or personalities, is not certain. But it seems that they depend on the same eternal dualism, classicistic–anti-classicistic or static–dynamic, that the chapter on the eighteenth century will discuss in greater detail. The trends of the later seventeenth century, in many respects more classicistic than those around 1600, might have favored greater strictness. Qualities well befitting the speechlike emotional freedom of the early Florentine-Mantuan monody were out of place in the architectural regularity of the Neapolitan *da capo* aria and the fugues of the North. Not even the later 'dry,' unaccompanied *recitativo secco* of the Italians had expressive shades. The singer, anxious to get to the showy bravura of his aria, skimmed over the introductory recitative in what was no longer free tempo and rhythm, but simply neglect.

All this shows once more how little we are entitled to generalize. The sweeping classification "older music" is totally unfounded.

Since musicians and music lovers are probably more interested in Bach or Couperin than in Frescobaldi, Froberger, or Muffat, it seems unavoidable to take sides in the question as to whether or not the last measures in the compositions of the two leading masters in Germany and France should be slowed down. Our answer must of necessity be tentative.

The adherents of free tempo, Frescobaldi and even his pupil

Froberger, belonged to the early Baroque with its subjective, emotional trends. In their anticlassicistic attitude, they avoided polyphony and concentrated upon the free, rhapsodic, and almost improvisatory form of the toccata. Muffat, the enemy of yielding tempi, on the other hand, represented the French-inspired classicism of the end of the century, the age of Louis XIV. To him, a well-wrought, often polyphonic form was paramount.

Bach—not to speak of Couperin—was closer to Muffat than to Frescobaldi. He did not spurn toccatas, to be sure; but they were exceptions in his work. The essence of his compositions, though never stiff or pedantic, followed strictest form—canon, fugue, Italian *da capo* aria; and experience shows that rigid form entails a steady tempo, and vice versa.

To be sure, there might be changes of tempo even within as short a form as the prelude. But such changes denote new sections within a piece; and they are sudden, not gradual. We might think of the end of Prelude II in *The Well-tempered Clavier*, Part I, with its six measures of presto, two of adagio, and four of allegro; or of the organ prelude, I, 2, with its adagio coda of eleven and a half bars. But the deflation *ritardandi* of final cadences that the naive performer takes for granted are entirely against the architectural spirit of Bach.

Speaking of this master of masters: Bach's obituary, written by his son Carl Philipp Emanuel and Johann Friedrich Agricola and published four years after his death, states that he took his tempi "very lively"; and Johann Nicolaus Forkel's pioneering book *On Johann Sebastian Bach's Life, Genius, and Works* (1802) confirms that "in the execution of his own pieces he generally took the time very brisk." [21] One more disillusionment for his many ever-solemn performers!

BAROQUE CLASSICISM. This discussion has carried the reader beyond the end of the early Baroque to the classicistic reversal mentioned in the introduction of this chapter. The Italians, basically fond of well-wrought form and of singing for the sake of singing, were fed up with shapeless monodies—*tedio del recitativo*

[21] Hans T. David and Arthur Mendel, *The Bach reader*, New York, W. W. Norton, 1945, p. 312.

they called what they were feeling. Drawing away from naturalism and over-expressiveness, they were estranged from rhythmical freedom and strove for clear-cut, regular rhythm.

Despite classicistic reversals, the Baroque could never grow static. Even in times of restraint, it was eager, where possible, to display dramatic, acting, driving forces. With Shakespeare, Calderón, Corneille, it had created the modern spoken tragedy; with Peri, Caccini, Monteverdi, the opera. In every one of its phases, it cherished emphasis on vigorous, often theatrical, gesture and steady movement in all the arts. And even façades of churches and palaces, often curved in and out, seem to move rather than stand.

This ceaseless movement is one of the first characteristics of rhythm and tempo in the Baroque. Nothing could be more Baroque than the striding basses which, even, majestic, and sometimes pompous, support the melody in a steady, unexcited drive, in the strongest balance of motion and rest. We all know them—Monteverdi's *ostinati*, the knightly beginning of Purcell's *Golden Sonata* for two violins, or, in the *Credo* and the *Dona nobis pacem* of Bach's B minor Mass, the mighty basses, which, starlike, seem to move in all eternity through space and time and carry the listener's attention beyond the bounds of bars and sections in that horizontal expanse so dear to the age in all its arts.

Very close to these basses in even strides are the frequent iambic basses in 3/4, as we know them best from Bach's great *passacaglia* in C minor on a theme by the French organist Raison.

Since the *passacaglia* and the closely related *ciaconna* are dance forms, we come to realize the very typical connection of the rhythms in the Baroque with the dance. An age so solidly built on movement could hardly avoid a decisive influence on the part of the most movemental of the arts, the less so, as the composers had no other starting points. Eager to replace the roving, shapeless monody by steadfast forms, they had no models in the flowing polyphony, vocal or instrumental, of the Renaissance; no models either in the irrational, oratorical *stile senza misura* of the early century; no models, finally, in the free, improvisational styles of instrumental music. The dances of the time, clear-cut, divisive, accentual, symmetric, were the only point of departure.

But even so exclusive a position would not wholly explain the enormous influence of dance rhythms as one of the most essential traits of the Baroque. The dance itself had an importance greater than ever before or after. Social dancing in aristocratic circles was an art—nobody would have dared present himself on the floor without having studied for years and years. The ballet on the stage had its heyday as one of the leading art forms—from Beaujoyeux's *Ballet de la Reine* through Monteverdi's *Combattimento di Tancredi* and *Ballo delle Ingrate* to Lully's *Ballets de Cour*, of which Louis XIV was the star.

Instrumental music led the way to divorce the characteristic patterns of rhythm and structure from actual dancing. It re-created them, above all, in the so-called *suite* of concert dances—an aggregate of contrasting forms, of rhythms and tempi, solemn and gay, slower and faster, binary, ternary—to be played outdoors, in squares and in parks, and later even indoors, indeed, on the harpsichord. The suite had a special significance as the mother of the *sonata da camera* and as one of the most important roots of the symphony, which, down to Beethoven's time, kept a remainder of the old dance connotation in its minuet movement. So dominating was the influence of dance music that the *allemande* and kindred forms were used to express lament and mourning in the numerous *plaintes, tombeaux,* and *lamentations* of the age.

The influence of characteristic dance rhythms even reached into vocal music: beginning with Giovanni Giacomo Gastoldi's earliest attempts in 1591, there emerged, in Italy as well as in England and elsewhere, catchy *Balletti per cantare, sonare & ballare*, as a re-fusion of dancing, singing, and playing and their aftermath in the choruses of the nascent opera. Moreover, as the following section will show, many songs of the seventeenth and early eighteenth centuries were written in the patterns of the saraband and other dances.

TRIPLE AND QUADRUPLE TIME. The leadership of 4/4 is unquestioned also in the seventeenth century. German sources refer to it as *schlichter Takt*, 'plain' or normal time, which is the exact equivalent of British 'common time.'

The last remainders of 'perfection' disappear; every note, as represented by an original symbol without an additional sign, is normally binary: the whole note equals two halves; the half note, two quarters; the quarter note, two eighths. Ternary character was considered against the norm and was therefore denoted by the original (binary) symbol *plus* an auxiliary dot: ♩. = ♩ ♩ ♩ .

And still, despite the leadership of 4/4, ternary time was in a way the distinctive pattern of the Baroque, no longer as an over-size *perfectio* in a Gothic sense, nor as an undersize *tripla* or *sesquialtera* in the sense of the Renaissance, but as an independent configuration with various tempi of its own, for which we have examples as early as the sixteenth century.

This new, or almost new, *ternalitas* is most striking in the well-defined field of dance music.

In the sixteenth century there had been a definite predominance of binary dancing. Among the seventeen types of dances in that age discussed in the author's *World History of the Dance*,[22] nine, or more than half, have unconditional duple time: *pavane, passamezzo, courante, bergamasca, danse des bouffons, branle double, branle de Montirandé, branle de Bourgogne, gavotte.* Four others are ambiguous: the *danse des Canaries* occurs both in 3/8 and in 2/4; the *cascarda* has 12/8, which is duple rather than triple in performance—"*a tempo di quattro battute*" says a contemporary; and even the *sarabande* and the *chacona* appear in 4/4 as well as in the 3/4 that we take for granted today. Less than a third of all dances—*galliarde, tourdion, volta, branle gay,* and the *triori* of Brittany—are definitely in ternary time.

The ratio is more than reversed in the seventeenth century. Out of ten dances eight are in all cases ternary, among them the leading courtly dances of the time, *menuet* and *courante.* The two binary exceptions, *bourrée* and *rigaudon,* are unaristocratic folk dances and as such not really significant; and the *bourrée,* at that, is sometimes ternary.

A similar survey in the broader field of music outside the dance is hardly feasible; and the ratio would by no means show a majority of ternary time; 4/4 was still 'common.' But nobody familiar with the seventeenth and early eighteenth centuries could overlook the comparatively frequent use and the importance of triple time.

In the first half of the century, ternary pieces, still following in

[22] Curt Sachs, *World history of the dance,* New York, 1937, pp. 356–413.

the wake of the old *proportio sesquialtera*, were generally faster than common time. A momentous change took place not much before the mid-century. Pregnant examples from that early time can be easily found in the scores of Carissimi (d. 1674). But the most delightful, truly Baroque example is the lament of Hecuba in Cavalli's heroic opera *Didone* (1641), with the noble stride of an *ostinato* bass in a hesitant iambic meter and the frequent dotting of the second beat: ♩ ♩. ♪|♩ .

The pattern is familiar. It shows the characteristic rhythm of the *Folía* or *Folie d'Espagne* and, eventually, of the saraband. But in order to set right an all too frequent mistake, it should be emphasized that as late as the second half of the century the saraband had often only a simple 3/4 time without the dotted second. Among the three sarabands in the first volume of Lully's ballets (1654–1657), only one is dotted.[23]

The broad, almost majestic *folía* rhythm reached its climax in the late Baroque and made its most beautiful appearance with Almirena's aria *Lascia ch'io pianga* in Handel's opera *Rinaldo* of

Ex. 93. Handel, Opera, *Rinaldo*, aria, *Lascia ch'io piango*

1711. But it had offshoots down to the last quarter of the nineteenth century: the slow movement in Beethoven's piano trio, Op. 97, in B flat (1811), the *Grandioso* in Liszt's B minor sonata (1853), the solemn Valhalla motif in Wagner's *Ring des Nibelungen* (1854), and the famous aria *Mon coeur s'ouvre à toi* in the second act of Saint-Saëns' *Samson et Dalila* (1877).

Ex. 94. Beethoven, piano trio, Op. 97 in B flat

Ex. 95. Liszt, B minor sonata for piano

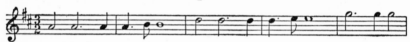

[23] Jean-Baptiste Lully, *Oeuvres complètes: Les Ballets*, Vol. I.

Ex. 96. Wagner, *Der Ring des Nibelungen*, Valhalla motif

Ex. 97. Saint-Saëns, opera, *Samson et Dalila*, aria, *Mon coeur s'ouvre*

Typically late Baroque, in these sustained ternary rhythms, is the initial stretch, the anticipative widening of the first note to often four times its proper value. One example, at least, is universally known: an aria from Handel's otherwise forgotten opera *Serse* ("Xerxes," 1738), since arranged for all combinations of in-

Ex. 98. Handel, opera, *Serse*, Act I, Scene 1, *Largo*

struments and popularly called the *Largo*, where the initial phrase has five instead of four measures because the first note is tied backwards to fill a whole introductory bar. Similar examples can be

Ex. 99. Steffani, chamber duo, *Occhi perchè piangete*

found in the chamber duets of Agostino Steffani (1654–1728), that is, one generation before Handel.

Speaking of ternary rhythm and dances, one cannot well pass in silence the juxtaposition of national playing styles in the preface to Georg Muffat's *Florilegium*.[24] It shows how the Germans and the Italians would bow a certain minuet, and how the Lully-educated French would do it. Lully's phrasing is truly ternary, with an accented down-bow on every first beat and an unaccented up-bow on every second and third beat. The Germans and the Italians, on the contrary, start on an up-bow and proceed in a

[24] Georg Muffat, *Suavioris harmoniae florilegium secundum*, Passau, 1698, reprinted in *Denkmäler der Tonkunst in Oesterreich*, Vol. II, ii, Vienna, 1895, p. 21.

regular alternation so that, as a rule, the first beats are alternately given an up- and a down-bow.

This procedure is too close to the old *tactus* habits to be accidental. It reminds one very much of the confusing discrepancy between the beaten and the musical measure mentioned earlier. The *tactus*, rigidly duple in quality, even beat ternary measures in a persistent up-and-down, so that the first of the three units fell now on a downbeat and the next time on an upbeat. This seemingly absurd procedure was acceptable only because the *tactus* did not convey any accent to a music that did not know much actual stress. By analogy, the alternate bowing of Germans and Italians at the end of the seventeenth century seems to indicate that these two nations still clung to the nearly stressless old performance even in instrumental music and in their very dances, while the school of Lully represented the modern accentual system.

HEMIOLA. Soon after the middle of the century, the novel dance of the day, the minuet, embodied a curious rhythmic anomaly. Its music was written in 3/4. But the regular step pattern consisted in a long bending step with the right foot, extending over two of the three quarter notes, and another long bending step with the left foot, also extending over two quarters and therewith ignoring the bar line, plus two straight and shorter steps, coinciding with one quarter each. In notation:

$$\text{music:} \quad 3/4 \quad \text{♩ ♩ ♩ |♩ ♩ ♩}$$
$$\text{dance:} \quad 3/2 \quad \text{♩ ♩ ♩ ♩}$$
$$\text{r} \quad \text{l} \quad \text{r} \quad \text{l}$$

Hence, the dancing master Giambattista Dufort felt compelled to recommend in his *Trattato del ballo nobile* (Naples, 1728) that the accompanying musicians should not stress the first beats of the even-numbered bars.

In short, the minuet dancer countered the 3/4 of the melody in a 3/2 hemiola.

The minuet was by no means the only hemiola dance, though none but the minuet had attracted the attention of a theoretician. Similar cases had occurred in the sixteenth century, especially in the galliard and the tourdion.

Outside dancing, the quick regrouping that we call hemiola

was a stock requisite of the Baroque as it had been back in the fourteenth and fifteenth centuries, both in melodic succession and in polyphonic coincidence: six units (written either in one or in two measures) are understood, now as two times three, now as three times two; they are either binary with ternary subdivisions or else ternary with binary subdivisions.

This omnipresent contraction of two 3/4 bars into one 3/2 measure with the help of a tie across the inner bar line has been proudly credited as a "two-length" bar to an anglicized Handel and his English predecessors.[25] Alas, this cryptic rhythm is neither specifically Handelian nor specifically British. It is the age-old and quite supranational hemiola, which the reader has met and will meet in almost each of the chapters of this book, from the ancient Orient to the modern West.

The dragging quality of all the ternary rhythms just discussed— the augmented iamb or *orthios* short-and-long, the retarded third beat of the *folía* and the sarabande, the elongated initial beat, and the three–two hemiola—gave melodies once more a broad horizontal expanse.

A similar dragging quality was sometimes achieved by overstretching a melodic line beyond the bar, as in the beautiful violin introduction to the soprano aria *Laudamus te* in Bach's B minor Mass. Both melodically and harmonically, the breath-taking tension in measure 5 comes to a peak only with the second eighth of measure 6. Measure 5 has actually 4 + 5 eighths.

Ex. 100. Bach, B minor Mass, *Laudamus te*

On hearing such rhythms, the listener has a truly Baroque experience. Architecture of the time expanded horizontally in much the same way, avoiding tallness and towers; within the enormous left–right span of the palace of Versailles even the church has no steeple. An unusual number of paintings were given an oblong

[25] H. H. Wintersgill, *Handel's two-length bar*, in *Music and letters*, Vol. XVII, 1937, pp. 1–12. Cf. also Rudolf Steglich, *Zur Kenntnis der sechsteiligen Takte*, in *Zeitschrift für Musikwissenschaft*, Vol. III, 1921, pp. 449–458.

form rather than the upright, vertical shape that the Renaissance had preferred. And social dancing no longer tolerated the leaps that once the galliard, *volta, nizzarda* had had. For, says the dancing master Rameau, "it is not seemly for great personages to leap and toss themselves about."

CHAPTER 13

Le Style Galant and the Age of Enlightenment

The great reversal of the 1720's had different aspects in different countries—it appeared as rococo or *style galant,* as middle-class movement, sentimentalism, or enlightenment. It was aristocratic and democratic; it opened the door for emotion and also for reason. But as far as music was concerned, it had one common goal: to abandon *la musique savante,* the dusty style of scholars and pedants, of cantors and organists. In the field of rhythm, the 'moderns' must have frowned at the archaic, turgid counterrhythm in the Resurrexit of Bach's B minor Mass, where the *basso solo* sings *Judicare vivos* in strictest 3/4 while a long 4/4 passage of the instrumental basses ignores the deceptive bar lines.[1]

Ex. 101. Bach, B minor Mass, Resurrexit, *Judicare vivos*

In its later days, to be sure, the century yields one example of particular rhythmical interest out of the ordinary and in its com-

---

[1] Complete edition of the *Bach-Gesellschaft,* Vol. VI, 1856, p. 206. I am indebted to Arthur Mendel for drawing my attention to this passage.

plication seemingly reminiscent of Flamboyant polyrhythms: the
famous scene in the ballroom in Mozart's *Don Giovanni* (1787),
where no less than three dance orchestras on the stage play in
3/8, 2/4, and 3/4 against each other. Actually there is not much
complication: the 2/4 orchestra shares all its bar lines with the
3/8 orchestra; and after every two measures of the 3/4 orchestra,
the bar line goes all through the three staff groups. Not to forget
that once in a while two allegedly conflicting voice parts duplicate
one another in octaves.

Ex. 102. Mozart, opera, *Don Giovanni*, ballroom scene

Indeed, the two generations after Bach and Handel strove for
clarity, lightness, simplicity. They banished fugues and kindred
forms of polyphony; they immobilized and sterilized the middle
voice parts and relied basically on melody and bass.

Such a trend was hardly in the interest of rhythmical life. The
simplest pattern would do. Rameau's operatic scores have pages
and pages of uniform quarter beats, many of Domenico Scarlatti's
harpsichord sonatas run off in a stream of perpetual sixteenths,
and even Handel provides examples: witness his F major suite for
harpsichord in its Allegro movement.[2]

CIRCUMLOCUTION, FEMININITY, AND *DOUCE MA-
NIÈRE.* While rhythmical life developed but little, melody as such
was given a refinement beyond our comprehension. Melody in our
sense—indeed, the melody as it was then written and printed—

---

[2] G. F. Handel, *Suite de pièces pour le clavecin*, London, 1720.

was nothing but a blueprint to be realized and enlivened in the performer's personal way. Slower melodies were dissolved into glittering coloraturas beyond recognition, whatever the musical medium was, the voice, the violin, the harpsichord. But also individual notes were affected; a direct and simple attack as it stood on paper would have been against the spirit of the *style galant*. The author cannot help thinking of a passage in Casanova's memoirs: when the Italian adventurer, some time around 1750, was traveling to France, a French *abbé*, his fellow-traveler in the mail coach, rebuked him for answering *non* to a question he had asked him and suggested a longer, well-polished, roundabout negation. "Where is the difference?" asked Casanova. And the smiling priest replied: "The difference? That the one form is polite, and the other one isn't." When a *c* was necessary, Casanova's contemporaries, and particularly in France, wanted it the "polite" way, in a circuitous statement and with its accent concealed rather than stressed. The direct approach was profoundly disliked as too vulgar and clumsy.

Musical circumlocutions, technically known as the *agréments*, were meant, in Carl Philipp Emanuel Bach's expression, to join "notes smoothly together." This statement testifies to the same ideal of close, gliding movement so striking in the courtly dance of the time, especially in the minuet and its next of kin. Dainty, flexing steps were dominant; no leaps, no energetic strides, no gestures were permitted. "Close movement reigns supreme. . . . The *douce manière* is the most pleasing. . . . It is only gentle and gracious movements which do not take from the body the dignified air. . . ." [3]

Like every close movement, the *agréments* had quite obviously a strictly feminine character. The eighteenth century itself felt this; Johann Adam Hiller (1728–1804), expressing the idea the other way around, praised the exceptional adagio performance of the famous violinist Johann Georg Pisendel (1687–1755) as 'devoid of unnecessary graces and thoroughly *virile*." Feminine trends in music are only natural where elegant Rococo and tearful sentimentalism reign. Once more, we realize how right the

[3] Gottfried Taubert, *Der rechtschaffene Tantzmeister*, Leipzig, 1717, p. 616.

Greeks had been in contrasting rhythm and melody as forces virile and feminine: the feminine eighteenth century, little interested in rhythm, gave all its energy to melodic refinement.

Nowhere was the feminine character more obtrusive than in the appoggiatura of the time. And nothing could be more typical than the fact that the appoggiatura was compulsory in all the fields of music, whether or not it was prescribed in notation. This ornament consistently replaced what prosody calls a masculine ending on one accented syllable or note by a feminine ending on two with the second one unstressed.

This feminine articulation of eighteenth-century music is particularly impressive in view of the fact that the Renaissance had had almost exclusively masculine cadences, with the final note on the strong beat.

APPOGGIATURA. An appoggiatura from the Italian verb *appoggiare,* 'to lean upon'—can be described in a general way as some grace note, written in smaller size if at all, which glides into an ordinary note from above or below. But different definitions must be given—one for the seventeenth and eighteenth centuries, and another for the nineteenth and twentieth centuries. Indeed, the modern appoggiatura is more or less the opposite of what it was in older times.

Today's appoggiatura, very short and stressless, takes a tiny bit from the *preceding* note and snaps or bounces into the following ordinary note, which keeps its unimpaired duration and accent. It has a pointed, prim, and often humoristic effect (as in Wagner's characterizations of the shaky, deceitful midget Mime in *Siegfried* or of the tottering tailors in the *Meistersinger*).

In the seventeenth and eighteenth centuries, on the contrary, the appoggiatura—then called *backfall* in England—took an essential part, sometimes two-thirds, from the *following* note. It fell *upon* the beat and carried the accent.

In the Baroque, down into the eighteenth century, the player had been rather free to balance the two notes against one another. The notational symbols used at the time for the appoggiatura—a lunula, an apostrophe, or even the modern small-sized grace note —left the choice between equal values, straight dotting, and reverse dotting. In the first of these three ways of interpretation, the written note kept only half of its allotted duration and left the first half to the appoggiatura. In the second way, the written note claimed only the last quarter of its allotted duration and left three quarters to the appoggiatura. In the third case (the Lombardian taste or Scotch snap), the appoggiatura usurped the accented first quarter and left the remaining three-quarters to the ordinary note. This choice, however, was not arbitrary. It followed certain rules, which are beyond the scope of this book.

After the end of the Baroque, in the 1750's, the appoggiaturas, like all the other circumlocutions, had already deteriorated from meaningful, improvised graces to mannerisms often empty and glued on—just like those of Casanova's French *abbé*. Once stereotyped, they were thoughtfully classified and brought into a system that had to be learned as the essential part of musical education.

J. J. Quantz, C. P. E. Bach, Leopold Mozart, and many others tried their best—not without at times contradicting one another. Here, too, the present author will refrain from giving too many details, exceptions, or special cases. It might suffice to speak of the time values meted out to the ordinary notes and the appoggiaturas. These are, after all, the main concern of modern performers.

Generally speaking, an appoggiatura before an (undotted) binary note takes half of the latter's duration. An appoggiatura before a (dotted) ternary note takes two-thirds of the latter's duration. Thus, when the appoggiatura precedes a half note (in writing), it actually assumes one quarter and leaves the second quarter to the written-out note; when the appoggiatura precedes a dotted half note, it takes possession of an (undotted) half note, while the ordinary note shrinks to a quarter. In 6/8 and 6/4 rhythms the appoggiatura is given three units: the measure is binary.

Sometimes, a measure consists (in writing) of an appoggiatura, an ordinary note, and a rest. In this case, the rest must be ignored and its place taken by the ordinary note, while the appoggiatura is given the whole duration of the ordinary note as it appears in writing.

Only one special case is worth mentioning: chains of thirds with 'passing' appoggiaturas. These passing notes can be realized in three ways:

(1) by giving all the notes except the first an equal duration and letting the passing notes carry the stresses (which violates the law of metric alteration in a set of equal shorts);

(2) by organizing them in Lombardian taste, with the appoggiatura accented and short;

(3) by dotting the ordinary notes and appending the subsequent appoggiaturas as shorts.

The last arrangement anticipates the modern form of snapping short appoggiaturas before the beat.

It seems that the whole practice of older appoggiatura notation, so utterly against our modern concepts, was mainly due to the practice of playing the figured bass. The keyboard performer, with a watchful eye on the bass and on the melody in order to improvise a well-wrought harmony between the two without hesitation, would have been exposed to unavoidable mistakes if dissonant appoggiaturas were presented as parts of the melody. A treble *e* above a bass on *c* clearly demanded a simple triad; but a dissonant *f* in the treble would have suggested any choice of chords except the correct one. The decline and close of the figured bass accompaniment in the last third of the eighteenth century coincided logically with the degeneration of the older uncertain notation. There was no longer any reason for hiding appoggiaturas in so cryptic a way. From that time on most of them were written in ordinary note sizes as a rightful part of melody. Only the so-called short appoggiatura kept the small-size symbol, because otherwise it would have necessitated a complicated dotting or double-dotting of the preceding note.

At the beginning of the nineteenth century, Koch's *Musikalisches Lexikon* [4] still treats the appoggiaturas of measurable duration in the old way, and it is not easy to make out whether he describes an actual survival or just bows to Quantz and Philipp Emanuel (whom he quotes) in an archaism so common in older writings. Nevertheless, on the last two pages of the article he presents the modern appoggiatura of shortest duration with the

---

[4] Heinrich Christoph Koch, *Musikalisches Lexikon*, Offenbach, 1802, p. 1726.

accent on the following main note. Curiously, his examples show the appoggiaturas *on* the beat, against this definition. He explains, however, that the grace note or group of grace notes that serve as an appoggiatura snap so quickly into the main note that practically the latter loses nothing of its actual duration.

The reluctance to approach a note directly appears most strongly in an *agrément*, very typical of *la douce manière* and called *coulé* in France, *tirata* ('drawn') by the Italians, *Schleifer* in German, and *slide, fall,* or *double appoggiatura* in English. An early mention of the voice "being carried gracefully" to the level on which the accent should be produced can be found in Artusi's booklet *Delle imperfezioni della moderna musica* (1600),[5] and an early example in the monody *Vergine bella che di sol vestita* by the Florentine composer, Domenico Belli (fl.1610–1616), on the syl-

Ex. 103. Belli, *Vergine balla che di sol vestita*

lable *Ver-*.[6] But one might just as well go back to the Gregorian chant with its innumerable instances of written-out *tirate,* such as:

Ex. 104. Gregorian *tirate*

The last of these three examples is dated eleventh century. A late, indeed contemporary, instance is in the first words that the hero sings in Stravinsky's opera-oratorio *Oedipus Rex* (1929):

Ex. 105. Stravinsky, *Oedipus Rex*

[5] Cf. Oliver Strunk, *Source readings in music history,* New York, 1951, p. 398.
[6] Reprinted in August Wilhelm Ambros, *Geschichte der Musik,* Vol. IV, ed. Hugo Leichtentritt, Leipzig, 1909, p. 800.

In the eighteenth century, the *tirata* was meant to bridge any interval wider than a second—oftenest a third or a fourth—so that the leap was avoided and replaced by a few very short tones and semitones in the same spirit that drove architects to wedge connecting, smoothing volutes into the angular outlines of church façades. This ornament set in on the beat that the aimed-at note should have had and pushed the latter back to an unaccented position between the beats. A slide upwards was in older England called *whole fall* or *elevation;* moving down, it was a *double backfall.*

Still more complicated was the case of dotted slides, which can be better shown than described.[7] The main note was, here too, reduced to a merely ornamental role.

Most *agréments* other than the appoggiaturas and slides have little rhythmical interest and will therefore be disregarded. But the two concepts of alteration and dotting are important enough to be discussed in greater detail.

METRIC ALTERATION [8] had existed long before the eighteenth century and even outside western civilization: on the island of Okinawa, ♫ is performed as trochaic triplets—♩♪.[9]

At least from the sixteenth century on, equal time values in groups of shorter notes—eighths or sixteenths—were avoided as far as possible. Sequences of such notes could be written in uniform symbols; but they were expected to be performed as alternately 'good' and 'bad' notes, the good ones being somewhat lengthened out and accented at the cost of the bad ones. By exception, the good ones, though accented, could be shortened to the Scotch snap or 'Lombardian taste.'

Quite a number of theorists in the sixteenth century speak of such alteration, albeit often in a rather vague phrasing. As the earliest unambiguous evidence, Giulio Caccini mentions and even

[7] C. P. E. Bach, *Essay on the True Art of Playing Keyboard Instruments,* New York, 1949, pp. 139 ff.

[8] Mr. Sol Babitz, violinist in Los Angeles, was probably the first to draw attention to this phenomenon. I remember with pleasure his convincing demonstrations in my class during a summer term in the University of Southern California and a manuscript that he had prepared and given me to look over. This paper has since been published in *The Musical Quarterly,* Vol. XXXVIII, October, 1952.

[9] Seihin Yamanouchi, *The Music of the Ryūkyūs,* Vol. 1, Tokyo, 1950, p. 5.

illustrates it in the Foreword to *Le nuove musiche* (1601/02). Shortly later, in 1613, the Hispano-Italian, Pedro Cerone, demands that a bit be taken away from the time value of one note and added to the following note.[10]

At the end of the seventeenth century, L'Affillard says on three consecutive pages of his *Principes* [11] that of every two eighths the second one should be very short; and Georg Muffat, Lully's disciple, calls alteration a necessary device.[12]

The eighteenth century, beginning two years after the publication of Muffat's second *Florilegium,* gave alteration an important place in its theoretical books. Johann David Heinichen (1711 [13]) speaks of the "well-known" fact that of all notes of equal value, the first, third, fifth, etc., are *virtualiter longae,* while the second, fourth, sixth, etc., are *virtualiter breves. Virtualiter,* to him, is "according to their inner value," a terminology that Johann Gottfried Walther was going to resume. But since this account has grouped itself in chronological order, Walther must still be held back in favor of Louis XIV's eminent organist and harpsichord player, François Couperin *le Grand,* who in his method of 1717 said clearly:

"Our writing differs from our performance. This is why foreigners play our music less well than we play theirs. The Italians, on the contrary, notate their music with the true values which have been in their minds. For instance, we give dots to eighths in stepwise succession; and yet we write them in equal values." [14]

In 1732, a leading German dictionary of music [15] discusses alteration under an enigmatic heading and in equally cryptic terms: "*Quantitas Notarum extrinseca, & intrinseca* [*lat.*], the outer and inner value of the notes; the former term applies to notes of the same kind performed in equal lengths, since the odd part

[10] Pedro Cerone, *El melopeo y maestro,* Naples, 1613, p. 541.

[11] Michel L'Affillard, *Principes très-faciles pour bien apprendre la musique,* Paris, pp. 34–36, quoted from the undated seventh edition.

[12] Georg Muffat, *Suavioris harmoniae florilegium secundum,* Passau, 1698, reprinted in *Denkmäler der Tonkunst in Oesterreich,* Vol. II, 2, Vienna 1895, p. 24; examples on pp. 53 ff. of the same volume.

[13] Johann David Heinichen, *Neu erfundene und gründliche Anweisung,* Hamburg, 1711, p. 258; new edition, as *Der Generalbass,* Dresden, 1728, p. 258.

[14] François Couperin, *L'art de toucher le clavecin,* Paris, 1717, p. 39.

[15] Johann Gottfried Walther, *Musicalisches Lexicon,* Leipzig, 1732, p. 507. I am indebted to Arthur Mendel for this not easily accessible reference.

of a measure is long, and the even part of a measure, short." Nobody can understand this definition without a previous knowledge of the problem and its implications.

The fullest account, as always, can be read in the three big treatises of the 1750's, by Quantz, C. P. E. Bach, and Leopold Mozart.

Quantz is very eloquent. "In performance, one must distinguish between the principal notes (which are also called attacking or, in the Italian way, good notes) and the passing notes, which are called bad notes by some foreigners. Wherever possible, the principal notes must be more accented than the passing notes. By the same token, the fastest notes, be it in moderate tempo or in adagio, must be played a bit unevenly although they look alike; so that the attacking notes of every figure—the first, third, fifth, and seventh—are held somewhat longer than the second, fourth, sixth, or eighth. But this lengthening should not amount to a dot. By 'fastest notes' I understand quarters in 3/2; eighths in 3/4; sixteenths in 3/8; eighths in *alla breve;* sixteenths or thirty-seconds in 2/4 or common 4/4; but only as long as there are no figures of notes still faster or twice as fast. For in this case it is the latter ones that must be performed in the way just described. . . . Excepted from this rule are, first, very fast passages in a very fast tempo that leaves no time but to lengthen and stress the first of every four notes. Also excepted are all fast passages that the singing voice has to perform, unless they are meant to glide. Unevenness is out of place, since every note in such a singing passage must be detached and marked off by a gentle exhalation. Excepted are also notes with dashes or dots above or those which repeat the same tone; slurred groups of more than two notes, that is, of four or six or eight; and finally the eighths in gigues. All these notes must be played evenly in equal lengths." [16]

Carl Philipp Emanuel Bach repeats, at first, what Heinichen has said. Even the word *virtualiter* recurs.[17] But in a later passage he is more circumstantial.

Sixteenths "sound insipid in an adagio if dots are not played be-

[16] Johann Joachim Quantz, *Versuch einer Anweisung die Flöte traversiere zu spielen,* Berlin, 1752, Chapter XI, § 12.

[17] C. P. E. Bach, *op. cit.,* p. 196; original edition, Part II, Chapter 1, § 74.

tween them. It is advisable to correct this fault in performance. Because proper exactness is often lacking in the notation of dotted notes, a general rule of performance has been established which, however, suffers many exceptions. According to this rule, the notes which follow the dots are to be played in the most rapid manner; and often they should be. But sometimes notes in other parts, with which these must enter, are so divided that a modification of the rule is required. Again, a suave effect, which will not survive the essentially defiant character of dotted notes, obliges the performer slightly to shorten the dotted note. Hence, if only one kind of execution is adopted as the basic principle of performance, the other kinds will be lost." [18]

The account of Leopold Mozart's contribution can be brief: he recommended that the "good" notes be "not only a little stronger, but also a little longer." [19]

Let us end this survey with a quotation from Jean-Jacques Rousseau's Dictionary of 1768 under the heading *pointer*, which in French means dotting: "In Italian music eighth notes (*croches*) are always equal unless marked to be dotted. But in French music eighths are perfectly even only in 4/4; otherwise they are always a bit dotted unless expressly marked as 'even eighths.' " [20]

Incidentally, in modern swing, alteration is so much a matter of course that the arranger expressly indicates when a certain passage should proceed in even notes.

All the evidences, including those which speak of dotting, leave no doubt that the ratio in length between the odd-numbered and the even-numbered notes was doubtful, changing, indeed irrational.

Only one source, off the beaten track, provides us with actual figures. This source is Father Marie-Dominique-Joseph Engramelle's outstanding treatise on mechanical instruments. The ratio could not be left irrational where the decision was taken away from the performer and left to the manufacturer: a definite solution was required in the preparation of the then highly

---

[18] C. P. E. Bach, *op. cit.*, p. 372; original edition, Chap. 29, § 15.

[19] Leopold Mozart, *Versuch einer gründlichen Violinschule*, Augsburg, 1756, Chapter XII, § 10.

[20] Jean-Jacques Rousseau, *Dictionnaire de Musique* (Paris, 1768), Geneva, 1781, Vol. II, p. 119.

cherished music boxes with cranks or clockwork. Engramelle needed no less than five pages to indicate at what distances the plucking pins should be inserted in the revolving cylinder to provide the correct ratios in metric alteration.[21] The ratios that he proposed were 2:1, 3:1, 3:2, and 7:5. Three years later, the great organ theoretician, Dom Bedos de Celles,[22] referred to Engramelle's ratios, but insisted they should change with the character of the piece: "In merry tunes they must be sharper than in graceful, tender airs, and in marches more so than in minuets."

The evidences of alteration, consistent, irrefutable, and overwhelming, have a grave and hardly welcome practical consequence. They seem to mean nothing less than revising, among other pieces that we know and love, the whole work of Bach, and particularly his keyboard compositions. There is hardly a single prelude, fugue, or invention without a longer or shorter group of eighth or sixteenth notes, and some pieces consist in nothing else. The first, the second, and the third of the preludes in the *Well-tempered Clavier*—must they really be played in bumpy, rumbling trochees or dottings instead of flowing evenly?

There seems to be one point in favor of unaltered performance as suggested by the available printed editions. Prelude XVI in the second part of the *Well-tempered Clavier,* which we could easily fancy as running off in even sixteenths, is actually written in dotted groups throughout. Is this not an evident proof that Bach prescribed alteration where it was necessary, and that, on the other hand, he did not want it where he did not prescribe it expressly?

This argument is hardly valid. The dot played often, if not always, the role of a modern double dot: "Short notes which follow dotted ones are always shorter in execution than their notated length." [23] Prelude XVI has an oversharp jumpiness entirely beyond the scope of 'alteration,' where, as Engramelle proves, the two extreme ratios between the odd-numbered and the even-

[21] Marie-Dominique-Joseph Engramelle, *La tonotechnie*, Paris, 1775, pp. 30–34.
[22] Dom Bedos de Celles, *L'art du facteur d'orgues*, Vol. 4, Paris, 1778, p. 602.
[23] C. P. E. Bach, *op. cit.*, p. 157.

numbered notes were 2:1 and 7:5. They would never reach the ratio 7:1 that a double dot has.

Once the first shock has subsided, some of the pieces seem to win us over. Prelude II, for example, loses its etude-like character and assumes a more virile outline. And the same might be true of Prelude III.

But we should not give in too quickly.

An evaluation of the sources quoted above yields the following picture. The Italians mention alteration only at the beginning of the seventeenth century; in Rousseau's time their eighth notes are "always equal." The Germans mention the alternation of good and bad notes; but their good notes are sustained just "a little" longer. It was the French taste—and apparently no other taste— to dot the good notes and to take the bad ones "very short." After all, French music in the seventeenth and eighteenth centuries depended greatly on the dance and its springy, elegant style. But even the French, according to Rousseau's weighty testimony, did not alter their eighths in 4/4 time.

Thus, Bach's works should be only mildly subjected to alteration, except perhaps for the French Suites, which were expressly written in the taste of France. "Mildly": that would mean about the lowest of Engramelle's ratios, 7:5. Indeed, just "a little bit."

As a postscript to this section, it seems necessary to quote the Englishman, C. Mason, who shortly after 1800, with reference to his compatriot, "Mr. Gunn," decreed: "The general principle upon which accuracy in time depends, is a power of giving to every note of the same denomination, precisely the same length or duration." [24]

This means, unmistakably, no metric alteration.

'SCOTCH SNAP' OR 'LOMBARDIAN TASTE.' Metric alteration also could, and did, appear the other way round: by shortening the good, accented notes and lengthening the bad, unstressed ones. This reversed alteration was generally known as the Scotch snap or the Lombardian taste.

[24] C. Mason, *Rules on the times, metres, phrases & accent of composition*, London [1807?], introduction, p. [1].

Outstanding examples of the time are the first movement of Haydn's trio in E flat major of about 1762 and his quartet No. 59, Op. 59, No. 3, and Johann Christian Bach's quintet Op. XI, No. 6.

Ex. 106. Haydn, trio in E flat

Ex. 107. Haydn, quartet no. 59, op. 54, No. 3

As far as the Lombardians are concerned—or, for that matter, the Italians in general—this mannerism was, according to Quantz,[25] at most a passing fad restricted to the second quarter of the eighteenth century. "It looks," he adds, "like Scottish music; and twenty years before its appearance in Italy some German composers had used it, although not often. The Italians, then, can only claim to have imitated them." Had Quantz known the greatest of his German masters in the seventeenth century, Heinrich Schütz, he could have quoted the woe-depicting, sobbing snatches in the *Auferstehungshistorie* or 'story of the Resurrection' (1623), when the Evangelist relates that Mary stands by the tomb and weeps.

Nevertheless, in his national analysis Quantz has fallen a victim to the frequent combination of insufficient historical knowledge and a misled patriotism of the acquisitive species. He fails to mention two outstanding sources from France: François Couperin's *Pièces de clavecin* (1713–1730) and *L'art de toucher le clavecin* (1716), to refer just to these two works. And he also ignores an older Italian testimony that belies him: the weighty preface to Frescobaldi's *Toccate e partite* of 1614.

The snap, incidentally, is a favorite of the quite un-Scotch Hungarians, too, and can be found in many Magyar folk songs and often in pieces of Bartók and Kodály.

[25] Quantz, *op. cit.*, ch. XVIII § 58.

The ratio of the initial short and the subsequent dotted note is in every case undetermined. To be sure, we learn from J. G. Walther [26] that the dot indicated officially the orthodox ratio 1:3 or 3:1. Unofficially, it could denote any one long–short relation that the player's taste and the character of the piece required. And as a rule, the dotted note was held beyond its rightful duration, with the appended note as quick as possible.

DOUBLE DOT. It was a symptom of weakened tradition and hence of growing literalness after the decay of the Baroque Age when musicians, feeling the need for a more specific symbol, introduced the modern device of a double dot to indicate the addition of a half plus a quarter to the value of the preceding note. Theoretically at least. Actually, nobody added just 75 per cent; a double dot marked simply the extreme shortening of the appended note.

Some modern authors attribute the double dot to J. J. Quantz, some to Leopold Mozart.

Quantz, the older man, does not come into question. He mentions the double dot only in the last sentence of Chapter Five, § 21. There he describes a thirty-second with "two dots" (*zweene Puncte*), but calls them in the following last line of the paragraph a "one-and-a-half dot" (*anderthalb Puncte*), which indeed indicates the time-value correctly. Nowhere does Quantz say that he has "invented" the symbol, or even that it is something novel.

Carl Philipp Emanuel Bach's *Versuch über die wahre Art das Clavier zu spielen*, one year after Quantz, ignores the double dot completely.

Leopold Mozart's discussion,[27] on the contrary, can—although not necessarily—be interpreted as a claim to invention. He says that, when a dotted note of regular length would sound "too lazy and rather sleepy," one should sustain it a bit longer and "steal" the additional time from the following note. "It would be very good to mark this longer dot with a special symbol. I for my part

[26] Johann Gottfried Walther, *Musicalisches Lexicon*, Leipzig, 1732, p. 504.
[27] Leopold Mozart, *Versuch einer gründlichen Violinschule*, Augsburg 1756, I iii, § 11.

have done it often and shown what I wanted with two dots and a shorter following note. At first sight it looks strange. But what of it?"

Leopold Mozart's recommendation starts from the necessary exaggeration of the dot in "certain passages" and curiously ends in the general statement that even a single dot ought in all cases to be lengthened; otherwise the performance would be sleepy. Shortening the short note after the dot provides animation; and it also keeps the player from the common misdemeanor of rushing.

Quantz [28] confirms the exaggeration of the dot. "In *alla breve* and in 3/4, in the *loure*, the saraband, the *courante*, and the *chaconne*, the eighths after dotted quarters must not be played literally, but very short and pointed (*scharf*). The dotted note is energetically stressed; the bow is lifted after (*unter*) the dot. One deals in a similar way with all dots whenever the time permits it; and when after a dot or a rest three or more thirty-seconds occur, they are, particularly in slow pieces, not always played in their proper values but at the extreme end of the time allotted them, and at the greatest speed, as often in overtures, *entrées*, and furies. But each of these rapid notes must be given a bow of its own; there is little slurring."

These precepts must not be indiscriminately projected backwards. They are valid for the later part of the seventeenth century, but certainly not for its beginning. Jean Titelouze (1563–1633), the great French organist, explains that "the dot placed after a note does not have a fixed value. . . . Sometimes it is half-plus," and he would dot a half note tied to a following eighth note, thus lengthening it by a quarter, not a half, of its original value.[29] Every player of Bach and Handel knows numerous passages where the dot stands for a quarter of the preceding note.

DUPLETS AGAINST TRIPLETS. A third form of alteration was the adjustment to be made in the execution of (generally dotted) duplets in one voice part moving against triplets in another part. How often has it been a stumbling block to all of us!

[28] J. J. Quantz, *op. cit.*, Chapter XVII, vii, § 58.
[29] Quoted from Eugene Belt, *Three seventeenth century French organ composers*, New York University master's thesis, 1951, p. 19.

Alas, not even masters living and writing at the same time in the same city of Berlin agreed upon the meaning and performance of this intriguing combination.

Carl Philipp Emanuel Bach (1753) gives a very simple recipe: "With the advent of an increased use of triplets in common or 4/4 time, as well as in 2/4 and 3/4, many pieces have appeared which might be more conveniently written in 12/8, 9/8, or 6/8." [30] The music example accompanying this statement adapts the dotted group to the triplet: the short note after the dot is made to coincide with the last note of the triplet; the group forms a triplet itself.

Two years later, in 1755, Friedrich Wilhelm Marpurg in Berlin sided with Carl Philipp Emanuel. In mingling binary and ternary groups in different voice parts, "the two first notes of a triplet are always played against the first note of the duplet . . . even if the first of the two binary notes happens to be dotted." [31] In other words, the two notes of a duplet must coincide with the first and the last note of the triplet, whether or not the first note is dotted. Duplets yield their identity to accompanying triplets.

The agreement of these two comparatively modern masters illustrates in a way the (temporary) decline of rhythmical interest and inspiration in the mid-century.

Quantz, more conservative than Marpurg and Carl Philipp Emanuel, has exactly the opposite opinion about dots against triplets. In § 22 of Chapter V he writes: "One must play the short note of the dotted group not with, but after, the third note of the triplet. Otherwise there would be 6/8 or 12/8 time." Indeed, he adds, the note after the dot should be shortened beyond its notational value. "Giving the dotted notes below triplets their natural values would be very poor and silly, not brilliant or majestic."

The double-dotting is in agreement with the aesthetic law that any distinction must be made clear as such.[32] The perceiver should not be left in doubt whether an all too little difference (in time or in space) is accidental or planned.

The reader is, of course, far more interested in the question of

[30] Carl Philipp Emanuel Bach, *Essay on the true art of playing keyboard instruments*, transl. William J. Mitchell, New York, W. W. Norton, 1949, p. 160.
[31] F. W. Marpurg, *Anleitung zum Clavierspielen*, Berlin, 1755, p. 24.
[32] Cf. Gustav Theodor Fechner, *Vorschule der Aesthetik*, 1876 ff.

how he should play the duplet-triplet passages in the works of
Johann Sebastian Bach, such as the violin-harpsichord Sonata

Ex. 108. Bach, sonata for violin and harpsichord No. IV in E flat

No. 4 and the Overture in D major. Whoever tries to find an answer in Robert Haas's volume on performance [33] will gather that
the master himself has given a solution in his *Clavier-Büchlein
für Wilhelm Friedemann Bach* (1720). Alas, there is no mention
of the device in this little method. Haas refers also to Dannreuther's well-known book. Alas, once more, this careful monog-
rapher of musical ornamentation says only that "similar passages in J. S. Bach must be taken *cum grano*," [34] which, albeit ob-
scure, is a confession of nescience. Haas's solution is high-handed
and unfounded. If Bach had a definite, unambiguous attitude, we
do not know it. And the performer is forced to make his own decision.

Such a decision is not hard in the case of the E-flat sonata mentioned above, where the smooth and tranquil flow of the violin
melody excludes the cramped jerks of double dots and makes an
adaptation to the accompanying triplets mandatory. And, I think,
the same applies to the tenth fugue (E minor) of the *Well-
tempered Clavier.*

Other occurrences are much more problematic.

TEMPO RUBATO has been understood in three very different
ways. Late in the eighteenth century it occasionally covered an
inversion of accents, letting the 'good' beats go unstressed and
giving sforzatos to the 'bad' ones. In the nineteenth and twentieth

[33] Robert Haas, *Aufführungspraxis*, in Bücken's *Handbuch der Musikwissenschaft*, p. 214.
[34] Edward Dannreuther, *Musical ornamentation*, Part I, London [1893–1895],
I, p. 191.

centuries the concept of rubato has been deteriorating to that of a flexible yielding tempo, now driving on, now holding back.[35]

These two rubatos, which have usurped their name improperly, are phenomena so current in the history of music that they had to be mentioned in most of the chapters of this book, although without this misleading title.

The authentic concept—the only one to be discussed in this section—is the freedom to change the time values of individual notes or to shift entire passages back or forward by just an eighth or a sixteenth without changing the tempo itself. Here, and nowhere else, the concept agrees with its name: tempo rubato is 'robbed' or 'stolen' time—a part taken away from the written time value of a neighboring note, to be restored at once or a little later to some following note so that the tempo itself does not suffer. Hence, the true rubato is closely related to metric alteration, but also to *portamento* and syncopation.

Once more: in rubato as well as in metric alteration, the tempo itself *did not* change: the bass went strictly on without rallentando or stringendo, and the melody made up for any delay or anticipation.

This rubato by alteration has doubtless an age-old pedigree. It occurs, already in notation—that is, de-improvised!—as early as the fourteenth century; for instance in Johannes de Florentia's madrigal *Nascoso el viso* [36] to depict the stealthy approach of the

Ex. 109. Johannes de Florentia (Giovanni da Cascia), *Nascoso*

poet who watches a girl bathing. As a specimen of the sixteenth century the Spaniard, Diego Ortiz, presents a *recercada* or set of variations for viol and harpsichord in his *Tratado de glosas* of 1553.[37] One of the most obvious examples around 1600 is the sec-

[35] Cf. H. C. Koch, *Ueber den technischen Ausdruck Tempo rubato*, in *Allgemeine musikalische Zeitung*, Leipzig, 1808, No. 33. Also Boris Bruck, *Wandlungen des Begriffes Tempo Rubato*, Erlangen dissertation (1929?).

[36] Printed in Johannes Wolf, *Geschichte der Mensuralnotation*, Leipzig, 1904, Vols. II and III, No. 39.

[37] Recorded in *L'Anthologie Sonore*, No. 40.

Ex. 110. Ortiz, *Recercada*

ond bar of Michael Praetorius' two-part chorale *Vater unser im Himmelreich*.[38] An illustration from the end of the seventeenth century is Purcell's *New Ground* for harpsichord.[39]

When Pierfrancesco Tosi wrote his famous *Opinioni de' cantori antichi e moderni* in 1723, rubato was already degenerating, even in its stronghold, the practice of Italian singers. Against the "gentlemen moderns" he held that "good taste" consisted, among other traits, in "stealing the Time exactly on the true *Motion* of the Bass." Later in his book, he explains that "whoever does not know how to steal the Time in singing, does not know how to Compose, nor to Accompany himself, and is destitute of the best Taste and greatest Knowledge. The stealing of Time, in the *Pathetick*, is an honourable Theft in one that sings better than others, provided he makes a Restitution with Ingenuity." And he adds an explanatory footnote that rubato occurs "when the Bass goes an exactly regular Pace, the other Part retards or anticipates in a singular Manner, for the Sake of Expression, but after That returns to its Exactness, to be guided by the Bass. Experience and Taste must teach it." [40]

Tempo rubato was redefined in Carl Philipp Emanuel Bach's *Versuch über die wahre Art das Clavier zu spielen* (1753–1762).[41] It was still described in a similar way, a generation later, in Daniel Gottlob Türk's *Klavierschule* of 1789: [42] "Most usually it means shifting the notes by anticipation or delay." And yet it had already in young Mozart's time degenerated to a mere relaxation of tempo rigidity, at least in Germany. On October 23,[43] 1777, Wolf-

---

[38] Davison-Apel, *Harvard Anthology of Music*, No. 167, p. 189.

[39] Henry Purcell, *The second part of Musicks' hand-maid*, London 1689, reprinted in Carl Parrish and John F. Ohl, *Masterpieces of music before 1750*, New York, 1951, p. 160.

[40] Pierfrancesco Tosi, *Opinioni de'cantori antichi e moderni* [1723]; quoted after a contemporary English translation: *Observations on the florid song*, transl. Galliard, London, 1742, Chap. viii, ix, pp. 129, 156.

[41] C. P. E. Bach, *op. cit.*, pp. 161 f.

[42] Daniel Gottlob Türk, *Klavierschule*, 1789, quoted from the second edition of 1802, p. 419.

[43] This letter has been wrongly dated October 24 in some present-day books.

gang wrote from Augsburg to his father: "They are amazed that I always keep time. Nor do they understand that my left hand knows nothing of the tempo rubato in an adagio. [When they play rubato], the left hand gives way." This is exactly what Chopin later said: "The left hand should act like a conductor: not for a moment must it waver."

Mozart's unpleasant experience with German pianists makes it rather probable that Chopin owed his rubato—of which he was the last representative—to the less forgotten traditions of Italian singing.[44] In a curious distortion of historical facts (which, how-ever, proves that the technique had otherwise fallen into oblivion) Liszt celebrated Chopin as the master who had "introduced" it and given it the name of "tempo rubato." In his turgid style, Franz Liszt described it as "a robbed, erose, yielding, ragged, and lan-guishing tempo, flickering like a blown-up fire and rolling like the grains of the field in a gentle breeze, or the tree-tops bending hither and thither."[45]

It might be worth mentioning that this highly improvisatory form had frozen into a notated mannerism by the mid-century (as so often in earlier ages). Good examples are in Carl Philipp Eman-uel Bach's Fifth Collection of *Sonaten für Kenner und Liebhaber* (1785) and in the harpsichord sonatas of Giovanni Platti (born *ca.* 1700). The frozen form had stragglers, of which the most curi-ous is the *Canzone napolitana* by Liszt, where for sixteen measures

Ex. 111. Liszt, *Canzone napolitana*

the right hand is consistently a sixteenth behind in whatever it does.[46] And the memory of Liszt evokes that of his friend and

[44] Lucian Kamieński, *Zum "Tempo rubato,"* in *Archiv für Musikwissenschaft*, Vol. I (1918), pp. 108–126.

[45] Franz Liszt, *Friedrich Chopin*, in his *Gesammelte Schriften*, Vol. I, 1880, p. 82.

[46] Franz Liszt, *Canzone napoletana*, New York, 1887, pp. 5 f.

son-in-law, Wagner, who has given one of the most beautiful quasi-ritenuto rubatos in *Parsifal* (music example 145).

THE RELATIVE TEMPO around the turn of the century is well discussed in the prefaces of Georg Muffat's two sets of suites, the *Florilegia* of 1695 and 1698. Though Muffat was a German and had his two collections printed in Bavaria, he speaks avowedly about the model practice of Paris and particularly about that of his adored master Lully.

Muffat's—and therefore Lully's—most important rule is doubtless "not to dwell longer or less on cadences than the notes imply." Neither should one hasten the last measures.[47] This cannot be too often repeated to our musicians and amateurs, who have been told, and blindly believe, that there must be a solemn ritardando at the end of every piece of "old music." But the reader should also remember that Muffat, representative of the French Late Baroque, is here completely at variance with Frescobaldi's Italian and Early Baroque conception at the beginning of the century.

In other respects, we learn from Muffat that the time signature 2¢ meant twice as fast as C. The signature 2—against the analysis of Saint-Lambert—is rather slow in overtures, preludes, and symphonies. Ballets are brisk but slower than ¢. The signature 3/2 indicates restraint. 3/4 is merrier in sarabands and airs, but not too much so. It is lively in rondeaux, and very lively in minuets, courantes, and the fugal movements in the middle of the so-called French overtures. The *canaries* and gigues have the fastest tempo.

The "very lively" tempo of the courante is remarkable and is in disagreement with the slow tempo of this dance in the surveys of Frenchmen. The contradiction might find an explanation in the fact that the original courante of the sixteenth century divided during the seventeenth into a lively dance, generally called by its Italian name *corrente*, and a slow and dignified courante proper.

The earliest tempo indications of the eighteenth century, and

---

[47] Georg Muffat, *Florilegium secundum*, Passau, 1698, in *Denkmäler der Tonkunst in Oesterreich, Jahrgang* II, Vol. 2, Vienna, 1895, p. 24.

French at that, can be read in Michel de Saint-Lambert's *Principes du Clavecin* (Paris, 1702).

Let us divide them up into binary and ternary times for the sake of clarity.

The binary times are:

C and ¢, both grave and slow in the tempo of a walking man and, between them, in the ratio 2:1

2, against Muffat's statement, gay and light and twice as quick as ¢

4/8, very fast and twice as quick as 2.

The ternary tempi are:

3/2, very slow (*fort grave*)

3, gay and light, twice as quick

3/8, very fast and twice as quick as 3.

The complex tempi are:

6/8, very fast, with each 3/8 twice as quick as 3/4 in the following 6/4

6/4, when binary as 2 × 3/4, *fort gay*, with each 3/4 at least as quick as the halves of 2

6/4, when ternary as 3 × 2/4, gay with its three beats in the tempo of those of 2.

The validity of Saint-Lambert's explanation is a bit dubious. In his stereotyped ratio 1:2 from signature to signature—"twice as quick"—he is still haunted by the restless ghost of the long-dead *proportiones—dupla, quadrupla, octupla*(!).

The metronomic sources of the time, which are also French, do not confirm, indeed they contradict, the somewhat clumsy oversimplification in Saint-Lambert's *Principes*.

METRONOMIC TEMPI. Subsequently, vague proportional indications like those of Saint-Lambert were in France replaced by precise metronomic numbers, more or less like our M.M.'s.

The decline of a generally accepted standard tempo with its proportional derivatives necessitated indeed a reliable method of conveying the composer's intention to the performer. J. J. Quantz's well-known attempt to create such a method on the basis of pulse beats was by no means a beginning but rather, as the reader has seen, the end of a practice more than two hundred fifty years old. The conservative master of Berlin knew, but ignored, the more exact devices contrived in the hundred years before him. To be more specific, he had only heard of Loulié's more than fifty-year-old chronometer but made short work of it, since "one could hardly carry along such a machine all the time; not to mention that the general oblivion into which it has fallen makes its practicality doubtful." [48]

The decline of tempo standardization had coincided with the advent of sciences, discoveries, and technical inventions characteristic of the Baroque Age. When in 1582 the physicist Galileo Galilei discovered the isochronism of pendulums by measuring a swinging lamp in the cathedral of Pisa with the beat of his pulse, he could not anticipate that one day the pendulum was to replace the pulse in gauging musical tempo. The leading French theorist, Father Marin Mersenne, born less than a quarter of a century after Galileo, made the first attempts in this direction. But his musical pendulum was far too long to be of practical use. [49] Thomas Mace, too, recommended a pendulum suspended from the ceiling, less to fix a tempo than to help the beginning lutanist in keeping time. [50]

The earliest serviceable, though hardly used, mechanism with an adjustable pendulum was the chronometer that Etienne Loulié, a Parisian, devised and described in his *Eléments ou Principes de Musique, mis dans un nouvel ordre*, [51] 1696. It was the one that Quantz had heard of and disapproved of.

---

[48] Johann Joachim Quantz, *Versuch einer Anweisung die Flöte traversiere zu spielen*, Berlin, 1752, Chapter XVII, vii, § 46.

[49] Marin Mersenne, *L'harmonie universelle*, Vol. I, Paris, 1636, p. 136.

[50] Thomas Mace, *Musick's monument*, London, 1676, pp. 80 f.

[51] Description, translation, and pictures in Rosamond E. M. Harding, *Origins of musical tempo and expression*, Oxford, 1938, pp. 9–11. Cf. also Sir John Hawkins, *A general history of music*, Vol. II, p. 777; Arnold Dolmetsch, *The interpretation of the music of the XVIIth and XVIIIth centuries*, London, 1915, pp. 27–52; E. Borrel, *Les indications métronomiques laissées par les auteurs français du XVIIIe siècle*, in *Revue de Musicologie*, Vol. XII, 1928, pp. 149–153; Ralph Kirkpatrick, *Eighteenth-century metronomic indications*, in *Papers of the American Musicological Society*, Vol. III, 1938, pp. 30–50.

One year later—if Eitner [52] is right—Michel L'Affillard published the first edition of his *Principes très-faciles*.[53] (The present author knows only the seventh edition, in the New York Public Library, which must have been printed after 1710, the year of the sixth edition). Its second part contains all sorts of contemporary compositions, on two staffs for melody and bass, with a two-digit numeral above the time signature.

These numerals express *tierces* (‴) or sixtieths of a second. They show how long a single beat—half note, quarter, or eighth—should be, not, as in our M.M.'s, how many of them would fill a minute. To transform the *tierces* into M.M.'s is very easy. The two numerals coincide at 60: there are 60 *tierces* in a second, and 60 seconds in a minute. All the other numbers represent inverse ratios: twice as many *tierces* (120) are half as many M.M.'s (30); 90 *tierces* are 40 M.M.'s. In short, the metronome figure is to 60 as 60 is to the number of *tierces;* or, still simpler, the M.M.'s are the quotient of 3600 divided by the number of *tierces*. If we know that a beat lasts 51 *tierces*, the M.M. must be 3600 ÷ 51, or 70½.

In rendering and transcribing L'Affillard's figures, we omit a number of nondescript *airs* and confine ourselves to music marked out as dances (some of which were still alive as social dances, and some, given up in the ballroom, as dances on the ballet stage).

	time	beats	*tierces*	M.M. per beat
bourrée	2	two ♩	30	120
canaries	6/8	two ♩.	34	106
chaconne	3	three ♩	23	160
courante	3/2	three ♩	40	90
gavotte	2	two ♩	30	120
gigue	6/8	two ♩.	36	100
	3/8	one ♩.	31	116
marche	6/4	six ♩	24	150
menuet	3	one ♩.	51	71
	6/8	one ♩.	48	75
passecaille	3	three ♩	34	106
passepied	3/8	one ♩.	42	88

[52] Robert Eitner, *Quellen-Lexikon der Musiker*, Leipzig, 1900, Vol. VI, p. 13.
[53] L'Affillard, *Principes très-faciles pour bien apprendre la musique*, Paris.

	time	beats	*tierces*	M.M. per beat
pavane	2	two ♩	40	90
rigaudon	2	two ♩	30	120
sarabande	3/2	three ♩	40	90
	6/4	six ♩	27	133

The tempi, once more, are impressively fast.

A few years later, in 1701, Joseph Sauveur devised an *Echomètre* with a metric scale; in 1732 and 1746, Pajot and William Tans'ur came out with similar contraptions; in 1796, J. G. E. Stoeckel described a *Chronometer;* [54] and eventually, Nicolaus van Winkel and Johann Nepomuk Mälzl presented the definitive solution of the problem in the *Metronom* of 1816.

Before returning to the French, mention should be made of the apparently very moderate tempo in England: in *A new musical grammar* of 1746, William Tans'ur, like Mersenne, gave the quarter note one second, that is, M.M. 60.[55]

The description of a new *métromètre* that Louis-Léon Pajot, Count of Ons-en-Bray or D'Onzembray, submitted in 1732 to the French *Académie Royale des Sciences* is, as would be expected, in the main a mechanical treatise without much musical interest.[56] What we do not expect is to find an entire page (p. 192) devoted to an exact metronomization of twenty-three actual and still available pieces by Lully (1632–1687), Colasse (1649–1709), Campra (1660–1744), Mato (*ca.* 1660–1746), and Destouches (1672–1749), all representative of French operatic and ballet scores during the most important forty years.

	signature	beats	*tierces*	M.M.
Bourrée (Lully, *Phaéton*)	2	2	32	112½
Gavotte (Lully, *Roland*)	2	2	37	97
Passecaille (Lully, *Persée*)	3	3	38	94½
Chaconne (Lully, *Fêtes de Bacchus*)	3	1	68	53
Gigue (Colasse, *Amadis*)	6/4	2	32	112½

[54] Magazine *Deutschland,* 1796, 6th *Stück* or fascicle.
[55] P. 44.
[56] *Description et usage d'un métromètre ou machine pour battre les mesures et les temps de toutes sortes d'airs,* in *Histoire de l'Académie Royale des Sciences, Année 1732, Mémoires,* Paris, 1735, pp. 182–195.

	signature	beats	*tierces*	M.M.
Loure (Colasse, *Thétis*)	6/4	2	32	112½
Ouverture (Colasse, *Thétis*— beginning)	2	2	56	64
Ouverture (Colasse, *Thétis*— reprise)	6/4	2	45	80
Passepied (Campra, *L'Europe galante*)	3/8	1	36	100
Rigaudon (Campra, *L'Europe galante*)	2	2	31	116
Menuet (Campra, *L'Europe galante*)	3	1	51	70½
Courante (Mato)	3	3	44	84
Sarabande (Destouches, *Issé*)	3/2	3	49	73½
Bourrée (Destouches, *Omphale*)	2	2	30	120
Menuet (Destouches, *Marthésie*)	3	1	51	70½

Campra's *menuet* is erroneously given a 2 signature. Our list has 1 beat where Pajot indicates 3 beats. From his own survey it is evident that one beat covers the whole measure.

The dance tempos in this survey answer one of the thorniest problems that face the modern performer:

a *passecaille* demands	M.M. 94½		for each of 3 beats in a bar
a *courante* "	M.M. 84		" " " " " " " "
a *sarabande* "	M.M. 73½		" " " " " " " "
a *bourrée* "	M.M. 112½–120	" " " 2	" " " "
a *rigaudon* "	M.M. 116		" " " " " " " "
a *gigue* "	M.M. 112½		" " " " " " " "
a *loure* "	M.M. 112½		" " " " " " " "
a *passepied* "	M.M. 100	" the 1 beat	" " "
a *menuet* "	M.M. 70½		" " " " " " "
a *chaconne* "	M.M. 53		" " " " " " "

(It is probably wiser to mark the tempos by beats than by note values—such as eighths or quarters or dotted halves—since the composers are not consistent in the choice of their symbols.)

Not long after Pajot, French dances (as types, not as individual pieces) were measured again by Jacques-Alexandre La Chapelle in 1737 [57] and by Henri-Louis Choquel in 1759.[58] From these three sources plus L'Affillard's *Principes,* we are able to deduce the following standard tempos of French dances during the first two generations of the eighteenth century:

allemande	—M.M. 120	for each of the 2 beats in a bar									
bourrée	—M.M. 112–120	"	"	"	"	"	"		"	"	"
chaconne	—M.M. 120–160	"	"	"	"	3	"		"	"	"
contredanse	—M.M. 132	"	"	"	"	2	"		"	"	"
courante	—M.M. 82–90	"	"	"	"	3	"		"	"	"
entrée	—M.M. 69	"	"	"	"	2	"		"	"	"
gavotte	—M.M. 97–152	"	"	"	"	"	"		"	"	"
gigue	—M.M. 104–120	"	"	"	"	"	"		"	"	"
loure	—M.M. 112½–120	"	"	"	"	3	"		"	"	"
menuet	—M.M. 70–80	"	"	"	"	1	"		"	"	"
passecaille	—M.M. 63–100	"	"	"	"	3	"		"	"	"
passepied	—M.M. 86–100	"	"	"	"	1	"		"	"	"
rigaudon	—M.M. 116–152	"	"	"	"	2	"		"	"	"
sarabande	—M.M. 63–80	"	"	"	"	3	"		"	"	"
tambourin	—M.M. 176	"	"	"	"	2	"		"	"	"

(The *sarabande* is generally written in quarter notes, but the so-called *sarabande tendre,* in half notes. The difference by no means implies the ratio of 1:2, but just a tiny shade in tempo.)

For the sake of completeness, the *polonaise,* a dance outside the scope of dancing in France but important in the ballrooms of central Europe, may be mentioned here as having been taken twice as slow as the minuet, that is, at about M.M. 105–120 for each of the three beats of a measure.[59]

These surveys from Muffat to Choquel, comprising more than sixty years, show one impressive fact: the vast majority of tempi were speedy, light and gay. Only in four French dances could the beat be slower than M.M. 80, and in the most important among them, the minuet, the actual beat comprised a whole meas-

---

[57] Jacques-Alexandre La Chapelle, *Les vrais principes de la musique,* 1.II, Paris, 1737.

[58] Henri-Louis Choquel, *La musique rendue sensible,* Paris, 1759.

[59] Christoph Gottlieb Hänsel, *Allerneueste Anweisung zur äusserlichen Moral,* Leipzig, 1755, p. 184.

ure, so that the individual quarter note, if beaten, would have amounted to M.M. 210–240 (against 120–126 in Beethoven's works). The *entrée* was an *alla breve* dance, in which the M.M. 69 left M.M. 138 to each of its quarters. This leaves only two dances, *passecaille* and *sarabande,* in the lower bracket of temporal ranges.

When Julien Tiersot notated the little pieces played by the musical clock of Marie-Antoinette in Versailles (whose date must be between 1786 and 1789), he failed, unfortunately, to metronomize these infallible witnesses of original tempo. But he remarked at least that one of them, an aria by Gluck, had "an animated (too animated) movement." [60]

And yet, as this chapter will presently show, French tempi were slow in comparison with German tempi of the time. (And this they are today as well. Gisèle Brelet writes: "We [the French] did not know before hearing Bruno Walter that certain finales of Haydn or Beethoven allowed for such rapidity." [61] Indeed, an obituary on Johann Sebastian Bach, printed in 1754, contains the remarkable statement that the deceased master had taken particularly vivid tempos. *Sehr Lebhaft,* says the original.

In the face of these unshakable testimonies, musicians should finally rid themselves of the traditional prejudice that the music of our ancestors was sleepy, slow, and grave. And still more so of the almost unbelievable misconception that there has been a "trend to increase the speed of tempo more and more which we observe [!] during the history of musical interpretation." [62] In what tempo, then, must the ancient Greeks, Sumerians, and Egyptians have sung! Too bad that even the best aestheticians and philosophers know so little of history and its laws.

As far as the eighteenth century is concerned, the very opposite was true. And this is natural enough. The eighteenth was the age of the *Régence* after the death of Louis XIV, and of the subsequent Rococo; it was the age of almost foamy decoration, of light, silvery colors, of pastels pale and frail, of a general dislike for anything ponderous.

[60] Julien Tiersot, *The musical clock of Marie-Antoinette,* in *The Musical Quarterly,* Vol. XVIII, 1932, p. 418.
[61] Gisèle Brelet, *Temps musical et tempo,* in *Polyphonie,* fasc. II, 1948, p. 16.
[62] *Ibid.,* p. 18.

We cannot leave the question of tempo without considering the conservative side, as represented by Johann Joachim Quantz in Berlin. Seven years before Choquel, in 1752, ignoring metronomic methods, he was the last to regulate tempo with the beats of his pulse. He counted 80 of them in a minute, although he was fully aware that "the pulse was slower in the morning than after the midday meal, and at night still faster than in the afternoon." [63]

According to his pulse—but converted into modern M.M.—French dances had the following tempi:

Bourrée	M.M. 80 the bar
Canaries	M.M. 80 the bar
Chaconne	M.M. 160 the ♩
Courante	M.M. 80 the ♩
Entrée	M.M. 80 the ♩
Furie	M.M. 160 the ♩
Gavotte	M.M. 80 the bar (or slightly less)
Gigue	M.M. 80 the bar
Loure	M.M. 80 the ♩
Marche	M.M. 80 the ♩
Menuet	M.M. 160 the ♩ [64]
Musette	M.M. 80 the ♩ (in 3/4), the ♪ (in 3/8)
Passecaille	M.M. 160 the ♩ (or rather a bit faster)
Passepied	M.M. 160 the ♩ (or rather a bit faster)
Rigaudon	M.M. 80 the bar
Rondeau	M.M. 160 the ♩
Sarabande	M.M. 80 the ♩
Tambourin	M.M. 80 the bar (or slightly faster)

Most of Quantz's figures are essentially faster than those of the French masters. It would probably be wise to ignore them. In the first place, French sources are more reliable in the matter of French music. Moreover, Quantz seems to oversimplify: while the French know finer shades, the Germans, somewhat clumsily, reduce all the tempi to a uniform M.M. 80 or its multiples. And lastly, he himself confesses that the dancers often need a slower

[63] Quantz, *op. cit.*, Chapter XVII, vii, §§ 46, 55, 58.
[64] Cf. Basilio's aria in Mozart's *Figaro*, Act IV: "*Tempo di menuetto.*"

tempo lest they lose the carrying power of their knees, especially in the *sarabande* and the *loure*.

The same questionable oversimplification appears in the tempos that Quantz allots to the usual Italian terms:

Allegro assai	
Allegro di molto—presto	M.M. 80 the 𝅘𝅥
Allegretto	
Allegro ma non tanto—non troppo—non presto—moderato	M.M. 80 the 𝅘𝅥
Adagio cantabile	
Cantabile—arioso—larghetto—soave—dolce—poco andante—affettuoso—pomposo—maestoso—siciliano—adagio spiritoso	M.M. 80 the 𝅘𝅥𝅮
Adagio assai	
Adagio pesante—lento—largo assai—mesto—grave	M.M. 80 the 𝅘𝅥𝅯

Quantz himself knows the basic and typically classicistic exception: "When a piece is repeated once or oftener . . . one plays it the second time a bit faster than the first time lest the listeners should get sleepy." [65]

On the other hand—although with the same intention of alleviating the boredom of repetition—the little daughter of Stein, the famous piano builder in Augsburg, played a repetition more slowly than the first occurrence of a section, and a second repetition still more slowly, as Mozart reported home with humor and disgust in his letter of October 23, 1777.

Half a century after Quantz, another teacher of the flute, Mason,[66] resumed the question of absolute tempo. His small book, undated but written probably after 1800, shows the most bewildering ignorance. A footnote claims: "N.B. The Times of Music never before published." And Mason is indeed completely nescient of his English, French, and German predecessors and of the metronome itself. His sole authority, he says, is "Mr. Gunn"—possibly the cello teacher John Gunn.

[65] Quantz, *op. cit.*, Ch. XVII, vii, § 55.
[66] C. Mason, *Rules on the times, metres, phrases & accent of composition*, London [1807], p. 1.

His, or Gunn's, tempos were based on the long-outworn empirical pendulum metrology. A pendulum, or "tape," 39 inches long yielded an eighth note in grave, and a length of one inch, a quarter note in prestissimo. Fortunately he added, as an actual tempo lead, that the eighth in grave lasted just a second of time. Hence, the quarter note in grave measured M.M. 30, as against the M.M. 40 of Quantz.

Except for grave the dozen tempos that Mason indicates are as such inapplicable because they are expressed in terms of length and nothing else. The only way to understanding is an evaluation on the basis of Galileo's formula, which equates the ratio of speed with the ratio of the square roots of the pendulum lengths, and to transform the results into M.M.'s. Here the reader must leave the author alone for an hour with his fractions and a table of logarithms, waive his claims to pages full of figures, and rest satisfied with the final results. These are, for the quarter note in

Grave	M.M. 30
Adagio	M.M. 31
Largo, Lento	M.M. 32½
Larghetto	M.M. 34
Andantino	M.M. 38
Andante	M.M. 41½
Allegretto	M.M. 53½
Moderato	M.M. 53½–117
Allegro	M.M. 117
Vivace	M.M. 134–150
Presto	M.M. 187½
Prestissimo	M.M. 375.

The gap between allegretto and allegro and the latitude of moderato are bewildering; but we probably cannot rely too much on Mason's figures in any case.

CLASSICISTIC AND ANTI-CLASSICISTIC TEMPO. Happy as we may be to possess so many exact metronomic data, we must not overrate their musical value—in the eighteenth century as little as in the preceding seventeenth and the following nineteenth century. There are imponderables beyond the figures of any metronome. "The true *mouvement* of a musical work . . . is beyond words," says Mattheson right at the time of the French metronomists. "It is the ultimate perfection of music, accessible only through eminent experience and talent." [67]

Moreover, we must remember that the treatises discussed in the preceding section merely reflect the ideas of their particular nations and times; and we must be careful not to apply these tempi to other nations and other times.

The worthiest witness around the mid-century, Bach's son Carl Philipp Emanuel, shows how great the contrast in national habits was: "In certain countries [that is, outside of Germany] there is a marked tendency to play adagios too fast and allegros too slow." [68]

C. P. E. Bach's remark can, and probably must, be supplemented and explained by the fact that Germany was in general less classicistic than her neighbors, England, France, and Italy.

As a matter of fact, tempo has always been intimately connected with the degree of classicistic or anti-classicistic attitude within a given country, time, or style. Classicism, it is true, appears in numberless shades. But all of them, whatever they are, share one leading quality—moderation. In terms of tempo, this means in the first place abstention from any extreme in speed and in slowness. Germany, less classicistic than her neighbors, would then have a wider range in tempo.

Does not young Mozart, then no more than fourteen years of age, confirm this contrasting attitude of Germany in his Italian adventures of 1770? Presto, as he played it, was in Italy so unprecedented and unbelievable that the native audience in Naples thought that only the magic forces of his finger-ring allowed him to go to such extremes. The Italian, Muzio Clementi, on the other hand, was in Mozart's eyes a charlatan because he would mark a sonata as presto, prestissimo, or alla breve, and play it just the same in a plain four-beat allegro. In another letter, written from Bologna on March 24 of the same year, the boy reported home that the Italians gave the minuet and other dances a surprisingly slow tempo. [69]

---

[67] [Johann] Mattheson, *Der vollkommene Capellmeister*, Hamburg, 1739, p. 173.
[68] C. P. E. Bach, *op. cit.*, p. 148.
[69] Miss Maedra Asch was kind enough to remind me of this passage.

This is good evidence. But matters were not always that simple. Seventy, eighty years earlier, the situation was apparently diametrically opposite. For Georg Muffat writes:

"In directing the measure or beat, one should for the most part follow the Italians, who are accustomed to proceed much more slowly than we do at the directions adagio, grave, largo, etc., so slowly sometimes that one can scarcely wait for them, but, at the directions allegro, vivace, presto, più presto, and prestissimo much more rapidly and in a more lively manner." [70]

In other words, around 1700, the Italians had been extreme, and the Germans moderate; fifty or sixty years later the Italians were moderate, and the Germans extreme.

The German contribution to this contrast finds a confirmation in one of Quantz's footnotes: [71] "In earlier times, very fast passages were played almost twice as slowly as nowadays. Their allegro assai, presto, furioso, and so on, was hardly faster than our allegretto. The many rapid notes in instrumental pieces of older German composers looked much more difficult and dangerous than they actually were. The French of today have generally kept the moderate speed of lively pieces."

The implication is that nationality alone cannot decide the type of tempo that we must read into a piece. Time is a factor just as important. Actually, the Germans and the Italians exchanged roles between 1700 and 1750 in all the fields of artistic expression. But let us stick to the musical field. Around 1700, Italy forsook the architectural forms of polyphony, created an emotional and attractive *cantabile* style, and devised, as its tools, the *gravicembalo col pian e forte,* or simply *piano,* with all its delicate shades of intensity, as well as the earliest *crescendo–decrescendo* of orchestral masses. Germany, at that time—the time of Bach—adhered to the polyphonic heritage in rigid forms. By 1750, however, things had changed completely. Italy had lost all interest in its own piano and had abandoned it to German builders and players, who also had given a new bloom to the emotional, flexible clavichord. Indeed, the Germans became custodians

---

[70] Georg Muffat, *Auserlesene Instrumental-Music, Passau,* 1701; quoted from Strunk, *op. cit.,* p. 451.

[71] Quantz, *op. cit.,* Chap. XVII, vii, § 50.

and protagonists of the once Italian *crescendo* and *decrescendo* in orchestral performances. The position had been reversed, and with it the attitude towards tempo. Extremes in tempo, characteristic of emotion and expressiveness, were at home in Italy around 1700, and in Germany around 1750; moderation of the tempo from both ends, characteristic of classicism, was at home in Germany around 1700, and in Italy around 1750.

A similar statement may be made regarding the tempo within a piece: in the one case it changes with the emotional content; in the other it is consistent, almost rigid.

The following paragraph on tempo, written by Carl Philipp Emanuel Bach, reads like a manifesto on the *stile rappresentativo* by Frescobaldi, the pioneer of anti-classicistic expressiveness a hundred and fifty years before:

"It is especially in fantasias . . . that the keyboardist more than any other executant can practice the declamatory style, and move audaciously from one affect to another. . . . Tempo and meter must be frequently changed in order to rouse and still the rapidly alternating affects. Hence, the metric signature is in many such cases more a convention of notation than a binding factor in performance. It is a distinct merit of the fantasia that, unhampered by such trappings, it can accomplish the aims of the recitative at the keyboard with complete, unmeasured freedom." [72]

Many Germans around Carl Philipp Emanuel Bach who followed the dynamic, emotional trends of the mid-century insisted on a flexible tempo in the interest of true expression and characterization. Even if the tempo obeyed certain standard laws at the beginning of a piece, it was bound to change subsequently, now slowing down, now driving on, in order to faithfully render sadness and energy, love and fury. "Every tempo, gay or slow, has its shades," said Leopold Mozart, and J. J. Quantz acquiesced, albeit somewhat *sotto voce*.[73]

On the whole, however, the conservative Quantz thought—as the classicistic Georg Muffat had done before him [74] that a piece should be played not only in its proper tempo but also in the same

[72] C. P. E. Bach, *op. cit.*, p. 153.
[73] Quantz, *op. cit.*, Chap. XVII, vii, § 36.
[74] Georg Muffat, *Florilegium Secundum*, Passau, 1698, reprinted in *Denkmäler der Tonkunst in Oesterreich, Jahrgang* II 2, Vienna, 1895, p. 21.

tempo from beginning to end.[75] Ralph Kirkpatrick's graphic words on a consistent tempo in the works of Bach may illustrate the point: "In most Bach movements," he says, "all harmonic and melodic detail is arranged in such a symmetrical relation to the whole phrase or movement that the musical structure can often be distorted by rhythmical fluctuations, like an elaborate Baroque façade mirrored in troubled water." [76]

In order to save us the trouble of coming back to these questions in the next chapter, a confirmation from the nineteenth century may be added here. Carl Maria von Weber branded the tyranny of "mill-hammer" (*Mühlhammer*) tempi: [77] he was a militant romanticist. Wagner, a militant romanticist too, was inclined to overdo the slower tempos: "The true adagio," he said, "can hardly be played too slowly." And he pilloried with his customary, let us say, straightforwardness, the reluctance to drive on or to hold back as "the classical playing" of "eunuchs of classical chastity" who fear expression. Mendelssohn and Brahms were "temperance leaguers."

The Wagner tradition of Bayreuth—especially under the baton of Felix Mottl (1856–1911)—has indeed overdone the slower tempos to such an extent that German musicians' slang coined the verb *vermotteln* for the exaggeration of *adagio* and *lento*. The new generation responsible for the *Bayreuther Festspiele* of 1951 has done away with drawn-out tempos.

[75] Quantz, *op. cit.*, Chap. XVII, vii, § 35.

[76] J. S. Bach, *The "Goldberg" variations,* ed. Ralph Kirkpatrick, New York, G. Schirmer [1938], p. xxiii.

[77] Carl Maria von Weber, Letter to Präger of March 9, 1824, printed in *Allgemeine Musikalische Zeitung* of July 11, 1827.

CHAPTER 14

Romanticism

BEETHOVEN'S TEMPO. The tempo questions discussed in the preceding section cut across the chapter line, just as many of our rhythms cut across the treacherous bar lines through our staffs. The early nineteenth century, heir to the currents and counter-currents of the eighteenth, shows an even deeper contrast between the two ever active camps, between the "eunuchs of classical chastity" and the more aggressive anti-classicists.

But the master whose name is the musical symbol of the initial quarter of the century was far above these camps. Beethoven cannot be squeezed into either of them.

There are a few witnesses among his friends and contemporaries. Around 1795, Wegeler tells us that the young master "had played a presto which he had never seen before so rapidly that it must have been impossible to see the individual notes." [1] Johann Friedrich Reichardt, once *Capellmeister* at the court of Prussia, heard Beethoven play his own Concerto in G, Opus 58, in 1808 "in the fastest possible tempo." [2]

So much for Beethoven's outer tempo. As to his inner tempo, the faithful Anton Schindler (1795–1864) relates that the master changed his tempo freely within a piece, but only in the later years of what he calls the third period. If he is right, then we behold

[1] *Beethoven, impressions of contemporaries,* New York [1926], pp. 17 f.
[2] Johann Friedrich Reichardt, *Briefe geschrieben auf einer Reise nach Wien,* Amsterdam, 1810; English translation in Oliver Strunk, *Source Readings in Music History,* New York, 1951, p. 738. About Beethoven's unclassicistic piano playing cf. also *Beethoven, impressions* (see note 1 above), p. 29.

once more the classicistic–anti-classicistic dualism, but this time
in the limited span of one single life. For in the first two periods
of his work Beethoven was no doubt predominantly a classicist.
When he entered the last third of his creative age, around 1817,
he had not become a romantic, to be sure, but he had swerved
from classical patterns and concepts to a quite personal way for
which there is not yet a handy label.

Whether Schindler's restriction of free tempo to Beethoven's
last years is correct must, however, be doubted. For Ignaz von
Seyfried, the Viennese conductor, who was the master's intimate
friend from about 1800 to 1806, relates that even then—twenty
years earlier—Beethoven "was very meticulous with regard to . . .
an effective tempo rubato" (this word being quite certainly taken
in the sense of uneven tempo), and also that "when, especially in
the scherzos of his symphonies, sudden, unexpected changes of
tempo threw all into confusion, he would laugh tremendously,
assure the men he had looked for nothing else, that he had been
waiting for it to happen, and would take almost childish pleasure
in the thought that he had been successful in unhorsing such rou-
tined orchestral knights." [3]

More generally speaking: with Beethoven, tempo became so
essential a part of the work of art that, as he said himself, without the proper tempo a work was beyond recognition and comprehension. Therefore, so he writes to his publisher Schott on De-
cember 18, 1826, "we can hardly have any *tempi ordinari* any
more, now we must follow our free inspiration." And since this free
inspiration, no longer bound to any generally accepted standard,
could not be gathered from the written notes or a noncommittal
heading like *Allegro,* Beethoven became the most enthusiastic ad-
herent of the newly invented metronome. Indeed, the matter of
correct tempi was so much on his mind that he published in 1817
two instalments of a *Fixation of Tempo* in terms of Mälzl's
metronome,[4] the first one containing the Septet and the symphonies except, of course, the still unwritten Ninth, while the second
one listed the quartets up to date. A few other metronomizations,

---

[3] *Beethoven, Impressions,* pp. 41, 42.

[4] Ludwig van Beethoven, *Bestimmung des musikalischen Zeitmasses nach Mälzel's
Metronom,* 1817.

including the Ninth, appeared in occasional letters or on the manuscripts themselves. The whole question of Beethoven's tempi has been authoritatively discussed by the great Beethoven player Rudolf Kolisch.[5]

An evidence of the general practice in Beethoven's earlier years may be found in the precepts printed in Daniel Gottlob Türk's authoritative *Klavierschule* of 1789 and 1802. Türk allows for a good many liberties in tempo, although in a moderate way. Even the question of a coda ritardando is answered with the greatest caution: "The passages at the end of a piece (or section), when marked diminuendo, diluendo, smorzando, and so forth, can be played a bit hesitatingly, too. Often, this restraint or hesitation is prescribed . . . by the composer himself." [6] This means that there *can* be a ritardando, but only "a bit," and not unless a diminuendo in intensity is prescribed.

An evidence of the general practice in Beethoven's later life, although not of his own practice, are the precepts printed in the authoritative *Clavierschule* by Joseph—not the famous Carl—Czerny of about 1825. According to this piano method, a ritardando was admissible in eleven cases: [7]

1. At the return of the principal subject;
2. when a phrase is to be separated from the melody;
3. on long notes strongly accented;
4. at the transition to a different time;
5. after a pause;
6. on the diminuendo of a quick, lively passage;
7. where the ornamental note cannot be played *a tempo giusto*;
8. in a well-marked crescendo serving to introduce or to terminate an important passage;

[5] Rudolf Kolisch, *Tempo and character in Beethoven's music*, in *The Musical Quarterly*, Vol. XXIX, 1943, pp. 169. Cf. also Jean-Louis de Casembroot, *Du mouvement de quelques oeuvres de Beethoven*, in *Revue internationale de Musique*, 1899, pp. 1364–1370; P. Bonavia, *Time, gentlemen, please*, in *Penguin Music Magazine*, IV, 1947, pp. 15–18; Stewart Deas, *Beethoven's 'Allegro assai,'* in *Music & Letters*, Vol. XXXI, 1950, pp. 333–336 ['enough' *versus* 'much'].

[6] Daniel Gottlob Türk, *Klavierschule*, 1789, quoted from the second edition of 1802, § 469, pp. 415 f.

[7] Quoted from the translation of Frederick Dorian, *The history of music in performance*, New York, W. W. Norton, 1942, pp. 206 f.

9. in passages where the composer or the performer gives free play to his fancy;
10. when the composer marks the passage 'espressivo';
11. at the end of a shake or a cadence.

There is absolutely no mention of a ritardando at the end of a piece.

In this context it seems necessary to consult a source available in almost every musical home: Bach's *Well-tempered Clavier*. Not for the sake of Bach, to be sure; but on account of the preface by Carl Czerny found in its most frequently used edition. Czerny says:

"In order to determine the tempo and the style of expression suited to each individual piece I have taken as the basis:

"1stly The indisputable character of each movement;

"2ndly The recollection (still so vividly impressed on my memory) of how I once heard Beethoven play a large number of these fugues."

We are meeting Beethoven once more.

The conception is totally—we cannot avoid the word—romantic. A continual change from *pp* to *p*, from *p* to *f*, from *f* to *ff*, is interrupted by crescendi, diminuendi, calandi, although not a single one of the keyboards in Bach's time was able to produce such shades and, more important, although these half-tones agree neither historically nor stylistically with the strictly structural art of the master. Worst are, in almost all of the pieces, the ending measures, which despite the change of energy in an ascending melody and in the concurrence of all the voice parts puff out in a pitiful diminuendo and rallentando and collapse in pianissimo.

We will probably never know how much of this unbearable sentimentalism is due to Beethoven, and how much to Czerny. But we realize that the early nineteenth century, whose misconception has been so unscrupulously forced upon our innocent students for more than a hundred years, was as far as possible from understanding the totally unromantic language of Bach.

> For what they call the minds of ages
> Is but the gentlemen's own mind
> In which the ages are reflected.
>   Goethe, *Faust*.

BEETHOVEN'S RHYTHM. The nineteenth century opens with a true apotheosis of rhythm. In Beethoven's works, the hearer's attention is often forced to withdraw from melody, harmony, color, and to concentrate upon the vigorous, all-dominating language of a rhythm that would persist as a pattern throughout a whole movement or interfere with peaceful continuity in unexpected counterblows. Well-nigh every page has some rhythmic fascination. To mention them all would disrupt the scope and economy of this book. Memory dwells on the continual offbeats in the piano sonata Op. 31 No. 1 (G major, 1802), on the adonic pattern (music example 2) of the slow movement in the Seventh Symphony (1812), on the lightning strokes in the scherzo of the Ninth (1823).

In the first allegro of the *Eroica* (1804), a long series of sforzatos move against the beat; Beethoven, conducting himself, "so completely put out the orchestra that it had to begin again from the beginning." [8]

But no example is better known or better suited to show the predominance of rhythm than his Fifth Symphony (1808). The melodic element in the initial movement is almost entirely restricted to the few notes of the soothing second theme. The principal theme and the development depend on the rhythmic figure 2/4 ♪ ♫♩|♪ which, in its hammering energy, could stand on its own without the melodic chance result that its successive entries on different pitches provide. Indeed, the scherzo of the same symphony takes it up once more in a slight 3/8 variant: ♫♩|♩. . (The case of this variant has been discussed in the Greek chapter.)

How truly Beethovenian this rhythm was can be seen from the sketch for the scherzo of a planned Tenth Symphony.

Again, he would, in the development of the *Eroica*, brutally interrupt the even progress of his 3/4 by the 2/4 of six lashing quarter-beat chords preceded and separated by breath-taking rests.

Ex. 112. Beethoven, *Eroica,* first movement

[8] Ferdinand Ries, in *Beethoven, impressions of contemporaries,* New York, 1926, p. 54.

Bolder than this hammering motive, and maybe his boldest inspiration, is the last movement of the *Emperor Concerto* (1809),
into which he bursts after an incomparable running start at the end
of the slow, preceding movement. The left hand of the pianist
proceeds in even 6/8; the right hand counters with a hemiola,
which, however, reaches beyond the bar line in what amounts to
7/8; and the ultimate trace of regularity disappears in the panting
rests of the right. How unique is this jubilant flight of the soul!

Ex. 113. Beethoven, *Emperor Concerto,* last movement

Incidentally, almost a century later, Beethoven's seven against
six found itself matched in the daredevil solo of the horn in Richard
Strauss' symphonic poem *Till Eulenspiegel* (1895), where the
melodic theme of seven eighths moves against a regular 6/8 time,
so that in its threefold repetition the individual notes fall each
time on different accents.

Ex. 114. Strauss, *Till Eulenspiegel*

From the viewpoint of comparative art history, it is worth notic-
ing that the span of Beethoven's life was coincident with the great-
est bloom that the 'virile' art of sculpture had had since the
Renaissance: with Antonio Canova (1757–1822), Johann Heinrich
Dannecker (1758–1831), Gottfried Schadow (1764–1850), Bertel
Thorwaldsen (1770–1844), and Christian Rauch (1777–1857).

Even the leading painters of Beethoven's time—Louis David
(1748–1825), Philipp Otto Runge (1777–1810), Jean Ingres
(1780–1867), Peter Cornelius (1783–1867)—found their language
in hard, inexorable drawing rather than in coloristic, blending effects.

Beethoven's, too, was a masculine art. In acknowledging this
often-voiced opinion, we remember again the wisdom of the

Greeks, who called melodic sets of notes and steps or "melodies" a matter without shape, which needed rhythm to join in as the shaping, life-giving force. Melody, they said, was passive and feminine; rhythm was active and virile.[9] Beethoven is the living evidence.

This is why Beethoven never would, or could, be a romantic master, although his romantic contemporaries claimed him emphatically as their brother-in-arms.

EARLY ROMANTICISM was basically a feminine attitude. It strove for feeling and longing rather than action, for personal experience rather than objective remoteness, for the mystic depths of night and death rather than the open clarity of day and life. In the quest for emotional atmosphere, it concentrated on the finer shades of harmony and orchestration, but neglected the driving, 'masculine' force of rhythm.

Of those born in the eighteenth century, Schubert, close to the rocklike Beethoven in many respects despite their basic disparity, might remind us of the greater master occasionally, as in both the lied and the quartet on *Death and the Maiden* with the throbbing dactyls so familiar from the slow movement in Beethoven's Seventh. But otherwise, he was too 'feminine' to find his expression in rhythm. And the same is true of Weber and the other romanticists of the time. Attention withdrew from rhythm to such an extent that there is some truth in Berlioz's pessimistic remark that "rhythm, of all the elements of music, seems today the least advanced." [10] (This is why he earnestly proposed to establish a class for rhythm at the Paris *Conservatoire*, to be attended by singers and players alike.)

The performer's shortcomings seem to have been on Berlioz's mind in the first place. But he also thought perhaps of certain composers, and particularly of the idol of the day, Rossini. In a review of *Guillaume Tell* (1834), he wrote disgustedly: "Our author would have done well to abandon the square-cut rhythms." But the overture, he says, is a masterpiece, "despite its lack of originality in theme and rhythm, and despite its somewhat vulgar use of the bass drum, most disagreeable at certain moments, con-

[9] Aristeides Quintilianus, translated by Rudolf Schaefke, Berlin, 1937, p. 228.
[10] Reprinted in Hector Berlioz, *À travers chants*, Paris, 1863.

stantly pounding away on the strong beats as in a *pas redoublé*
[a quick march] or the music of a country dance." [11]

It is true, to be sure, that in Paris, the center of musical life
after Vienna's abdication, at least operatic melodies were seldom
served without some rhythmical spices. But the pungent, pert,

Ex. 115. Auber, opera, *Fra Diavolo,* overture

and peppery dotting that we find so often in marchlike melodies
like those of Auber (and, as a leftover from the French *grand
opéra,* in Wagner's *Tannhäuser* [music example 88]) soon loses
its interest.

Speaking of marches, is it this rhythmical dearth that led to
the new position of the march, the lowest form of rhythmical movement?

Marches first appear in 'art' music with William Byrd's collection of pieces for virginals (that is, harpsichord), *My Ladye
Nevells Booke of* 1591. The march is a favorite of Lully's and the
masters around and after him, but mostly in a more dignified vein
than that of the military marches in the Elizabethan age. Even
the eighteenth century prefers the graver kind, such as the dead
march in Handel's oratorio *Saul* and the processions of priests in
Gluck's *Alceste* and Mozart's *Zauberflöte.* The modern era, with
marches of all moods from gravity to electrifying vividness, begins
with Mozart's *Figaro* (1785).

In the nineteenth century, the march became a stock requisite
to such an extent that any enumeration seems inadequate and cannot be more than just a suggestion of its importance and frequency.
The marches in most, if not all, of Spontini's operas are forgotten;
but those composed by Mendelssohn for the wedding in *A Midsummer Night's Dream,* by Meyerbeer for the coronation in *The
Prophet,* by Gounod for the soldiers in *Faust,* by Verdi for the
triumphant Egyptian army in *Aida,* and by Wagner for the guests
in *Tannhäuser,* the bridal procession in *Lohengrin,* and the parade
of the *Meistersinger* are universally known.

[11] Quoted from Strunk, *op. cit.,* pp. 810, 811 f.

One could object that these were stage marches, and their reason for being was less the music as such than the visual pomp of impressive processions in the best tradition of *grand opéra*. But there are a sufficient number of eminent marches outside the stage: those of Le Sueur, the funeral marches of Beethoven and Chopin, Schubert's military marches for piano, the Rákoczy March in Berlioz's *Damnation de Faust* and the March to the Gallows in his *Fantastic Symphony*, the march of the crusaders in Liszt's *Legend of St. Elizabeth* (just as far-fetched as the two preceding ones and quite unjustified but for the sake of stirring rhythms), and Wagner's three non-operatic marches, for his patron, King Ludwig of Bavaria, for the German emperor after the end of the Franco-German war, and for the Centennial Exhibition in Philadelphia (1876).

The march, with its uniform beats in groups of four, left–right left–right, is probably the lowest form in the musico-rhythmical field. It restores the pristine direct rapport with the body—a stronger rapport even than that of the dance, which suggests some more complicated pattern of movement. That so elementary a pattern can be in general favor seems to confirm Einstein's statement that the "union of the refined and the elemental" is "characteristic of all late periods in artistic development." [12]

Berlioz, the critic of rhythmical dearth, was himself a brilliant exception. The overture for his opera *Benvenuto Cellini* (1838) starts in a mystifying rhythm strangely at variance with the orderly *alla breve* that the composer has prescribed in the interest of the conducting baton. An analysis detects the erratic sum of

Ex. 116. Berlioz, opera, *Benvenuto Cellini*, overture

$3 + 2 + 3 + 2 + 2 + 2$ beats, confirmed in the brasses which, coincident with the tuba that our music example adds to the melody, leave in their hard, energetic blows no doubt about the

12 Alfred Einstein, *Music in the Romantic Era*, New York, 1947, p. 8.

metric intention. In *L'Enfance du Christ* (1854) we meet with

Ex. 117. Berlioz, oratorio, *L'enfance du Christ*, first part

7/4 time. Berlioz's *Fantastic Symphony* of 1830—written between Rossini's *Guillaume Tell* and Meyerbeer's *Robert le Diable*—was incredibly rich in rhythmic invention, stretching from the dreamy freedom of its ubiquitous *idée fixe* to the nightmarish syncopations of the March to the Gallows. How exceptional these rhythms were appears from Robert Schumann's review of this work in the *Neue Zeitschrift für Musik:* "The modern period has perhaps produced no other work in which equal and unequal mensural and rhythmic relationships have been combined and employed so freely as in this one." [13]

Schumann certainly knew. He had heard the polyrhythm in Spohr's symphonic *Tongemälde*, Op. 86, *Die Weihe der Töne* (1832), where in one section every three 3/8 measures coincided with two 9/16 measures in other instruments.[14]

But Schumann himself, together with Chopin, was a prominent leader in the rhythmic and polyrhythmic field. In their hands, the conflicting coincidence of different rhythms reached a new heyday in a merely musical capacity, without symbolic or poetic connotations.

In their pianistic polyrhythm, we can easily distinguish between two varieties: coincident beats, but conflicting accents; and again, conflicting beats, but coincident accents.

The 3/8 over 6/16 in Schumann's piano piece *Des Abends*,

Ex. 118. Schumann, *Phantasiestücke*, Op. 12, *Des Abends*

[13] Quoted from Alfred Einstein, *op. cit.*, p. 137.
[14] Dr. J. Braunstein of the New York Public Library kindly recalled this passage to my mind.

No. 1 in the *Phantasiestücke*, Op. 12 (1837), have the individual beats coincident, but oppose three accents in the melody to only two in the accompaniment, which creates a hemiola in principle not very different from that in Schubert's *Sentimental Waltz* in A major.

Ex. 119. Schubert, *Valse sentimentale*

Inversely, the quarter triplets over eighths in one of Chopin's F minor Etudes (in his *Drei Neue Etuden* [15]) have the two ac-

Ex. 120. Chopin, *Drei neue Etuden*, etude in F minor

cents in each measure coincident; but the unaccented beats do not coincide. The same is true of another F minor Etude (Op. 25, No. 2) [16] with 12/8 over 6/4.

Ex. 121. Chopin, etude, Op. 25, No. 2, in F minor

Later on, in Brahms' *Paganini Variations*, Op. 35, of 1866, both the beats and the accents disagree. There are both 2/4 over 3/8 and, the other way round, 3/8 over 2/4.

[15] Chopin, *Gesamtausgabe*, Vol. II, pp. 94 f.
[16] *Ibid.*, pp. 48 ff.

There is, on the contrary, no polyrhythm without a conflict of either accents or beats. Mendelssohn's *Song without Words*, No.18 or III 6, which Mathis Lussy claims to be 6/8 over 18/16,[17] is, as the composer has correctly notated, a perfectly harmless, smooth 6/8 with triplet accompaniment.

Once more we must revert to Chopin. His Ninth Prelude presents the age-old problem of dotted duplets against triplets. The reader will remember from the preceding chapter that this problem can be solved in two ways: either by adaptation or by distinction. In the case of adaptation, the dotted note coincided with the first note of the triplet, and the appended note with the last note of the triplet. In the case of distinction, the appended note of the duplet sounded after the last note of the triplet and was even shortened to make the distinction more obvious. Chopin doubtless counted on the latter form of execution; for in the bass, though not consistently, he expressly wrote double dots. A particularly difficult passage occurs in Chopin's B minor Sonata, Op. 58, where the right hand plays sixteenths against left-hand triplets with the second notes dotted.

Ex. 122. Chopin, sonata in B minor

Chopin is indeed a striking counter-evidence of rhythmical richness against the complaint of Berlioz. But with Chopin, the Franco-Pole, we also face the new impact of rhythms from the less impoverished treasure house of eastern Europe.

That such influence from without was possible—above all in music and maybe even more in the dances of the ballroom—was in large measure a consequence of the changing attitude of the time towards national features.

[17] Mathis Lussy, *Die Correlation zwischen Takt und Rhythmus*, in *Vierteljahrsschrift für Musikwissenschaft*, Vol. I, 1885, p. 153.

The rather cosmopolitan eighteenth century had been very little influenced by foreign styles as such. The almost romantic reversal around 1760, it is true, evidenced a growing interest in things exotic. Macpherson conjured the ancient spirit of the Scottish Highlands in his pseudo-Ossianic poetry, and Herder's *Stimmen der Völker in Liedern* contained translations of poems from all over the world, primitive and oriental, while the connoisseurs of furniture delighted in gold-varnished black and red *chinoiseries*.

The musical stage reacted with 'Turk' operas, like Gluck's *Cadi dupé* and *La Rencontre imprévue*, or Mozart's *Entführung aus dem Serail* and Grétry's *Caravane du Caire*, and numberless others. But the part that music had in all these operas was for the time being just a humorous toying with pseudo-oriental trifles; the exotic appetite of a smiling audience was fully satisfied with the modest local color that the noisy so-called Turkish music of a bass drum, a triangle, and a pair of cymbals provided whenever the 'Turks' marched onto the stage. The Spanish *fandango* after the wedding chorus in the third act of Mozart's *Figaro* (No. 24), which the

Ex. 123. Mozart, opera, *Figaro*, III, 24, *Fandango*

master actually took from Gluck's ballet *Don Juan* (1761), was hardly more than a brilliant exception.

Ex. 124. Gluck, ballet, *Don Juan*

But the nineteenth century, fostering the fanatic passions of nationalism instead of the older humanitarian one-world ideal, expected creative artists to be truly German or French, truly Polish or Russian. It wanted distinguishing traits in a deeper sense—in the first place those of one's homeland; but, in a strange reciprocation of such trends, it hailed and appreciated 'characteristic' traits of some foreign national stamp in a movement that we might call exoticism.

The best-known example of this novel romantic exoticism is probably the symphonic ode *Le Désert* (1844) by the French composer, Félicien David, fellow 'orientalist' of the leading romantic painter, Eugène Delacroix. But an older, though musically inferior, symbol is a set of six sonatas for violin and piano written in the fall of 1810 by Carl Maria von Weber (Op. 13), allegedly the most German of the romantics. The first sonata is in *carattere*

Ex. 125. Weber, sonata, *in carattere espagnuolo* for violin

espagnuolo on a bolero-like rhythm, and the others are based on a French *romance*, an *air russe*, an *air polonais*, a *siciliano*, and a *polacca*. Not even to mention the master's Asianism in the Chinese Overture (*Turandot*), with an authentic Chinese theme, the singspiel *Abu Hassan,* and his last opera, for London, *Oberon*.

EAST EUROPEAN RHYTHMS. The most invigorating influence came from the Slavonic East of Europe—in music as well as in dancing, and particularly in dance music. The Polish polonaise had been an old acquaintance of the West, to be sure. But the springy dactyls on the first beat were rarely present: the *Allgemeine musikalische Zeitung* [18] printed in 1813 two questionable polonaises of one Aloys Stolpe from Warsaw, because "the many polonaises that come out in all music-loving countries year after year are very far from genuine." From this judgment we should probably not even exclude the polonaises of Bach, Mozart, or Beethoven.

Ex. 126. Chopin, *Polonaise* No. 3, Op. 40

[18] *Allgemeine musikalische Zeitung,* Vol. XV, 1813, p. 211.

The true elastic and chivalric rhythm of the polonaise had hardly been known when Frédéric Chopin (1810–1849) made it at one stroke the common property of western music. But an even stronger impulse came from his mazurkas, which, subtilized though they were under the hands of the master, still betrayed the improvised, stamping, heel-clicking character of that vigorous folk dance with irregular accents on the first, second, or third of its three beats, on two, or even on all of them,[19] and usually with a little suspension on the second.

Ex. 127. Chopin, *Mazurka* Op. 6, No. 1

We know what a dominating and often bewildering role such suspensions played in the master's own performance; how he often did his mazurkas in 4/4 instead of the notated 3/4 without being conscious of any deviation from the print; and how one day the good friends, Chopin and Meyerbeer, parted in some irritation because the latter had loudly counted one–two, one–two, while Chopin stubbornly maintained that he was playing in 3/4.

The Magyar influx had already begun at that time, at first, it seems, with Weber's *Andante e Rondo Ungarese,* Op. 35, for bassoon (1813) and Schubert's *Divertissement à l'Hongroise* (Op. 54). It became obvious when Berlioz laid the first scene of his dramatic cantata, *The Damnation of Faust* (1846), in Hungary, though there is no other motivation for this astounding change of habitat than to have a pretext for closing it with the snappy rhythms of the age-old Hungarian *Rákóczy March,* among which we notice the presence, once more, of a 3 + 2 + 3. The heyday of the Magyar vogue came with Liszt's tribute to his native country—the Hungarian Rhapsodies, a symphonic poem *Hungaria* (1856), and a Hungarian Coronation Mass (1866/67)—and, in their wake, the Hungarian Dances of Brahms. But it would only be fair to mention that the generation of Bartók and Kodály has not been at all convinced of the Magyar character in the works of Liszt and still

[19] Cf. Curt Sachs, *World history of the dance,* New York, 1937, p. 440.

less so in those of Brahms. They think that the nineteenth century greatly mistook for Hungarian what in reality was Gypsy.

After the Magyar or pseudo-Magyar wave, we witness the advance of Czech rhythms with the works of Smetana and Dvořák; these were probably strongest in the former master's *Bartered Bride* (1866) and the latter's *Slavonic Dances for Orchestra,* Op. 72 (1886).

Ex. 128. Dvořák, *Slavonic Dances,* Op. 72, IV, 8

To what extent the older Russians affected the West is dubious. Borodin and Balakirev were but little known outside their homeland; and of César Cui the Second Suite, Op. 38 (1887), with pounding 2/8 within a 3/8 scherzo, was not too often performed

Ex. 129. Cui, suite No. 2, Op. 38, scherzo

in Germany or elsewhere. Mussorgsky and Rimsky-Korsakov made headway only when the nineteenth century had come to an end. To the West, the great Russian was Tchaikovsky; but to the East he was not 'Russian' enough, and the 'Mighty Five' representatives of Russian nationalism in music refused to include him. Tchaikovsky's name, at any rate, evokes the very Russian concept of five-beat time.

QUINTUPLE TIME, which so delightfully taxes our western ears, was in recent times indeed a gift of masters from Slavonic countries who had raised it from folk to art music. Every music lover knows the truly graceful 5/4 movement *Allegro con grazia* in Tchaikovsky's Sixth, *Pathetic Symphony* of 1893. But there had

Ex. 130. Tchaikovsky, Sixth Symphony, 2nd movement

Allegro con grazia ♩ = 144

been an older Russian example—the women's chorus in Glinka's *Life for the Czar* of 1836; and a more or less contemporary one—the first scene of the third act in Rimsky-Korsakov's opera *Pskovityanka* (1873/1895). Among their Polish fellow Slavs, Chopin gave 5/4 to the slow third movement of his C minor sonata, Op. 4, and Paderevsky, to the *Andantino mistico* in his *Chants des Voyageurs*, No.4.

Ex. 131. Glinka, *A Life for the Czar*, women's chorus

Ex. 132. Rimsky-Korsakov, opera, *Pskovityanka*

Ex. 133. Chopin, C minor sonata, Op. 4, 3rd movement

Among the non-Slavs, Boieldieu (who had spent eight years as a conductor at the Russian court) used it on the words *déjà la nuit* in the *Cavatina* (Act II, Scene 2) in the most famous of his operas, *La Dame blanche* (1825); Johannes Brahms, in a lied,

Ex. 134. Boieldieu, *La Dame blanche*, cavatine

Agnes, Op. 59; and Wagner, in *Tristan,* in the disguise of alternating 3/4 and 2/4, to convey the restless anticipation before Isolde's arrival at the castle in the second scene of the third act. In the nineties, two Frenchmen used quintuple time for slow movements in chamber music: Saint-Saëns in his second piano trio in E minor (1892), and Vincent d'Indy in his second string quartet, Op. 45 (1897). In the very last year of the nineteenth century, 1899/1900, quintuple time occurs where it would be expected: in the symphonic poem *Finlandia,* in which Sibelius portrays his native country, the land of five-beat songs. These rhythms, it is true, must

be laboriously read from the score in which Sibelius shamefacedly
conceals the 5/4 under artificial, misleading 4/4 signatures.

Ex. 135. Sibelius, *Finlandia*

The last example ranges with the Slavonic 5/4 against the western examples: it is 'numerical' in a typically East European way,
proceeding in steady groups of five quarter notes, whose internal
accents are insignificant in the absence of any metrical organization. The western 5/4 melodies are metrical and accentual in a
western sense and are, rather, a continual alternation of three and
two beats.

The quintuple time of the nineteenth century had had a few
precursors in the eighteenth. Handel used it in his opera *Orlando*
of 1732 (Act III, scene 11); and in Italy Benedetto Marcello

Ex. 136. Handel, *Orlando,* Act II, Scene 11

(1686–1739) prescribed it as a pitfall for players in a cantata for
soprano and harpsichord, where—quite in the spirit of Guillaume
de Machaut and the end of the fourteenth century—the comment
is written into the text: *Senza gran pena non si giunge al fine*
("Without hard labor one cannot get to the end"). The last aria in
this cantata, which is in 5/4 time, is, the composer says, "*di novità
stravagante.*" [20] Incidentally—has Marcello taken this motto from
the pious ejaculation at the end of Frescobaldi's Toccata No.
IX: "*non senza fatiga si giunge al fine*"?

Marcello's claim to *novità* was not quite justified. In the preceding centuries, too, composers had known and occasionally written in quintuple time. Two examples from the seventeenth are
Heinrich Albert's German arias (1638–1650), where five, six, and
four beats alternate; [21] and one of the intradas in the *Conviviorum
deliciae* of 1608 by Christoph Demantius.[22]

[20] Benedetto Marcello, *La stravaganza, cantata a una voce sola,* aria No. 2.
[21] Arnold Schering, *Geschichte der Musik in Beispielen,* Leipzig, 1931, pp. 233 f.
[22] *Ibid.,* pp. 158 f.

Ex. 137. Albert, *Arie*

Ex. 138. Demantius, *Intrada*

Ex. 139. von Bruck, *Komm heiliger Geist*

As far back as the sixteenth century, Arnold von Bruck's chorale setting *Komm heiliger Geist* (1534) [23] ends with a broadening, free *Hallelujah* in 5/4. One last example might even reach back to the fifteenth century: the episode *Qui tollis peccata mundi* in the *Gloria* of Obrecht's Mass *Je ne demande*, though shrouded in the conventional ¢ signature of mensural notation, is an unmistakable 5/4.[24]

Ex. 140. Obrecht, Mass, *Je ne demande*, Gloria

The 5/4 of eastern Europe is often doubtful. Is it 3 + 2 or 2 + 3? When Mussorgsky prints the ever recurring *Promenade* in his *Pictures at an Exhibition* (1874) as an alternation of 5/4

[23] *Ibid.*, pp. 108 f.
[24] Jakob Obrecht, *Werken*, Vol. I, p. 8. Also Arnold Schering, *Takt und Sinngliederung in der Musik des 16. Jahrhunderts*, in *Archiv für Musikwissenschaft*, Vol. II, 1920, p. 475.

and 6/4, he sets the bar line quite arbitrarily and misleads the player. Actually, the signature should be 11/4—the only time symbol under which the phrases could be placed without inconsistency (music example No. 7). There is no divisive rhythm, to be neatly halved, quartered, or doubled; the quarter note is the motor unit, and the rhythm is once more, as in the Orient, an addition of units.

The same is true of the introductory chorus in his *Boris Godunov* (1874). The time signature—3/4, except for 5/4 in the third measure—is as arbitrary as the underlying harmony. Even if one

Ex. 141. Mussorgsky, *Boris Godunov*, Act I, Scene 1

decides on two 5/4 measures, *arsis* and *thesis* remain uncertain, and, we may add, pleasantly so. Again, there are eleven additive quarters, whose even flow does not stand divisive organization.

This can be said of a good deal of Russian music, down to Stravinsky.

To a certain extent, the many offbeat sforzatos in this kind of music lose their seeming anomaly: where there are no grouping accents, a sforzato anywhere cannot be a counteraccent.

FREE AND FLEXIBLE RHYTHM. Even within the realm of western means of expression, with its complicated interweaving of rhythm, harmony, and form, it was only natural that Romanticism at its peak, striving for freedom from patterns and rules, tried to break the strictness of rhythm as much as its bar-lined, baton-beaten scores permitted.

Much of this freedom was a time-honored heritage from earlier generations and within the "rules." One device to ease the fetters of measure was—once more—the hemiola or alternative subdivision of six units. It is frequent in the piano works of Chopin and Schumann, as in the latter's *Davidsbündlertänze*, Op. 6, No. 10

(written between 1837 and 1850); and it is almost a mannerism in the scores of Brahms (1833–1897). The following two quotations from the master's Second Symphony (1877) show them both ways—as a tightening and as a broadening contrivance: in the

Ex. 142. Brahms, Second Symphony

first case the 3/4 changes to a sharply marked 6/8; in the second case two 3/4 change to one 3/2.

We are somewhat inclined to attribute such formal informalities to composers of a more conservative cast who insist on purely musical means of expression. But they can also be found in the opposite camp: when in the second act of *Die Walküre* Sieglinde, exhausted, has fallen asleep after her elopement, an impressive hemiola widens the tender melody of the strings before the dismal,

Ex. 143. Wagner, *Die Walküre*, Act II

ominous tubas cause her lover Siegmund to lift his eyes from his bride to the death-heralding Brünnhilde. They can be found in the *Tristan* prelude with the entry of the full-chordal orchestra to slow and widen the glance of him who beholds the beloved one;

Ex. 144. Wagner, *Tristan*, prelude

and also in *Parsifal*, when the solemn strides in 6/4 of the so-called Motif of Faith slow down—both ways: in the duplet-after-

Exs. 145/146. Wagner, *Parsifal*

triplet form (3/4 + 6/8) and as a widening from 3/4 to 3/2. And let us not forget Strauss' *Eulenspiegel* who, idly trotting along— *gemächlich*—misses a step now and then and veers from a none too certain 6/8 to an outright 3/4 (cf. music example 114).

Another conspicuous case of hemiola might be quoted from Rimsky-Korsakov's *Sheherazade*.

Ex. 147. Rimsky-Korsakov, *Sheherazade*

The rarer case of a 2/4 rhythm squeezed into the bar lines of a 3/4 can be found in the third movement of Gustav Mahler's Fifth Symphony (1902).

Ex. 148. Mahler, Fifth Symphony, 3rd movement

Beyond such flexible rhythms, later Romanticism proceeded, circumstances permitting, to a more or less complete freedom.

Many examples can be heard in *Tristan*. The whole first page of the full score is free rhythm in the disguise of 6/8 measures. The duration of the sustained notes in the cellos, being too long for direct perception, is arbitrary; there could be four, six, seven beats just as well as five, if they must be counted and are countable at all. And arbitrary are the durations of the subsequent woodwind chords as well as the protracted rests between the seven timeless returns of the languid motive of love. Twice in *Tristan* Wagner even breaks the fetters that an orchestral score imposes and writes

Ex. 149. Wagner, *Tristan*, prelude

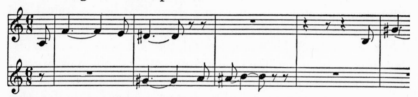

free-rhythmic melodies in a true folk-song style without accompaniment: in the tune of a seaman high up on the mast at the begin-

Ex. 150. Wagner, *Tristan*, Act I

ning of the first act; and later, when the curtain rises for the third
act, in the melancholy *Hirtenweise* of the faithful shepherd who
searches the sea for Isolde.

Ex. 151. Wagner, *Tristan*, Act III

Parsifal begins with the seeming paradox of a beatless melody
within a strictly beaten rhythm. The so-called motif of the Holy
Communion which mystically sounds from the orchestra pit is
embedded in a setting of regular 4/4 time; but its first seven
notes, drawn out over two measures, and again the last notes, are
all off beat and convey a perfect impression of free rhythm.

Ex. 152. Wagner, *Parsifal*, prelude

Melody against the bar lines and beats, reminiscent of flowing
Renaissance polyphony, was indeed one of the new ideals. It
found a strong expression in the conducting of Liszt, who, after
deserting his brilliant career as a piano virtuoso, had turned to
the orchestra without the technical education of firm, reliable

beating and with a deep aversion to its mechanical down–left–right–up. Answering the protesting storm that his emotional and probably showy gesticulation had caused at the music festival at Karlsruhe in 1853, he wrote against the "efficient time-beaters" that in modern music "the crude preservation of the measure and of each of its parts might interfere with sense and expression. . . . I do not see the advantages of a conductor adopting the function of a windmill. . . . We are helmsmen, not galley slaves." [25]

CLUSTERED UPBEATS—if the reader will let this neologism pass—display the condensed energy characteristic of a good many romantic melodies. The author understands by this term an intensified upbeat in which the simple quarter note (or, for that matter, the simple dotted group) is replaced by a whole cluster of notes, a triplet, a quadruplet, or a dactyl. The oldest example in the century is not quite flawless, since the sixty-fourth upbeats in the funeral march of Spontini's opera *La Vestale* (1807) imitate drum rolls. For a similar reason, we should hesitate to quote the trumpet triplets on *c* sharp at the beginning of Mahler's Fifth

Ex. 153. Mahler, Fifth symphony, 1st movement

Symphony or, for that matter, those on *c* natural in the Wedding March of Mendelssohn's *Midsummer Night's Dream* (1843).

Ex. 154. Mendelssohn, *A Midsummer Night's Dream,* wedding march

Better examples are the triplets in the overture of Weber's

Ex. 155. Weber, *Euryanthe,* overture

[25] Reprinted, for example, in Julius Kapp, *Franz Liszt,* Berlin, 1909, p. 277.

Euryanthe (1823) and the whipping upbeats in Berlioz's orchestration of the *Rákoczy March* in the *Damnation of Faust* (1846).

Ex. 156. Berlioz, *Rákoczy march* from *La Damnation de Faust*

But the best evidences come from Wagner's works. We think in the first place of the spirited triplets in the introduction before the

Ex. 157. Wagner, *Lohengrin*, Act III, prelude

third act of *Lohengrin* (1847). How much the clustered upbeat is indeed a trait of Wagner's (and his time), can be seen from

Ex. 158. Wagner, *Die Meistersinger*, parade

the parade of the *Meistersinger*, because in its model, an authentic melody printed in J. C. Wagenseil's book *Von der Meister-Singer Origine* (Nürnberg, 1697), the upbeat appears as a simple, rather insipid quarter.

In a recent example, Paul Hindemith opens the third *Bild* of his opera *Mathis der Maler* (1937) with a quick triple upbeat.

Ex. 159. Hindemith, *Mathis der Maler*, 3rd *Bild*

A specially fascinating, energetic variety is the clustered upbeat on the downbeat, if the reader will allow me to add a paradox to a neologism. The paradox arises when the leading melody shifts its upbeat to coincide with the downbeat of the other voice parts and leaves the principal accent—whether actually stressed or not—to the second beat in the bar; in other words, when the upbeat of the leading voice rebounds from the downbeat of the orchestra and the listener, forced out of his 4/4 routine unawares, is given an invigorating shock treatment.

Venerable precursors of the clustered upbeats in the early eighteenth century were Handel's *Concerto grosso* in C major and Bach's concerto for two violins, the *Doppelkonzert*. Almost a

Ex. 160. Bach, double concerto for two violins

hundred years before, another German, Heinrich Albert (1604–1651), had started his aria *Auf mein Geist* [26] in a similar way, and so

Ex. 161. Albert, aria, *Auf mein Geist*

had Froberger in his *Capriccio IV*.[27] But in dealing with such examples, one must make sure as far as possible that the "clustered upbeat on the downbeat" does not stand for a written-out *tirata*, in which case it would be "feminine" rather than energetic.

Excellent examples from the nineteenth century are the stirring Coronation March in Meyerbeer's *Prophet* (1836), an instance of

Ex. 162. Meyerbeer, *Le Prophète*, coronation march

the vivid rhythmical life in French and Italian operatic scores of the time; also the chorus of Norwegian sailors in *The Flying Dutch-*

Ex. 163. Wagner, The Flying Dutchman, mariners' chorus

[26] Reprinted in Davison-Apel, *Historical anthology of music*, Cambridge (Mass.), 1950, Vol. II, No. 205, pp. 42 f.

[27] *Denkmäler der Tonkunst in Oesterreich*, Vol. VII, p. 84.

man (1842), where the apparent upbeat in a 2/4 rhythm strikes consistently on the first quarter, and the apparent downbeat on the second; the inverted rhythm of the galloping Valkyries, with

Ex. 164. Wagner, *Die Walküre*, Act III, introduction

the stress on the fourth of 9/8: and the energetic entry of the orchestra when chorus and organ are finishing the chorale at the beginning of the *Meistersinger* (1867):

Similar shifts of stress occur in the first act of *Parsifal* (1882), in

Ex. 165. Wagner, *Parsifal*, Act I, No. 88, first violins

the first violins at No.88 of the full score, and in the *Meistersinger* prelude, measure four, in which the accent and climax is actually on the second beat instead of the first. But the most fascinating examples are Berlioz's overture *The Roman Carnival* (1830's), where the crest of the first wave is reached on the fourth sixth of a bar, and the master's Rákoczy March from *La Damnation de Faust* (1846) with its whipping triplet upbeats and Hungarian offbeat accents.

Clustered upbeats come to a climax in Gustav Mahler and Richard Strauss. At the beginnings of Mahler's Second and of Strauss' symphonic poem *Don Juan* the upbeats reach the length and density of seven sixteenths in running starts of unprecedented

Ex. 166. Mahler, Second Symphony

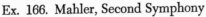
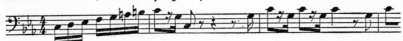

Ex. 167. Strauss, *Don Juan,* beginning

energy and driving force. Other examples are Strauss' operas
Salome and *Ariadne on Naxos.* Their function was what the procatalectic beginnings had been in the seventeenth century: an
opening of space and form in pursuit of fleeting impressions, as it
shows so strikingly in paintings of the leading schools, those of
Barbizon and of the 'impressionists' from Manet and Whistler to
Monet and Sisley.

Ex. 168. Strauss, *Salome*, beginning

Ex. 169. Strauss, *Ariadne on Naxos*

(The eventual emergence of the theme out of the shapeless mist
of tremolo strings or a rolling bass drum, as in Beethoven's Ninth
or Strauss' *Zarathustra,* is a different means to a similar end.)

RHYTHMIC *GESTALTEN.* Every rhythmical pattern is in a
way a *Gestalt* or configuration in the sense of modern psychology.
Even the simplest dactyl does not appear to the listening ear as
an assemblage of one long and two shorts, or of one strong and
two weaker units, but has a meaning only as an indivisible whole
(just as a figure 8 is psychologically different from the two heart-
shaped outlines that seem to "compose" it). In this book we might,
however, be allowed to use the word *Gestalt* exclusively for those
very complex cases in which any attempt to perceive recurrent
lengths, recurrent accents, or recurrent numbers of units would
fail.

Take the beginning of Strauss' *Don Juan,* which in more than
sixty years has nothing lost of its demoniacal urge (music example 169). Nobody will doubt that its breath-taking momentum is
due, not to melodic, harmonic, or coloristic traits, but to rhythm.
What we hear does not fit in any category; it is not metrical, not
accentual, not numerical, and yet it partakes of all these qualities.

Any description that we might venture, such as seven (procatalec-tic) sixteenths, followed by a half note, followed by a triplet of eighths, followed by something else, would be nonsensical. The parts are meaningless within the whole, and nobody could recon-struct the daredevil resilience of those first four measures from so lame a description.

That complex *Gestalten* occurred long before Strauss and his contemporaries is obvious; the end of the second and the begin-ning of the last movement in Beethoven's *Emperor Concerto* (music example 113) shows one of them three generations before *Don Juan*. But their importance increased in the current of the nineteenth century. The new ideal of art was dynamic: it re-flected action, progress, and drive not only of outer events but also of thoughts unspoken and often subconscious. Drama became the central subject, be it on the musical stage, or in the lied, or in symphonic, chamber-music forms.

Dramatic art relies on rapid changes rather than on static ex-panse. All means of musical expression—melody, harmony, coun-terpoint, orchestration—learned the skill of swift, unhesitant adap-tation to sudden shifts in emotion and circumstances. Where there had been a long stretch of melody in one key and one orchestral color, the nineteenth century needed laconic 'motives,' fast modu-lation, and ever changing timbres.

Rhythm had likewise to learn the skill of quick adaptation and the art of expressing character, thought, emotion, and motion in brief configurations of trenchant descriptive power. Such is, among the earlier examples, the limping off-beat rhythm in the strings when Tannhäuser drags along on his remorseful pilgrimage to Rome.

Many of these formulas have since Wagner's days been known as *Leitmotive,* or leading motives, to accompany, herald, or evoke significant objects, persons, or concepts—'the sword,' 'Siegfried,' 'the curse.' Such a *Leitmotiv* is a melodic and often rhythmic organism, pregnant enough to be recognized and re-understood without difficulty and short enough to be completed before the flashing thought or gesture or action that the composer wants to render has yielded to a subsequent happening. Rhythm is quicker in action and reaction than melody can ever be. The motif of

Hunding, Siegmund's gloomy slayer in *Die Walküre*, is such a brief characterization. Its melodic content, that is, the sequence of its pitches, has little meaning in itself. But the barking meter, dismal and menacing, would not lose its nature if the notes, devoid of pitch, were struck on a single drum. Pregnant in a similar

Ex. 170. Wagner, *Die Walküre*, Hunding motif

Ex. 171. Wagner, *Der Ring des Nibelungen*, fire motif

way are the double-dotted, crackling motifs of Loge's fire and the galloping dactyls of the Valkyries (music example No. 164, prefigured in the piano accompaniment of Loewe's ballad *Erlkönig*).

Some of these *Leitmotive* appear in various rhythmical shapes or metamorphoses: while the melodic sequence of the notes is consistent in expressing the unchanging identity of the person described, rhythm, the sequence of time values, develops with his age and destiny. Thus Siegfried's personal symbol is, in the drama *Siegfried*, still a gay and careless horn call in 9/8, but changes in *Die Götterdämmerung* to several solemn 4/4 forms with vigorous offbeat accents when the youth has grown up to be a hero.

Ex. 172. Wagner, *Siegfried*, Siegfried motif

Ex. 173. Wagner, *Die Götterdämmerung*, Siegfried motif

These rhythmic *Gestalten* are also one of the characteristic traits of Richard Strauss' post-Wagnerian style. The galloping, clattering dactyls of Wagner's Valkyries return in a new, quite personal way at the end of *Elektra* (1909) in the brutally pound-

Ex. 174. Strauss, *Elektra*, No. 56

ing, convulsive dactyls of the final, eerie dance of triumph; and in a clipped inflection, more concise than any of Wagner's, the principal motif of the drama, the conjuration and never-absent thought of Elektra's murdered father Agamemnon, takes its origin from the very name pronounced in frenzied passion and hurry: *Agamem—non.*

Ex. 175. Strauss, *Elektra*, beginning

Such significant motives can grow together in strange *proportiones.* Wagner evokes, indeed, the memory of flamboyant polyrhythm at the end of the *Götterdämmerung* (1875), when after the recovery of the fatal ring and Siegfried's and Brünnhilde's reunion on the pyre, Valhalla, burning with the dying gods and heroes, appears through the smoke. The key then changes from E flat to D flat, and the motifs of Valhalla, of Brünnhilde's love, of the jubilant daughters of the Rhine are heard at the same time in a breathtaking polyrhythm: Valhalla's in the brasses under the signature 3/2, that of the daughters of the Rhine in woodwinds and strings under 6/8, and the love motif on top of both in flutes and violins under 2/2.

Ex. 176. Wagner, *Die Götterdämmerung,* closing scene

Even though such impressive superimposition might be called flamboyant, it has very little in common with the truly Flamboyant polyrhythmic webs of the late Gothic style. In the first place, Wagner's cumulation of motives is not polyrhythm or even polyphony in any stricter sense. His motives alternate rather than coincide and at best overlap by lengthening out initial and final notes. And then, the masters of the fifteenth century had piled up their often bewildering Masses and motets from sheer delight in audacious, intricate structures; Wagner, the romantic, remote from any interest in structure for the sake of structure, expressed in the reunion of audible symbols the bond between the destinies of his *dramatis personae*.

The famous three-theme counterpoint in the middle of the *Meistersinger* prelude seems to be of a different brand. Walter Stolzing's enthusiastic theme above, the weighty motif of the masters below, and between them the theme of their solemn parade

Ex. 177. Wagner, *Die Meistersinger*, prelude

expressed in lighthearted diminution in *proportio dupla*—all of the voice parts follow strictest 4/4 time without providing any special interest in their superimposition except the truly playful and musicianly delight in the discovery that they lend themselves so easily to a brilliant combination, albeit not quite in agreement with the rules of Palestrinian counterpoint. The whole opera, like this counterpoint, symbolizes a reconciliation of "the masters" and the unmasterly Walter, of tradition and freedom, of inherited craft and independent genius. And yet it seems that the passage owes its existence in the first place to musical inspiration. A symbolic interpretation comes *post festum*.

REBIRTH OF ADDITIVE RHYTHM. From the middle of the century on, we feel that additive rhythms are coming to the fore after centuries of divisive rhythm. Quintuple time, discussed in an earlier section of this chapter, had been a spicy exception. It was still an exception when, away from all the beaten tracks and from the prevailing atmosphere of nineteenth-century rhythm, Joachim Raff (1822–1882), a prominent master of the Lisztian camp, wrote the vivid movement (*Sehr rasch*) of his second *Grosse Sonate für Pianoforte und Violine* of ca. 1859 in an alternation from bar to bar between 3/4, 5/4, 4/4, and 2/4. This amounts almost to an Arabian or Indian 14/4 and foreshadows the complicated additive rhythms of the twentieth century.

Liszt himself did not go that far. But about the time of Raff's sonata, he confronted the audience of his *Faust Symphony* (1854–

Ex. 178. Liszt, *Faust Symphony*, first part

1861) with a perpetual change from 3/4 to 4/4: his symphonic polyphony followed a quite monodic *espressivo* style in which a uniform pattern of beats would weaken the emotional intensity just as it would have done two hundred and fifty years earlier in the Italian *stile recitativo e rappresentativo*.

The next move came from the Russians. Mussorgsky's additive trends were illustrated in the first chapter. The eleven beats of the *Promenade* recur in the first chorus of his *Boris Godunov* (1874), although disguised under time signatures changing from 3/4 to 5/4 (music examples 7 and 141). Rimsky-Korsakov was more consistent when he prescribed 11/4 in the final chorus of his

Ex. 179. Rimsky-Korsakov, *The Snow Maiden*

opera *Snow Maiden* (1882). The second act of *Boris* has a fascinating scene in 3/4 + 5/4, which amounts to 3 + 3 + 2.

Ex. 180. Mussorgsky, *Boris Godunov*, Act II

From the 1890's on, the number of such examples increased in every country. In England, Elgar contributed a 3/4, 4/4, or 3 + 4

Ex. 181. Elgar, *Caracterus*

in the Lament of his cantata *Caractacus* (1898). Around the same year, the Frenchman, Gabriel Pierné (1863–1937), must have been working at his sonata for violin and piano, Op. 36, where the first, *allegretto* movement leads the 6/8 of the violin against 10/16

Ex. 182. Pierné, violin sonata, Op. 36

of the piano. Additive rhythms are very frequent in Debussy's works. Suffice it to mention one piece of chamber music, the 15/8 or 9 + 6 in the second movement of the first string quartet (1893),

Ex. 183. Debussy, First String Quartet, 3rd movement

and one orchestral score, the *Rondes de Printemps* of 1912 (last

Ex. 184. Debussy, *Rondes de Printemps, Images*

part of his *Images*), also with 15/8. (Actually, this rhythm had occurred as early as 1864 in the 9 + 6 eighths of the *chanson de*

Magali in the second act of Gounod's opera *Mireille*.) Between the two Debussys, Gustav Mahler alternated in the scherzo of his Sixth Symphony (1904) from 3/8 to 4/8. But this is a particular case, since his 7/8 derives from the age-old *Zwiefacher* of Bavaria and Bohemia, a folk dance in rapidly alternating steps and rhythms, as the name implies.

Ex. 185. Mahler, Sixth Symphony, scherzo

The transition to the twentieth century, touched upon in Mahler's and Debussy's examples, is completed in the Third (*Ilia Murometz*) Symphony (1909–1911) by the Russian, Reinhold M. Glière, where the English horn and the bass clarinet proceed in a continual change, from 6/8 to 4/4, 5/8, 8/8, and finally pay their tribute to the purest 3 + 3 + 2.[28]

Ex. 186. Glière, Third Symphony

[28] The author is indebted to Dr. Joseph Braunstein of the New York Public Library, Music Division, for knowledge of this score.

CHAPTER 15

The Present

The twilight of Romanticism was rhythmically perhaps more ambiguous than other times of crisis. For Romanticism itself, in its endeavor to encompass all facets of expression, had reached for the most divergent forms of rhythm: for its exaggeration and for its utter neglect, for an iron one–two, one–two discipline and for shapeless freedom. It had condensed dramatic characterization in rhythmic *Gestalten;* it had led the regularity of divisive rhythm to a climax, and had re-opened the way for a bloom of long-forgotten additive rhythms.

Debussy's impressionism, emerging in 1892 with his symphonic poem *L'Après-midi d'un Faune,* led rhythmical life in many respects to a nadir. In all its iridescent flux the impressionistic work actually does not move. It has no growth or action, no driving force or will. Melody does not stride; it wavers, glides, and soars. Harmony has lost its 'function.' It is coloristic, not dynamic; it creates emotional atmosphere, but does not progress from chord to chord in keeping with any rules. Rhythm, once derived from our body's urge and experience and meant to impart a clean-cut structure to time, has given up its intrinsic nature in a style that, contrariwise, seeks disembodiment, dimness, and timeless passivity.

Let us get this straight: the impressionistic disintegration did not entail an impoverishment of rhythm, just as the subservience to speech that the Florentine monodists around 1600 imposed on melody was far from being a deathblow dealt to melody. The actual foes of rhythm had been people like Rossini, who, indifferent to the expressive power of rhythm, persevered in hackneyed stereotypes and thus destroyed its life.

While impressionism disembodied rhythm in the interest of an immaterial presentation of moods and a hazy rendition of atmospheric phenomena, the strong rebellion against both the romantic and the impressionistic ideals early in the twentieth century reversed the stand, withdrew from musical disintegration, and gave a new supremacy to the virile, shaping forces of rhythm.

One symptom, whose importance should not be underrated, is the world-wide acceptance of Emile Jaques-Dalcroze's rhythmo-gymnastic system for the education of children and adults, of laymen and professionals, less than a generation after Hugo Riemann, like Hector Berlioz before him, had complained, "Rhythmics is really the stepchild of musical theory and is not taught as a special subject at any music school." [1]

NEW TIME SIGNATURES. The name of Jaques-Dalcroze as an educator is too well known all over the world to require a special discussion in this brief survey. Less well known is his attempt to improve and modernize time signatures by replacing the often arbitrary time unit by the unmistakable beat value and, hence, to re-establish the close relation between rhythm and the body's movement. He uses fractions, too; but his numerators indicate the actual number of beats, and his denominators, their values expressed in notes. When a 6/8 is too fast to be played in six eighths [as for instance in the languishing Tristan prelude], but rather in two beats, it is written as 2/♩.; and a 12/16 accordingly as 4/♪. .

Another suggestion to improve time signatures has come from Carlos Vega in Argentina: [2] the denominator indicates the unit, according to whether they are halves, quarters, or eighths, and the numerator the number of units in a measure. While this is not new, the two figures are braced by a smaller figure to the right to

---

[1] Among Jaques-Dalcroze's writings: *Eurhythmics*, New York, 1930; *Rhythm, music, and education*, New York, 1921. Also J. Pennington, *The importance of being rhythmic*, New York and London, 1925.—Hugo Riemann, review of Westphal's *Theorie der musikalischen Rhythmik*, in *Literarisches Centralblatt*, 1881, p. 582.

[2] Carlos Vega, *Fraseología*, in *La Música popular argentina*, Buenos Aires, 1941, Vol. I, pp. 48, 49.

indicate the subdivision. Our (and his) 6/8 gets a figure 3, because the two feet are ternary, and our 3/4 can appear as a 6/8 with a figure 2, because its three feet are binary. This, however, seems to be confusing, since the figure 2 interferes with the ternary character of the measure, and 3, with the binary character of 6/8.

FUTURISM. The dying Romanticism had itself led the way to a revival of rhythm: in some of Gustav Mahler's symphonies percussion became autonomous, although with a strongly sentimental weft. The author remembers how Mahler stopped the drummers at a rehearsal and told them to "sing," and how the men, nonplussed, stared at him but quickly complied with the new leading role assigned to their instruments. Even in later works—as in the symphonic poem *L'Homme et son désir* by Darius Milhaud—the new front position of drums and gongs, of triangles and castanets, has in its primitivistic character a deeply moving, human element. In the score of Stravinsky's *L'histoire du soldat* (1918), only six melody instruments counterbalance the six percussion instruments.

Only a few years later, in 1925, Béla Bartók published a composition for strings, percussion, and celesta. In the following year, 1926, he silenced the orchestra in the second movement of his piano concerto and restricted the accompaniment to kettledrums, a snare drum, a bass drum, and cymbals. In the same year, Virgil Thomson wrote *Five Phrases from Songs of Solomon* for a singer with percussion accompaniment. In 1934, he came out with *Medea Choruses* and a second *Missa brevis*, both for women's voices and percussion; and Henry Cowell joined him in an *Ostinato pianissimo* for xylophone, piano, kettledrums, bongos, rice bowls, and wood blocks. In 1941, Bartók wrote a concerto for two pianos with nothing but percussion instruments instead of the accompanying orchestra. A *Ritmo Jondo* by Carlos Surinach (1952) uses even hand clapping. On May 6, 1952, a whole concert of such pieces was performed at the Museum of Modern Art in New York—a *Percussionists' Hey-Day*, as Jay S. Harrison reported in the New York *Herald Tribune*.

While on this occasion the New York *Times* praised the clapping hands in Surinach's *Ritmo Jondo* for giving "a sense of humanity that was oddly moving," percussional rhythm had become dehumanized in a definite estrangement from romantic emotion. Italian *futurismo,* or *bruitisme* as the French, and *Geräuschmusik* as the Germans say, had tried to banish melody completely.

Futurismo proper has hardly enriched or deepened our rhythmical language. But in suppressing or denaturalizing melody instruments and granting a monopoly to percussion, it has certainly stressed its significance.

Noise music was inaugurated by two Italians. Francesco Pratella took the initiative in 1912 and was joined by Luigi Russolo in 1914. Their aim was to adapt orchestral art to the world of today, "to render," as Pratella said in the preface of his *Musica futurista,* "the musical soul of the crowds, of big industrial plants, of trains, of liners, cruisers, cars, and planes; to add to the dominant motives of musical poetry the rule of the machine and the victorious reign of electricity." Two years later, the painter Luigi Russolo chimed in with his manifesto *L'arte dei rumori:* "We want to let the motley noises speak and to control them in harmony and in rhythm."

The futuristic school has not covered too much ground; but it found a fertile field of action in the movies of the twenties and thirties. Two 'classics' of movie *bruitisme* are unforgotten: Edwin Meisel's *Potemkin* (1925) and Honegger's *Pygmalion* (1938).

Even outside the world of films, the futuristic school has had followers or at least fellow riders to this day. To this day indeed. Upon concluding this book, the author came across a critical column in the New York *Times* of March 7, 1952, in which Olin Downes reviewed a piano concerto by Jean Rivier as "an orchestral jangle and boom that suggests nothing so much as the revolution of machinery, maybe the tractors of tanks or steel riveters or machine guns."

Of the masters in between, the most powerful figure is the Corsico-American Edgar Varèse (born 1885), who created *Ionization* (1931), based on the theory of electrolytic dissociation. This is a composition for thirteen performers with up to three rhythmical instruments each, including, besides the ordinary percussion, West Indian twin drums, Cuban sticks, rattles and scrapers, Chinese blocks, slapsticks, sirens, anvils, sleigh bells, and a piano to

be played with the full forearm—suggesting, in the words of Paul
Rosenfeld,[3] "the life of the inanimate universe." This is a truly
extraordinary piece in extraordinary rhythms and counterrhythms,
and perhaps the greatest rhythmic inspiration ever materialized.

Another follower of the futuristic school is Arthur Honegger in
his *mouvement symphonique* of 1923, *Pacific 231*, but only because
it is the glorification of a railroad engine and its pounding, jubilant,
delirious race. There are no actual noise instruments; the standard
orchestra is sufficient for his purpose. Otherwise Honegger, too,
renounces melodic and harmonic expression completely and de-
picts the puffing engine gaining momentum in a purely rhythmical
climax, of which we just describe the outer surface when we present it as a stepwise growth from whole notes, via dotted and undotted half notes, up to fullest speed in triumphant, irresistible
sixteenths.

Ex. 187. Honegger, *Pacific 231*, score No. 199, p. 45

A sidetrack has led from the percussionists proper to those composers who avail themselves of typewriters, thunderbolts, struck
and ultimately breaking window panes, to speak their rhythmical
language. A typical example is John Cage's piece *Amorosa*[4] of
1943 for a "prepared" piano with rubber, bolts, and screws (one
of the screws "with loose nut") inserted between the strings, for
nine "tomtoms," a pod rattle, and a wire brush. Among its rhythms
we find the 3 + 5 and 3 + 3 + 2 patterns that will be discussed
in the following section.

Ex. 188. Cage, *Amorosa*, No. IV

This was by no means just a transitory fad. For in the New
York *Times* of January 2, 1952, we find a review of a concert to

[3] Paul Rosenfeld, in *The New Republic*, April 26, 1933.
[4] Published in *New Music*, New York, 1943.

which "those interested in experimental piano music turned out in force. . . . There was a pause while Mr. Tudor 'prepared' the piano for the pieces by Christian Wolff. This meant shaking objects out of a series of envelopes and inserting them between the strings of the piano so that a variety of sounds would be produced, which included the twanging of slack wire, off-pitch chimes and the vibrating of paper."

RAG AND JAZZ. The earliest reaction against the anemic rigidity of duple and triple time in folk and popular music came from America.

In an enormous circle movement, the complicated rhythm of the Middle East had conquered Negro Africa, had crossed the Atlantic with the Negro slaves, had put its indelible stamp on the music of both Americas, and ultimately found its way back east to Europe and to the Middle East. Although the Negroes had in Catholic South America much better opportunities to keep their musical heritage alive, the driving force of Afro-American music got its momentum in the South of the United States. It was given its first public sanction when out of the cakewalks, buck-and-wings, and jigs of early minstrel shows a certain style developed about 1890, to be known as *ragtime* or, literally, 'time in tatters.' [5]

Ten years later, these unwonted rhythms reached the Continent, when John Philip Sousa (1854–1932) began to tour the world outside America with his well-trained band (1900) and the latest American dances—cakewalk, one-step, tango—began to conquer Europe.

Rag became the sire of musical styles since known as blues, hot jazz, sweet jazz, swing, fox trot, Charleston, rumba, and what not. It was also closely related to the Negro spirituals. Jazz has never been, and probably cannot be, properly defined. For the purpose of this book it will suffice to comprehend the styles of all these

[5] The best discussion of these and kindred forms is Winthrop Sargeant's *Jazz*, New York, 1938, new edition 1946. Two more books at random: Maud Cuney-Hare, *Negro musicians and their music*, Washington, 1936; Wilder Hobson, *American jazz music*, New York, 1939. The latest discussion of African influence is Richard A. Waterman's *"Hot" rhythm in Negro Music*, in *Journal of the American Musicological Society*, Vol. I, 1948, pp. 24–37. An interesting parallel between jazz and the Baroque, also in matters of rhythm, can be found in Hans-Peter Schmitz, *Jazz und alte Musik*, in *Stimmen*, No. 18, 1949, pp. 497–500.

Ex. 189. Negro spiritual, *When Isrel was in Egyp lan'*

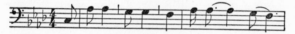

species as musical concepts in which the rigidity of four even quarter-beats per measure is counterbalanced by the irregularities of 'primary' or 'secondary' rag.

'Primary rag' is often quite colorless, as it consists in tiny shifts within the accentual pattern. Often it anticipates the second note of a bar, either in the form of a so-called Scotch snap, say, an eighth followed by a dotted quarter, or of a feminine ending in reverse, such as a quarter on the first beat and a half note on the second beat, instead of a lengthening of the accented, and a shortening of the weaker, beat. The other way around, there might be a retarding rest on the beat with an offbeat syncopation. In either case, the syncope does not necessarily appear in the printed music, but may

Ex. 190. Blake, *Coon's Breach*

be left to the player's improvisation.

'Secondary rag,' leading directly into jazz, implies in the first place the even, unaccented throb in 4/4 of the bass drum and the string bass, which in its immovable steadiness and lack of accentual weight allows the melody instruments to have their fling in the extreme freedom of what appears to the paper-educated listener as ceaseless rubatos, offbeats, ties.

Most of the devices in which the melody-bearing instruments move against, and independent of, the bass are known to the readers of this book from other countries and from previous ages.

One of the favorite devices proceeds in even eighths against the even quarters of the compulsory bass, so that every odd-numbered eighth coincides with a quarter note. This seems to be rather simple and conservative.

Actually, the melody is ternary and contradicts the 4/4 of the bass:

It is the well-known principle of the hemiola. Only the 4/4 ground time (instead of the orthodox hemiola 3/4) makes an extension imperative: the 3/8 and the 4/4 do not reach a coincidental end before the lapse of three 4/4 measures. It is not, as elsewhere, 3×2 against 2×3, but 8×3 against 3×8.

Of minor importance—from the viewpoint of this book—are two very frequent characteristics: that the upbeat falls as a rule on the sixth, not on the last eighth; and that the most salient note of a pattern shifts within this pattern from a strong to a weak and again to stronger spots, thus changing its weight from occurrence to occurrence.

By far the most fascinating 'irregularity,' very frequent in ragtimes, Negro spirituals, and jazz proper, is notated as a 4/4 measure with a tie that connects the fourth and the fifth eighth note, thus bridges the center of the measure, and destroys its two-times-two structure. Everybody knows it as the typical foxtrot

Ex. 191. Cook, *Down de lover's lane*

rhythm. A jazz specialist, Don Knowlton, and a modern composer, Aaron Copland,[6] have placed it correctly: the tie is a misleading notational expedient; there is no true syncopation, but rather an unsyncopated additive pattern—3 + 5. If we break down the unwieldy addendum 5 into its natural elements, we face once more the age-old dochmiac pattern 3 + 3 + 2, George Gershwin's "Fascinating Rhythm," which has so often come to the attention of the

Ex. 192. Gershwin, *Fascinating Rhythm*, p. 5

I   get up with the sun

[6] Aaron Copland, in *Modern Music*, January–February, 1927.

author and his readers in the chapters on the Near and Middle East, on India, Greece, the Middle Ages, and the Renaissance.

Quite similar is the rhythm of the Cuban *rumba,* performed by a clacking woodblock over the drumming of the gourd rattles.

Ex. 193. Cuban rumba

To be sure, it will not do to squeeze the whole unpapery complex of jazz rhythm into a few devices easily rendered on paper. More than in any chamber or concert-hall music, rhythm is here often intangible, irrational, and inaccessible to cold analysis. More than in most of our western music, it is the moving force that drives the melody on, now smoothing its flow, now rushing it forward head over heels, and always giving it the continuous spirited impulse that the jazzer calls by the beautiful, untranslatable word 'the swing.'

Not the swing, but at least the 'devices' of rhythmic flexibility have been imitated in many ambitious 'art' compositions in and outside America. However convincing such devices are in improvisation, they have not always been convincing on paper. And yet they have enriched our musical language; indeed, they have been new blood transfused into the exhausted body of Romantic music.

RAG AND JAZZ IN HIGHBROW MUSIC. A good many pioneering composers of serious music have eagerly reached for the idioms of both ragtime and jazz and tried to absorb them, in the hope of getting away from the rhythmic sterility of post-Romanticism, or at least from its divisive even beats, which were no longer in keeping with the new trends of the earlier twentieth century.

The ragtime period in highbrow music lasted from the *Golliwog's Cakewalk* in Debussy's *Children's Corner* (1908) via one of the three dances in Stravinsky's *Histoire du Soldat* (1918), his *Rag-*

Ex. 194. Debussy, *Children's Corner*, cake-walk

time for eleven instruments (1918), and one for piano (1919) to one of the two dances in Hindemith's *1922 Suite für Klavier* (1922).

Jazz proper seems to have been first grafted on serious music in the second decade of the century, and to a great extent in France. There is Satie's ballet *Parade* of 1917; there are Milhaud's two ballets *Le Boeuf sur le Toit* (1920) and *La Création du Monde* (1923), Honegger's *Concertino* for piano and orchestra (1925), and Ravel's *Sonata* for violin and piano (1927), with a blues as the second movement. Outside France, we witnessed in the same year, 1926, Ernst Křenek's opera *Jonny spielt auf*, Aaron Copland's

Ex. 195. Krenek, *Jonny spielt auf*, jazz

Concerto for piano and orchestra, and, in the conservative atmosphere of the Metropolitan Opera House, John Alden Carpenter's *Skyscraper Ballet*. Then came the end for the time being with

Ex. 196. Lambert, *Rio grande*, beginning

Constant Lambert's *Rio Grande* for chorus, orchestra, and solo pianoforte (1928), and a few distinguished stragglers—Dmitri Shostakovich's *Suite* for jazz orchestra (1934) and Stravinsky's *Ebony Concerto* for clarinet and swing band (1945).[7]

They all make ample use of three–five or three–three–two and, in general, of additive rhythms.

---

[7] Cf. also: Rex Harris, *The influence of jazz on English composers*, in *Penguin Music Magazine*, II, 1946, pp. 25–30; M. Robert Rogers, *Jazz influence on French music*, in *The Musical Quarterly*, Vol. XXI, 1935, pp. 53–68.

A postscript may be taken from a London cable of the Associated Press of April 18, 1952. It quotes *The Church of England Newspaper* as calling "for a revival of 'stunt evangelism' to make the 'music of heaven' as familiar to the people as the tunes crooned by Bing Crosby. It must be taught them, even if it has to be done through percussion band, drum and fife, bebop trio or any other instruments that are understandable to them."

ADDITIVE AND NUMERICAL RHYTHMS. The absorption of jazz in the works of leading 'serious' composers has been much more than just a tribute to passing fads. When the twentieth century buried Romanticism and, with it, the tradition of five hundred years of musical evolution, clean-cut divisive rhythm with its neat 4/4, 3/4, 6/8 was losing its hold. Following the law of the pendulum, other forms of rhythm had to come to the fore again. One of them was jazz. Another one was frequent or consistent use of additive quintuple or even septuple times. And still another one—foreshadowed in Raff—was the shifting from one irregular group to another in successive measures.

In Béla Bartók's *Mikrokosmos* for piano, the short piece No. 140 in the sixth fascicle, which takes only one minute and forty seconds (according to the composer's indication), has on its four pages no less than thirty-five time signatures in a continual change between three, four, five, six, seven, eight, nine eighths and two quarters. The measure is no longer the rhythmical unit. You cannot divide or multiply, but can only add individual groups of notes. The climax of additive patterns is found, in the *Mikrokosmos*, in a number of pieces "in Bulgar rhythm," as the composer headed them. Not the individual beats, but whole measures, now of five, now of seven units, form the cells of shape and perception.

Such "Bulgar" rhythms are not confined to the *Mikrokosmos*. In one of Bartók's piano pieces, *Outdoors*, No. 4 (1926), the listener finds himself in a similar whirl of five, six, seven, eight sixteenths.

From his free compositions the way leads back to Bartók's arrangements and actual transcriptions of Magyar and Balkan music as his source of inspiration. The scholarly notations of Hungarian folk music [8] show additive rhythms of all kinds with from five up to ten units; and the orchestration of Rumanian dances presents us even with an impressive three–three–two, barred throughout as an alternation of two 3/4 and one 2/4.[9]

The master's work confirms once more the rule that rhythm necessarily withdraws to a subordinate role wherever expression focuses on melodic invention; but that melodic invention accepts a rear position wherever rhythmic intricacies engage the central attention. There is a basic polarity similar to that of outline and color in painting.

The picture is similar in the works of Igor Stravinsky. The brilliant last movement of the *Fire Bird* ballet (1910), from No. 203 of the full score on, proceeds in rapid quarter notes under the

Ex. 197. Stravinsky, *The Fire Bird,* end

signature 7/4, alternately 3 + 4 and 4 + 3. The first page of his *Rite of Spring* (*Le Sacre du Printemps*) of 1912/1913 opens with solos *ad lib.* of the bassoon and the horn, in tempo rubato with fermatas, triplets, quintuplets, and perpetual changes of time signature. It is, under the disguise of precise time signatures, a completely free rhythm—a rhythm as free as that of a shepherd's shawm on the boundless steppes of Russia.

Ex. 198. Stravinsky, *Le Sacre du Printemps,* beginning

The genuine Stravinsky appears in the last movement, a sacrificial dance, where the full, gigantic orchestra moves in rapid sixteenth beats, each at M.M. 252 in ever changing measures of 3/16, 5/16, 3/16, 4/16, 5/16, 3/16, 4/16, and so on almost from bar to bar. And as a rule there is a rest on the beat while the chords

[8] Bela Bartók, *Hungarian folk music,* London, 1931.
[9] Bela Bartók, *Roumanian folk dances,* Vienna, 1922.

whip down offbeat. Counting, if it were possible at all in so fast a tempo, would probably unhorse the players—this is an old oriental, additive style in a new occidental form of orchestral rhythm, with infinitesimal cells and an enormous span.[10]

Sometimes, Stravinsky combines perpetual change in one of the voice parts with vertical conflicts. In the movement called *The Little Concert* in *L'Histoire du Soldat* (No. 21 of the score) the clarinet and the trombone move from bar to bar in 5/4, 3/8, 4/4, 3/8, 2/4. For the purpose of easier reading and beating, the composer has given the same signatures to the other instruments, too. Actually, they do not change at all, but oppose some consistent accentual pattern of their own to the vagaries of the upper voice: bassoon and double bass a 4/8, the cornet a 4/4, and the violin a 3/8.

This is the instrumental side of modern rhythmic conception. For the vocal side, Stravinsky—he who, in Copland's unforgettable words, has given a "rhythmic hypodermic" to European music— availed himself of another national heritage: the numerical rhythm of ancient Byzantium. The powerful score of his choral ballet, *The Wedding Feast* (*Les Noces*) of 1917, is a unique apotheosis of

Ex. 199. Stravinsky, *Le Sacre du Printemps*, sacrificial dance

Ex. 200. Stravinsky, *Les Noces*, No. 24

this kind of rhythm. The chorus hammers down in breathtaking eighths, without regard for long and short, but in correct accentuation of the (original Russian) text. In a perpetual change of time signatures—4/8, 5/8, 6/8—some sections form in patterns of a purely numerical type: the bridesmaids would, in a genuine Byzantine way, lay out their monotonous song in eleven, twelve,

[10] A short attempt to analyze this piece and its three rhythmical cells is made in Pierre Boulez, *Propositions*, in *Polyphonies*, fasc. II, 1948, p. 66.

five, six, seven eighths or syllables. Such patterns can be carelessly
violated like those of primitive man; when the text requires a
change, a few notes are dropped or inserted without hesitation.
Even a series of apparently regular five-beat measures must not
be mistaken for additive rhythm; one might be $3 + 2$, and the
next, $2 + 3$, which does not occur in additive patterns. The bar
lines mean very little; all voice parts may have an accent on the
second beat, so that the bar seems misplaced; or the characteristic
beginning of a pattern may stand now after, now before the bar
line.

Ex. 201. Stravinsky, *Les Noces*, No. 55

Stravinsky has many predecessors in this form of rhythm. The
most recent seems to be Nicolai Rimsky-Korsakov, who concludes
his opera *Snegurotchka* or "Snow Maiden" (1882) with a chorus in
rapid 11/4, all notes being uniform quarters except for two eighths
to replace the sixth of the quarter notes in each bar (music example 179).

There is doubtless a causal connection with the Russian orthodox liturgy, which relies, on the whole, upon a non-metrical, little-
accented numerical rhythm of even eighth or quarter notes length-

Ex. 202. Russian liturgy, *Alleluia*

ened out on some, though by no means on all, of the word accents
in the text. The relations of Russian and Byzantine chant are obvious.

From about 1920 on, Stravinsky himself shifted away from
numerical rhythms, as he abandoned inspiration from Russian
folk music. Works like the oratorio-opera *Oedipus Rex* (1927) and

the *Symphony of Psalms* for chorus and orchestra (1930) differ in
their rhythmical attitude very little from the concepts of the nineteenth century.

Arnold Schoenberg was little interested in rhythmic expression.

The younger masters are to various degrees complex and often
confusing in their rhythmical idioms. To a great extent they favor
additive concepts. Just at random: the Austrian, Egon Wellesz,
superimposes half-note triplets upon the 5/4 of the basses in the

Ex. 203. Wellesz, *Die Bakchantinnen*, Act II

second act of his opera *Die Bakchantinnen* (1930); the Russian,
Dmitri Shostakovich, proceeds in regular alternations of binary
and ternary measures in his sixth and seventh symphonies of 1939

Ex. 204. Shostakovich, Sixth Symphony, Op. 53

Ex. 205. Shostakovich, Seventh Symphony, Op. 60

and 1941; the American, Roger Sessions, veers in his first piano
sonata of 1931 from 7/8 to 8/8 [in 3 + 3 + 2], 4/8, 5/8, and 4/8,
and throws in a 7/16 before the end to make the coda even more
breathless; and the Italian, Alfredo Casella, changes on the very
first page of his *Concerto* (1923/24) from 4/4 to 3/4, 4/4, 2/4,
3/4, 4/4, 7/8, 4/4, 2/4, 5/4, 7/8.

Indeed, "the occurrence of unusual looking time-signatures, especially in ambiguous form, is one of the commonplaces of modern music," wrote Daniel Jones in 1950.[11] As a composer, quite un-

---

[11] Daniel Jones, *Some metrical experiments*, in *The Score*, June, 1950, pp. 32–48.

aware of oriental parallels, Jones indulges in, and recommends,
repetitive patterns of an accentual nature. In the paper just quoted,
he prints a sonata for three kettledrums, in which the fourth movement has the time signature 3/4 9/8 2/4 6/8 4/4 3/8, and
the second movement, the probably unsurpassed signature $3 + 2$
$+ 3 + 2 + 2 + 3 + 2 + 2 + 2 + 3 + 2 + 2 + 3 + 2 + 3 + 3 + 2$
$+ 3 + 3 + 3 + 2 + 3 + 3 + 2$ quarters.

(In the same year 1950, Elliott Carter wrote a *Suite for Tym-
pani.*)

A special paragraph is due the eminent rhythmicist of modern
France, Olivier Messiaen (born 1908) who, rightly or wrongly,
has been credited with a language derived from Hindu, Greek,
and Gregorian rhythms.[12] Indeed, a rhythm like $3/4 + 7/16$,
which the composer claims to be *la formule-type de nos amours
rythmiques*, could easily be compared to Indian patterns, while
the alleged Greek and Gregorian ancestries are less convincing.
Whatever his "influences" may be—if we understand by this misused word an affinity that consciously or unconsciously produces
the same or similar results—the nearest or most important parent-
age seems to be the rhythm of the later Gothic Age. 'Canonic artifices' in the spirit of the French around 1400 are predominant
in Messiaen's technique: actual rhythmical canons in *stretto* at
the distance of a quarter note, the augmentation and diminution,
exact or approximate, of the constituent values of a rhythmical
pattern, and even crab canons where not the melodic steps but
the individual time values backward from the end to the middle
of a piece correspond to those from the beginning forward to the
middle notwithstanding the progress of melody—these are truly
Flamboyant, even if Machaut and de Vitry did not use devices of
this very coinage.

It is hard to say what the immediate future will bring. Sometimes, as in Hindemith's works, a reaction towards divisive rhythm
seems imminent. But it would be premature and improper to classify or even discuss the ultimate trends of today before a greater

---

Dr. Joseph Braunstein of the New York Public Library, Music Division, drew my
attention to this paper.
[12] Cf. Marcel Frémiot, *Le rythme dans le langage d'Olivier Messiaen*, in *Polyphonie*, fasc. II, 1948, pp. 58–64. Also Pierre Boulez, *Propositions*, *l.c.*, p. 67.

distance has erased accessory details and displayed the general outlines that matter in the long run.

THE BALLET. Beyond the rhythms that jazz has imparted, the dance, in the widest sense of the word, is playing a role more vital than ever since the seventeenth century. At that time, the French *ballet de cour* could hold its own against Italian opera— so much so that it could hinder the latter from entering France for more than two generations; an essential part of instrumental music stylized pavans, galliards, *courantes* in the form of the suite; and even vocal music took characteristic rhythms from the ballroom.

Around 1700 interest began to withdraw from the dance: the ballet decayed, and the suites developed into danceless sonatas and symphonies. Two hundred years later, opera reached a peak for the time being with Wagner and Strauss, with Verdi and Puccini.

Led by the Russians under Diaghilev, the old ballet came to the fore again, an eloquent challenge to romantic and naturalistic trends, and has replaced the opera almost completely, not only in the attention of the public, not only in the impressive frequency of new creations as against the retrospective repertoire of our opera stages; the most decisive fact is that the ballet, as in the days of Lully and Rameau, has found its musical partners in the leading composers of the day, from Stravinsky to—Stravinsky, from the *Fire Bird* of 1910 to the *Orpheus* of 1947,[13] with Bartók, Satie and Milhaud, Hindemith, Piston and Copland (to take a few names at random). Even Richard Strauss, last flag-bearer of the old, romantic music drama, had bowed to the victorious ballet in *Josephslegende* (1914) and *Schlagobers* (1924).

TEMPO, no longer regulated by any set standard and little affected by binding traditions, is often meticulously described beyond the usual metronome figures. A label pasted in the full score of Mahler's Sixth Symphony of 1904 urges the conductor to give the first movement twenty-two, the second fourteen, the

[13] Cf. *Strawinsky in the theatre*, a forum, in *Dance Index*, Vol. VI, 1947, Nos. 10–12.

third eleven, and the fourth thirty minutes. And Béla Bartók carefully timed every single piece in his *Mikrokosmos* in minutes and seconds.

Where such is not the case, the speed is left to the player's taste and temperament. Alas, everybody knows how widely opinions differ, and "the greater the composer the greater the doubts, since a richer imagination must surely suggest more alternatives, more ideas, more thoughts." [14] By the same token, music lovers are likely to fly into a rage in discussing these opinions.

This being as it is, we reach with pleasure for the informative paper that a music-minded psychologist in Berlin, Dr. Alfred Guttmann, wrote in 1932 on *Das Tempo und seine Variationsbreite*,[15] or 'Tempo and the latitude of its variance.' He had followed the performances of first- and second-rate conductors for a good many years with notebook and chronometer and had jotted down in minutes and seconds the duration of whole works and often of their sections. The details can hardly be of interest in this context. But the general results have a bearing on our topic. They are:

1. The inherent tempo of a certain piece is stronger than the temperament of the performing conductor. When the latter dominates, the piece appears in distortion.

2. The individual tempo of a conductor changes from performance to performance, but its latitude is much smaller than the span between conductors slow and rapid by temperament.

3. In symphonies and similar cyclical works, the largest variance occurs in the first movement.

4. The greatest variability found in performances of the same work under the baton of the same conductor—in Guttmann's case, of Beethoven's Fifth Symphony directed by Richard Strauss—was 20 per cent. The greatest variability of the same work directed by several conductors—Wagner's *Siegfried Idyl*—was 32.2 per cent.

5. The conflicting claims, frequently voiced, that individual con-

---

[14] P. Bonavia, *Time, gentlemen, please,* in Penguin Music Magazine, IV, 1947, p. 16. Cf. also E. O. Turner, *Tempo variation,* in Music & Letters, Vol. XIX, 1938, pp. 308–323. Hans Gál, *The right tempo,* in Monthly Musical Record, Vol. LIX, 1939, pp. 174–177.
[15] Alfred Guttmann, *Das Tempo und seine Variationsbreite,* in Archiv für die gesamte Psychologie, Vol. 85, 1932, pp. 331–350.

ductors grow progressively either slower or faster with age could
not be substantiated.

These five rules will do. There are, of course, some shortcomings in Guttmann's experiments. The worst is probably the rather
restricted number of tested conductors and the emphasis on those
who were Berliners or regular guests with the orchestras of the
German capital and, hence, the complete exclusion of non-German
conductors. The national side of the question remains untouched.
Yet the results, though limited, are valuable as a testimony that
variations of such a latitude were possible in a time when the
novel trend of an objective, impersonal rendition was already restraining the romantic subjectivism of the performers.

Incidentally, the conscientious harpsichordist Ralph Kirkpatrick, on editing the *Goldberg Variations* by Bach, has added a
comparative table of the tempi that he was taking at the time of
publication and of the tempi that he had taken eighteen months
before. Result: most tempi had originally been faster—up to 14
per cent. Only a few had been slightly slower.[16]

Though very limited in scope—one player, one work, one instrument—Kirkpatrick's unassuming notes can be more elucidating than Guttmann's heterogeneous experiments. For the latter
records must rest on one assumption: that tempo is a quality in its
own right.

If this right exists, it is perceptibly impaired. The performer depends not only upon his personal temperament and interpretation,
but also upon a number of ponderables and imponderables. The
same metronomic speed might be correct, too fast, or too slow, de-
pending on the medium in which it materializes.

Orchestration is one factor: the same melody at the same metronomic speed might appear too slow on a xylophone [17] and too fast
on an organ; the broken line that a staccato creates must be con-
tracted in comparison with the sustention of notes in thick or even
viscid organ combinations.

The *tessitura,* or range in which a voice part falls, is another

[16] Ralph Kirkpatrick, in J. S. Bach, *The "Goldberg" Variations,* New York [1938],
p. xxvi.
[17] André Souris, *Le rythme concret,* in *Polyphonie,* fasc. II, 1948, p. 6.

factor: low registers quite often need a slower tempo, unless a particular characterization, humoristic or otherwise, is intended.

A third factor is the density of writing. A bare, monophonic setting is necessarily faster than a polyphony of twelve or sixteen parts.

Fourth factor: the density provided by bigger masses of performers and the multiple harmonics that they create. A specific experience comes to the author's mind: when once in his presence the massive *Wacht auf* chorus from the third act of the *Meistersinger* was for a certain occasion sung by a chamber ensemble in an apartment without any action or scenery, the customary, original tempo became insufferably slow: the texture seemed disrupted. Every musician, to be sure, has been exposed to similar tests.

Fifth factor: the acoustical conditions of the performing room. Echoes, so frequent in churches, impose a slower tempo.

Sixth factor: a similar case, and of even greater importance today, is the different effect of a musical piece, heard three-dimensionally in a tone-reflecting concert hall and even seen with the concurrence of the performing bows and the baton of the conductor, and of the same piece under the same conductor, heard two-dimensionally in the flattening projection of microphones and loudspeakers and without the concurrence of visual impressions: all broadcasts and recordings need a slight acceleration.

And yet, the outer conditions are the lesser powers in modeling the speed of a piece.

"You know," wrote Schumann in 1835, "how little patience I have with quarrels over tempi and how for me the movement's inner measure is the sole determinant. Thus the relatively fast allegro that is cold sounds always more sluggish than the relatively slow one that is sanguine. In the orchestra it is also a question of quality—where this is relatively coarse and dense, the orchestra can give to the detail and to the whole more emphasis and import; where this is relatively small and fine . . . one must help out the lack of resonance with driving tempi." [18]

Arnold Schoenberg, the last and most punctilious of our witnesses, has printed incredibly detailed orders about the correct

[18] Robert Schumann, *Davidsbündlerblätter*, 1835; quoted from Oliver Strunk, *Source readings in music history*, New York, W. W. Norton, 1950, p. 837.

380 RHYTHM AND TEMPO

way to perform his Fourth String Quartet, including minute accenting and lengthening of individual notes. But on tempo, the preface says:

"The metronome marks must not be taken literally—they merely give a suggestion of the tempo." [19]

And from the last witness the eye reverts to one of the older ones, to Bach's contemporary Mattheson and his sagacious words: "Many a one would like to know how the true *mouvement* of a musical work can be known. Such knowledge, alas, is beyond words. It is the ultimate perfection of music, accessible only through great experience and talent." [20]

Against this human, anti-mechanistic attitude, the ever more influential machine has risen even in music to a dehumanizing power of the first magnitude. The length of a recording groove and the inexorable, often tragicomic timing impositions of broadcasts, movies, or television force the performers and even composers into an often unmusical, antimusical straitjacket. Indeed, recording firms and movies have reached for *ad hoc* composers with deadlines of duration expressed in seconds. Roy Harris has good-humoredly responded to this coercion by giving a phonograph-sponsored composition of his the probably unprecedented title *Four minutes and twenty seconds for string quartet and flute* (1934).

In the recording field, the straitjacket has been loosened with the introduction of disk-turning, automatic 'players' or 'record-changers,' which allow the performer to go on, and the listener to hear, beyond the ending groove of the individual disk; and still more so with the invention, in the fall of 1948, of 'long-playing' records, which have given the music infinitely more latitude in length and tempo.

These are good omens. They give hope that man, creative, soulful, and warm, will ultimately master his machines, and not, as did the Sorcerer's Apprentice, succumb to the evil spirits he has conjured.

[19] Frederick Dorian's translation in his *History of music in performance*, New York, W. W. Norton, 1942, p. 332.
[20] [Johann] Mattheson, *Der vollkommene Capellmeister*, Hamburg, 1739, p. 173.

Index